Lost in the '80s

by

John Williams

DEDICATION:

To the journey.

CONTENTS:

CHAPTER 1: THE BOY FROM ROCHDALE

October 1978

The kitchen of our terraced house always felt too small for four bodies, never mind four Parrys: fifteen-year-old me, my parents, and my younger sister Sarah, all shoehorned together by six o'clock for the ritual of tea. I sat at the end of the table, hunched over a mountain range of O-level textbooks, battered folders, and sheaves of A4 that bled with the blue ink of my own desperate revision. My notebooks had begun to curl at the corners from proximity to the kettle's endless vapour, each page a palimpsest of crossed-out answers and margin grumblings. Every time I looked down, I found a new fleck of potato or gravy dotting the cover.

Beneath the table, my right knee jogged in counterpoint to the angry hiss and spit of the open fire behind me. The thing was old as the house and seemed to express its grievances on the hour, every hour, sometimes drowning out the telly's six o'clock news. The linoleum underfoot was cracked and yellowed, its pattern a memory of better days, and the threadbare curtains trembled in a draught that had resisted all of Mum's improvised remedies - rolled towels, cellophane, the lot.

Dad's steel-toe boots made a test match out of the linoleum, pacing a groove by the oven while Mum set down a steaming casserole dish. The ceramic lid clattered against the counter, the sound sharp enough to pull Sarah's head out of *Smash Hits* and summon a flinch from me. The smell was a mix of stewed meat, stock cube, and the faint sourness of old coal dust that nothing could ever quite erase.

Dad, never one to let a silence breathe, started in before the condensation had even formed on the window glass. "Another bloody strike on Monday," he barked, slamming his open palm on the table so the salt pot did a little dance. "This country's gone soft. You lot think the world owes you something for showing up." I sometimes had to remind myself that my father actually *was* a trade union convenor.

I kept my head down, reading the same sentence over and over about osmotic gradients, the words blurring until they looked like code. Mum moved between stove and table with her usual quiet efficiency, pouring tea the colour of tar into thick-shouldered mugs. She never flinched at Dad's volume, nor did she ever quite meet his gaze. Instead, she offered her opinion sideways, like she was dropping a hint for a crossword.

"He's got a good brain, our Liam," she said, setting my mug beside my hand. "Let him use it."

Dad scoffed, reaching for the casserole as if it might run off if he didn't secure it with both hands, "he'd be better off on a football pitch. Instead, he's wasting his time with all that fancy-arse studying." His eyes flicked toward me, fierce and weary, "they won't be needing philosophers down at the mill, lad."

"Not planning to work at the mill, am I," I muttered to myself. With anyone else, I would have spoken loudly, or even found some humour with a sarcastic comment, but with my dad, I had learnt over the years that silence, or near silence at least, was best.

Sarah's mouth twisted in a smirk, "if your head gets any more stuffed with facts, it'll explode. I'll be left scraping brains off the wallpaper." She stabbed at her mashed potatoes with a fork, but I noticed she made sure to get the last word.

Dad ignored her, focusing instead on me, "what's the point then? You think you're better than the lot of us, sat there with your books?"

I fought the urge to look up. If I made eye contact, I knew he'd see the answer written plain on my face: Yes, sometimes I did think I was better, and the shame of that was an extra coat of weight on my shoulders. Instead, I pinched my pen and started underlining at random, giving the illusion of busyness.

"Don't be daft, Patrick," Mum said, her voice a little firmer now, "he's just trying to make something of himself. You should be proud."

" 'Proud', she says," Dad snorted, buttering a thick heel of bread, "last time I was proud, United were top of the league." He looked at me sidelong, a glint in his eye that was either challenge or warning.

Sarah, emboldened, flicked her fringe out of her eyes and grinned at me, "maybe our Liam can get famous and buy you season tickets? So, leave him alone, Dad. At least one of us might get out of here someday." The words tumbled out of Sarah's mouth without any drama, but their effect was like flipping a switch. Dad's jaw worked silently for a moment before he went back to his stew. Sarah had never felt the back of dad's hand and so could get away with such boldness with him.

Mum shot her a look, part gratitude, part annoyance, and then turned her attention to the chipped teapot, refilling the mugs with military precision. I exhaled a long, measured breath. The pressure behind my eyes eased just enough for me to see the text on the page: *'The selective permeability of cell membranes permits regulated diffusion of substances into and out of the cytoplasm.'* It made sense in a way: barriers, gates, things let in or shut out according to rules you didn't set yourself. The table, the kitchen, this whole house was like a cell. If I was lucky, I'd find my way across the membrane before I went to rot.

Dad finished his meal with the efficiency of someone on a time clock. He wiped his mouth with the back of his hand, then reached across to switch the telly from news to the football scores, the volume suddenly a thunderclap. Sarah retreated to the corner with her magazine, feet tucked under her, humming along to *Blondie*. Mum cleared the plates, her hands deft even as the water ran scalding hot in the sink.

The silence that followed was neither comfortable nor absolute. I felt it in my bones, the expectation, the unspoken dare to be worth all this effort.

I read and re-read the same sentence until I could say it backwards, my fingers picking at the edge of the page, leaving crescent-shaped indentations in the paper.

Above me, the lightbulb hummed, a dull white orb casting every flaw in the wallpaper into high relief. Mum's soft footsteps, Dad's low grumble, Sarah's half-mumbled lyrics; all of it wove together, tight and inescapable. I wondered if there was any science in the world that could explain how a family could love you and not see you at all.

I turned the page, careful not to let it rip.

The next morning at school, the corridors smelled of disinfectant and adolescent panic. I moved through the haze of fluorescent light and echo, skirting clusters of boys who traded insults and flicked rulers at the back of passing heads. My own locker had acquired a new gouge since yesterday, a diagonal slash through the sticker I'd never dared to remove, a sort of badge for the noncombatants. I ran a finger over the scar, then tucked my bag beneath my arm and made for the one place where the noise never quite reached: English classroom, first floor, end of the hall.

The air in there was a blend of chalk dust, floor polish, and the lingering bitterness of stale cigarettes from teachers who thought no one noticed. The windows rattled with every gust, and the radiators, even older than the ones at home, hissed in a language only the truly bored could decipher. Mrs. Buckley, whose hair was the colour of wet iron and whose cardigan had seen three monarchs, perched on the edge of her desk, reading out the day's assignment with funereal dignity.

"'*Wuthering Heights*,' chapters nine to twelve. Who can summarise Heathcliff's motivations in this section?" Her gaze swept the room, pausing only to mentally mark out the usual suspects.

My hand shot up, almost involuntary, a reflex built on equal parts fear and hope. A faint smile flickered at the corners of her mouth, like she'd been waiting for me all along.

"Yes, Parry?"

I recited, verbatim, the paragraph I'd rehearsed over breakfast, voice steady despite the chorus of snorts from the back row. "Heathcliff's anger isn't just about revenge; it's a protest against his own powerlessness, a refusal to accept the order of things as they are." I felt the words settle in the air, heavy and deliberate.

Mrs. Buckley nodded, more to herself than to me. "Very good. And what does that tell us about the nature of…"

A cough from the far side of the room, loud and theatrical, "teacher's pet's at it again," someone stage-whispered, just shy of the teacher's hearing but plenty loud for everyone else.

"Hasn't got time for birds, has he? Too busy romancing the Heathcliff." Another snigger, this one a direct hit from Callaghan, whose breath always reeked of vinegar crisps and low expectations.

A flush crept up my neck, hot and shameful, but I kept my eyes on the text. I'd learned by now that if you ignored them, they grew bored eventually - like wasps. Or so the theory went.

Mrs. Buckley, oblivious or perhaps just immune to the background radiation of cruelty, scribbled something on the blackboard and then gestured for us to open our copies of the novel. The rest of the lesson passed in a blur: her voice reading passages, the rasp of chalk, the constant undercurrent of muttered jokes and chair legs scraping. I took notes in microscopic handwriting, a habit borne of trying to occupy as little physical space as possible.

When the bell rang, it was like the starter pistol for a footrace. I gathered my books quickly, head down, and made for the door. The corridor was already filling with bodies, the noise cranked to maximum. Callaghan and his echo were waiting just outside.

"Oi, Parry," he called, blocking my path with a well-practiced lean, "you coming out Saturday, or have you got another date with your boyfriend Heathcliff?" The words were coated in a venom that didn't need context. His mate, more muscle than brain, brayed a laugh and flicked the back of my notebook as I edged past.

"Probably doesn't even know what to do with a girl," the other one sneered, like it was the punchline to a joke everyone, but me, found hilarious.

I felt my face go cold, the heat of earlier replaced by a numb, distant ache. I kept my mouth shut and pushed through, refusing to look back. They followed for a few paces, then peeled off toward the canteen, hunger for chips greater than the need to humiliate me further.

I ducked into the boys' loos, shut myself in a stall, and waited until the tide of bodies receded. My hands trembled slightly as I fished out a biro and started scribbling equations on the inside cover of my English book, anything to convince myself I was immune.

When I finally emerged, the corridor was almost empty, save for a few stragglers and a caretaker with a mop. I kept my head down, shoes squeaking on the polished floor, and made for the library. That was the plan anyway, always was.

The library was colder than the rest of the school, though I always imagined it was a deliberate choice, as if the books themselves required a certain chill to keep from igniting under the pressure of so many words. I claimed my usual spot at the far end; an alcove wedged between the encyclopaedias and the window that looked out over the car park. The glass was streaked with rain, refracting the rows of beige *Vauxhalls* into smudgy ghosts. Here, the soundtrack was the distant clack of typewriters from the office, the soft shuffle of rubber soles, the papery sigh of a page turned with reverence.

I unloaded my bag in stages: maths revision workbook for camouflage, then the real prize, wrapped in the camouflage of last term's exercise book. The cover was worn, the spine split, and the first pages were scored with the scrawls of a dozen prior borrowers. Oscar Wilde's *The Picture of Dorian Gray*. It had been stamped out to me so often that I worried the librarian would catch on, but so far no one cared what a lad read as long as he returned it on time.

I pressed the book open, careful not to let the covers creak, and picked up where I'd left off. The words were oxygen, dizzying and forbidden. Wilde's sentences curled around my thoughts, drawing out feelings I pretended not to have, mapping desires I'd barely dared name. There was something in the cadence, the unspoken signals that ran like current beneath the story's surface, something that made my heart jackhammer, even in the dead hush of the stacks.

I caught myself smiling at a line, the way someone might at an in-joke only they understood. My fingers traced the italicised words: *"He wondered if he would ever be more to her than a bright, fascinating shadow."* The idea of being a shadow, of existing in the margins, struck me as both deeply sad and, for reasons I couldn't explain, oddly comforting.

Footsteps sounded from the main aisle. I snapped the book shut and, with a practiced motion, slid it inside the maths workbook. A moment later, the librarian passed by, steering a squeaking trolley stacked with returns. She was young, maybe mid-twenties, and had a fringe that hung just above her eyes, perpetually in need of a trim. She paused in front of my table, glanced at the textbook with professional disinterest, and then nodded, as if to say, *'good lad, keeping up with your studies'*.

I kept my eyes on the workbook until her footsteps faded, then eased the Wilde back into view, this time setting it flat on my knees beneath the lip of the table. It was a ritual, the secret reading, the thrill of hiding in plain sight. If anyone came close, I'd flip the maths book back on top and pretend to be deep in quadratic equations.

I read for as long as I dared, letting the outside world dissolve. The clock above the reference desk ticked in slow motion; lunch break felt infinite, a precious suspension. I was only interrupted when the boy from my English class, the one who always looked like he was about to say something but never did, drifted past and paused at the row opposite. He caught my eye for a second, then pretended to browse the dictionaries, his ears burning red.

I looked down, heart thumping. *Did he know? Did he care?* I'd never spoken to him outside of class, but there was an intensity in the way he paid attention during lessons, a fierce hunger to know things. I wondered if he had his own secrets, or if I was just projecting mine onto the nearest available body.

Eventually, the bell sounded, sharp and final, and I shut the book with a soft thud. I tucked it back in my bag, buried it deep, then swept the crumbs of a stolen biscuit into my palm and dropped them in the bin. As I left the alcove, I glanced back at the shelves, Wilde sandwiched between Hardy and Woolf, both of whom I'd get to in due course. There was something reassuring about the permanence of the books, even as everything else felt temporary, uncertain.

I lingered at the exit, waiting for the corridor to clear. When I finally stepped out, the smell of old paper clung to me like an invisible shield. I wondered if it would be enough.

Evenings in my bedroom had always been my safe zone. The desk was a cheap plank balanced on filing cabinets, but it faced the window, out over the backs of the other terraces, rooftops stacked like dominoes all the way to the main road. The light in my room was a jaundiced yellow from the overhead bulb, not quite strong enough to chase away the corners, but perfect for hiding in plain sight. I arranged my books in two neat stacks, one for subjects I liked and one for subjects I merely tolerated and tried to wedge my mind into the narrow gap between.

I'd only managed half a page of chemistry revision before the voices from below began to rise, a tide that wouldn't be held back. At first it was just sound; vowels and consonants tangled up with the scrape of a chair and the muted thunk of the fridge. Then the words themselves started to travel.

"I'm telling you; we can't afford it!" Dad's voice was a battering ram, meant to take down doors and resistance alike.

Mum replied, softer but with a tensile strength that didn't break, "you're thinking small again. He's not like us. He's got a shot at university, Patrick. He's clever enough."

"He's too smart for his own good, if you ask me. All this talk about Manchester and Leeds, who's going to pay for it, Maggie?"

The words scraped at the walls, found the gaps beneath my door. I abandoned my seat and padded across the carpet, pressing my ear to the cold wood. I heard the whirr of the meter, the kettle clicking off, the shuffle of Sarah moving through the hallway, always alert for trouble.

"He deserves better than what we had, and besides he will qualify for a grant," Mum said, almost pleading. "You want him to end up at the mill? Or on a building site? There's nothing left here but the dust."

Dad's reply was sharper now, but also more tired, "you don't know what you're wishing on him. Those places, they eat lads like him alive. You think he's ready for the likes of them?"

There was a pause, a silence stretched so thin it threatened to snap. I imagined them standing on opposite sides of the table, Mum still in her apron, Dad gripping the back of a chair like he could will it to hold him upright.

From the landing, Sarah's voice came in a sarky stage whisper, "maybe they'll kill each other and we can get a telly upstairs." She was sitting cross-legged outside her own tiny bedroom, flicking at her nail varnish, but her eyes were on me, narrowed in the half-light.

I shushed her with a glare, then pressed my ear harder to the door. Downstairs, the argument had shifted from academic to existential.

"And who's going to pay for it? The fairies?" Dad's tone was half-joke, half-resentment.

"Will you be told, he will get a grant," Mum's voice was slightly raised.

"And what makes you so certain?" Dad countered, not believing that Mum might know more than he does.

"I've already been in to the Town Hall to check," Mum said silencing my dad. *'Checkmate'*, I thought.

I let go of the doorknob and slunk back to my desk, hands shaking hard enough to make the biro rattle on the wood. I picked it up and forced myself to finish the equation I'd started, but the numbers were meaningless now, the words in the textbook swimming in and out of focus. Instead, I stared at the window, the sodium-lit rooftops beyond, and tried to picture what any of it would look like when it was all memories; when I was finally away from here, somewhere I could breathe.

In that moment I wanted, more than anything, to believe that it was possible to be both myself and good enough. But the voices below kept bleeding into my chest, and the draft that curled around my ankles reminded me that no room, no matter how small, was ever truly a fortress.

I closed my notebook and let my head fall into my hands, listening to the slow, inevitable footsteps of my parents circling each other on the floor below. If there was a future in any of this, I couldn't see it, not yet.

But I kept the Wilde hidden in my bag, just in case.

CHAPTER 2: APPEARANCES

September 1979

Sixth form college was meant to be a liberation, a year zero, a fresh start with only the past twelve years of uniformed humiliation and daily pecking order as ballast. In reality, it was a set of connected demountables and three-storey cinderblock, crouched at the edge of town, with walls painted the colour of undercooked liver and windows permanently clouded by either drizzle or the breath of two hundred hormonal teenagers.

I learned, in the first hour of my first day, that nothing in my all-boys grammar had prepared me for the savage chaos of a mixed sixth form. Girls were everywhere, and not the theoretical girls I'd encountered on the high street or in the distant haze of family weddings. These were real, too close, too loud, armed with perfume and opinions and an uncanny ability to spot the cracks in your composure from a dozen paces. Their voices stitched through the corridors, high and brittle, and their hair caught on your jumper when they passed in a rush, leaving the ghost of shampoo or, worse, actual conversation.

The timetable said History, double period, so I ducked into the first open classroom and took the desk closest to the wall, a reflex from years of avoiding notice. The tables had all been scuffed and battered by prior generations, deep knife marks, hearts carved through the veneer, *'SUE = SLAG'* written in a fading *Bic* rainbow. The teacher arrived late, a harassed woman in her forties who wore her tweed skirt like a battle flag and took attendance with a voice that rang out over the chatter like a police siren.

"Parry, Liam."

I raised a hand.

She peered at me over the rims of her glasses, "new boy, are you?"

"Just transferred," I said.

"Well, let's see what you're made of," she said, turning to the board and firing off a question about the reform acts. I answered automatically, half-remembered from last term, and a girl two rows back smirked as some wag farted audibly. When the teacher pressed me for more, the same girl yawned, loudly, stretching so her cardigan slipped off her shoulder and exposed a freckled patch of skin. I felt my face burn and fumbled the rest of my answer.

The next forty minutes passed in a haze of dates and legislation, punctuated by the scrape of chairs and the rustle of note-passing. The girl from before, she had a name, Amanda, which I clocked during roll-call, caught my eye a few times, though always with a layer of irony so thick you'd need a mining permit to dig through it. I wanted to hate her, or at least not care, but every time her pen flicked up to meet my gaze, I got a knot in my chest like the aftershock of a missed step on the stairs.

Break came, and with it a stampede of bodies into the corridor. I tried to go the opposite direction, but the flood carried me down toward the canteen. The queue for tea was a rugby scrum of elbows and snide comments, the air thick with chip fat and *Lynx*. I waited my turn, collected the world's weakest instant coffee, and made for a table at the edge of the room, only to find Amanda already there, boots propped on the plastic chair, mug in hand.

"You're one of the new ones from the grammar school," she said, as if confirming a theory. Her eyes were blue, not the washed-out blue of most Northerners but electric, like a *Bunsen* flame.

I nodded, "bit closer to home and better choice of subjects here."

She made a face, "all boys wasn't it?"

"Yeah."

"So you've never..." She paused, considering, "been to a real school before?"

I looked at the steam rising from my cup, "suppose not."

Amanda leaned forward, "it's not so bad, as long as you don't mind everyone knowing everything about you within a week. Are you one of the clever ones or the ones that sneak behind the bike sheds for a smoke?"

A trick question, I guessed, "bit of both."

She grinned, showing slightly uneven teeth that, on anyone else, would have been a flaw, "good answer."

We sipped our coffee in silence for a moment. I felt the tickle of self-consciousness under my skin, what did my hands look like, were my glasses fogged, was there butter on my shirt from breakfast? Amanda didn't seem to mind, or at least was professional enough to hide it.

"Everyone says the staff here are crap compared to where you were," she said, tipping her chair back, "but the politics teacher's alright. He lets you argue back. D'you do politics?"

I nodded, "yes, in fact that's really why I came here - no politics A level at my old school."

Amanda's eyebrows shot up, "you like arguing, then?"

I shrugged, "if it's about something real. I suppose I get it from my dad; he's a union convener."

She gave me a slow, appraising look, "I'm in your history class," she said, as if letting me in on a joke, "I'm Amanda. You probably guessed."

"I did."

"Most boys don't notice," she drained her cup in one go, then got up, "I'll see you later."

I sat for a full minute after she left, trying to reassemble the mask of indifference that had got me through five years of male-only education.

My intent was not to make new friends but simply to pass my A levels as a route out of Rochdale to university somewhere. But, I kept bumping into Amanda over the next few weeks, and we moved on from a quick smile of acknowledgment to short chats about our classes. One day just before half-term I was sat in my usual place in English Lit, when I noticed Amanda bounding in as she usually did, but instead of taking her seat with the girls, she headed for me.

"Swapsies," she said, elbowing a weedy lad out of the chair next to me, "move."

He did, muttering something about 'bossy cows' but not meeting her gaze. Amanda flicked her hair, shot me a sideways look, and opened her battered *Penguin* edition to the correct page. The teacher, a pale and birdlike man, started reading, but Amanda didn't even try to hide her disinterest. Instead, she passed me a note, folded so tight it looked like an origami animal.

Inside, she'd written: "you read a lot? Or into music?"

I wrote back, "depends who's asking."

She snatched the paper, grinned at my answer, and scribbled: "I work at *HMV* on Saturdays. Staff discount. If you ever want to borrow records, say so."

The exchange was childish and exhilarating and terrifying all at once. I was convinced the teacher would see, or that the class would, but nobody did. Instead, Amanda spent the entire lesson pretending not to notice me, only occasionally nudging my foot with hers under the desk. Each contact sent a shot of cold lightning up my leg, and I had to dig my nails into my palm to keep from yanking my foot away.

Afterwards, she caught up to me in the corridor, "you've got politics next, yeah?"

"Room twenty-three?"

She smiled, "I'll walk with you."

It was a declaration, or maybe a challenge. The eyes of passing students tracked us as we walked together, people noticed, as Amanda had said they would. We reached the classroom, and she hesitated at the door.

"Don't let them get to you," she said, meaning the others, "it's all bollocks anyway."

The politics teacher was as good as advertised at the beginning of term, a lean, bearded man who ran the room like a debating chamber, firing out hypotheticals and letting the class tear them to shreds. I volunteered, once, and the rush of words was like a floodgate opening. My answer earned a slow clap from the teacher, and Amanda's sidelong glance was almost proud.

The rest of the afternoon passed in an unreal blur. I made it through two more periods without completely humiliating myself. When the final bell rang, I drifted toward the exit, not expecting Amanda to be waiting by the door.

"You going into town?" she asked.

"I usually get the bus home."

"Come with," she said, "just for a bit."

She led me down Drake Street, past the record shop where she worked, and into a café so dimly lit it felt like entering a womb. Amanda ordered for both of us, tea for her, coffee for me, and claimed a table at the back, out of sight of anyone who might know us.

For a minute, neither of us spoke. Then Amanda leaned in, "you're not like the other lads," she said, matter-of-fact.

I almost choked on my coffee, "in what way?"

She grinned, "for a start, you don't stare at my tits when you think I'm not looking."

I felt my face go beet red, heat crawling up from my collar, "I didn't think you'd want that."

"I don't," she said, "but it's interesting." She sipped her tea, eyes never leaving mine. "Are you shy?"

"Maybe."

Amanda nodded, "I like that. Means you actually listen."

We sat in silence, the sounds of clinking cups and distant traffic filling the space between us. After a while, she reached across the table and placed her hand on mine. Her fingers were cold, but her grip was firm.

"Is this okay?" she asked, voice barely above a whisper.

I willed myself not to flinch, "yeah."

She squeezed my hand, then released it, "I'm just saying, if you want to hang out again, I'd be up for it."

I tried to summon the correct response, but all I managed was a nod and a strangled, "sure."

She stood, dropped a pound note on the saucer, and gave me a final, appraising look, "you'll get used to it. See you tomorrow."

After she left, I sat with the dregs of my coffee, hands trembling slightly. The day had been a gauntlet of newness and old fears, eyes watching, judgments forming, the unspoken rules of a universe I didn't know how to navigate.

Walking home, I replayed the moments in my head. The hand on mine, the easy way she talked about everything, the fact that she had chosen to sit with me when she could have been anywhere else. It was all evidence, stacked and incontrovertible, that I was expected to perform normality, to pass as a person for whom this was all real and uncomplicated.

At the front door of our house, I stopped and looked at my reflection in the window: hair too long, shirt already wrinkled, the new tie a shade brighter than it should have been. I let myself in, the familiar smell of damp and fried onions settling over me like a blanket.

In my bedroom, I put the Wilde back on the shelf, this time behind a row of battered redundant chemistry textbooks. If I was going to survive sixth form, I needed to learn how to hide in plain sight all over again.

But my hand still tingled where Amanda had touched it, and the feeling lingered, equal parts thrill and terror, for hours afterwards.

The ritual at our house was always the same: tea at six, TV at seven, then a slow unwinding toward bedtime while the evening cooled the walls and the coal fire shrank to a dull orange core. Tonight, there was a sense of occasion, or at least an undercurrent of it, because I'd come home not only with a decent mark on my history essay but with news that, for once, Mum could brag about without the familiar twist of anxiety. I told her about coffee after college.

"She's called Amanda, is she?" Mum said, her hands never still, folding the tea towel into neat quarters before attacking a smear on the kitchen table, "that's a lovely name, that is. Nice and classic. Is she local?"

I mumbled something about her being from the other side of town, a half-lie that was easier than explaining the map of alliances and rivalries that defined the sixth form's social geography. Sarah snickered from her post at the fridge, where she was picking the raisins out of a stale Eccles cake.

After some thought, Mum's eyes went wide, "well, you dark horse!" She dabbed at her face, then gave me the look, the one that said, *'we both know you're too clever for your own good, but I'll pretend for your sake'*. "I hope you were a gentleman."

"He was," Sarah said, hopping up onto the counter. "Sat there like a robot, he did. Nearly spilled his coffee when she touched his hand."

I shot her a look, *'how do you know?'*, but then realised my sister would know Amanda from school, it only made her grin. Mum didn't notice, lost in the possibilities, "you should bring her round sometime," she said. "I'll do my corned beef hash, or maybe the fish on Fridays, some people don't eat meat, you know, even now."

I nodded, already dreading the prospect, "maybe."

Behind us, Dad's boots thudded down the stairs, then across the hallway. He entered the kitchen in his usual end-of-shift uniform: thick work shirt, trousers stained at the knees, a faint aura of tobacco and diesel that never fully left his skin.

"Evening," he said, but his eyes were on the casserole. He scooped a ladleful onto his plate, took a seat, and started in on the food without ceremony. For a minute, it was just the scrape of cutlery and the tick of the wall clock, the only soundtrack to the day's debrief.

Mum poured herself a cup of tea, then settled at the table, "our Liam's got himself a girlfriend," she announced, like she was breaking the result of a cup final.

Dad's fork hovered mid-air, "oh aye?"

Mum's pride softened her voice, "a nice girl, goes to his college. He had coffee with her after school."

Dad nodded, chewing, "about time you found yourself a bird, lad. Can't spend your whole life with your head in them books."

The words landed with the usual mix of sarcasm and expectation, "she's got blue eyes," Sarah offered, "and she talks twice as much as he does."

Dad's attention was briefly on Sarah, then on me, "you treat her right, son," he said, voice pitched low for maximum importance. "None of that messing around you hear about nowadays. Take it slow, and keep your hands to yourself, if you know what's good for you."

Mum tsked, "don't embarrass him, Patrick."

He shrugged, "just saying. World's gone mad since I was a lad." He spooned another lump of casserole onto his plate, "all them stories on the telly, I sometimes wonder if there's any point in rules at all."

Mum shot me an apologetic glance, but her pride was still shining through, undimmed, "she sounds nice, Liam. I'm sure she'll be good for you."

Sarah hummed tunelessly and waggled her eyebrows at me when Mum wasn't looking.

I busied myself with the food, but the kitchen felt airless, every conversation now subject to the laws of surveillance and mutual suspicion. The old enemy, the sense of being observed, studied for fault lines, hadn't left with my move to sixth form. It had only changed address. Apparently, through this observation, I had got myself a girlfriend without me even knowing it myself.

After dinner, Dad commandeered the living room armchair, feet up on the ottoman, packet of Embassy tucked into his shirt pocket. The telly was already blaring, the *BBC* news anchor's voice like gravel poured over glass. On screen, Thatcher's face loomed, spectral and implacable, talking about cuts and unions and the need for sacrifice.

Dad growled, "bloody woman'll be the death of us."

Mum, perched at the end of the settee, nodded along as if the conversation was a duet she knew by heart, "maybe she'll shake things up. Sometimes you need a strong hand."

Dad laughed, "you just like her because she does her own hair."

Mum smacked his arm, grinning despite herself, "she's the Prime Minister, Patrick. Show some respect."

He scoffed, lighting a cigarette, "respect, is it? When she wants to destroy the unions and every other town up north on the breadline?"

Sarah, who had been sitting cross-legged by the fire, chimed in: "they said on the news the schools'll be next. More cuts."

"Wouldn't surprise me," Dad said, "sooner have the lot of you on the dole than with a proper education and challenging them."

I watched all this from my corner of the settee, picking at a loose thread on my jumper, jaw clenched so tight it felt like my teeth would splinter. The news rolled on, a parade of disasters and talking heads, while Dad muttered commentary between drags.

"There's your future, lad," he said, nodding at the TV, "enjoy it now while it lasts."

I wanted to say something back, something incisive or clever or at least true, but the words caught somewhere behind my tongue. Instead, I let the silence settle, filling in the cracks with the tap of ash against the tray and the occasional sniffle from Sarah, who was now half-buried under a pile of discarded newspaper.

When the news ended, Mum flicked off the telly and stood, "I'll make a brew," she said, already halfway to the kitchen, "anyone want?"

Dad grunted, "just a splash for me."

Sarah shook her head, "I'm going upstairs."

She shot me a look as she passed, the barest suggestion of sympathy or warning, hard to tell which, in the gloom. Left alone with Dad, I felt the tension build like static on a wool blanket. He studied me for a moment, then said, "don't let them girls distract you from your schoolwork, hear?"

I nodded.

He stubbed out his cigarette, voice softening a fraction, "you'll do good, Liam. You've got the brain for it. Don't waste it on daft things."

The words should have reassured me, but they didn't. Instead, I felt a twist in my gut, the unspoken knowledge that everything Dad said about the world, the old rules, the dangers lurking at the edge, was only going to get worse now that I had more to lose. Or more to hide.

Mum returned with tea, and the moment broke. She handed Dad his cup, then sat beside me on the settee.

"You know," she whispered, "if you ever want to talk about anything, you can. I won't judge."

"I know," I said, not meeting her eyes.

She squeezed my hand, "you're a good lad."

Dad turned the TV back on and raised the volume.

I sipped my tea, watching the world shrink and harden outside our frosted window. Every day, it seemed, there was a little less room to manoeuvre, a little less air to breathe.

When it was finally time to retreat to my bedroom, I closed the door behind me and sat on the edge of the bed, head in hands. The world outside was changing, and fast, but in here the same old rules applied: keep your secrets close, trust only what you can carry in your head. I let the silence fill the room, and waited for the comfort of sleep to come. I concluded that I had not lied about Amanda being my girlfriend, but instead just been the victim of unchallenged assumptions. I felt a little bit safer.

Parry family parties were, by design or accident, a species of controlled detonation. The entire downstairs was rearranged to maximize capacity, table pressed against the wall, armchairs conscripted into the perimeter, every surface cleared for plates or bottles or stray limbs. By seven, the place was full: my parents, my sister, three aunts in varying states of decibel and makeup, two uncles, four cousins under the age of ten, and a neighbour who always turned up when sherry was on offer. The windows fogged over with breath and cigarette smoke

within the first hour, turning the house into a submarine patrol-
ling the depths of working-class England.

I spent the first half hour fending off well-meaning
aunts who pinched my cheek and commented on my 'new man'
hair, or who asked if Amanda was "steady" and what her father
did for a living. They prodded at my future with the hopeful intensity of fortune-tellers: would I study at university, would I be
a doctor or a lawyer, would I marry before thirty. I answered in
monosyllables, then handed the conversation to Sarah, who
could distract any adult with a few bars of *Blondie* or by narrat-
ing the latest spat between teachers at her school.

The uncles, meanwhile, had colonised the kitchen,
where they talked politics, football, and occasionally work,
though never for long enough to suggest they actually liked
their jobs. My dad, as always, played host and referee, keeping
the beer cold and the ashtrays clear. Uncle Frank, his older
brother, commandeered the sink with a pint in one hand and a
cigarette in the other, lecturing anyone within earshot about the
decline of everything since 1972.

"Kids these days, they don't know they're born," Dad
said, voice raised above the squall of the children, who were
pelting each other with matchbox cars, "look at our Liam, brain
the size of a planet, but ask him the offside rule and he goes all
glassy-eyed."

I felt my ears redden but forced a smile.

Uncle Frank grinned, flashing the gold crown on his
front tooth, "if you're not careful, your balls'll shrivel and fall
off," he said, cackling, "that's what too much reading does."

The kitchen laughed with him, the joke old as dirt but
always good for a laugh. I excused myself, claimed I had to help
Mum in the lounge, and made for the relative safety of the TV
corner.

Mum and the aunts were in full gossip mode, trading
stories about neighbours and old classmates and who'd had a
breakdown or a baby. Sarah was on the carpet with the youngest cousin, showing her how to peel the foil off a toffee without
mangling it. The room smelled of boiled onions, embrocation,
and the sickly-sweet scent of cheap sherry.

I positioned myself near the window, the glass slick with condensation, and tuned in to the news on the telly, and leaned in close to hear the headlines: inflation, strikes, trouble in Northern Ireland, the US embassy crisis in Iran. Then, for a split second, the news cut to a brief film of a demonstration, the words "Gay Rights Protest" emblazoned on a placard before flicking away to footage of riot police in Brixton.

Uncle Frank came in from the kitchen just in time to see it. He jabbed a finger at the TV, beer sloshing onto the carpet, "look at that. Bloody poofs. Should be locked up, the lot of 'em. World's gone soft, that's the trouble."

His laugh was infectious, Dad, the other uncles, even two of the aunts snickered, "you know what they say," Frank went on, winking at the room, "if God had meant men to love men, he'd have given 'em tits."

The laughter rolled through the room, echoing against the low ceiling and the close-packed walls. I felt the blood rise in my face, a flush so hot it stung the corners of my eyes. I mumbled something about needing the loo and pushed past the crowd.

The bathroom was small, the sort of cell you could cross in two steps. I locked the door, ran the tap, and splashed cold water on my face. The mirror above the sink was fogged, but I could make out my own shape: pale, hunched, a shadow behind steam. My hands trembled, and when I tried to steady them, they only shook harder.

I stood there until the party noises faded to a muffled blur, until the water ran lukewarm and the voices outside sounded like they belonged to a different species.

The rest of the night passed in a kind of dissociation. I helped clear plates, poured drinks for the aunts, fetched a blanket for one of the cousins who fell asleep on the settee. Nobody seemed to notice my absence from the jokes, or my silence when the conversation turned to "real men" and what they were made of.

After the last relative had stumbled out the door and Mum had done a quick sweep for stray children, I made my way up to my room, shut the door, and dropped onto the bed. I lay there in the dark, the house finally quiet, save for the rhythmic tick of the landing clock and the clunk of the boiler cycling on and off.

I waited until I could be sure nobody was listening, then fished the battered notebook out from my shoebox. I opened to the first blank page, smoothed it with my palm, and started to write.

It came in a rush: the memory of Amanda's hand on mine, the way her hair caught the light in the canteen, the sound of my own heartbeat when she called me by name. Then the flash of Frank's joke, the laughter, the sick certainty that if anyone ever guessed the truth about me, there'd be more than just jokes, there'd be shame, disgust, maybe even hate. I wrote until the cramp in my fingers was worse than the ache in my chest, and still the words kept coming, line after frantic line, until the page was a tangle of ink and anger and fear.

When there was nothing left to say, I ripped out the pages, careful not to tear them, and slipped them into the back pocket of my jeans. I crept out to the bathroom, locked the door, and lit a match. The pages curled and blackened, the words turning into bright flakes that drifted down into the toilet bowl. I watched until the last ember went out, the only evidence a few smudges of ash and the acrid bite of burnt paper in my nose.

I flushed, watched the ashes swirl away, and stood for a long minute staring at my hands. They were still shaking.

Back in bed, I waited for the world to still itself. I listened to the house breathe and settle, the tick of the clock, the faintest creak from the floorboards above my parents' room. I closed my eyes and let the darkness rise, until the only thing left was the memory of flame and the echo of laughter, looping and endless, just under the surface of sleep.

Appearances, it seemed to me, mattered if I was to avoid the vitriol of men like my father and uncles. A realisation that terrified me.

CHAPTER 3: MANCHESTER CALLING

March 1981

The envelope waited for me on the kitchen table, swollen and official, its thick ivory belly stamped with the *University of Manchester* crest. The sight of it sent a jolt through my arm and straight into my lungs, as though I'd touched the business end of a live wire. I hovered in the doorway, backpack still on, uncertain whether the thing was bait or bomb.

Mum was first to break the stalemate. She wiped her hands down her apron, leaving a pair of floury ghosts at her hips, and called up the stairs for Sarah to come down, her voice ringing with the command reserved for emergencies and special occasions. Dad was already in his seat, a permanent dent in the faded vinyl, but he made a show of hiding behind the *Evening News*. Only his knuckles betrayed him, white against the print.

"Go on, love," Mum said, nudging me forward. The table was laid for four, though the cutlery never matched and the plates were all different patterns, bits and pieces scavenged from the jumble sale at *St. Anne's*. The steam from the kettle drew slow rivers down the kitchen window, and for a moment I wished I could dissolve into the condensation and be gone.

I sat, the envelope in front of me, its flap heavy with the fate of my next three years. The rest of the mail, water bill, takeaway flyers, a pale blue envelope for Dad, was shunted to one side.

Sarah clattered down the stairs, two at a time, and burst into the kitchen on a cloud of *Impulse* and adolescent energy. She took in the tableau: me, the envelope, Mum wringing her hands, and immediately went to the fridge, as though the drama had nothing to do with her.

"Open it before I do, lad," Dad said, not lowering the newspaper, "you're turning it to mush with your sweating."

I hesitated a half-beat longer, then wedged my thumb beneath the paper seal and tore along the edge. The rip seemed to echo in the small space, sharper than the scrape of the chair legs on lino. Inside was a letter and a pack of glossy pamphlets, the university's name screaming in burgundy and gold.

Mum craned her neck to read upside-down, but I brought the letter up to my face, scanning for words that mattered: *"pleased to inform," "conditional offer," "congratulations."* My heart hammered as if I'd run a mile. I handed the letter over without a word.

Mum's eyes darted across the page. She read silently at first, then aloud, stumbling on every academic term as though it were in a foreign tongue. *"'…conditional upon achievement of grades ABB… commended for your interview… look forward to welcoming you in September…'* Oh, Liam. Oh, love." She clapped her hand over her mouth, and the tears came instantly, bright and stupid.

Dad grunted. He folded the newspaper with military precision, set it on the table, and reached for his mug. "Well, that's that, then." He took a sip of tea that had gone cold, grimaced, then looked straight at me, the way he did when he wanted me to remember who'd paid for my shoes.

"I suppose you'll be after new clothes now," he said, "got to keep up with the city set."

Mum wiped her eyes, half-laughing, half-crying, "don't mind him, love. He's proud as anything. He just can't show it."

Dad bristled at that, but said nothing more, eyes locked on a point just past my shoulder. I felt a strange urge to thank him and to apologise all at once.

Sarah finally stopped digging through the fridge, a wedge of *Red Leicester* in her hand. "What's it say, then?" She didn't wait for an answer, just snatched the letter from Mum and scanned it, her lips moving. "ABB? I could do that standing on my head. D'you get a crown when you go, Professor Parry?"

I snorted, the joke landing right where she wanted it to. "It's not even a proper university," I shot back, though the words had no venom. "Not like Oxford or Cambridge."

"But it's not one of those *'Poly'* things," she replied, grinning. "But you'll fit right in. All those brains and nowhere to put them."

Mum pulled me in for a hug, nearly choking me with the strength of it, "I always knew you'd get out of here," she whispered. Her breath smelled faintly of onions and soap.

Dad stood, his chair screeching against the floor, and went to the sink. He didn't look back as he spoke: "hope you know what you're doing. It's not easy, living among them who think you're less than nowt." He stared out the window, as if the answer might be drifting down the street with the clouds of coal smoke.

"Better than dying of boredom," Sarah said, licking cheese crumbs off her fingers.

Mum smacked her arm, "don't say that. Your father's just being…"

"Realistic," Dad finished. He rinsed his mug and left it in the sink, then paused, "but well done, son." The words were clipped, final, but heavier than the letter itself.

For a moment, the room was silent but for the hiss of the kettle and the tick of the cheap plastic clock over the stove. Then Sarah jumped onto the nearest chair, striking a mock-regal pose, "all hail his majesty, Liam Parry, first of his name, king of the bookworms!" She cackled and ducked as I flicked a tea towel at her.

Mum started laughing again, a proper laugh this time, and wiped the tears from her cheeks with the hem of her apron, "let's celebrate, shall we?" She opened the tin of broken biscuits, her version of a party, and pushed it into the centre of the table.

I watched the little family drama, the parade of pride and sarcasm and love so gnarled it barely recognised itself, and felt the relief blossom in my chest, sharp and overwhelming. This was it, then: my ticket out, written in black ink and sealed with a city's crest. All that was left was to survive the summer, the exams, and whatever else life in a terraced house could throw at me. I reached for a custard cream and let Sarah's laughter fill the room, already tasting the future in the dry sweetness of its crumbs.

If I'd had a choice in the matter, I'd have picked a different film, but Amanda loved comedies with American teenagers who looked nothing like us; sharp-toothed, tan-skinned kids who threw parties in houses bigger than our entire terrace. Rochdale's only cinema stank of mildew and the slow decay of decades-old velvet; the walls were nicotine yellow and the air never quite lost the aftertaste of last night's crowd. We took our usual seats in the back row, left-hand side, within easy reach of the fire exit.

We'd been together for just over a year, my ultimate and most shameful concession to peer pressure, though the word *'together'* felt like a misnomer. We held hands because it was what people did, not because it made sense. The first time Amanda laced her fingers through mine, the shock of skin on skin had nearly made me jolt. Now, my palm just sweated until I found a reason to scratch or shift in my seat, breaking contact for a blissful half-second of reprieve.

Tonight, Amanda wore her hair up in a knot, the little wisps at her neck making her look oddly vulnerable. She was already taller than me in her platforms, but when she sat, she curled inwards, making herself smaller. She picked at the cardboard tub of popcorn in her lap, never really eating it.

The lights went down and the film started with a shriek of synth and canned laughter. The previews before the main feature were for aftershave, lager, a new brand of oven chips, all filmed with a level of polish that made our whole world seem even duller by comparison. Next to us, a couple that looked barely out of first year snogged so loudly it was almost comical. Amanda snickered, nudged me, and mouthed "Gross," but I just shrugged, eyes fixed on the blurry half-light ahead.

The projectionist must have been half-blind; every reel change came with a rattle and a ten-second misalignment where the image wobbled, smearing the actors' faces into ghosts. The laughter in the audience was scattered, polite, and it seemed to die entirely during the love scenes. Amanda leaned her head on my shoulder at one point, but the angle made my neck ache, so I shifted, pretending I needed a drink.

At intermission, I bought a *Fanta* and two *Mars bars*, standing in the garish light of the foyer. The concessions girl wore blue eyeshadow all the way to her eyebrows, and I wondered if she'd practiced the look on a mannequin before bringing it out into the world. I caught sight of our reflection in a cracked mirror: Amanda's lips set in a straight line, my own face washed pale and sickly in the glow of the fruit machine.

When I sat back down, Amanda looked at me like she expected something, a line, a compliment, a gesture. Instead, I just handed her the *Mars bar* and rustled the wrapper on mine, eyes glued to the screen. The film had already restarted, the sound slightly out of sync.

It went on like that: bodies sharing space but not heat, laughter that didn't quite reach the eyes. The actors onscreen finally got together, the big romantic payoff, and I forced a laugh when Amanda squeezed my arm. In the dark, I could pretend that my stiff posture and rapid heartbeat were due to nerves and not the crushing fear that I was faking everything. I wondered if she could tell.

When the credits rolled, we filed out with the rest of the punters into the wet Rochdale night. The town centre was half-deserted, the only light coming from the kebab shop and a few flickering sodium lamps. Amanda pulled her coat tighter around her, then stopped just outside the cinema, beneath the faded awning.

"Did you like it?" she asked, voice uncertain, as if the answer mattered.

"Yeah, it was funny," I lied, "reminded me of that time at yours when…" I trailed off, realising too late that the anecdote I was reaching for wasn't ours at all but one I'd overheard at school.

Amanda smiled, but it flickered, on and off. We started to walk in the direction of her house, the street slick with rain. Our footsteps echoed in tandem, two parts of a four-legged animal that didn't quite know where it was going.

For a while, we talked about nothing: Mrs. Buckley's meltdown in English, the new PE teacher with his obscene whistle, the rumour about Sarah getting caught smoking behind the bike sheds. Amanda laughed at the right bits, even making a few jokes of her own, but there was a brittleness to it, as if she were pulling teeth one by one and waiting for someone to notice the blood.

Halfway to her house, Amanda stopped and turned to face me. We were by the gates of the cemetery, beneath a streetlamp that buzzed with dying insects. The music from the pub across the road seeped into the night.

"Are you okay?" she asked, her face pinched in concern.

"Course I am," I said, maybe too quickly, "why?"

She hugged herself, coat pulled in so tight it seemed she wanted to disappear inside it. "You just … sometimes you go quiet, and I don't know what you're thinking."

I tried to muster a reassuring smile, but the muscles refused to cooperate, "probably just tired. I've been up late, revising."

Amanda nodded but didn't look away, "you ever think about, like, what it'll be like? When you're gone?"

"Gone?" The word caught in my throat.

"To university," she smiled, but not with her eyes. "You'll meet people. New people. I bet you won't even remember me."

The idea of forgetting Amanda was laughable; she was too deeply embedded in every routine, every expectation. But I was already picturing the city, rows of glass and stone, coffee shops, people who didn't look twice at boys with books and mismatched shoes. I was already halfway there.

I didn't say any of that, though, "I could never forget you," I managed, and instantly hated myself for it. It sounded like something from one of her films, and even she looked pained by the cliché.

We reached her house in silence. The porch light was off, but the window above the front bay glowed blue with telly light. She stopped at the gate, hands in pockets, rocking on her heels.

"Do you want to come in?" she asked, quietly.

I glanced at my watch. It was barely ten, "I should get home. Dad'll kill me if I'm late again."

She hesitated, then nodded. "Okay." She looked up at me, eyes round and solemn, "you know you can talk to me, right?"

"Yeah," I said, but even to my ears it sounded flat, "I know."

Then, in a move so choreographed I almost saw it coming in slow motion, Amanda leaned in for a kiss. She stood on tiptoe, her hand on my shoulder, and closed her eyes. I could see the faint shimmer of lip balm, the furrow in her brow, the way her eyelashes fanned out against her cheek. I wanted, for her sake, to want it.

But all I could think about was how it would look: the neighbours, the dark street, the shape of us framed against the houses opposite. I froze, lips grazing hers for a second before I recoiled, pulling away as though the contact had burned me.

Amanda's face crumpled, confusion giving way to something like resignation, "it's okay," she said, too quickly. "We don't have to. I just … I thought maybe you wanted to."

I scrambled for an excuse, "I do. I just … respect you, you know? I don't want you to think I'm …"

She put a hand up, stopping me, "don't be daft." She looked away, her smile stitched up like a wound. "You're the only lad in Rochdale who thinks too much."

I laughed, because it was the only thing left to do, and the sound echoed in the empty street, bouncing back with twice the sadness. Amanda stepped back, wrapping her arms around herself.

"See you tomorrow?" she asked.

"Yeah," I said, already backing down the path. "See you."

She watched me go, standing perfectly still under the streetlamp, until I turned the corner and she disappeared from view.

I walked home fast, head down, hands in pockets. The sky threatened more rain, and the damp crept through my trainers, chilling my toes. Every step hammered the same thought into my skull: *she knows, she knows, she knows*.

At home, Mum was on the phone to her sister and Dad was already asleep in his chair. I slipped up to my room, and shook off my wet clothes and burrowing under the covers with my revision notes. But the words on the page blurred, the sentences collapsing into shapes I didn't recognise.

I lay there in the dark, thinking about Amanda, about the way she closed her eyes, the way she tried so hard to make it easy for me. I wondered if she understood, really understood, or if she was just too kind to say it out loud. Maybe it didn't matter. Maybe, like everything else, it would dissolve when I crossed that invisible border, when I started over as someone new.

But I knew better. You couldn't shed your skin and expect not to bleed. Not in Rochdale, not anywhere.

I sat at my desk after midnight, the rest of the house dead except for the pipes shuddering every time the central heating hiccupped. My walls were lined with bookshelves made from leftover planks and bent nails, nothing matched, but I liked the feeling that I'd built this cell myself, a place to store up knowledge and hide in plain sight.

The university packet was spread in front of me like a game board. I'd read the cover letter a dozen times, but it still didn't seem real: *Parry, L., we are pleased to invite you*. The phrase *"conditional upon grades"* had been underlined by my own hand until the paper nearly tore. Beyond the official paperwork, there were leaflets for student societies, union clubs, glossy photos of the campus at improbable angles, a letter from a second-year *"buddy"* named Tim who claimed to love hiking, and a campus map so intricate you'd need a week and a compass to survive it.

I looked for clues on every page. There was the *student union*, apparently open till two in the morning; the *poetry society*, which met at a pub with a name I couldn't pronounce; a list of international student associations, each with their own cryptic acronym. I traced each line of text for some secret signal that it would be okay to be different, that there were others who'd walked out of a town like this and found themselves on the other side.

Beneath the university pack I kept a stack of local newspapers, for research. At first, I'd thought they might help me acclimatise, but mostly they reminded me of home: petty crime, council meetings, the occasional scandal about misused funds. Tonight, flicking through the brittle pages, I spotted a headline tucked between the classifieds and the death notices: *"Student Protest at University: Dozens March on Victoria Park."* The photo was grainy but arresting, a crowd of kids with a banner and wild hair, one of them in a leather jacket that looked like something from a dream.

I held my breath and read every word. The article was about student grants and *"solidarity with striking workers,"* but what made my heart knock was the mention, at the bottom, of *"multiple campus groups—including the newly formed Gay Soc—voicing demands for inclusion."* It was the first time I'd seen the words in print outside of a slur, and it sent a cold rush up my spine.

I read the line over and over. I imagined the person who'd said it out loud, maybe even in a microphone, and tried to picture what that would feel like: to say it and not shrink, to own the word and stand in a crowd, not alone.

With trembling fingers, I found the scissors and cut the article out with a precision I'd never managed in Craft at school. The snip of each cut was painfully loud in the quiet, but I kept at it, even folding the edges so it would fit neatly in the battered shoebox under my bed.

The shoebox was a reliquary. Inside it I kept the poems I wrote and never dared show to anyone; a concert programme from when Mum took us to see *Romeo and Juliet* at the *Octagon*; a photo of Sarah as a toddler, her face smeared with ice cream; ticket stubs from the library's poetry night; and a few pages I'd torn from library books and hidden here, convinced even the *Dewey Decimal System* couldn't protect me if the wrong person found out.

I added the article to the box, sliding it between my copy of *'Auden's "Selected Poems'* and a flyer for a gig I'd never went to. The box was almost full. Sometimes I worried what would happen if Dad ever found it, whether he'd bother to read the poems or just torch the lot in the backyard.

I pressed the lid shut and hid the box again, then turned out the lamp and let the darkness flood the corners. My eyes adjusted, and I could see the outline of my own body, lean and knobbly, stretched out on the mattress. I counted the weeks until I'd leave for Manchester, ticking off the days in my head like a prisoner etching marks into the cell wall. Part of me wanted to run from all of it, to lose myself in the city, to become someone else entirely. But another part, smaller and sharper, wanted to keep everything: the box, the poems, the memory of Sarah laughing, even the awkward weight of Amanda's hand in mine.

I listened to the silence, feeling the heat of my own breath against the pillow, and wondered what the future would make of me. I imagined standing in the middle of that campus, banners waving, voices raised for things that mattered. I thought about the kids in the article, their arms thrown up in defiance, and wondered if any of them had sat up at night, alone, scissors in hand, cutting hope out of the daily news.

I didn't know if I'd ever be brave enough to join them, but for now, it was enough to know they existed. I closed my eyes, feeling the weight of the shoebox under my bed, and let myself dream of the city where maybe, just maybe, I'd find the others like me.

CHAPTER 4: CROSSING CLASS LINES

October 1981

They made a show of getting lost, even though I'd memorised the route from the admissions packet twice over: through the mean squares of central Manchester, past the lopsided post-war terraces and the curry shops, until the streets got wider and the gardens trimmed down to military length. My father's knuckles bleached to bone on the steering wheel as the car entered the university precinct, the hand-painted white arrows on the tarmac leading us under a low arch of blackened stone. The *Escort's* suspension groaned like a pensioner. My mother, never one for silence, offered a running commentary about every building, "that must be the library, look at the windows!" as if she could convince herself this was a place for people like us.

We joined a hesitant parade of cars in the quadrangle; bumpers shined for the occasion and registration plates from counties I'd only ever seen on quiz shows. As dusk approached, the lamplight here was autumnal and syrup-thick, puddles catching yellow and scattering it back onto the brick. Students wheeled trolleys and dragged suitcases, some pausing to smoke, others with parents in tow who wore that same mix of pride and panic. My own mother twisted in her seat every ten seconds, checking the back, as though my bag might have staged a break for it.

"Are you sure you've got the room number right, Liam?" she asked, flicking at the corner of the letter in her lap. It was already creased into transparency at the folds, "it says here B-block, but on the map it …"

"It's B-block, first floor," I said, not looking up. The space between the front seats felt like a moat.

"See? He knows what he's doing, Mags," Dad grunted, searching for a spot to park. There was a line of staff in hi-vis vests, waving at us to move along, but Dad took his time, sizing up the competition. Next to us, a family in matching raincoats unloaded a hatchback so new it still had showroom stickers on the glass.

I slipped out the rear door as soon as we stopped, grateful for the rush of damp air and the opportunity to put my hands to use. My bag was wedged in the footwell, heavier than I remembered, and I grunted as I heaved it over my shoulder. My dad had insisted on packing the trunk himself, a game of *Tetris* he won every time, and now he fussed over which box to take first, "get the heavy one out, then you don't have to come back," he said, like he was prepping me for a shift at the depot.

Mum, already blinking fast to keep from tearing up, grabbed the handles of my pillow and duvet, still in the plastic sack from the market, "let's have a look at your room, then," she said, marching ahead as if by taking the lead she could will away the last twenty years of her life.

Inside, the air was warmer, smelling faintly of new paint and yesterday's sweat. A thin, nervy student in a purple t-shirt, *Hall Rep*, according to the badge, greeted us at the door. He tried to shake my hand, fumbled the gesture, then pointed up the staircase, "B-block, left at the landing, you can't miss it." The accent was RP, or close enough; my dad rolled his eyes as soon as the rep turned away.

We climbed the stairs in single file. Each landing was painted a different shade of green, like the decorators couldn't decide if they were in a hospital or a primary school. My room was at the far end of a corridor that hummed with fluorescent tubes. The door stood open, keys dangling from the lock.

Mum gasped, genuinely delighted, "it's bigger than your room at home!" It wasn't, but I let her have the illusion. The single bed was a wire-mesh special, mattress thin enough to feel every spring. The desk was bolted to the wall, and a wardrobe with two warped doors leaned against the far side. Someone had left a welcome pack, a mug with the university logo, a map, and a can of baked beans, on the window ledge.

Dad set the box down with a thud, "could've done with a lick of paint," he said, testing the desk with a fist. "Still, you won't be sleeping much, will you?"

He meant it as a joke, but the room swallowed the sound. My mum went to the window, drew the thin curtains aside, and looked down at the quadrangle below, where new arrivals milled about in a confusion of suitcases and farewells. Her hand lingered on the glass.

I took a minute to absorb the space. It was nothing special, but it was mine. The walls were off-white, marked with *blu-*

tack stains; the radiator hissed faintly under the sill. Through the window, you could also make out the clock tower of the main building, bathed in sodium light.

I turned and caught my dad watching me. He looked older in here, his hands too big, his voice less certain, "you'll be all right, won't you?" he said, but it wasn't really a question.

I nodded, then looked away, "yeah, I will."

We unpacked in silence, Mum lining the dresser with tea towels "to keep the dust off," Dad assembling a pyramid of tinned goods by the kettle. He rifled through the shelf of battered books I'd brought, picking up a dog-eared copy of Orwell and flipping to the first page. "Heavy stuff, this," he said, eyes skimming the blurb, "thought you were here to read about history?"

"History and English Lit. And maybe teaching's after," I said, knowing he wouldn't get it.

He grunted, put the book down. Mum had found the laundry schedule pinned to the wall and was copying it word for word onto her palm.

I heard laughter from the corridor, a snort, a string of swear words, someone banging on a door down the hall. I felt my shoulders tense, then relax. I was supposed to be part of that noise now, wasn't I?

After a while, Mum said, "well, we'd better get going before it gets too late." She checked her watch even though the time had never mattered less.

Dad held out his hand. When I took it, he squeezed hard, as if daring me to squeeze back, "don't let them take you for a mug," he said, voice low, "you're just as good as the lot of them."

I managed a laugh, "thanks, Dad. I'll remember."

Mum hugged me, harder than I expected, her breath damp on my collar, "you ring me if you need anything, love. Doesn't matter what time."

"Okay, Mum," I said, my own throat going tight.

We walked down together, dragging out the descent as long as possible. Outside, Dad opened the car door, then closed it again. Mum tucked a five-pound note into my palm, like she was giving me secret instructions, "for a treat," she said, and I nodded, knowing I'd probably spend it on the laundry.

They got in the car. I watched through the window as Dad started the engine, hesitated, then gave a little wave before pulling off. I stayed on the step long after the *Escort* had disappeared through the gates, feeling the weight of every eye in the windows above. Alone, finally, just as I'd hoped, and terrified, just as I'd expected. I went back inside, feeling the silence settle around me, and tried to decide what to do next.

I'd expected to unpack in solitude, but the hall was already alive, a living thing pulsing with voices and slamming doors. The clatter from the kitchen at the far end suggested someone had started a party, or at least the early negotiations for one. I set about making my cell habitable, lining the desk with my books, each with a carefully rehearsed story about where I'd got it. The battered *Penguin classics* were charity shop rescues, true, but I arranged them as though they'd been collected over years of continental travel. Forster went spine-in, sandwiched between a battered poetry anthology and a heavy history text; Mum would have said I was being daft, but I didn't want to risk it being seen by the wrong set of eyes.

My shirts, crisply ironed and still faintly scented with the ghost of our detergent, went into the wardrobe. I ran a hand along the edge, feeling the ridges where the iron had pressed too hard, proof, if I needed it, that I had not been born to this sort of order. On the desk, I set up the two pens I'd bought from *Woolworth's*, arranging them parallel with the edge as though precision alone might fend off the chaos I knew was waiting.

It didn't take long before there was a knock at my open door. I tensed, then turned, putting on the smile I'd practiced for exactly this sort of encounter.

First in was James, whose handshake nearly detached my arm at the socket, "James. Law. Surrey," he said, as if reading from a nameplate. His accent was soft but polished, vowels so elongated I almost lost track of the words. He wore a rugby shirt with the collar up, and his hair was cut like he'd just stepped off a prospectus.

I gave my name, but before I could finish, he'd already moved on to "what school were you at?"

"Sixth Form College, Rochdale," I said, but instantly regretted it. The words felt flat, monochrome against his technicolour past.

"Oh, right," he replied, giving me a blank look before filling the silence himself. "I took a gap year, did Thailand for six months. Could've stayed, honestly, just beaches and *Chang* beer all day. You been abroad much?"

"France on a school trip," I said, and then, grasping at social driftwood, "but my aunt lives in Cheshire. Near Knutsford." It was true, technically, though I'd only been twice and the last visit ended in a two-day standoff over a borrowed coat.

James nodded, satisfied, and glanced around my room, eyes landing on the books. "You're into literature, then? Not my thing, but my girlfriend's all about it. Keeps quoting poetry at me. We're meeting her for a pint later, you should come."

"Yeah, maybe," I said, and he was gone, off to the next door.

After James came Rupert, whose haircut must have cost more than my entire wardrobe, "name's Rupert," he said, leaning in the doorway with the authority of someone used to standing in them. "Did you go to the freshers' meeting yet?"

"No, just unpacking," I said.

He peered into my room, sizing it up. "I was at Harrow, so this is a bit of a come-down," he joked, but there was no real self-mockery in his tone. "You can always tell who's public and who's not, can't you?" He smirked, scanning my shoes and the plain bedding Mum had insisted on. "Still, anyone's better than the idiots on C-block. You drink?"

"Yeah," I lied.

He nodded approval, "we'll get on, then."

He left, and I was alone again for a minute before a third figure appeared, this time leaning in without knocking.

"I'm Steve. Business," he said, "you play football?"

"A bit," I said, not wanting to confess that PE at my college was more about survival than sport.

"My family's got a place in the South of France. We always have a kick-about on the beach. You should come out sometime, Easter or summer. Depends on what the old man's doing with the house." Steve's confidence was so effortless I wanted to punch it, but instead I nodded and made a note to consult an atlas and find out where, exactly, the South of France even was.

He looked past me, at the window, then said, "decent view. You into music?" He gestured to the radio I'd set up on the sill.

"Yeah, *Motown*, *Stevie Wonder* mostly, and ..." I caught myself, unsure if admitting to liking *Motown* would get me classified as weird. "And rock," I said, as a hedge.

Steve shrugged, "haven't heard much of that." He shrugged again. "See you downstairs?"

I said I would, and he wandered off, leaving a faint trail of aftershave and ambition behind him.

The corridor quieted after that, and I sank onto the edge of the bed, picking at a stray thread in the cheap poly-cotton. I thought about finding a pay phone and calling Amanda, or maybe Sarah, but the idea of admitting how lost I felt made my stomach twist. I'd spent so much energy rehearsing my new self, the one who could pass, who could talk about holidays and aunts in Cheshire and not betray the terraced house behind the accent, that now, with no one watching, I felt even more fake.

I stared at my reflection in the small rectangular mirror opposite the bed. The overhead light cast weird shadows on my face, pulling the skin taut over bone, making me look older, or maybe just more brittle. I tried on a few smiles, polite, wry, confident, but they slid off before they could settle. The eyes, at least, were honest: tired, a bit scared, and deeply unconvinced.

A burst of laughter erupted from the kitchen. I listened, straining to catch a word or two, but it was just sound, undifferentiated and strange. Maybe I'd go to the freshers' do after all. If nothing else, it would give me a new story to tell.

For now, I turned the radio on, tuning to *Radio One*, a station that played nothing but *Top 40*. I let the music fill the room, masking the emptiness with something predictable and safe, and wondered how long it would take before I could believe the version of myself I was working so hard to invent.

I hovered at the edge of the wood-panelled common room, clutching my bottle of *Pils* like it might sprout a second head and save me from small talk. The place looked like it had been stripped from a stately home and bolted onto the back of the modern halls: huge stone fireplace, a pair of antlers above the mantel, armchairs that creaked if you breathed within five feet of them. Clusters of students orbited the beer table, already forming the alliances that would carry them through the rest of the year. Every conversation seemed pitched just loud enough for me to overhear the words "gap year," "private tutor," or "internship with my dad's firm."

I circled the room twice before settling into a niche beside the radiator, watching the newcomers as they measured each other up. It was the same dance as at home, but the stakes felt higher, like everyone here was auditioning for some unspoken role. I checked my watch twice, thinking I could slip away after a socially acceptable twenty minutes, but my legs wouldn't move.

The door swung open with a gust of cool air, and for a moment, everyone looked up. He strode in with the confidence of someone who'd already done this a dozen times: tight, brand-new jeans that clung just enough to be illegal in some countries I imagined, and a canary-yellow jumper. His hair was sun-bleached and artfully messy, and his face was tanned in a way that suggested he'd actually seen sunlight during the English summer.

He scanned the room with a quick, knowing smile, then caught me staring. Our eyes locked for half a second, and something fizzed in my chest, a cold spark that left me almost winded. I looked away fast, cheeks going hot.

He didn't hesitate. He bee-lined straight to me, threading through the crowd with the grace of a footballer dodging a tackle.

"Evening," he said, voice light and assured. "I'm Alex. Alex Hughes. Geography." He pronounced it "Geo," with a hard "g," like he was daring me to correct him.

"Liam Parry," I managed, my accent flaring up for the first time since I'd walked in, "History and English Lit."

His handshake was dry, firm, and lingered a millisecond longer than necessary, "from round here?" he asked, eyes narrowed but friendly.

"Rochdale, more or less," I said, instantly wishing I'd lied.

Alex grinned, his teeth perfect in a way that should have been annoying, "nice. I'm from the Wirral, but don't hold it against me. Just means I'm a *posh scouser*." He leaned in slightly, like we were already conspirators, "you enjoying the welcome show so far?"

I glanced around the room, at the kids in blazers and the girls in heels stabbing the cheap carpet, "it's…something."

"That's about right." He took a long pull from his own bottle, *Stella,* imported, and gestured with it toward the far corner, where James and Rupert were loudly arguing about rugby. "Already feels like school again, doesn't it? You ever get the sense we're all in the wrong place?"

"Every single day," I said, the words tumbling out too fast. I braced for him to laugh, but instead he gave a knowing nod.

Alex dropped into the armchair next to me, legs stretched out, ankle resting on knee, "so, Liam, English. Who's your favourite?"

I blinked, "sorry?"

"Author. Poet. Whatever. You're an English type; you must have a favourite. Unless you hate all of them, which would be more interesting."

I hesitated, suddenly shy about my answer, "probably Auden," I said, and then, "or Wilde."

He let out a soft whistle, "bold. You going to quote *The love that dare not speak its name'* at me, or should I buy you a drink first?"

It caught me so off guard I nearly choked. I looked up, trying to see if he was taking the piss, but his grin was so open that it disarmed me completely.

"I don't really do poetry," Alex continued, "but I had a teacher who was obsessed with Oscar Wilde. Used to read us bits from *The Importance of Being Earnest* and then cackle like a loon. He got fired, actually, bit of a scandal."

I laughed, the first real one since arriving, "scandal's part of the job description for English teachers."

He toasted me with his bottle, "that's what I keep telling myself."

The conversation hit a rhythm I'd never managed before, not with anyone outside of Amanda or the teachers who saw through me. Alex was quick, but not sharp in a way that cut; he made it easy to keep up. He asked about my courses, my books, what music I was into, and every answer felt like it unlocked something else between us. I barely noticed the crowd getting louder, the air growing thick with beer and anticipation.

Every now and then I'd catch a look from one of the others, the kind that catalogued me and filed me away under *"Northern"* or *"Working Class"* or, worse, *"Try-Hard."* But Alex didn't blink. He seemed to relish the awkward pauses, filling them with stories about getting lost on the train to Manchester, or about the time he'd dyed his hair blue to annoy his father and then forgotten to wash it out before family photos.

By the time the beers ran out, I felt less like a stranger and more like a version of myself I'd never had the nerve to be. Alex said he was heading out for a smoke, and some quiet and asked if I wanted to come. We stepped into the cool corridor, the sudden chill shocking the sweat off my skin.

He lit up, passing me the pack without comment. I took one, more for the company than the nicotine. We leaned against the railing, looking out over the quad. The lamps were on now, the courtyard below empty and echoing.

"So, what made you pick Manchester?" he asked, after a long silence.

I shrugged, "anywhere but home, really."

He nodded, flicking ash over the side, "same."

There was a quiet, expectant moment between us. I didn't want to ruin it by talking, so I let the silence stretch.

Alex glanced at me sideways, "you know, you've got a great accent. Don't hide it."

I almost dropped the cigarette, "what?"

"You keep trying to smooth it out when you talk," he said, matter-of-fact, "but it's way better *au naturelle.*"

I laughed, but it came out tight, "doubt most people here would think so."

"Most people are idiots." He looked at me full on, his gaze even and unembarrassed, "anyway, you stand out. That's better than blending in."

The words sent a shiver up my spine that had nothing to do with the cold. I didn't know what to say, so I just nodded, letting the meaning hang between us.

He finished his smoke, stubbed it out on the railing, "there's an after-party in C-block, if you're up for it. Supposed to be a bit mad."

"Yeah," I said, before I could second-guess myself, "yeah, I'll come."

He grinned, and this time it was more than just friendly. "Good man," he said, and clapped me on the back, sending a pulse through my whole body.

As we walked back in together, I felt the old nerves flicker, but something else, too, like a pilot light had caught in my chest and was burning away the self-doubt by degrees. For the first time since arriving, I didn't care if anyone else was watching. I was too busy watching Alex.

We stepped into the chaos of the common room, side by side, and I realised I hadn't thought about home, or Amanda, or even the day's induction activities for nearly an hour. The feeling was electric, dangerous, and impossible to ignore. For the first time ever, I suspected that another man might be interested in me beyond wanting to copy my homework. It would be days before I'd let myself name it, as perhaps 'attraction', but for now, it was enough just to feel it blazing under my skin.

CHAPTER 5: DOUBLE LIVES

The November wind had teeth and little mercy; it chased me down the concrete chasms of campus, stinging every exposed inch of skin until I remembered to duck my head and huddle deeper into my coat. The sky was gunmetal grey, the air sour with the ghost of rain yet to fall, and even the scrappy magpies loitering near the humanities building looked pissed off to be alive. I kept my textbooks clamped to my chest like a breastplate, knuckles red and cracked, each step a metronome of get to the library, get to the library, get to the library until, like always, the plan derailed.

"Oi! Parry!" Alex's voice cut through the wind, a clean, unbothered whistle. He trotted up from behind, no coat, just a battered fisherman's jumper and faded jeans, like he'd never once been cold in his life, despite not carrying a pound of fat on his body for insulation.

I slowed, partly out of caution and partly because the sight of him always did something strange to my pacing, "you'll catch your death dressed like that," I said, trying to make it sound like a joke instead of an accusation.

He shrugged, "it's all in the blood, mate. Wirral lads don't even own proper coats. Didn't you know?"

"I must've missed that memo about the hardiness of the *'posh scouser',*" I said, forcing a smile. My breath fogged up the lenses of my glasses; I wiped them clean with the hem of my jumper, which only made things worse.

Alex fell in step beside me, his hands tucked in his pockets, "you off to the library again?" He made *"again"* sound both impressed and faintly alarming.

"Just thought I'd get some reading in before lunch," I said, "they've got the new set texts on reserve, but you have to be quick or the law students nab them."

He grinned, "you're the only person I know who does homework before it's due."

I hesitated, "you don't know many people."

"Ah, but the ones I do know are exceptional." He turned his grin up a notch, then nudged me with his elbow, "fancy grabbing a coffee at the *Union* instead? My treat, if you can stand the company."

Every warning system in my head lit up. Alex was not the sort of person you met for coffee unless you were sure of yourself, which I manifestly was not. But I said yes anyway, because the prospect of declining and then watching him walk away was somehow worse.

We peeled off toward the *Student Union* building, the doors gaped wide, coughing out the smells of burnt toast and tobacco, instant coffee, and wet carpet. The inside was warmer, lit by yellow bulbs that made everything look slightly dingy but also safe. I followed Alex through the lobby, past the notice-boards and the vending machines, and into the coffee area, a collection of misfit tables, threadbare armchairs, and students pretending not to be alone.

Alex selected a table in the back corner, near the pinball machine and a half-dead Ficus. He slid into the seat, then gestured for me to do the same. "I'll grab the drinks," he said. "What's your poison?"

"Just a black coffee," I said, but he was already gone, weaving through the line with a confidence I would never master. I set my bag on the floor and tried to look occupied, flipping through the highlighted pages of a reading packet until the words swam.

He was back in record time, two steaming mugs in hand, "I told them you were an intellectual, so they gave you the fancy stuff," he said, pushing the cup my way.

"Cheers," I said, wrapping both hands around the mug. The warmth hit me like a drug.

Alex sipped his own, then looked me dead in the eye, "so what's got you buried in books this early? Essay?"

"Just background for a seminar," I said. "French Revolution. The lecturer's obsessed with Robespierre, and if you haven't read at least three biographies, you're dead in the water."

He whistled, "I remember Robespierre from school. *The Terror*, right? Lopping heads left and right."

"That's the one," I said, relieved at a conversation I could manage. "He was a fanatic, but also ..." I broke off, suddenly self-conscious.

Alex leaned in, his expression open, "but also?"

I forced a laugh, "it's stupid. I just think he was more complicated than anyone gives him credit for. Like, everyone focuses on the guillotine, but nobody talks about the years he spent trying to make things better before it all went to hell."

Alex nodded, the corner of his mouth lifting, "I get it. Heroes and villains are easier when you keep them simple." He stared into his coffee for a second, then said, "I always liked the messy ones best. The ones who never really knew what side they were on."

I looked away, heat prickling my neck, "you sound like you've got a bit of sympathy for the devil yourself."

He laughed, low and unbothered, "only if he buys the first round." He then took out his pack of *Benson and Hedges*, and tossed me one across the table.

For a few seconds, the only sound was the low rumble of the other students, the mechanical clank of the pinball machine and the sparking of a match. I risked a glance at Alex, who seemed perfectly at ease, slouched back, eyes half-lidded, like he was immune to awkwardness.

"What about you?" I asked, exhaling a cloud of smoke. "Geography, wasn't it?"

He nodded, "coastal erosion and glaciation. You wouldn't think it, but it's sexy as hell. Most people just see a map and think it's boring, but the stories underneath, tectonic shifts, ancient floods, the whole world getting re-sculpted by invisible forces. It's chaos, but it's beautiful."

I watched his hands as he talked. They moved in lazy arcs, sketching out invisible coastlines and river deltas. There was something hypnotic about it, and I had to fight to keep my eyes on his face.

"Did you always want to study that?" I said, if only to break the spell.

Alex shrugged, "not really. Dad wanted me to do economics or law, but they're hard! I always preferred the parts of the world nobody bothered to pay attention to. The places that get washed away, and that I found easier." He paused, searching for something in my reaction. "What about you? Always a bookworm?"

I hesitated, then nodded, "my mum says I learned to read before I could walk. Or at least, before I could walk without falling over."

He grinned, "I'm picturing you in a nappy, clutching a volume of Shakespeare."

"More likely *The Beano*," I said, and he laughed, loud enough to turn a few heads.

The noise startled me. I shrank into my seat, suddenly conscious of how visible we were, two blokes in the corner, one of them flamboyantly handsome, the other a textbook case of *"trying too hard."* I tugged at my sleeve and busied myself with the coffee and cigarette, though my hands trembled just enough to slosh some onto the saucer.

Alex must have noticed, because he sobered, leaning in so his voice dropped to a near-whisper, "you all right, Liam? You seem tense."

"I'm fine," I lied, "just tired."

He nodded, not convinced, "you get used to it, you know. The whole…scene." He gestured around the room, at the clusters of students, the invisible pecking order.

"I'm not sure I want to get used to it," I said, surprising even myself.

Alex's eyes flickered, a brief glint of something like admiration, "Then don't," he said, voice steady, "do it your way."

We sipped in companionable silence for a minute, finishing our cigarettes as the world narrowed to the orbit of our table. I found myself relaxing by degrees, letting the warmth seep in, letting my guard slip just enough to feel human.

"So, Rochdale," Alex said, "you ever miss it?"

"Every day," I said, and meant it, "but I don't think I could go back. Not now."

He nodded, then said, "I'm the same. Parents still live in the old house, but every time I go back it feels smaller. Like I'm too big for it now." He grinned, "not in an arrogant way. Just … like the walls moved in."

I smiled, recognising the feeling, "yeah. Like you're visiting someone else's life."

We traded stories then, back and forth. His were mostly about growing up near the river, sneaking into pubs at sixteen, the epic fights with his older brother. Mine were about the way the town shrank every year, about Mum's legendary Sunday roasts and Sarah's crusade to outwit every teacher at her school. We orbited the topic of family for a while, careful not to mention relationships or girlfriends; that ground was booby-trapped, and we both seemed to know it.

Somewhere in the middle of a story about his brother's failed attempt at running away to Wales, Alex said, "you ever read *The Swimming-Pool Library*?"

I shook my head, "don't think so. What's it about?"

He hesitated, then leaned in conspiratorially, "it's about this guy, Will. He spends his life drifting between clubs, never quite belonging anywhere. But it's also about secrets, and how sometimes the things you hide end up running your whole life."

I felt my stomach knot, "sounds intense."

Alex grinned, a flash of challenge in his eyes, "it's banned in most public libraries, you know. Too much…content."

I blushed, knowing exactly what he meant, "I'll add it to my list."

He laughed, easy and full-throated, but softer than before, "I bet you will, Parry."

The conversation drifted, but I couldn't shake the feeling that something had shifted, some secret hand of cards now on the table, waiting to be played. I focused on the patterns in the coffee foam, willing my hands not to betray me.

At some point, Alex's knee brushed mine under the table. I jerked back, sending a minor tidal wave of coffee over the rim and onto the saucer. He reached across, steadying my hand with his.

"Sorry," I muttered, voice scraping my throat raw.

He didn't let go, "you okay?"

"Yeah, this time just clumsy," I said, but the tremor in my voice made it sound like a confession.

Alex squeezed my hand once, then released it, "you'll get the hang of it," he said. "Promise."

I swallowed, not trusting myself to answer.

We sat there a little longer, letting the conversation drift to exams and Christmas holidays and which halls had the worst heating. I wanted to keep talking, to sit here all afternoon and peel the world away until it was just the two of us in this dim, battered corner of the *Union*. But the sense of being watched, of every passing student cataloguing our strangeness, grew until I felt like a specimen pinned to a board.

"I should get going," I said, finally, "I've got a tutorial in ten."

Alex stood, draining his coffee, "right you are," he said, "we'll do this again, yeah?"

"Yeah," I said, and meant it.

He clapped me on the shoulder as we walked out, the touch brief but electric. We parted at the main doors, he with a wink and a backwards wave, me clutching my books so tight I thought they'd leave bruises on my ribs.

Outside, the wind had dropped, but the cold felt sharper. I hurried towards my tutor's room, head down, the ghosts of our conversation burning in my chest. I didn't know what any of it meant, or what would happen next, but for the first time since arriving, I felt like maybe, just maybe, I wasn't the only one making it up as I went along.

The rest of my day blurred into a fog of tutorial notes and footnotes, but somewhere around four, as the sky surrendered to the early dark, I found myself weaving through the logjam of students that clogged the campus's narrowest passage, officially *'Arts Link'*, but everyone just called it *The Gauntlet*. The air was heavy with fried onions from the burger van and the tang of wet wool. I shouldered through with my usual low profile, eyes on my boots, until I heard the voice again, that Wirral lilt unmistakable even at a whisper.

"Liam! Hang on."

I paused, heart jumpstarting in my chest. Alex jogged up, his cheeks pink from the cold, and fell into step beside me like it was the most natural thing in the world. We were jammed shoulder to shoulder by the press of bodies, the heat and friction making my face sting with self-consciousness.

"Good tutorial?" he asked, grinning like he knew the answer already.

"Not bad. We spent half an hour arguing about whether revolutions ever really succeed or if they just swap one bunch of bastards for another."

He laughed, "sounds like my dad's take on politics. *'New government, same shite, different haircut'.*"

I snorted, then immediately regretted making any noise at all. The crowd pressed us closer; our arms brushed, and I tensed so violently that my books nearly shot out from under my elbow. For a moment, the corridor funnelled all sound into white noise, just the two of us locked in orbit, my skin burning where he'd touched it.

Alex didn't flinch. If anything, he seemed to enjoy my discomfort, his eyes dancing with secret amusement, "you all right, mate? You look like you've seen a ghost."

"Just cold," I muttered, though I could feel the heat radiating from my ears.

The squeeze of bodies forced us to slow, and in the jam-up, a second, heavier contact, his hand grazing mine, knuckles brushing in the most accidental way possible. My reflexes betrayed me: I jerked back, colliding with a girl in a rugby top, and my folders exploded across the walkway.

Papers everywhere. Fuck.

I dropped to one knee, scrabbling for the loose sheets. Alex crouched beside me, scooping up pages and handing them over with a deadpan efficiency that made the whole thing somehow worse.

"No harm done," he said, though everyone in a ten-foot radius had seen my little meltdown.

I mumbled a thanks, shoving everything back into my bag. The rugby girl glared, but Alex flashed her his best smile, and she just rolled her eyes, moving on.

We picked up our pace, emerging from *The Gauntlet* into the relative quiet behind the *Union*. My hands shook as I refastened the zipper on my bag, but I tried to keep it together.

"So, uh. Plans for the weekend?" Alex said, tone casual, but there was a sidelong glance that landed like a challenge.

"Nothing much," I lied, then caught myself. "Actually, Amanda's coming down from Stirling. She's got a break before Christmas to visit her parents."

He nodded, the smile on his face not quite reaching his eyes. "Nice. How long you two been together?"

I did the maths, "just over a year. We met in sixth form."

"Sound," he said, and for a second there was an edge to the word, a blade behind the syllables. Then he shrugged, the mask of easy confidence snapping back into place, "I suppose you'll be playing tour guide, then?"

"Something like that," I said, my mouth dry.

He looked at me, really looked, and I felt like a specimen pinned under glass, "you ever get the feeling you're not cut out for this place?"

"All the time," I admitted, surprised at my own honesty.

Alex smiled, softer now, "me too."

We walked in silence for a minute, the campus suddenly vast and empty. The wind whipped up, rattling the bare branches overhead.

At the door to the hall, he stopped, hands jammed in his pockets, "well. Have fun with your girlfriend."

I tried to read his face, but he was already halfway to his usual grin, "thanks. I'll see you around?"

"Always," he said, and with a backwards wave, he was gone.

I stood in the cold for a moment, watching his retreating figure, the unspoken things piling up inside me like snow on the windowsill. Then I let myself back into the warmth of the building, every nerve on fire and nowhere to put it.

Saturday came with a hangover of November sleet, the sky so low you could scrape it with your knuckles. The concourse at *Manchester Piccadilly* was packed, rucksacks and umbrellas jostling in wet procession, the tannoy barking out delays in a voice so flat it could have been a joke. I found Amanda before she found me, her hair shorter than last time, the new fringe framing her face in a way that made her look older, or maybe just more certain of herself.

Her suitcase came first, clattering along the platform, and then she followed, wrapped in her duffel coat, cheeks blotched pink from the train ride and the sharp wind. She broke into a smile as soon as she saw me, the real kind that cracked her face wide open.

"Liam!" She barrelled in for a hug, suitcase abandoned mid-step. I let her hold me as long as she wanted, but my arms stayed a shade too loose, a secret I hoped she'd forgive.

"You look knackered," she said, pulling back and searching my eyes for the joke.

"Long week," I said, and tried to make it sound like anyone else's.

We squeezed into the greasy spoon across from the station, Amanda already talking a mile a minute about her flat mates in Stirling, the impossible pace of lectures, the late-night kitchen confessions that were the real education. I listened, or tried to, but every time the door jingled open, I glanced up, half-expecting to see Alex's sun-bleached hair or hear his voice slicing through the crowd. Instead, it was just rain-soaked students, truant granddads, a procession of lives with no relevance to mine.

"Are you even listening?" Amanda said, waving a chip in front of my nose.

"Of course," I lied, then repeated the last sentence she'd said. "The one from Ayr keeps burning toast and nearly set off the alarm."

She smirked, satisfied, then leaned in, voice dropping, "I missed you, you know."

I felt something twist in my gut, guilt and longing and something else that didn't have a name yet. "Same," I said, and this time it was almost true.

I played tour guide for the rest of the afternoon, showing her the *Union* ("It looks just like on the telly, but dirtier," she pronounced), the main quad ("Did you know every building here is haunted?"), and the narrow alleys between the lecture halls where I half-lived. At every turn, I checked the crowds, scanned the faces, waiting for the world to collapse in on itself. Amanda noticed, because she noticed everything.

"You walk like you're expecting to be mugged," she said, linking her arm through mine.

"It's Manchester," I replied, shrugging.

She laughed, the sound sharp and genuine, "you were never this jumpy at home."

We ducked into the library to escape the rain, Amanda gawking at the sheer size of it, "we've got three shelves at Stirling, and one's just *Mills & Boon*." She wandered the stacks with childlike awe, fingers trailing the spines, before spinning to face me in a patch of cold sunlight.

"So, what's it like?" she asked, "really."

I knew what she meant, but pretended otherwise, "it's university," I said. "Everyone's smarter than you and pretends not to care about anything."

She rolled her eyes, "come on. You love it, don't you?"

"It's not what I expected," I said, which was the best I could do.

Her eyes softened, and she stepped closer, close enough that I could smell the clean, sharp scent of her shampoo, "you can tell me if you're lonely, you know."

I almost laughed, if only she knew the truth of it, but instead I squeezed her hand, hard. "I'm all right, honest. Better now you're here."

She smiled, but it was a small, careful smile, "good. Because I've missed having someone who gets my jokes."

We spent the rest of the afternoon in the student cafe, the radiators rattling and the windows steamed up with other people's conversations. Amanda told stories about her classes, her friends, her new life two hundred miles north. I played along, asked the right questions, but I kept one eye on the door at all times, nerves wound tight as piano wire.

At one point, Amanda leaned across the table, both hands around her mug, and said, "you seem a thousand miles away today."

I forced myself to meet her gaze, "sorry. I just, there's been a lot on my mind."

She nodded, eyes searching, "you'd tell me, right? If something was wrong?"

"Of course," I said, squeezing her hand tighter than necessary. "Nothing's wrong. Not with us."

She bit her lip, unconvinced, but let it slide. I watched her for a moment, the curve of her jaw, the light in her eyes, the way she fit into my life like an old, much-mended jumper. I wanted, desperately, to want this more than anything.

"I'm glad you came," I said, and the words almost stuck in my throat.

She smiled, this time wider, and brushed her foot against mine under the table, "me too."

We killed the rest of the evening in my room, talking nonsense, listening to tapes, Amanda curled up on the bed in her pyjamas while I sat at the desk, hands clasped between my knees. We watched the city glow from my window, sodium lamps blinking to life in the drizzle, the campus shrinking to an island of warmth and sound.

She dozed off before midnight, head on my pillow, breathing slow and even. I sat for a long time watching her sleep, feeling the weird ache of being both too close and not close enough. At some point I drifted too, the night pressing in, the world outside briefly forgotten.

In the small hours, I woke to Amanda's hand on my arm, her eyes searching for mine in the dark.

"I know you," she whispered, "I know when you're lying."

I wanted to confess it all: the confusion, the fear, the thing inside me that wasn't meant to be spoken. Instead, I just pulled her close, held her until the sun started leaking through the curtains. In the half-light, everything looked softer, almost possible.

We spent Sunday morning like it was borrowed time, wandering the empty campus, Amanda taking pictures with her disposable camera, forcing me to pose in front of statues and stairwells, "one day you'll want to remember this," she said, snapping a shot of me squinting into the drizzle.

I tried to believe her. I tried to believe I was someone worth remembering.

After lunch, the city's drizzle upgraded itself to proper rain. Amanda wanted to see the university shop before she left; something about a gift for her dad, who collected novelty tea towels from every place she visited. We ducked under the portico by the union, waiting for a break in the downpour, Amanda huddled into my side for warmth. I was telling her about the time my own dad tried to brew beer in the bathtub and promptly lost it all when Mum pulled the plug out by accident. The doors behind us swung open and I heard Alex's laugh, a sound you could spot in a crowded stadium.

I turned, heart hammering, and saw him striding out with a girl on his arm. She was tall, blonde, and so classically pretty it hurt to look at her. Her raincoat was candy-apple red, her lipstick a perfect match. The sight of them together, her arm looped through his, his hand on the small of her back, knocked the air from my lungs.

Alex spotted us and broke into a grin. "Liam! Fancy seeing you out in this weather."

I faked a smile, already regretting every choice that had brought me to this precise moment. "Amanda wanted to see the campus shop before she headed back to her parents."

Amanda beamed, sticking out her hand with her usual confidence. "Hi, I'm Amanda."

"Alex Hughes," he said, shaking her hand, "and this is Caroline. My girlfriend." The word hung in the air, sticky as tar.

Caroline smiled at Amanda, a quick up-and-down that took in her shoes, her hair, her whole life in a single glance. "Lovely to meet you," she said, voice smooth and expensive.

For the next five minutes, we made small talk about courses, accommodation, the city's weather (always worse than home, wherever home was). Alex asked Amanda about Stirling, about how she liked Scotland, and she answered with a bright politeness that barely concealed her nerves. I said as little as possible, watching the way Caroline leaned into Alex, the way he rested his chin on her head like he'd done it a thousand times before.

I squeezed Amanda's hand so tight my knuckles went white. She shot me a quick, searching look, but said nothing. The rain picked up, drumming a rhythm on the plastic bin nearby.

Eventually, Caroline checked her watch, "we should get going, or we'll miss the start of the film."

Alex grinned, squeezing her shoulder, "nice to meet you, Amanda. Liam, see you in the trenches."

"Yeah," I said, barely hearing myself.

They vanished down the steps, heads bent together. Amanda watched them go, then looked at me sideways.

"He's posh, isn't he?" she said, tone light but edged.

I shrugged, trying for nonchalance, "you get all sorts here."

She smirked, "I like her coat."

I laughed, a brittle little sound, "yeah, me too."

We bought the tea towel, dodged puddles back to halls, and killed the last half hour in the common room, Amanda perched on the arm of my chair, swinging her legs. The whole time, my mind ran the loop: Alex and Caroline, Alex's hand on her back, the easy, practiced way he'd said "girlfriend." I wanted to hate her, or him, or myself, but mostly I just felt tired. Tired and empty and skinless.

At the station, on the way back to her parents' house , Amanda hugged me goodbye, the squeeze longer than necessary.

"Are you sure you're okay?" she whispered, her breath warm on my neck.

"Fine," I lied, "just hate goodbyes, but say hello to your mum and dad for me."

She smiled, sad but forgiving, "you'll call?"

"Course."

She got on the train, found her seat, pressed her hand to the window as it pulled away. I watched until the carriages blurred into the rain, then stood alone on the platform until the guard shooed me out.

The walk back to my room felt longer than ever. Every step echoed, every corner bristled with ghosts. When I got in, the room was silent. I dropped onto my bed and stared at the ceiling, counting the cracks, trying to outlast the noise inside my head.

In the dark, I could still feel Alex's hand on mine, the heat of it, the weight of everything unsaid. I wondered if he remembered it at all, or if it was just another story he told himself about how the world worked.

I curled tighter, wishing I could make myself small enough to disappear. But the ache in my chest wouldn't let me, and neither would the memory of a voice that made me feel, for one impossible second, like I was seen.

I closed my eyes and let the future creep in, one cold breath at a time.

CHAPTER 6: THE BREAKING POINT

It was the last Friday before Christmas break, and the common room had been converted into a chemical spill of lager, crisps, and manufactured joy. The windows steamed with the heat of too many bodies, and the air was thick enough to make your teeth taste of smoke. I wedged myself into the corner beside the radiator, next to a table buckling under the weight of *Tesco's* finest party food and tried to look like someone who belonged there.

Most people had swapped real clothes for fancy dress: shepherds, elves, one Mary in a blue bedsheet, several Jesuses. The pre-med boys had synchronised to the minute when to rip off their shirts and pour beer over each other; it was a reenactment of something, maybe birth or death or both. I watched with clinical detachment as two future solicitors, already pink with booze, tried to assemble a human pyramid using three unwilling engineers as the base.

I picked at the sausage rolls. The pastry was pale and undercooked, the kind that left a paste on the roof of your mouth. I downed a cup of warm lager to clear it. The volume of the room surged as someone produced a plastic trumpet and began playing what might have been *"God Save the Queen,"* or possibly the theme from *Match of the Day*. A girl in tinsel antlers tried to teach her boyfriend how to waltz, but he tripped over his own trainers and went down hard, nearly taking her with him. They laughed, legs tangled, and she sprawled across his chest, their hands finding each other as if magnetised.

It was, in theory, everything I'd ever wanted: anonymity, noise, the chance to be rewritten by proximity to other lives. Instead, I felt like an extra in someone else's hallucination.

I had clocked every person in the room, as was my habit. Rupert, already sloshed, danced atop a coffee table, yelling the lyrics to *"White Riot"* while clutching a can in each hand. James worked the room, shaking hands and dispensing back slaps like a local MP. Steve, the football evangelist, was somewhere in the kitchen, leading a conga line and shouting for more "lad juice." Every ten minutes, the door would bang open and a new wave of people would surge in, trailing cold air and strange perfumes.

I searched for Alex, though I never let myself admit that was what I was doing. He was usually at the centre of any crowd, arm wrapped around someone, voice a little too loud, laughter booming out over the lesser noises. But tonight, he was nowhere to be seen.

I finished my drink, wiped my hands on my jeans, and decided to try the corridor. The kitchen was a riot of spilled drinks and instant noodles, the floor sticky and the air so dense with steam you could barely see across the room. I spotted Caroline by the fridge, blonde hair in a glossy ponytail, holding a bottle of wine and surrounded by half the rugby team. She glanced up and saw me, then turned her head, as if the sight of me was too awkward to acknowledge. I didn't blame her.

Outside, the hallway was a tundra by comparison, the echo of the party bouncing off painted brick and fire doors. I considered heading back to my room, but a sound, quiet, almost muffled, caught my attention. I followed it to the far end, where the last door was ajar, a wedge of orange light slicing into the gloom.

Alex's room was smaller than mine, but neater: bed made with military corners, desk aligned with surgical precision. The only disorder came from the stack of books next to the lamp, a sprawl of paperbacks and highlighted lecture notes. A poster of *The Clash*, mid-explosion, covered half the wall above his pillow. Alex sat cross-legged on the bed, a bottle of *Famous Grouse* between his knees, reading by the yellow spill of his desk lamp.

He looked up, surprise flickering for a second before he smiled. "Liam," he said, "you look like someone's run you through the mangle."

"I could say the same for you," I replied, forcing a grin.

He gestured to the floor, "take a seat. There's cups in the drawer, if you want one."

I sat, folding myself into the narrow space between bed and wardrobe. The floor was cold through my jeans, but I welcomed the shock of it. Alex reached for the bottle, poured two inches of whisky into a mug, then pushed it towards me across the carpet.

The first sip was all fire and cleaning fluid, but the second was smoother. I let it burn a path down my throat, felt the heat ripple out to my fingers.

"So, what's your excuse for skipping the fun?" he asked, rolling the bottle between his palms.

"I could ask you the same."

He shrugged, "needed a break. It's all a bit much, isn't it?"

I nodded, surprised at the honesty, "yeah. It is."

A silence settled, not quite comfortable but not hostile, either. I watched the way his hair fell over his eyes, the way his hands never stopped moving, tapping the glass, tracing the rim, worrying at the edge of his sleeve. I took another sip and tried not to stare.

"Caroline's out there," I said, not really a question.

He made a noncommittal sound, "she likes a crowd."

"That's... good?"

He shrugged again, but slower, "it is what it is."

I felt the shape of a question forming, but let it die.

"When are you going home for Christmas?" Alex asked.

"Tomorrow. Mum would kill me if I missed my cousin's nativity play. She's a sheep this year. They didn't trust her with lines after last time." I grinned, despite myself. "What about you?"

He tipped the mug to his lips, drained it, and refilled, "we're doing New Year in the Wirral. Parents are trying to kill each other, so I'll stay here as long as possible."

"You could stay with us, if you wanted." The words tumbled out before I could stop them, "it's not posh, but you'd get a decent roast."

He looked at me, the full weight of his attention landing squarely between my ribs, "maybe I will," he said, voice lower now.

Another silence. The party was a distant roar, punctuated by the occasional crash or peal of laughter. I felt the whisky working, stripping away the insulation between me and the world.

Alex reached for the bottle, refilled his mug, then poured a splash into mine. His hand brushed mine, and I felt the static crackle up my arm.

"You ever feel like we're just... going through the motions?" he said, staring at the wall.

"All the time."

He laughed, but it was a bitter, frayed sound. "I thought uni would be different. That it'd be ..." He broke off, searching for the word.

"Freedom," I supplied.

"Yeah. Instead, it's just more of the same. Different uniforms, same rules."

He leaned back, propping himself up on his elbows. The muscles in his forearms tensed, the veins visible under the skin. I realised my own hands were trembling. I curled them into fists, hid them between my knees.

He watched me, eyes sharp but not unkind. "What about Amanda?" he asked, voice softer. "She seems nice."

"She is," I said, and meant it. "But it's …" I trailed off, not sure how to finish.

He finished for me, "it's hard to be what people want, sometimes."

I nodded, "she thinks I'm someone I'm not. I think I want to be that person, but I don't even know who he is half the time."

Alex looked at me for a long second, and his gaze lingered. I felt the whisky working, making everything loose around the edges.

He smiled, a quick flash of teeth, "you're all right, Liam." I liked it when Alex used my Christian name and dropped his public school conventions.

"So are you."

He poured again, less for the taste than for the ritual of it. We sat in companionable silence, the only sound the distant thrum of the party and the ticking of the radiator as it cooled.

He nodded, as if this confirmed a private theory. The air between us hummed with the things we weren't saying.

I drained my mug, set it down, and wiped my palm on my jeans. My fingers still shook, but now it was harder to tell if it was nerves or the whisky.

Alex reached out, fingers grazing mine in a gesture so casual it could have been accidental. But his hand lingered, just a beat longer than necessary. We sat there, hands barely touching, the promise of something electric suspended in the tiny space between our skin.

From the corridor came a shout, an open invitation to the kitchen for drink and food. We didn't move. I felt the weight of his hand, the warmth of it, the pulse. For a moment, the world narrowed to that single, fragile connection.

Neither of us spoke. Neither of us needed to.

We just sat, suspended, waiting for the next moment to arrive. Time bent in on itself, elastic and unreliable, while we sat with only the radiator's ticking to keep us honest. The bottle of *Grouse* hovered between us, its neck shining greasy in the lamplight. I watched the amber surface rise and fall in the mug, a tide chart for how much of ourselves we were willing to lose.

After a while, Alex got bored of the silence and uncorked the cap on politics, "you see what they're doing with the student union fees?" he said, mouth twisted with contempt, "first they cut the grant, then they act like we should be grateful for the crumbs. Bunch of wankers."

I shrugged, unsure if I was allowed to agree, "better than being on the dole, though. That's what my dad says."

He made a face, "your dad ever had to live on tinned beans and rationed heat? Mine has, and he's still a bastard. Thatcher's got her foot on everyone's neck and half the country's begging for more."

I laughed, bitter and quick, "you make it sound like we're all living in a dystopia."

He looked at me sideways, "aren't we?" The question was a joke, but the way he held my gaze said otherwise.

We spiralled through the usual catalogue, lecturers on strike, teachers on the march, the endless rounds of student protest. Alex had a talent for making everything sound like a dare. He got wound up about the injustice but never seemed to worry that anything truly bad could stick to him. For my part, I kept my opinions sanded down to the grain. Letting people know what you cared about was just another way to get hurt.

At some point, Alex reached behind him and fished out a battered paperback, tossing it so it landed in my lap, "you ever read this?" he said. "Changed my life. And I don't say that about books."

The cover was blue, worn at the edges, the title scuffed but legible: *Maurice*. I'd seen it before, locked in the faculty library behind a "restricted" sticker, as if the contents might jump out and infect the unprepared.

I picked it up, felt the dry rot of the spine, "isn't this …"

He cut me off, "it's a love story, yeah. But it's more than that. It's about refusing to become what they want. Even if it means…" He trailed off, leaving the rest unsaid.

I turned the book over in my hands. Alex watched, waiting for a verdict.

"What's it like?" I asked, and immediately regretted the childishness of the question.

He grinned, but his eyes were serious, "it's like finding out you're not the only one. Even if it's just on the page."

We let that settle for a moment, the air thick with smoke and possibility. I flipped the book open at random, read a line, then closed it again.

Alex poured us each another round, the liquid sloshing unevenly from his unsteady grip, "they don't teach you that in school," he said, voice gone rough, "they teach you how to hide."

I nodded, and the words spilled out before I could rein them in, "do you ever wish you could just be…" I hesitated, searching for the shape of the thought. "Someone else?"

His smile faded, replaced by something softer, almost broken. "Sometimes," he said, "but mostly I just wish I could be the same person in front of other people as I am in here."

He was leaning closer now, his knees drawn up, the space between us shrinking with every syllable.

"Why do you care so much?" I asked, not sure if it was an accusation or a plea.

Alex shrugged, but the motion was slow, deliberate, "because I see you trying so hard not to feel anything. I used to be like that. Still am, when it counts."

I looked away, fixating on the warped wood of his desk, "you don't know anything about me."

He let out a small laugh, not unkind, "I know enough."

The whisky had made my limbs heavy, my tongue loose. I felt a flush crawling up my neck, prickling under my collar.

"We should probably go," I said, not moving, "they'll be heading to the clubs by now."

Alex shook his head, "let them. It's shit out there, anyway."

He reached out, then thought better of it, hand hovering above my knee before dropping back to his own lap.

"Are you scared?" he said, voice low.

I bristled, "of what?"

He didn't answer, but his eyes never left mine.

I tried to laugh it off, "you're the one who's always got to push things," I said, but the tremor in my voice gave me away.

"I just want you to stay," he said, "that's all."

The room went very still. I stared at the floor, at the cracked linoleum and the shadow of his foot beside mine. He touched my wrist, fingers gentle but insistent, thumb pressed just above the pulse. My skin felt electrified. I swallowed. My body wanted to run, but my heart hammered a different message, faster and louder than the radiator's ticks.

"Okay," I said, barely audible.

He leaned in, closing the gap, and our foreheads bumped, clumsy as children. His breath was sweet with whisky and something else, a tang of sweat and hope. He tilted his head, awkward, and our lips met, harder than I'd imagined, almost violent, teeth knocking. I jerked back on reflex, but he followed, hand cupping my neck, steadying me.

We stayed like that, pressed together, until the panic overwhelmed the pleasure and I broke away, gasping.

"I'm sorry," I blurted, "fuck, I'm sorry, I didn't mean ..."

He silenced me with a finger on my lips, "it's fine, Liam. It's fine." He kissed me again, slower this time, giving me space to breathe. My whole body was trembling, but I didn't pull away.

His hands were everywhere at once, my back, my shoulders, the ridge of my jaw. He smelled of cold and smoke and salt, and I breathed him in like oxygen.

Somehow, we made it onto the bed. The lamp cast long, gold shadows across the room, turning our skin unfamiliar and new. My hands fumbled at his shirt, buttons slipping and popping free. He laughed, a low, nervous sound, and then his own hands were at my waist, tugging my jumper over my head.

The air was sharp on my bare skin. My heartbeat so loud I was sure he could hear it. We undressed in a tangle of limbs, urgency at war with uncertainty. My hands shook as I touched him, unsure where to linger, how hard to grip. He guided me, gentle but determined, his lips on my collarbone, then my throat.

He rolled us over, pinning me beneath him, his knees bracketing my hips. I felt small and exposed, but also invincible, like nothing outside this bed could ever touch us.

He kissed me again, and I let myself respond, matching his rhythm, my hands digging into his hair. The sensation was overwhelming, every nerve ending lit up and screaming. I wanted to stop, to run, to hide. But I wanted to stay more.

He pressed against me, hips grinding into mine, and I arched up to meet him. Our bodies fit together, clumsy and perfect, sweat slicking our skin. I gasped, shuddered, and he buried his face in my neck, biting down to keep from crying out.

We moved together, frantic and graceless, neither of us speaking, just the sound of breath and flesh and the distant thump of music through the walls. The first time was over almost before it began, both of us shuddering, limbs locked, muscles tense. After, we lay tangled, chest to chest, hearts galloping.

My mind was a storm. I wanted to apologise, to explain, to ask if this meant anything or if it was just the whisky and the hour. He stroked my hair, the motion slow and steady.

"You're shaking," he whispered.

"Sorry," I said again, and this time it sounded like the truth.

He pulled me closer, wrapped his arms around me, and we lay like that, sticky and spent, while the world fell silent outside the window.

I stared at the cracked plaster of the ceiling, at the flicker of the lamp, at anything but his eyes. My hands trembled still, even as he laced his fingers through mine. We didn't speak. We just lay, bodies pressed together, listening to the radiator cool and the whisky settle in our blood.

Somewhere in the hallway, the partygoers returned, their voices loud and drunken. I listened to the footsteps pass, the slamming of doors, the laughter. I wondered if any of them would ever understand what it felt like to be this alive and this afraid.

Alex's breath slowed. He squeezed my hand, just once, as if to say, I'm here.

I squeezed back.

We stayed like that, silent and unmoving, until the world outside faded and nothing remained but the warmth between our skin. I drifted in and out of sleep, buoyed by the warmth of Alex's arm and the aftershocks in my limbs, until the corridor came alive again with another stagger of returning bodies. Voices ricocheted off the walls, each laugh or slam a fresh test of whether I could keep from flinching.

We lay side by side, not touching now. The sweat between us cooled and dried, and the sheet felt scratchy on my bare skin. Neither of us spoke. The silence stretched, sharp as wire, pulling tighter with every second. I watched the play of shadows on the ceiling, waiting for Alex to break the spell or at least acknowledge it, but he just stared straight ahead, one hand behind his head, the other tracing circles on the thin coverlet.

I tried to match his calm, but my heart was sprinting again, panic refuelling where pleasure had been. A door banged somewhere down the hall, closer this time. I heard someone cough, a wet hacking sound, and then the clatter of bottles rolling across cheap linoleum. The clock by Alex's desk read 3:17. The minute hand trembled, refusing to settle.

I swung my legs off the bed, found my jeans on the floor, and started to get dressed. My hands shook so badly I could barely find the button, let alone thread it. My jumper was inside out, but I left it that way. I wanted out, now, before the world could catch us in the act.

Alex propped himself up on one elbow, watching. His face was unreadable in the half-light. He didn't say anything, didn't ask me to stay, didn't apologise for what we'd done or try to make it mean something.

I laced up my trainers with numb fingers. I could feel his eyes on me, waiting for a crack or a confession, but I kept mine fixed on the floor. My chest felt hollowed out, like something vital had been scooped free and replaced with cold air.

At the door, I paused, hand on the knob. The urge to say something, anything, burned in my throat, but I couldn't form the words. I glanced back, just once.

Alex gave a tiny, crooked smile. His hair was wild, his skin flushed and shining. For a moment, I saw the boy from the first week of term, sun-bleached and sure of himself. But I also saw the shadow underneath, the part of him that wanted, desperately, to be seen.

"Goodnight, Liam," he said, voice barely above a whisper.

I nodded, jaw locked and let myself out.

The corridor was empty but for a line of empty cans and the distant thump of a radio. My footsteps echoed, each one a small admission of guilt. I moved past doors with names taped on, the neat print and coloured stars suddenly obscene in their innocence. Somewhere, someone was crying, low, muffled sobs. I wondered if it was joy or despair, and whether it made a difference.

At my own door, I hesitated. The impulse was to bolt the lock and never come out again, but the room smelled stale and unfamiliar, as if someone else had moved in while I was away. I left the light off and sat on the edge of the bed, hands gripping my knees, breath coming fast and ragged.

I replayed everything, the taste of Alex's lips, the heat of his hands, the shame and terror that followed. The body betrayed itself, even when the mind shouted no. It was a kind of violence, but also a relief. I looked at the clock on my bedside table. 3:32. Ten minutes had passed, or maybe a whole lifetime.

I stood, crossed to the window, and shoved it open. The night air was icy, sharp enough to burn away the last traces of sleep or longing. I leaned out, sucking in lungfuls, watching the city's sodium lights blur and twinkle. On the street below, taxis crawled past, their drivers hunched over steering wheels, faces lit green by the meter.

I thought about home, about Amanda and Sarah, about Dad's warnings and Mum's hopeful lies. I wondered if they'd ever know this side of me, or if I'd spend the rest of my life carving it into tiny, hidden rooms like this one.

I could never go back. Even if I tried, something irreversible had split me clean through. I stayed at the window until the sky paled, the first frost tracing lines on the quad below. When I finally crawled under the covers, every inch of me felt different, raw, alive, unfixable. I shut my eyes and tried to sleep, but the feeling wouldn't let me. It pressed in, hard and unrelenting, reminding me at every breath that I was still here, and that the only way forward was straight through.

CHAPTER 7: THE ART OF DISCRETION

Alex and I had parted for the Christmas holidays without seeing each other again. I'd rehearsed a thousand versions of that conversation; sometimes I told him it was a mistake, sometimes I begged to do it again. I spent the holiday at home in a half-sleep, replaying that night until the memory wore thin in places. One moment I'd feel my skin burn with wanting him; the next I'd picture Amanda's face crumpling if she ever found out. I prayed Alex would forget while simultaneously hoping he remembered every detail.

In January we finally bumped into each other in the corridor of the hall of residence. His easy smile and warm wishes for the new year left me both relieved and devastated. Had he forgotten? Or was he just better at pretending?

That first night a soft knock jolted me upright. I swung my legs off the bed and opened the door to find Alex standing there, sheepish, clutching the half-empty *Famous Grouse* we'd shared before the holidays. My heart kicked against my ribs as my mind flipped between relief, maybe he'd come to say we couldn't see each other, and dread, maybe he wanted more. Both ideas sent a tight tingle through me. I stepped aside.

"Thought we should finish this, and ..." he said, lifting the bottle, then faltered as if the words tasted sour in his mouth.

"And talk?" I blurted, grabbing mugs from the shelf by the kettle. I dreaded it but knew it was inevitable. Alex perched on my bed, then leaned back against the wall, patting the mattress beside him.

"Please?" he murmured when I hesitated.

I let myself sit at the top of the bed, a safe distance, or so I told myself. He sighed, uncorked the whisky, and poured two generous measures. He leaned over to set the bottle on my bedside table and I caught the familiar mix of his scent, warm tobacco and something uniquely him. He straightened and lifted his glass.

"Happy New Year, Liam." Our mugs met with a soft clink. I wondered if he meant to press his knuckles to mine or if it was accidental, but the spark shot through me regardless.

"Happy New Year, Alex," I replied. We drank, and the warmth slid down my throat, loosening a knot I'd been carrying since term ended

He gave me a slow smile, then chuckled, "you look like a puppy being taken to the vet to have his balls cut off."

I couldn't help grinning at the brutal honesty, "maybe that's what we both need," I teased, though my stomach twisted at the thought.

"Fuck that," Alex snapped, eyes blazing a clear blue. "I'm keeping mine, and I hope you keep yours." His gaze pinned me like an accusation, or an invitation. My carefully built resolve, the guilt over Amanda, the shame I'd packed into my suitcase, all of it crumbled into dust. My face must have given me away.

He leaned forward, glass resting on my thigh, "so what is it, Liam? Balls or no balls?" I felt hypnotised, powerless to move, until my free hand rose on its own, settling over his.

"We keep the balls," I whispered.

Relief flooded him, and he collapsed against me, head finding my shoulder. His breath trembled, "I thought I'd fucked everything up at the end of term. I was sure I'd scared you off, or disgusted you."

He sobbed softly into my shoulder, and that raw vulnerability cut me deeper than any fear. I'd never imagined feeling this close to a man beyond desire. An ache swelled in my chest.

"I'm sorry if you thought that," I admitted, "because I've been thinking the same. I've spent the holidays dreading your return, terrified you'd just ignore me."

"I could never ignore you," he said, lifting his head with a grin that was half pride, half relief. "You're far too fit and sexy for that." He squeezed my thigh. My cheeks heated, no one had ever called me that before. I laughed, incredulous at how ridiculous and wonderful it sounded.

"Are we good then?" I asked, voice catching.

"We will be very soon," Alex whispered, and emptied his glass. He took mine from my trembling hand, set it down, then slid down the wall, pulling me on top of him.

Afterward, we lay topless in our shorts, my skin cooling in the draft from the window, my mind racing between elation and panic.

"I think we need some rules," Alex said, tracing circles on my shoulder. "So nobody has ammunition." I nodded, stomach knotting. "Nobody can find out."

"Be subtle," I suggested, already calculating the thousand ways we might slip.

"Exactly." His certainty both reassured and terrified me.

"I feel sick about Amanda," I said, shame rising like bile, "one minute I'm convinced this is worth any price, the next I hate myself for betraying her."

Alex's fingers stilled, "Caroline's different, my parents practically arranged it. We've never even..." He trailed off.

"Amanda was just...expected," I admitted, then winced at my own callousness. "But she trusts me. She writes these letters..." I couldn't finish.

"With Caroline, I've made no promises," Alex said, propping himself up. His face hardened slightly. "The long-distance thing never works anyway. You could just be distant until she ends it."

I nodded, hating how reasonable it sounded, hating how readily I agreed. "Let's just see how things go," he murmured, and I nodded again, already wondering which version of myself I'd hate more: the one who ended it with Alex, or the one who didn't.

The winter air gnawed at us with iron teeth, eating through scarf and coat and whatever else you thought might protect you from the long freeze that started at your skin and worked inwards. It was the first day of lectures, and the two of us walked side by side but not close enough to draw notice, boots scraping rhythm on the salt-streaked pavement of the main quad.

"Forecast says more snow by Friday," Alex muttered, voice low enough to vanish in the wind.

"Brilliant," I said, pulling my bag higher on my shoulder, "as if the library's not cold enough already."

He smiled in profile, lips chapped, eyes narrowed against the wind. In daylight he was even more striking; that shouldn't have mattered, but it did, so much so that I caught myself cataloguing the details as a kind of self-torture. His hands, ungloved, knuckles red from the cold; the arch of his cheekbone where the January sun bothered to hit; the way he tucked his chin into the collar of his fisherman's jumper when he thought no one was watching. Only I always was.

We turned onto the shortcut behind the *Science Tower*. Alex drifted a little ahead, then checked himself, slowing so our steps would sync again. "So. Timetable?" he said, the codeword for how do we see each other alone.

"Seminar in B7 at ten. Then a two-hour break before Modern Lit."

He shot me a sidelong glance. "You want to meet up after? I can make it to the *Law Library* by quarter past."

"Fine. But we use the third-floor annex," I said, "nobody goes up there unless it's revision season."

He nodded, a barely-there tilt, "it's a date, then," he whispered, and for a split second his hand hovered at the edge of mine, a single exposed nerve. But we kept walking, never once touching, both pretending the half-metre gap was there by accident.

We skirted the main entrance of the *Student Union*, where the crowd was thick and impossible to dodge. The smell of burnt coffee and over-boiled radiators rolled out as we fought our way through. I could feel every eye on us, even if it was my own paranoia that made it so.

Alex peeled off at the foot of the central stairs, muttering something about "Glaciation at nine," and left me at the doors to the History building. I watched him climb away, part of me desperate to follow, another part desperate to run in the opposite direction.

The History seminar room was already filling with the usual suspects: three mature students at the front, notebooks open and pens poised like weapons; a cluster of rugby types at the back, making a project out of slouching; and the handful of us in between, the ones who cared enough to show up but not enough to advertise it. I slid into my usual seat, far enough from the front to avoid being a target, close enough to look like I was trying.

Dr. Henderson appeared a minute after the hour, long coat flapping, hair stuck up in a way that implied he'd slept in it, which he probably had. His glasses caught the light and turned his eyes into white coins. He started writing dates on the chalkboard, voice echoing even before he spoke.

"Right, gentlemen," he said, and it was always *'gentlemen'*, despite the presence of two women in the class. "French Revolution, part two. As you'll recall from last semester, we left Robespierre on the cusp of *The Terror*. What I want to know today is, was it inevitable? Or was there a moment, a single hinge, where it all might have turned out differently?"

He turned, chalk dust drifting from the elbows of his jacket. "Liam. Thoughts?"

A dozen faces pivoted my way, some openly entertained. I felt the rush of blood to my neck, the way my hands always seemed too big in these moments. "Uh. It was inevitable," I managed, the syllables scraping at my throat.

"Why?" Henderson pressed, his gaze sharp behind the smears on his specs.

I cast around for my prep notes, but the words had dissolved into static, "because… the forces that caused the revolution never went away? They just got redirected."

He frowned, "be specific. Which forces?"

I fumbled for a foothold, "economic collapse. Food shortages. The pressure from the *sans-culottes*. The inability of the *Assembly* to control the populace."

"Better," he said, but his voice implied it was only marginally so, "and do you see any modern parallels?"

I opened my mouth, then shut it, "maybe," I said, and let it die there.

He stared at me a second longer, then moved on to interrogate the next in line. I sank back in my seat, breath tight, sweat prickling under my arms even as the radiator did its best impression of a broken fridge.

The hour passed in a blur of names, dates, and the shuffling of paper. Every time Henderson paced the aisles I felt his shadow fall over my desk. He had a way of knowing when you weren't prepared, of sniffing out the precise moment you tried to coast. I both hated and admired him for it.

As the seminar drew to a close, Henderson clapped his hands once, abrupt as a gunshot. "Liam, stay behind a moment, would you?"

My stomach dropped. The rest of the class filed out, some with not-so-subtle glances over their shoulders, as I packed my bag with more care than was strictly necessary. Henderson leaned against the edge of the desk, arms folded, waiting.

"Relax, Liam," he said, and I flinched at the sound of my first name. He only used it when he was either very pleased or very disappointed.

"Sorry," I muttered, hovering halfway between seat and exit.

He smiled, but it was thin, "you know, you're more than capable of leading these discussions. Your written work shows a grasp of nuance I rarely see at this level. But in class, you disappear."

I shrugged, the old routine, "I'm better on paper."

"That's a dodge, not an answer," he said, "you have something to say. I'd like to hear it."

I didn't know where to look. At my shoes, at the window, anywhere but his face.

After a beat, he let the silence stretch, then said, "you're not in trouble, Liam. But I want more from you. Consider this… encouragement."

He handed me a reading list, a week ahead of the rest. His eyes crinkled at the corners. "Take the lead on Robespierre next time. I want your point of view."

I nodded, pocketed the paper, and mumbled, "thanks, sir."

As I turned to leave, "oh, and can you pop into my office around lunchtime too?" he added. I nodded, "but if you can't we can do it some other time."

I felt the weight of his expectations settle between my shoulders, heavier than any backpack. What else did he want, I wondered? But, I also felt something else, a spark, maybe, or the start of one. I wondered if he saw through me, or just past me.

In the corridor, I stood for a minute, letting my pulse slow before heading toward the *Law Library*, where I knew Alex would already be waiting, keeping a table warm on the third floor, like nothing out of the ordinary had ever happened at all.

We didn't have long, but we chatted quietly about our mornings. I recounted my interaction with Henderson and his invitation to go and see him.

Alex leaned in conspiratorially, "maybe he fancies you too?" I pulled my best *'most disgusted'* face and we laughed quietly.

Alex was first to leave and as he stood up he said, "I'll be finished about four pm, come to my room when you're finished?" I nodded quickly and then watched him walk to the door. I suppressed the urge to wolf-whistle which amused me.

Dr. Henderson's office was a shrine to the idea that knowledge could be stacked, catalogued, and bent to a man's will, provided he had enough shelving and not enough time for dusting. The walls were lined floor to ceiling with books, some spine-broken, some pristine, all jammed in together like a crowd waiting for the last train. The window was half-frosted with condensation, lamplight giving the whole place a yellowed, late-afternoon glow that felt both safe and a little oppressive.

He motioned me toward a battered leather chair that looked like it had outlived its original owner, "sit, please," he said, then perched himself on the edge of his own desk, which was so loaded down with papers and folders that the surface was visible only in patches.

I sat, setting my bag on my lap, hands tangled tight in the strap.

"You know why I wanted a word, I assume," he said, glasses low on his nose.

"No," I said honestly.

He let the silence expand, then said, "your last essay on the Girondins was excellent. Not just good. I've shown it to two colleagues and both commented on the clarity and force of your arguments." He shuffled through a stack, fished out a folder, and tapped it for emphasis, "you have a talent for picking apart the causes from the noise. That's rare, especially for first-years."

I managed a muttered, "thank you, Dr Henderson," but it came out croaky and thin.

Henderson gave a rare, real smile, the kind that made you wonder what he was like before the world got to him, "I wanted you to know there's a summer research post for a month in the department. For undergraduates who show promise. Paid, plus board, though the room is less grand than you might hope." He paused, eyes sharp, "I think you should apply."

I blinked. The idea of spending a summer here, of being hand-picked for anything, felt alien. Like it must have been meant for someone else. "I don't know if..."

"Let me be clear," he said, leaning forward, "you'd be wasted in some temp job. You have the makings of an academic, if you want it. And I want you on the shortlist."

I swallowed. "Okay," I said, voice barely audible. "Thank you."

He nodded, satisfied. Then he changed gears, his tone going casual, but in the way that only signalled a new line of questioning, "you settling in all right? I know it's a bit of a culture shock, coming up from a place like, Rochdale, was it?"

"Yes," I said, a reflex. I heard the caution in my own voice and cringed.

Henderson folded his arms, "you're ahead of the curve, but you act like you're always waiting for the rug to be pulled out. Why is that?"

I tried to smile, but I felt my mouth jerk instead, "just don't want to mess up," I said, "my family ..." I faltered. "They're proud, but this is... not their world."

He nodded, like he'd heard this before, "that can be a strength, you know. Not belonging, I mean. It forces you to see things others miss."

He let that settle, then picked up a new thread, "you mentioned in your entrance essay that you had a girlfriend back home. How's that going?" His voice was neutral, but the question felt loaded.

My heart rate doubled, "still together, yeah. She's at university too, in Scotland."

He made a sympathetic face, "long distance. Hard work."

"Yeah," I said, wishing my hands would stop moving.

He leaned back, chair creaking, "well, if you ever want to talk, my door's open. About the job, or anything else."

"Thank you," I said, already halfway to standing.

He smiled again, thinner this time, "don't let the others intimidate you. Most of them are winging it, too."

He handed me a blue folder with the summer scheme logo on it, then returned to the heap of papers on his desk, already moving on to the next crisis.

I stood, folder in hand, and let myself out, feeling the weight of the conversation pressing at my ribs. In the corridor,

I leaned against the wall for a minute, willing my pulse to slow, trying not to think about how easily he'd read through me.

As I walked back toward the *Law Library,* I pressed the folder flat against my chest. My hands shook, just a little, and I told myself it was only the cold. But I knew, with the sick certainty of someone who'd spent a lifetime hiding, that it was something else. I was being watched. Maybe even seen. And I had no idea if that was a blessing or a curse.

Alex's room felt smaller after dark, the walls creeping in as if they meant to smother the day's noise and leave us untouched. The radiator in the corner wheezed a steady background of complaint, but the place was warm, at least, and the curtains were drawn tight over the frost that spidered the glass. When I let myself in, Alex locked the door behind me with a quick, practiced flick, then checked it twice, which became his habit.

He was stretched out on the bed, ankles crossed, shirt untucked and a battered textbook propped on his stomach, "you look like you've seen a ghost," he said, not glancing up.

"I might as well have," I said. I dropped my bag onto the chair and started pacing, my boots leaving wet tracks on the thin carpet.

"Let me guess," Alex said, voice bored but eyes sharp. "Henderson."

I stopped. "How did you…"

He closed the book, sat up, and smirked, "apparently, he does the same to everyone who gets top marks. Calls you in for a 'chat,' pokes around, makes you feel special and terrified at the same time."

I frowned, still feeling the echo of Henderson's gaze, "he asked if I was adjusting. Then he asked about my…" I hesitated. "He asked if I had a girlfriend. Specifically."

Alex's smirk broadened, "did you tell him about Amanda, the great love of your life?"

"I said she was at university in Scotland," I muttered.

"Perfect," he stood, closed the distance between us in two steps, and tilted his head like he was sizing me up for a suit. "You're not a natural liar, Liam. Your ears go red when you're nervous."

I folded my arms, "I'm not nervous."

He grinned, then reached out and pinched my earlobe between thumb and forefinger. "Liar," he said, gentle, "but it's cute."

I pulled away, but only half-hearted, "this isn't funny. What if he knows?"

Alex shrugged, "so what if he does? It's not illegal."

"It is until we are twenty-one," I said, and immediately regretted it.

He let go, the amusement draining a little from his face, "listen. People see what they want to see. Henderson's not looking for closet cases. He's looking for prodigies he can put his name to."

I sat on the edge of the bed, rubbing the base of my palm into my temple, "you make it sound easy." We sat on the bed, Alex close enough that our thighs touched, "it is, if you keep your stories straight. Want me to show you?"

I made a face, "show me what?"

He kicked off his shoes, tucked one leg under him, "all right. You're at a party. Someone asks about your girlfriend. Go."

I rolled my eyes, "she's at university. Stirling. Studying…" I blanked, panicked, then blurted, "music."

Alex gave me a teacher's smile, "good. What's her name?"

"Amanda," I said, maybe too fast.

He wagged a finger, "be more casual. Like you're bored of saying it. Also, make her real. Say something only she would say."

I tried. "Amanda … she hates jazz. Says it's just showing off for the sake of it."

He snorted, "excellent. What's the weirdest thing about her?"

"She alphabetises her records, but not her books," I said, surprised to find I believed it.

Alex clapped, soft, "that's it. See? Easy. Nobody's going to question you if you sound bored. Just don't let your voice go up at the end. That's another tell."

We went back and forth, him inventing awkward social scenarios and me responding, until it started to feel less like a test and more like a game. Each time he called me out for hesitating or fidgeting, I wanted to hit him, but then he'd laugh and touch my knee, and the anger would melt, and then I wanted to kiss him.

After a while, the game slowed and the silence took over. I lay back, stretching across the narrow mattress, and let my arm fall so our hands were side by side. Alex slipped his fingers between mine, lacing them together.

"This is the bit nobody tells you," he said, voice barely a whisper. "The hiding's easy. It's the remembering not to forget each other that's hard."

I looked at the ceiling, at the crack that ran above the window and split the plaster into two unequal halves, "what if I don't want to hide?"

Alex was quiet for a long time, "then you're braver than I am," he said.

His hand tightened around mine, and for a moment I felt the world shrink to just the two of us, suspended in the warmth and the dark. He rolled onto his side, propped his head up, and looked at me in that way he had, unblinking, amused, unafraid of being caught.

"Do you ever regret it?" I said, almost too soft to be heard.

"Regret what?"

I hesitated, "this. Us."

He grinned, slow and sly, "every second we're apart."

He leaned over and kissed me, not urgent, just there, real, mouths pressed together with the lazy confidence of a secret repeated until it became muscle memory. I let him, and for a while there was no outside, no Henderson, no cold or fear.

Eventually, we lay back, side by side, bodies curled together under the single blanket. The radiator rattled and spat, but the bed was warm. Alex's breath slowed; he drifted first, head on my chest, hand resting just above my ribs.

I stared at the ceiling, thinking of Henderson and his open-door policy, of Amanda and her unalphabetised books, of home and everything that waited for me outside this room. The world out there was sharp and hungry, but in here, I could almost believe we had all the time we wanted.

I traced the line of Alex's shoulder in the dark, then let myself slip under, just for a while, into a place where nothing needed hiding and the rules were written by hand.

CHAPTER 8: POLITICAL AWAKENINGS

April 1982

I watched the Falklands War break out from a cracked leather sofa in the *Union* common room, surrounded by a tangle of voices that knew everything and nothing all at once. Someone had nicked the remote, so the telly blared at full volume, Thatcher's cut-glass vowels slicing through every conversation, her face alternating between grave and imperious as she explained why a windswept colony seven thousand miles away required the massed might of Her Majesty's Navy.

The room was dense with the morning's hangover and the stink of instant coffee. Radiators banged and spit, barely keeping pace with the churn of bodies crammed onto mismatched armchairs or propped against windowsills. Every table hosted an argument in miniature: the hard left lads hunched over their *Guardian* dailies, the rugger crowd slagging them off two metres away, the usual noise of students trying to build themselves from sound alone.

Alex had gone off for a run before breakfast, something about clearing his head, and so I sat solo, clutching my second mug of coffee, scanning for anyone I could claim as a friend. News of the war crackled through the radio mounted above the bar, the presenter working herself up into a lather about patriotism and "unjustified aggression." Some wag had put a sticker of Thatcher's face on the radio dial; every time the needle swung left, her eye glared down, unblinking.

The tension in the air wasn't just international; you could feel the lines being drawn around every table. On the rug in front of the telly, two politics students were already halfway to a brawl, one red-faced and thundering on about imperialism, the other snorting about "Argies" and "traitors in our midst." Most everyone else pretended not to listen, but every head turned when the words got loud.

I tried to melt into the upholstery, but it was impossible. The soft whine of the fridge behind the bar, the scrape of a chair leg across the tiles, every sound spiked, every motion doubled. I felt like a dandelion seed drifting through a hailstorm.

It was in the midst of this that the flyer found me. Someone must have stuck it to the pillar overnight, a splash of neon red on cheap A4, blaring '*SOCIALIST WORKERS' STUDENT SOCIETY,*

MEETING TONIGHT, ALL WELCOME'. The words *"Anti-war Emergency"* were underlined twice in thick black marker. Below, in scrawled biro, someone had written *"*B*ring your own anger."*

I cast my mind back to all the political leaflets I'd seen as a kid when my Dad was heavily involved with his trades union. At the time, I had not understood the significance of any of the words I had read then, but now I felt some kind of resonance with my father's activism. For the first time, I perhaps understood him better, and the anger he often displayed in the dark days of the mid-1970s.

I reached up, peeled off the leaflet and ran my thumb over the edge. The ink bled onto my hand. It was the most alive thing in the room. I pocketed it, drained my mug, and stood, stretching out the knots that overnight study had put in my neck. As I headed for the door, I caught the eye of one of the hard left regulars, a lad with hair like a broken mop and a scarf that looked older than Thatcher herself. He nodded, a flicker of solidarity, and I found myself nodding back before I realised what I was doing.

Outside, the air was bright and brittle. The quad was packed with students moving in clots, hands jammed in pockets or waving cigarettes. A pair of lads in air force-blue blazers marched past, faces set in identical sneers, and I trailed them with my eyes, half-sure I'd be on the receiving end of a jibe. Instead, one of them peeled off, headed for the building across from the *Union*, the poshest lecture hall on campus, all glass and marble, a holdover from when the university still pretended it was a part of the real world.

I paused under the *Union* portico, shivering as the wind cut up under my jumper. I saw Alex in the distance, striding across the quad with the same easy confidence he wore everywhere. He'd changed out of his running gear into a crisp navy blazer and grey slacks, uniform for the *Conservative Association*, which met Thursday afternoons in the *Johnson Suite*. I watched as he greeted his mates outside the doors, all of them laughing a little too loud, all hair gel and polished shoes. He caught my gaze, gave a sly little wave, then turned and vanished into the building.

I looked down at my own reflection in the window. My jumper was two years out of fashion, the collar stretched and patched where the wool had started to go. My jeans were clean, at least, but only because I'd spent half an hour last night scrubbing out the remains of curry sauce. I ran a hand through my hair, which would not be tamed, then squared my shoulders and set off for the other side of campus.

The *Socialist* meeting was held in the basement of the old chemistry building, a place even the custodians seemed to have given up on. The hallway leading down smelled of wet concrete and a century of cigarettes, each step echoing up the narrow stairwell. At the bottom, a battered door hung half off its hinges, the *Socialist Workers* star painted in red above the handle.

Inside, the room was a furnace. The windows had been painted shut decades ago, and the only ventilation came from a clunky fan that stuttered in the corner, its cage caked in nicotine. Fifty students, maybe more, were packed in, squeezed onto folding chairs and along the back wall. The heat and smoke and sweat fused into a single thick cloud; it stung my eyes and clung to the roof of my mouth.

At the far end, a makeshift table was piled with pamphlets, most of them stamped with the same red star as on the flyer. A girl with cropped dark hair and eyes the colour of old pennies handed out leaflets with rapid-fire efficiency. Her voice, low and raspy, cut through the din: "Take one, take two, pass them back. Nobody sits this out."

I found a seat at the edge, jammed between a girl in a leather jacket and a bloke in an *Iron Maiden* t-shirt who looked like he'd been up for three days. The girl clocked my nervousness and offered a sly smile; her eyeliner smudged into wings that gave her a permanent look of suspicion.

Up front, the meeting's chair banged a mug on the table for order. "All right, comrades! We've had enough of Thatcher's lies. The only war we should be fighting is against her!" A ragged cheer went up; someone in the back whooped loud enough to start a ripple of laughter.

The cropped-haired girl, Diana, according to her badge, stood to speak. Her voice was even rougher than before, as if she'd spent the morning chain-smoking *Camels* and arguing with traffic wardens. "We have to organise, and fast," she said, scanning the room with eyes that didn't flinch. "They're going to draft, conscript, and silence anyone who doesn't toe the line. That's what history tells us, if we're paying attention." She launched into a litany of past government betrayals: Vietnam, Northern Ireland. With each point, she hammered her palm onto the table, and the crowd responded with a thrum of assent.

The passion in the room was a living thing; it surged and twisted, passing from speaker to speaker, growing louder with every accusation. I felt myself drawn in, my usual cynicism dissolving in the face of such certainty. Even when I disagreed, when a bloke two rows ahead suggested torching the university flag in protest, I couldn't help but admire the force of belief.

Halfway through, Diana spotted me hovering at the edge, her gaze pinning me like a specimen. She beckoned me forward, patting the empty chair beside her.

"New face," she said, not a question, "name?"

"Liam," I said, nearly tripping on the word.

"First time at a meeting?"

I nodded, suddenly aware of how much I didn't know. She smiled, and this time it was almost gentle, "you'll get the hang of it. Just shout when you're angry and listen when you're not." She thrust a pamphlet into my hand. "Read this after. It's got the real story, not the BBC version."

The debate shifted from war to gender politics, with Diana taking the lead, her voice gaining strength as she tore into the government's stance on women's rights and the military, "they want to send boys off to die so the next crop of girls can be secretaries and nurses and nothing else. That's the future they're selling."

The crowd rumbled, a mix of grunts and applause.

A bloke at the back yelled, "what's your solution, then?"

Diana didn't miss a beat, "solidarity. Real, messy, dangerous solidarity. Not just marching, but organising. If the government wants to play war games, let's make it hell for them at home."

I found myself nodding, swept up by the certainty of her words. For a minute, I imagined myself on the front lines, not with a gun, but with a banner, a bullhorn, maybe even a brick.

The meeting wound down with a call for volunteers to organise a march. I almost raised my hand but chickened out at the last second. Instead, I joined the queue for coffee at the side table, where two volunteers poured it black and bitter into polystyrene cups. The coffee tasted like burnt toast, but the caffeine hit with surgical precision.

Diana caught up with me by the sugar packets, "don't worry about not speaking up," she said. "Everyone's nervous the first time. Next week you'll be shouting like the rest of us."

I mumbled a thank you, feeling the heat rise up my neck. She regarded me for a moment, as if gauging my worth, then nodded once, satisfied.

Outside, the air hit like a slap. I walked the quad in circles, the flyers and slogans echoing in my head. Through the windows of the *Johnson Suite,* I could see Alex and his crew, perched on the edge of well-lit armchairs, neat as chessmen. Someone in the group was laughing so hard he doubled over, his navy tie bouncing against his chest.

I looked down at the pamphlet Diana had given me. The cover was a fist, drawn in thick black lines, smashing through a barbed wire fence. Inside, someone had written a note in blue ink: "Read this. Then come to the march."

I tucked it into my pocket, then walked home past the *Union*. In the distance, the radio still blared, and Thatcher's voice lingered on the wind, promising justice, discipline, and victory. I tried to imagine a world where anyone I knew believed her.

Back in my room, I laid the pamphlet on my desk, next to my unread history texts. I stared at the cover for a long time, the fist growing bolder in the lamplight, until it seemed to pulse with its own private life.

In the quiet, I heard Diana's voice: "solidarity. Real, messy, dangerous solidarity." I thought about Alex, about the line that ran through the city and the campus and right through the middle of my own head. I didn't know which side I was on yet. But for the first time in months, I wanted to find out.

The next morning, I met Alex at the coffee shop by the library, our regular haunt, though neither of us would ever admit to having a routine. The place was a converted banking hall: tall ceilings, battered marble, sunlight slanting through high, grimy windows to illuminate the chipped *Formica* tables and the slow-motion ballet of the staff. At this hour, it was all students and staff, the air sharp with the tang of espresso and academic panic.

Alex was already there when I arrived, sprawled in the corner booth with the *Financial Times* spread open and a pencil in his mouth, highlighting an article about the war. He'd gone for the full prep-school look: crisp shirt, slim grey tie, the blue blazer from the Conservative meeting still sharp at the cuffs. He looked like he'd stepped out of an ad for expensive education.

I slid in across from him, shoving the *Socialist* pamphlet deeper into my jacket pocket, "morning," I said, though I hadn't slept for more than a few hours.

Alex didn't look up straight away, but when he did, his eyes had that same quick, dangerous glint they got when he was about to start something, "you're alive, then. Thought you might have been conscripted already."

I tried to laugh, "if they draft anyone, it's the rugger lads. I'd be in the intelligence corps, armed with a biro and bad opinions."

He smiled, briefly, then closed the paper with a snap, "so, what's the news from the revolution?"

That was my opening. I told him about the Socialist meeting, how crowded it was, the electricity in the air, Diana and her "solidarity" speech. I went all in on the details: the clouds of smoke, the sweat, the way people actually seemed to believe in something. I waited for him to take the piss, to point out the clichés, but for a few minutes he just listened, eyes half-lidded, fingers drumming on the tabletop.

When I finished, he said, "you really got into it, didn't you?"

I felt my face burn, "I don't know. It was just… different. People actually cared."

He picked up his coffee, swirling the dregs, "or they just like having something to shout about."

I shrugged, "maybe that's better than having nothing."

He laughed, but the sound was thin, "you ever notice that the people who shout the loudest are the ones who'll never have to put anything on the line?"

I bristled, "Diana's parents were both on strike during the bin-men walkout. She's not exactly Eton-educated."

Alex looked at me, flat-eyed, "it's easy to be radical when you've got nothing to lose. That's why the rest of us have to clean up after."

Something in me snapped, "you mean like your dad? Raking it in off the back of people who actually work for a living?"

He set his cup down with a hard click, "careful, Liam. You sound like you're accusing me of something."

I glared, "maybe I am."

We stared at each other, the air between us going dense and bitter. Around us, the café noise seemed to hush; even the hiss of the espresso machine faded.

Alex leaned forward, voice low, "let me tell you something about how the world works. You can protest all you want, but in the end, the people who run things aren't the ones marching in the streets. They're the ones who've learned to play the game."

I shook my head, "that's bollocks and you know it."

He gave a small, vicious smile, "you're so desperate to be different you'll join any crowd that lets you. But when it comes to actually doing something, you'll just write an essay and hope for a pat on the head from Dr. Henderson."

The words stung more than they should have. I looked down at my hands, knuckles gone white around the mug.

Alex sat back, running a hand through his perfect hair, "you want to know the real difference between you and me? I know who I am. I'm not ashamed of it."

I looked up, voice shaking, "neither am I."

He laughed, cold, "you're so full of it. You don't even know who you want to be. Last week you were quoting Auden, now you're ready to join the Red Army."

At this, I slammed my mug down, sloshing coffee over the rim. Heads turned. The girl at the next table, one of the hard left from last night, was watching, eyebrows raised.

I spoke, louder than I meant to: "at least I'm not hiding behind a fancy shirt and a family name."

Alex's face went flat, all the air gone out of it. For a second, I thought he'd swing at me, but instead he just stood, pushing the chair back so hard it screeched. He reached into his pocket, dropped a fistful of change onto the table, and walked out, his steps measured and slow, not looking back.

I watched him go, heart jackhammering in my chest. The café noise returned, but this time it felt like a million miles away. I stared at the table, at the spilled coffee and scattered coins, at the place his hand had been.

After a minute, I got up, grabbed a napkin, and tried to mop the mess. The girl at the next table caught my eye and gave a knowing half-smile, like she'd seen this fight before, a hundred times. I left the money where it was and walked out into the cold.

The quad was empty, the wind pulling at my jacket. Across the way, the *Johnson Suite* glittered with lunchtime chatter, the glass polished to a shine. I thought about Alex, about his easy stride, the way he could belong anywhere he wanted. I thought about Diana and the basement, and the way it felt to be part of something, even if only for an hour.

I walked in circles until my feet went numb. When I finally headed back to my room, the world felt thinner, the colours drained out. I sat on my bed and pulled the Socialist pamphlet from my pocket. The cover was smudged now, the fist less certain, the ink half-vanished from being handled too much.

I tried to read the words, but they swam. All I could see was the look on Alex's face, the final, flat disappointment in it. I wondered if I'd ever get the hang of choosing a side, or if I'd just spend my life stuck in the crack between them, waiting for something to tip me one way or the other. I lay back, closed my eyes, and waited for the feeling to pass.

The next day, I found myself knocking on Dr. Henderson's office door, more out of habit than hope. The corridor was silent; the kind of hush you only get in old buildings designed to impress and intimidate. I stood outside for a minute, reading the brass nameplate until my heart slowed.

He called out, "come," and I eased inside, blinking at the sudden change in light. Henderson himself was at the desk, glasses perched on the end of his nose, marking something in red so fiercely I half-feared the page would catch fire.

He glanced up, "Parry. You're early."

"Sorry, Dr Henderson. I can come back…"

He waved a hand, "nonsense. Always time for the keen ones. Sit." He gestured at a battered armchair, its fabric patched and re-patched, the springs protesting as I sank in.

On the wall behind him, a framed photograph caught the sunlight: a mob of students in some ancient city square, banners waving, police in full battle gear at the edges. At the front, young Henderson, hair longer and darker, arm thrown up in a gesture somewhere between defiance and ecstasy. The caption, lettered in fading biro, read: *'Paris, 1968'.*

He caught me looking, "different world, that. Or so we thought." He set the pen down, turned his full attention to me.

I pulled the essay draft from my bag, hands sweaty despite the cold, "I wanted to ask about the research project. The one on Victorian unions."

He nodded, "good. What's your angle?"

I launched into my prepared speech about the crossovers between Chartist activism and later syndicalist movements, but my heart wasn't in it. I stumbled, lost my thread, and ended up mumbling something about solidarity and "the contradictions of working-class leadership."

He smiled, gently, "you've been to the meetings, then."

I blinked, "what?"

"The *Socialist Society*," he said, eyes bright, "I hear they're recruiting half the first years this month. You strike me as someone who'd want to see for himself."

I felt my face go hot, "I just … wanted to understand it. Not as an insider. Just… academically."

He leaned back, chair creaking, "you'll learn more from an hour in a union hall than a year in this office, but you're welcome to try both."

I nodded, not trusting myself to speak.

Henderson took off his glasses, polished them on his sleeve, and set them down on the battered copy of some memoir that lived at the corner of his desk, "you didn't come here to talk about Victorian unions, did you?"

He let the silence stretch, then added, "it's all right. This office is off the record."

I swallowed, "I just ..." I fumbled for words. "I had a fight. With a friend. About politics. It got out of hand."

He looked at me for a long time, then nodded, "it always does, at your age. At any age, really."

He laced his fingers together, thoughtful, "in '68, we thought we'd change the world overnight. End every war, tear down every hierarchy. What we learned was that most change happens in private. Quietly. Person to person."

I didn't know what to say. I watched the dust motes drift through the sunlight, the slow movement of the shadows across the rug.

Henderson continued, softer now, "a friend of mine once told me: *you can't truly stand for something unless you're willing to stand as yourself*. Took me thirty years to understand it."

He glanced at the photo, then at me, "and even longer to live it."

I felt the meaning hit, slow, then hard. All the compartmentalised parts of my life, the way I kept each piece away from the others. The argument with Alex, the meeting in the basement, the way I performed different versions of myself depending on which room I was in.

Henderson slid the battered memoir across the desk, "take this. It's out of print. There's a chapter on the General Strike: page 113. I think you'll find it clarifies a few things."

I picked up the book. The spine was broken, the margins filled with notes in blue and black ink, whole sections bracketed in Henderson's neat, looping hand.

He watched me, the sunlight making a pale halo on the thinning hair at his temples, "try to be kind to your friend," he said. "We're all figuring it out."

I stood, clutching the book. My voice was thin, but steady, "thank you, sir."

He smiled, warmer than I'd ever seen, "I'll expect a draft by next Thursday. If you need to talk before then ..."

"I know where to find you." I smiled.

I let myself out, the corridor dazzling after the cave of his office. The book felt heavier than it should, as if the arguments inside had weight beyond the page.

I wandered back across the quad, replaying the conversation in my head. The words about standing as yourself stuck, looping over and over. In my room, I opened the memoir to page 113 and started reading, the annotated lines leaping out at me like a secret map. Outside, the afternoon faded into dusk. Inside, for the first time in ages, I felt the walls between things begin to thin.

That night, I sat at my desk with a blank sheet of paper and a list of lies I would not write. The lamp threw a sickly yellow over the desktop, pooling around my hand as it hovered, useless, above the page. I could feel the thump of my own pulse in the tips of my fingers, every beat a reminder that the time for hiding was running out.

I started over half a dozen times. The wastebasket filled with false starts and apologies that rang hollow, my own handwriting turning traitor as it sloped off the page, desperate to escape. In the end, I kept it short, two careful paragraphs, each one trimmed to the bone:

Dear Amanda,

I'm sorry. This isn't easy to say, but I don't want to lie to you. The truth is, things have changed since I came here. I need to focus on my work, and I don't know if I'm who you thought I was. I'm not sure who I am, to be honest, but I know it's not fair to keep pretending everything is the same. You deserve someone better than a ghost.

Please forgive me. I hope you're happy, whatever happens next.

Yours,

Liam

I read it three times, eyes stinging. Nowhere did I mention Alex, or what we'd done, or the way my entire life had turned inside out in a matter of months. I didn't have the courage. I told myself that was kindness, but it felt like another kind of fraud. I folded the letter with trembling hands, pressed it flat, and slipped it into an envelope. My writing was shaky, the pen almost digging through the paper.

I sealed it, then set it on the desk, staring at the way my own name looked alien and unearned in the top corner. For a long time, I just sat, watching the envelope as if it might open itself, or disappear, or catch fire.

At midnight, I slipped out of the room and padded down the corridor in socks. The hall was silent, the only light a sodium strip above the staircase. The post-box was at the end, by the doors, a battered blue slot that swallowed secrets for the price of a stamp.

I stood there, letter in hand, thumb running the seam of the envelope. I hesitated, fighting the urge to turn around, to unwrite the words, to keep living with the lie a little longer. In the end, I let it drop. The clang was louder than I'd expected, ringing up the empty stairwell and echoing after I'd gone.

I walked back to my room, hollowed out but light, as if something had been scooped from my chest and replaced with air. I lay on my bed and stared at the ceiling, waiting for regret to kick in, for the wave of grief that always came after endings. But what I felt was relief, bright and clean and terrifying.

I drifted for a while, thoughts skipping like stones, Amanda's laugh, Sarah's half-mocking smile, Dad's voice on the phone, and always, always, Alex: the way he looked at me when he thought I wasn't watching, the weight of his hand on the back of my neck.

It was half past one when I gave up on sleep and pulled on a jumper over my pyjamas. The corridor was cold, the carpet rough under my feet. I stopped outside Alex's door, listened for a moment. Nothing.

I knocked, soft. Once, then again, the second time barely more than a tap. He answered, hair wild, wearing only a t-shirt and boxers. His eyes were bleary, but when he saw me, something in them sharpened, anger or hope, I couldn't tell.

We stood in the doorway for a long second, the silence thick with everything we hadn't said. Then I stepped forward, closing the gap, and he moved aside to let me in. He locked the door behind us with a click that sounded final and sweet.

We didn't talk. We just stood there, staring, both of us stripped of whatever performances we usually wore. He reached for me first, his fingers rough on my jaw, his breath whiskey-warm. He kissed me hard, not gentle or slow but with a hunger that left no room for doubt.

I pushed him back against the door and kissed him again, mouths mashed, teeth scraping. He grabbed my hips, hauled me closer, and for the first time in weeks, I felt the last of the fear bleed away, replaced by something urgent and clean.

He lifted my jumper, pulled it over my head, and I let it fall. His hands were everywhere at once, palms rough against my ribs, my back, my neck. We tumbled to the bed, limbs tangled, skin against skin.

I could taste salt on his shoulder, feel the heat of his body, the way his muscles tightened every time I touched him. He bit down on my lip, just shy of drawing blood, and I bit him back, and we both laughed, low and shaky.

Clothes scattered, covers kicked off. We fucked with the lights on, the lamp throwing huge shadows onto the ceiling, our bodies twisted into shapes that felt as old as the world. There was no choreography, no softness, just noise and sweat and the desperate need to get as close as possible, to make the distance go away for a little while.

After, we lay side by side, chests heaving, not touching but not letting go. He reached for my hand, found it, and squeezed hard enough to hurt. I squeezed back, then let my head drop onto his shoulder.

In the hush, I could hear the faint noises from the quad, voices shouting, car horns, a distant police siren. The world was still out there, waiting to drag us back into its cold machinery.

Alex spoke first, "what now?"

I didn't answer straight away. I traced the line of his arm, the curve of his wrist, the pale scar that ran just below the thumb. I thought about Henderson's words, about standing as yourself. I thought about the letter in the post-box, already speeding away from me at a hundred miles an hour.

"I don't know," I said, voice raw, "but I think I'd rather fuck it up with you than get it right alone."

He laughed, a sound so unexpected, it made my eyes sting, "you're such a nerd," he said, but he held me tighter.

We lay there, letting the world shrink to the small rectangle of his bed, the warm spill of the lamp, the scent of sweat and detergent. We both knew it wouldn't last, that the morning would bring back the old games, the hiding, the cold drift of things unsaid.

But for now, in the battered little room, we were whole.

We lay together in the dark, our bodies tangled and marked, the walls paper-thin but solid enough for the night. I thought of the quad outside, the war blaring on every radio, the lines being drawn and redrawn by people with louder voices and safer lives. I thought of the march, the meetings, the arguments yet to come.

I thought, too, of Amanda, and hoped she'd understand, in time.

I pressed my face into the hollow of Alex's neck and let myself believe, just for a while, that love could outlast the rest of it.

And when I finally slept, I dreamed of a place where none of us had to pretend.

CHAPTER 9: SUMMER ON THE WIRRAL

June 1982

Heswall was all air and elevation, a place built for people who could afford not just a view, but the distance that came with it. The taxi traced a slow curve up the hill; past gardens squared off by stone walls and driveways so clean you could've eaten a Sunday roast off the gravel. Each house loomed, set back and apart, as if allergic to the sight of its neighbours. We'd barely spoken since the train; Alex had a way of going silent in transit, coiling up his energy for the main event. He watched the horizon with a soldier's focus, letting the minutes spool out as if he could slow time by ignoring it.

I'd dressed up, by my standards, a shirt that hadn't seen a laundry cycle in a fortnight, borrowed tie, trousers that didn't make my knees look like a pair of conspiracy theorists. Still, next to Alex, I looked like a council house kid in borrowed kit. His hair was freshly cut and his shoes could have doubled as mirrors.

The car rolled to a stop outside a house that wasn't so much a building as a declaration. Victorian, triple-gabled, with a stained-glass window above the main door that glowered in the last of the light. The front garden was weedless, not a single blade of grass out of alignment. A pair of stone lions flanked the porch, mouths open in identical, silent judgment.

Alex paid the driver, then squared his shoulders, "ready?" he said, voice brisk, as if we were about to walk into a viva rather than his family home. I nodded, fingers tight around the handle of my duffel bag. My palms left sweat stains on the plastic.

The door opened before we reached it. Mr. Hughes, never "Alex's dad," always "Mr. Hughes" in my head, stood framed by the light, sleeves rolled precisely, jaw clenched just enough to suggest there was a correct way to carry tension. He had the look of a man who could read a room and invoice it in triplicate.

"Alexander," he said, hand out, voice like a half-remembered radio drama, "good to see you."

"Dad," said Alex, barely a pause before they did the handshake, quick, dry, no nonsense.

"And you must be Parry," said Mr. Hughes, turning to me with the smile he used for clients he intended to out-bill, "welcome to our humble home."

I took his hand, trying not to flinch at the grip. It was surgical, designed to test for weakness, "thank you, Mr. Hughes," I said, hoping my accent wouldn't set off any alarms.

He sized me up, eyes flicking from my shoes to my hairline as if cataloguing liabilities, "travel all right?" he asked, though he didn't wait for an answer, "excellent. Let's get you both inside, bit of a wind this evening."

We followed him through the entryway, which was panelled in a dark wood so shiny you could trace your reflection down to the skirting board. The floors were scrubbed to within an inch of their lives, every rug lined up as if inspected by a drill sergeant. Coats hung on a row of brass hooks, all identical but for a single *Barbour* that must have belonged to Mrs. Hughes.

The drawing room was a museum of comfort, overstuffed leather chairs, side tables bristling with decanters and cigarettes, a fireplace grand enough to cremate a horse. A grandfather clock ticked so loudly I thought at first it was a trick of the acoustics, but the room just amplified everything, even the sound of my own breathing.

"Gin, Parry?" said Mr. Hughes, not a question but an expectation. He poured without waiting for an answer, two fingers' worth into a crystal tumbler and handed it over with a wink that said, *I won't tell if you won't*. "Helps take the edge off the commute."

Alex was already at home, hands in pockets, doing a slow circuit of the room as if checking for new additions. His mother entered with the grace of someone accustomed to timing, neither too soon nor too late. She was smaller than I remembered, all bones and cheek, her hair the exact shade of a well-worn coin.

"Alexander, darling. And Liam, is it?" Her smile was generous, but it never quite crossed the border into warmth. She kissed Alex on both cheeks, then offered me a hand, which I shook, unsure if I was supposed to kiss it or just hang on. Her perfume was floral, a note of lilies undercut with something sharper.

"Thank you for having me, Mrs. Hughes," I said, struggling to keep my voice even.

"Nonsense, Liam," she said, "always happy to meet Alex's friends." She pronounced "friends" with a capital F, the kind of tone that left plenty of room for interpretation.

She led us to the sofa, gesturing for me to sit as if awarding a prize. Alex took the armchair, folding himself into it with practiced ease.

"So," said Mrs. Hughes, settling beside me with a cup of something too delicate for my hands, "tell me about yourself, Liam. Are your parents in teaching as well?"

I blinked, caught off guard, "no, my mum works in a bakery. Dad's a contractor, does a bit of everything."

She arched an eyebrow, then smiled, as if this explained a private theory, "how industrious," she said, "and you're from...?"

"Rochdale," I said, bracing for the reaction.

She didn't miss a beat, "that's quite a journey, isn't it?" She turned to Mr. Hughes, who was already smiling over the rim of his glass.

"Oh, it's nothing these days," he said. "The trains are much improved. Of course, you need to know how to avoid the worst of the crowds." His eyes lingered on me, an unspoken challenge.

I nodded, not trusting myself to speak. I could feel the accent swelling in my mouth, desperate to escape.

Mrs. Hughes sipped her tea, "are you enjoying Manchester, then? I hear it can be a bit... rough, in places."

Alex rolled his eyes, "Mum, it's not Beirut. There's a Sainsburys on every corner now."

She laughed, touching her throat, "of course, darling. I'm just being maternal."

I stared at the carpet, which was pale blue and so plush you could lose a shoe in it. I thought of our carpet at home, threadbare from years of foot traffic and dog hair. The contrast made me want to apologise for every second I'd spent on their furniture.

"So, Alexander tells us you're quite the scholar," said Mr. Hughes, refilling his glass, "top marks in History, and some research work before you start next term?"

I coughed, nearly spilling my gin, "yes. It's mostly luck, though."

He gave a bark of a laugh, "nonsense. Luck favours the prepared. I always said that to Alexander, but he's never been one for deferred gratification." He shot his son a look, half-admiring, half-exasperated.

Alex smirked, "you just wish I'd gone into law."

His father shook his head, "too sharp to waste in a courtroom. You're better suited for business. Or Parliament."

Alex shrugged, as if neither option held much interest.

Mrs. Hughes patted my knee, an intimacy that startled me, "so what are your plans, Liam? After university, I mean."

I had the answer ready, Dr. Henderson's research project, maybe teaching, keep the options open. But under her gaze, it sounded childish, like I was reading from a careers brochure.

"I'm not sure yet," I said, voice shrinking, "maybe postgraduate, if I can swing the funding."

She nodded, the smile flickering, "very wise. The world is changing so fast, isn't it?"

Alex jumped in, steering the conversation away, "Liam's also in the *Socialist Society*. He's practically a card-carrying member."

The words hung in the air like a bad smell.

Mr. Hughes arched a brow, "you'll be storming the Winter Palace next," he said. "Don't let my old friends at the club hear, or you'll never get an interview at the Bar."

I smiled, but it felt brittle, "I doubt they'd have me anyway."

He grinned, pleased by the retort.

The conversation skittered on, talk of strikes, university politics, the Falklands, the latest scandal in the Conservative party. Each topic was a test, and I could feel myself measured, weighed, and filed in the correct cabinet. Every time I let my guard slip, I saw Alex watching, lips curled in private amusement, as if daring me to break character.

Eventually, Mrs. Hughes stood, "why don't you boys take your things up? Dinner will be at seven sharp." She directed this at Alex, but I knew she was really talking to me.

Alex led me up the stairs, which creaked under our combined weight. The hallway was lined with family portraits,

Alex in cricket whites, Alex at some European ruin, Alex in a prefect's blazer, grinning with a certainty that made me want to punch him and kiss him at the same time.

His bedroom was at the end of the landing, bigger than any I had ever seen. The bed was made with military precision; the shelves held a neat row of trophies and books. A model of the *Cutty Sark* sat on the window ledge, sails pristine.

"Sorry about them," Alex said, dropping his bag by the desk, "they mean well. Mostly."

I collapsed onto the bed, careful not to muss the covers, "are you kidding? I could live in the garage and die happy here."

Alex flopped beside me; arms folded behind his head, "you did well. Dad only does the handshake of death if he thinks you're worth the trouble."

I let out a breath I didn't know I'd been holding. The room felt less oppressive, now, more like a set from a play than a museum.

"Do they always talk about you like you're not in the room?" I said.

He snorted, "only when they want me to know I'm disappointing them."

We lay there, listening to the house settle, each tick of the clock another reminder that time moved differently in places like this. After a while, Alex rolled onto his side, propping himself up on one elbow.

"You really okay?" he asked, quieter now.

I nodded, "yeah. Just… different. That's all."

He reached out, brushed a stray hair from my forehead. The gesture was brief, almost accidental.

"Tomorrow will be better," he said. "Dad's got golf and Mum's at bridge. We'll have the place to ourselves."

I smiled, letting the promise settle between us. For the first time, the idea of staying here didn't seem impossible. Maybe I could learn to fit, if only for a weekend.

"Sounds good," I said.

He grinned, then got up to unpack, leaving me to stare at the ceiling and listen to the echo of my own heartbeat, loud and stubborn in the quiet.

Downstairs, I could hear the clink of glasses, the low drone of voices. I imagined Mr. Hughes, already on his second drink, holding forth about the importance of tradition and the collapse of standards among the young. I imagined Mrs. Hughes, half-listening, eyes drifting to the clock, counting down the minutes until she could retire to her book and her gin.

I wondered what they thought of me, really. If I was a curiosity, a project, or just another of Alex's experiments. I closed my eyes, tried to picture the house from the outside, the windows glowing, the garden neat as a parade ground. I thought of our house in Rochdale, Mum's slippers by the door, Dad's jacket always on the banister. I thought of Sarah, probably eating crisps in front of the telly and laughing at some soap.

I missed them, more than I wanted to admit. But for now, I was here, in a room that smelled of lemon polish and the faint, persistent ghost of Alex's aftershave.

I opened my eyes, looked over at him, and said, "Thank you."

He didn't answer, but the smile he gave me was real, and for a minute, it was enough. He then led me up a narrow flight of stairs into the eaves to a small guest room. At least I had a small shower room and toilet to myself up there.

The gong for dinner rang at precisely seven, a sound that seemed to issue from the bones of the house. We filed down the staircase behind Alex's mother, who had swapped her earlier cardie for a silk blouse the colour of piano keys. Mr. Hughes waited at the foot of the stairs, hand poised over his watch, as if tallying the seconds lost to inefficiency.

The dining room was staged for theatre, mahogany table, six high-backed chairs, napkins folded with a kind of origami violence. Silverware gleamed in regimental lines, wine already breathing in crystal decanters. A portrait of a distant, hawk-nosed ancestor glared down from above the sideboard, daring anyone to eat without permission.

Alex held my chair, an affectation, I thought, until he whispered, "breathe," just loud enough for me to hear. I sat, folded my hands in my lap, and tried to look as though I'd always dined in places where a soup spoon existed, let alone required its own place in the order of battle.

"Liam, I do hope you're not vegetarian," said Mrs. Hughes as she settled opposite me, "I know it's the fashion among students these days, but we like to support the local butchers. I find it anchors one in the real world."

"Not at all," I said, trying to soften the Rochdale with vowels pilfered from BBC presenters, "my dad would kill me if I turned up my nose at a proper dinner."

Mr. Hughes let out a bark of approval, "good lad," he said, "none of that fad nonsense, eh, Alexander?"

Alex smiled, one corner only, "no, dad. I'm more of a steak and chips man."

We made it through the soup with only minor skirmishes, a few questions about my family ("is your father in a trade?"), some gentle ribbing about Manchester's "intake." I clung to the etiquette drills from school assemblies and the rare family weddings, watched Mrs. Hughes for cues, and mirrored her pace bite for bite.

The main course arrived, roast lamb, pink at the centre, ringed with a moat of gravy that dared you to drown in it. Mrs. Hughes ladled minted peas onto my plate.

"So, Alexander," said Mr. Hughes, as he carved with surgical precision, "your mother tells me you're considering postgraduate work. Is that really the best use of your talents?"

Alex hesitated, just long enough to be noticed, "it's an option," he said, "Dr. Adams thinks I'd do well in research."

Mr. Hughes snorted, "Adams is a dreamer. We're not in the business of subsidising perpetual students. Real ambition means entering the fray, not hiding in ivory towers." He speared a slice of lamb, savaged it, then pointed the knife at his son, "your friend here, Parry, sorry Liam, he seems to know what he wants. Teaching, is it?"

I nodded, but the attention felt like a bucket of cold water, "maybe," I said. "Or research, if I can get the funding. But teaching's solid. Respectable."

"Good," said Mr. Hughes, the word as final as a rubber stamp. "We need more people with their feet on the ground. Don't let the academics fill your head with nonsense, Alexander."

Alex didn't reply. He cut his food into geometric shapes, eyes fixed on the plate.

Mrs. Hughes dabbed her lips, then aimed her artillery at me, "do you enjoy the city, Liam? Manchester, I mean. You mentioned you joined some societies?"

I felt the wire tighten around my tongue, "some, yes. Socialist, mostly for the debate. I like hearing all sides."

"Oh?" Her eyebrows twitched, "and which side do you prefer?"

I picked up my water glass, hoping the coolness would slow my pulse, "depends on the issue," I said, voice bland. "I'm not much of a joiner. More interested in arguments than in dogma."

She nodded, filing this away, "so you're not a committed revolutionary, then?"

I smiled, rehearsed, "I'd rather read about them than become one." Alex shot me a look of gratitude. I caught it, squeezed it for all it was worth.

Mr. Hughes poured wine into my glass, generous, a silent dare, "you must have an opinion about the recent war," he said, "everyone does, these days."

I had seen this trap before, "it's complicated," I said. "History usually is."

He laughed, but the sound had no humour in it, "not to the families of the lads out there fighting for us. The country needs a clear victory now and then." Alex coughed into his napkin. I tried to keep my face flat, but my jaw ached from the effort.

Mrs. Hughes watched us both with hawk-eyed patience, "it's so much simpler when you know what you're fighting for," she said. "In my day, at least we had the decency to pick sides."

There was a silence, thick enough to cut.

Alex broke it, "Liam's got the right idea, Mum. Stay out of the trenches, let the world argue itself to death." He flashed me a quick, wicked smile, "he's much cleverer than he lets on."

I shrugged, the compliment burning more than the wine.

The meal carried on in the same vein, lamb, then trifle, then cheese and fruit for those who weren't already beaten. Every round, Mr. Hughes returned to the subject of ambition, to the necessity of "standing out" in a world gone soft. He needled Alex about sports ("you've not played since Easter, have you?"), about university politics, about the girls in Manchester.

Mrs. Hughes pressed me for stories about home, about "what the schools are like up there," as if Rochdale existed solely as a cautionary tale for the children of Cheshire. I answered with the same evasive moves I used with my own parents: humour, self-deprecation, the odd quote from a famous author. She seemed to enjoy these, even when I knew she'd never read them. But the real test came after the cheese, when Mr. Hughes topped up all the glasses and cleared his throat.

"To the Prime Minister," he said, voice ringing, "to victory. To restoring our place in the world."

He raised his glass, and I saw, in the flash of light on the crystal, a command rather than an invitation.

Alex caught my eye, a flicker of warning. I picked up my glass, hoping the tremor wouldn't show, and raised it with the others.

"To the Prime Minister," I repeated, the words sticking in my throat like gristle. We drank. The wine was sour, or maybe it was just the taste in my mouth.

Alex let the moment settle, then pivoted, launching into a story about a lecturer who'd set his own trousers alight during a chemistry demo. It was a ridiculous tale, and the way he told it, embellishing, drawing laughter from the table, reminded me why I liked him in the first place. He was brilliant at defusing, at taking the raw charge of a moment and channelling it into something almost bearable.

The mood thawed, a little. The rest of the meal passed with less interrogation, more stories, more laughter, most of it rehearsed, but real enough to keep the evening from cracking. The grandfather clock chimed the hour, and Mrs. Hughes rose, signalling the end.

"Thank you for the lovely company, boys," she said, brushing her hand over my shoulder as she passed, "you'll stay up, I'm sure. There's sherry in the drawing room if you fancy a nightcap."

Alex stood, polite to the bone, and waited for the door to close behind his parents before letting out a shuddering sigh.

"You, okay?" he whispered, leading me back toward the drawing room, where the fire still smouldered.

I nodded, but my tongue felt thick as glue, "do they always go that hard?"

He flopped onto the sofa, stretching out his legs, "only when there's new blood. You did brilliantly."

I sat beside him, feeling the stiffness in my spine begin
to dissolve, "I nearly lost it when your dad toasted Thatcher. I
thought you'd kick me under the table."

He grinned, "I considered it, but you looked like you
might shatter if I touched you."

We sat in silence, the crackle of the fire covering our
breathing. I listened for footsteps upstairs, for the faint clink of
glass as Mr. Hughes poured himself another, for the sound of
the house exhaling after a successful evening of pageantry.

"Thank you," I said, not sure what I was thanking him
for.

Alex reached over, took my hand, and squeezed it. His
grip was warm, reassuring, "anytime, Liam."

We stayed there, hands tangled, watching the shadows
lengthen and the wine sink to sediment in our glasses. In the
comfort of the drawing room, surrounded by the ghosts of old
victories and older secrets, I almost believed we could survive
this world together. I rested my head on his shoulder, and for a
minute, we belonged.

The house at night was a different species, soft-footed,
predatory, more alert than in daylight. The grandfather clock at
the end of the hall counted every minute with the pitiless patience of a judge. Alex led the way up the stairs, moving with a
lightness I tried to copy, the runner muffling our steps but not
the creaks that sang out whenever we missed the safe centre of
a tread.

His room was unchanged from earlier, but the dark
gave everything a new edge. The model ship on the sill cast sails
of shadow across the wallpaper; his old football medals winked
dully from their rack above the bookshelf. The door shut with a
click that might as well have been a gunshot. There was no
lock. I heard Alex draw a breath, slow and controlled, before he
turned to face me.

"Are you sure?" he whispered, voice so low I caught
only the shape of it.

I nodded, heart loud in my ears. He crossed the distance in three steps, hands finding my face, then my waist. His
touch was urgent, almost rough, but I could feel the restraint at

the edges, the way he measured every gesture against the threat of discovery.

We kissed, mouths barely parting, all the heat and force of a thousand silent arguments pressed into that one spot where his tongue found mine. The air in the room was thick, metallic, cologne, lemon polish, the ghost of a boyhood spent hiding from himself.

He tugged at my shirt, yanking it loose from the waistband with a desperation that made me want to laugh and cry at the same time. I slipped my hands under his jumper, fingers glancing off the warm skin at his ribs, the sharp edges of his bones. He shuddered at the touch, then pressed closer, our hips grinding together, the friction setting off a series of tiny, involuntary noises from both of us.

"Floor," he hissed, and I understood instantly, the bed would betray us with every spring, every inch of movement. We slid down, landing soft on the carpet, hands working at buckles and buttons, our movements clumsy in the dim.

There was no choreography. We fumbled, improvising, learning each other anew with every shift and sigh. I ran my tongue along the line of his jaw, tasting the salt of his sweat, the aftertaste of wine. He covered my mouth with his palm when I gasped, his own eyes wide with panic and delight.

"Shh," he breathed, and I nodded, the wordless agreement that we were in this together, for better or worse.

He pushed my trousers down, fingers trembling. I reached for him, pulled him on top, his weight pinning me to the floor in a way that made the whole world tilt. He bit at my neck, at my collarbone, careful not to leave marks above the line of my t-shirt. I pressed my knee between his legs, felt the sharp inhale, the way he stilled, muscles locked.

We moved like that, bodies pressed close, every muscle straining to make less noise, to keep the moment secret and sacred. I felt his breath hot on my ear, his heart hammering against my chest. When he came, it was almost silent, a soft, strangled moan, his face buried in my shoulder. I followed, the climax raw and sharp, biting down on my own fist to keep from crying out.

After, we lay there, limbs tangled, sweat cooling on our skin. I stared at the ceiling, at the curve of shadow where the plaster met the moulding, and tried to memorise every detail. The moonlight slipped in through the thin curtains, casting stripes across our bodies. Alex traced slow circles on my stomach, his fingertips feather-light.

I heard footsteps in the corridor, a slow, measured tread, pausing just outside the door. We froze, not even breathing, waiting for the sound to resolve into movement away or the rattle of the knob. After a long, endless minute, the steps moved on. I let out a breath, shaky with relief.

Alex turned on his side, propped his head on his elbow. "Tomorrow," he whispered, "we're free. Wales. Just us."

I grinned, the taste of him still in my mouth, "you think the sheep will judge us?"

He snorted, then clapped a hand over his own lips, eyes wide in comic terror. The sound was barely louder than a heartbeat, but it felt enormous. We stifled laughter into each other's necks, biting down on the joy and the fear together.

He brushed my hair off my forehead, then kissed me, slow and lingering. "I meant what I said downstairs," he murmured. "You're better at this than you think."

"Better at what?" I said, teasing.

"Surviving them," he replied, jerking his chin toward the ceiling, where his parents no doubt lay in parallel, cataloguing the day's performance. "Surviving all of it."

I thought about my own parents, about Mum, who would never have let me share a room with a girl, but would a boy. About Dad, who believed in fairness but not in deviation. I wondered what they would say, if they knew.

I pulled Alex close, pressed my forehead to his, "just keep holding on," I said. "That's all I want."

We lay like that for a long time, eyes open, waiting for sleep. At some point, I realised that the fear, the animal terror of being found out, of being caught, had not vanished, but it had been replaced by something else. A kind of pride, maybe. Or just the knowledge that, if the world wanted to crush us, it would have to work harder than this.

I drifted off with my fingers locked in his, the clock in the hall ticking away the minutes to morning. The house was still awake, listening, but in our little patch of carpet, under the moon and the silent stars, we were untouchable.

For once, the danger felt worth it.

The morning sun burned off the old fear, at least for a while. I woke to the whirr of the lawnmower somewhere out back, the perfume of cut grass sneaking in through a window that Alex must have cracked open after I fell asleep. He was already up, nowhere in sight, the dent of his head still warm on the other pillow. He checked for activity on the landing and quickly and silently ushered me up to the guest room.

Downstairs, the kitchen was all brightness and order. Mrs. Hughes moved between kitchen and table, orchestrating the meal with a precision that shamed any doubts I'd had about her authority. She wore a lavender housecoat over her silk blouse, the sleeves rolled to the elbow, hands flicking between egg pan, toast rack, and coffee pot as if each were a symphony section waiting for the baton.

I found Alex in the conservatory, reading the *Times*, legs crossed at the knee. He looked up and smiled, the same smile as last night, but dialled down for morning. I wanted to reach out, take his hand, but in the slant of sun and glass it felt impossible. He patted the seat beside him, and I sat, the air between us thick with what we'd left unsaid in the dark.

"Sleep well?" he asked, eyes trained on the crossword, but voice aimed at me.

"Yeah," I said, "your floor's more comfortable than my bed at home."

Mrs. Hughes called us to breakfast, her voice measured but unmistakable. We filed in, took our places. Mr. Hughes was already there, reading the *Financial Times*, every page squared to the inch. He nodded at me, then at Alex, as if inventorying his property before the start of business.

The table was set with everything, grapefruit halves, boiled eggs, a silver rack of toast. There was a low hum of domesticity, almost peaceful.

I'd just reached for a slice of toast when Mrs. Hughes cleared her throat, "Alexander, I've just heard from Caroline. She'll be joining us for lunch today, before you two head off to Wales."

The words dropped into the room like a tray of glassware. I choked on my tea, spluttered, caught the edge of the cup with my elbow, and nearly sent the whole thing into my lap.

"Are you all right, Liam?" she asked, concern layered under amusement.

"Fine," I managed, mopping the spill with my sleeve. "Just went down the wrong way."

Alex didn't look at me. He kept his eyes fixed on the crossword, circling clues with methodical detachment, "that's great," he said, a beat too late to be believable. "Hadn't realised she was back from the States so soon."

Mrs. Hughes smiled, relishing the surprise, "she said she might bring you something from her trip. I thought it would be nice to catch up as a family before you leave."

There was a pause, during which Mr. Hughes rustled his paper and said, "will she be joining you in Wales as well?" The question was tossed at Alex, but I felt it land somewhere deep in my chest.

"No, just lunch," said Alex, still not looking at me. "She's got her own plans for the summer."

I stared at the tablecloth, tracing the blue-on-white *fleur-de-lis* pattern with a shaking finger. My mouth was dry, but my hands wouldn't stop sweating. I tried to replay the last twenty-four hours, searching for any mention of Caroline, any hint or warning that might have prepared me.

Nothing. Only the hard, clean silence of a secret too well kept. Breakfast became an exercise in willpower. I chewed each mouthful, swallowing hard against the urge to gag. Mr. Hughes put down his paper and turned to me, smile sharp as a guillotine.

"So, Liam. Is there a young lady waiting for you at home?"

The question was a cliche, but in this context it felt like a test. I nodded, falling into the script I'd learned by heart. "Amanda. She's in Stirling. We've been together since sixth form."

He grinned, pleased with the answer, "very good. You'll want to keep your options open, though. My advice: never settle too soon. Life has a way of changing your priorities."

"Thanks," I said, forcing a smile, "I'll remember that."

Mrs. Hughes poured more coffee, her hands steady, eyes never leaving me, "is Amanda your first serious relationship?"

The question startled me; it sounded almost kind, as if she were trying to reach through the noise to the person underneath. I hesitated, then nodded, "yeah. First real one, anyway."

She nodded, as if this confirmed a long-held suspicion, "you must miss her."

"Sometimes," I said, which was both true and not.

Across the table, Alex finished his eggs, set down his fork, and finally met my eyes. There was apology there, or maybe just regret. I looked away, unable to hold the gaze.

Breakfast ended in silence. Mr. Hughes folded his paper, stood, and announced he had an appointment. Mrs. Hughes began clearing plates, humming softly. Alex touched my arm as we rose, but I shrugged him off, not out of anger but because I was afraid my own touch would betray everything.

We walked back upstairs, neither of us speaking. In the bedroom, I collapsed onto the bed, staring at the ceiling and counting the slow whir of the lawnmower as it looped round and round the perimeter of the house.

After a few minutes, Alex sat beside me, hands folded in his lap.

"I should have told you," he said, voice flat.

"Why didn't you?" I whispered, though I already knew the answer.

He shrugged, helpless, "it's what they expect. What everyone expects. I thought it was just for show, and now ..." He trailed off.

I stared at the wall, fighting the urge to cry. "Is that what I am, then? The thing you hide until it's safe to let it out?"

He flinched, as if I'd slapped him, "no. I just ..." He looked away, jaw tight, "it's not that simple."

I sat up, the anger and the sadness colliding somewhere in my throat, "it is for them," I said, meaning the parents, the world, the millions of people who would never know what it cost to keep this kind of secret. "It is for me, most days," he reached for my hand, and this time I let him. His grip was fierce, almost painful.

"I don't want to lose you," he said, "but I can't lose them either. Not yet."

I nodded, swallowing the words I wanted to say. I should confront him about Caroline, but instead I heard myself ask, "Who's the judge bloke in the picture at the bottom of the stairs?" I tried to change the course of the conversation and my voice sounded hollow even to me.

Alex's laugh seemed to come from somewhere far away, "I wondered if you'd notice Grandpa. He was not just any judge, a High Court one."

"Impressive," I said, though what impressed me more was how quickly we'd slipped into this safer conversation, "is that what your father's aiming for too?"

"He wishes," Alex's eyes flashed with something like triumph, "simply not good enough according to Grandpa."

I watched him savour the words, and felt a stab of guilt for enjoying his family's fractures.

"What about your mum's parents?" I asked, then immediately regretted prolonging this charade.

Alex's laugh had an edge now, "oh, you've fallen for the accent and all that prim and proper rubbish."

"What do you mean?" my hand twitched toward his, then retreated.

"Mum's actually from Bootle, over the water. Proper scouser," he paused, his face softening. "Evacuated during the war. Stayed after her parents died in the Liverpool Blitz."

"That's sad," I offered, though what felt sadder was how we were both avoiding the real conversation.

"She did alright. Adopted by a wealthy childless couple," he shrugged, not meeting my eyes. "Learned early that to get on she had to pretend to be something she wasn't."

The irony hung between us, too obvious to mention.

"Grandpa used to say: *'you can take the girl out of Bootle, but you can't take Bootle out of the girl'.*"

"We are what we are," I said, "but no harm in trying to change."

"Until the mask slips," he replied, and I couldn't tell if it was a warning or a wish

We sat together, letting the words settle, until the clock in the hall struck eleven. Then, with a precision I admired and hated, we packed our bags, zipped them shut, and went to face the rest of the day.

Lunch would come, and with it Caroline, a new fiction to add to the shelf. But for now, we sat on the edge of the bed, two actors between scenes, waiting for the next cue.

It would be a long drive to Wales.

CHAPTER 10: FREEDOM UNDER CANVAS

Lunch came with all the inevitability of a courtroom summons. The dining room was a kind of mausoleum, thick curtains drawn against the sun, a rug so deep you lost sensation in your ankles, a sideboard polished to near-weaponised gleam. The table was set for five, each place a miniature theatre: silverware fanned in concentric arcs, napkins folded into origami swans, crystal glasses lined up like a firing squad. I had never in my life seen so many forks, and already doubted my capacity to wield any of them without incident.

Caroline arrived at twelve-thirty sharp, delivered by a new *Jaguar* the colour of a hearse and driven by a silent manservant whose only job, apparently, was to open the rear door and hover until she'd reached the porch. She looked every inch the diplomat's daughter: tan trench, navy blouse, cream skirt, legs that started at her earlobes and went on past the horizon. Her hair was the kind of blonde you only get in a laboratory or a French spa, and her handshake was cool, precise, almost calculated.

"Liam," she said, with the briefest flicker of recognition. "Alex has told me so much about you." Her voice was mid-Atlantic, each syllable sanded free of local bias.

"He lies," I said, aiming for dry, but it sounded like I'd got something caught in my throat.

She smiled, a show of perfect white teeth, "that's what I'm hoping for."

Mrs. Hughes shepherded us towards the dining room and the waiting table, smoothing the way with small, clinical compliments. "Caroline is just back from New Haven, darling. An exchange at Yale. We're so proud."

"I see Alex survived the term, then," said Caroline, as she took the chair opposite me. "He usually needs at least one medical intervention per term."

Alex managed a rueful grin, "kept myself mostly out of A&E this time. Though the campus bar nearly finished me."

There was a round of laughter, which I tried to join, but my mouth was suddenly too dry.

The first course arrived, melon and *Parma* ham, arrayed in a spiral that could have doubled as a biology diagram. The silverware felt heavy, alien, cold against my palm. I watched Caroline slice a neat crescent of melon, then imitated the gesture, missing the mark and chasing my fruit across the plate with a fork that clanged, loud as a dinner bell.

"So, Liam," said Mrs. Hughes, in a tone that suggested she was about to take my measurements, "are your family still in Rochdale?"

"Yes, Mrs. Hughes," I said, putting every vowel through the filter of elocution class and hope.

Caroline cocked her head, eyes narrowing just a fraction. "And you're at Manchester, too? I thought Alex said you were in different colleges."

"We are," I said. "But we're both in halls, so we see each other. Sometimes more than we'd like. I think we may have met just before Christmas."

Alex barked a laugh, but it sounded like a slip of the tongue. "He's the only person who knows where the library is. I need him for reference."

"That's not what you need him for, I'm sure," said Caroline, the smile not quite matching her eyes. She then returned with to me, "didn't you have your girlfriend with you?"

I saw the conversational landmine a millisecond before I stepped on it, "yes, Amanda," I said, keeping my gaze on the fork. "She's in Scotland, at Stirling."

Caroline nodded, slow and deliberate. "Long distance, then. That's hard to make it work."

Mrs. Hughes intervened, "Caroline's father is in the diplomatic service," she said, as if this explained the whole of British society. "She's hoping to join them after she finishes her degree."

"Maybe," said Caroline, with a practiced humility that wasn't humility at all, "but, I've got the summer placement lined up. Alex, are you still set on going the legal route?"

Alex shrugged, the motion so subtle it might have been a muscle spasm, "Dad wants me to," he said, "but I haven't decided."

Mr. Hughes beamed, topping up Caroline's glass with a flourish. "Alex is being modest, as usual. He'll have his pick of chambers after next year. *Brindle and Smythe* would be lucky to have him."

"I'm not sure the world needs another barrister," said Alex, voice light but with a quiver underneath.

"Nonsense," said Mr. Hughes, "the world is run by them." He winked at Caroline. She laughed, but the sound was brittle, like glass at a high note.

The main course was chicken chasseur, served from a porcelain platter the size of a coffin lid. Mrs. Hughes ladled generous portions onto our plates, careful not to spill even a drop. The sauce was deep red, the meat pink and perfect. I tasted nothing but adrenaline.

Caroline steered the conversation back to academics, "so, Liam. Do you have plans for after graduation? Manchester's got a strong teaching program, right?"

"I'm thinking about it," I said, "teaching, I mean. Maybe even staying on for research. I'm not much for competition."

She smiled, but it was more of a reveal than a gesture, "I'm sure you'll do brilliantly. Alex always did say you were the clever one."

"I didn't," said Alex, but he was smiling, too.

Mrs. Hughes folded her napkin with a snap, "you must bring Amanda round, next time you visit. I do love a northern accent." I nodded, the lie landing somewhere in the middle of my chest.

The talk drifted to politics. Mr. Hughes and Caroline ran the table, volleying takes on the Falklands, the miners, the inefficiency of the public sector. Alex played along, chiming in with the odd counterpoint, but his eyes kept drifting to the window, as if mapping the shortest escape route.

I focused on the food, counting each bite. Dessert was lemon tart, so sharp it made my mouth water even before I tasted it. The table relaxed, the edge dulled by wine and the choreography of meal's end. Mrs. Hughes produced a silver tray of chocolates, offering them first to Caroline, then to Alex, then to me, with an encouraging, "go on, have two, you're all skin and bones."

After coffee, Mr. Hughes pushed back from the table, stretching to his full, imposing height, "well, ladies and gentlemen," he said, "I'm for a walk in the garden. Give the boys a head start on their camping, eh?"

Mrs. Hughes smiled, but her eyes held a warning: "don't get lost, Alexander. You know how your father is if you're not on time."

Caroline stood, gathering her things with a grace that looked expensive, "it was lovely to meet you properly, Liam," she said, and for the first time, I believed she almost meant it. She leaned in, air-kissed my cheek, then Alex's, before gliding out with Mrs. Hughes on her heels. Alone, Alex and I sat in the thick, unbreathable silence left by their exit.

"Sorry," he said, after a while, "she's not usually that…"

"Efficient?" I offered.

He laughed, sharp and brief, "yeah. It's like being cross-examined."

"She likes you," I said, and I hated the edge in my voice.

He glanced at the empty door, "doesn't matter. It's not real."

We cleared the plates in silence, stacking them by the sink with the mechanical precision of people who'd learned, young, how not to leave fingerprints. Upstairs, we packed for Wales, rolling sleeping bags and rationing socks, pretending not to hear the echo of Caroline's voice in the hallway below.

When we descended with our bags, Mrs. Hughes was waiting by the front door, lips pursed as she checked the kit, "do be careful on the roads," she said to both of us, "they're not like in the towns. Single track for miles."

"We'll be fine," said Alex. He hoisted his bag, shot me a look of conspiracy, "we know how to survive in the wild."

Mrs. Hughes kissed him on the cheek, then looked at me with an expression I couldn't parse, pride, or perhaps the recognition of a fellow outsider, "you'll keep him in line, Liam?"

I smiled, said, "I'll do my best."

The front door closed with a sigh, and we stood for a second on the porch, the sun glinting off the stone lions. As we turned to head for the garage, Alex reached out and squeezed my hand, just once, hard enough to leave a mark.

Neither of us said anything. There wasn't time. We had miles to cover, and a world to escape. We'd barely made it down the drive before Alex's mother re-materialised in the entryway, clutching a second set of keys and a smile that looked like it had cost her something to produce, "just a minute, boys," she called, waving us back.

We exchanged a glance, then retraced our steps, expecting a forgotten sandwich or a last-minute injunction about the roads. Instead, she beckoned us around the side of the house, past a rhododendron as tightly manicured as her voice, to the garage, a whitewashed bunker that must have housed a dozen secrets.

She pressed a button, and the electric door rose, slow as a funeral curtain. There, half-buried under tarps and two lifetimes of boxed detritus, was a blue *Ford Escort*, the paintwork still shiny in the bits that weren't covered with dust.

"Alexander," she said, turning the keys in her palm like a rosary, "your father and I wanted to surprise you. You earned it, darling. Completing your first year."

Alex stared, then managed a dry, "thanks, Mum," before she enveloped him in a hug, a performance both brisk and almost savage in its intensity. She gave me a quick squeeze on the shoulder, "drive safe, for all our sakes," then left us to inventory the miracle.

Alex ran a hand along the bonnet, knuckles pale, "fuck me," he whispered, "she's actually done it. I never thought they'd …"

He stopped, then laughed, the sound sharp and bright, bouncing off the walls of the garage, "you realise we're going to get so lost."

I grinned, the sun cutting a square of warmth onto my face as we pulled the car into the light, "we'll be fine. You've got instincts, right?"

"I may be studying Geography, but I have no sense of direction."

"It's Wales," I said, "how hard can it be?"

We loaded the boot with sleeping bags, tarpaulin, enough instant noodles to fortify a siege. As we buckled in, I caught a last glimpse of Mrs. Hughes at the window, watching us leave with a look I couldn't read, hope, maybe, or the disappointment of letting go.

The first part of the drive was all A-roads and roundabouts, the world trimmed and measured. Alex played DJ, flipping between classic rock and news bulletins, the war now downgraded to a ticker in the background of British life. We passed business parks, new estates, a thousand petrol stations. The car still smelled of new vinyl, but Alex insisted on keeping the window cracked, letting in the air, the green, the lowing scent of summer on the turn.

Somewhere past Llangollen, the landscape unclenched. The hedgerows grew wild; the lanes shrank to ribbons. We switched off the radio and let the silence in, punctuated only by the rattle of loose gear in the back and the pop of gravel under the tyres.

It was impossible not to relax, at least a little. With each passing mile, the memory of the Hughes' dining room faded, replaced by an itch to see what lay beyond the next switchback. Alex rolled his sleeves, sang along to the wrong lyrics, made up stories about the villages we passed, who lived there, who hated whom, what secret affairs played out behind the net curtains. I laughed more than I'd planned to, the tension in my spine dissolving by slow degrees.

By the time we reached Beddgelert, the sky had gone the bruised blue of late afternoon. The campsite was set back from the main road, a clearing in a thicket of Scots pine and moss, the only structure at the entrance a battered sign listing the rules: *'No open fires, no noise after ten, no dogs unless on leads'*. There were three other cars in the gravel lot, but no sign of people. The place radiated stillness, as if even the wind had forgotten how to move. In the centre was a single brick-built block containing the toilets and showers.

We found our spot, number seven, on a rise overlooking the river, and got to work. The tent was second-hand, a relic of Alex's *Duke of Edinburgh* days, the smell of ancient polyester baked into every seam. We unrolled the canvas, hammered in the stakes, and spent five minutes cursing over the guy ropes until Alex, with a little flourish, tied a knot so neat and clever it made me want to take notes.

"Silver Award," he said, dusting off his hands, "we got lost in the Peaks and ended up camping in a cow field. Nobody told me cows don't sleep."

He showed me how to dig a shallow pit for the Trangia stove, how to bank the rocks so the wind wouldn't snuff the flame. I watched him work, the muscles in his forearms shifting with each motion, his mouth fixed in a line of focus. It was a new side to him, capable, practical, almost gentle.

We boiled water, made tea, and sat cross-legged on a ground-sheet as the sun melted behind the ridge. For the first time in weeks, I felt the world go quiet.

Alex passed me the mug, fingers lingering on the handle. "See?" he said, voice low, "surviving."

"I don't think we've been tested yet," I replied.

He shrugged, but the smile didn't fade.

As the light bled out of the sky, the woods filled with the ticking of insects and the distant chime of water over stone. We stretched out, backs against our rucksacks, and watched the first stars appear through the mesh of branches. The fire pit glowed with a mean little flame, orange on our hands and faces.

"Better than the Wirral?" I asked, after a while.

He nodded, head lolling against the pack, "infinitely."

The night was absolute, a black velvet that swallowed the road and all the noise we'd carried from home. We didn't talk about parents, or Caroline, or the lies we told to keep the world at bay. We just sat, letting the hush do the work.

When the last of the tea was gone, Alex reached for another bottle of *Famous Grouse*, poured a capful each, and held it up in a silent toast.

"To making it out," he said.

We clinked, drank, and let the whisky burn a line down to our bellies. The flame in the pit sputtered and died, but neither of us moved to relight it.

It was only then, in the dark, that Alex leaned in, shoulder pressing against mine, the contact deliberate but not urgent. We sat like that, fused at the seam, watching the embers cool to memory. For the first time since I could remember, I didn't want to be anywhere else.

We woke to the sound of rain on nylon, a gentle, arrhythmic tapping that made me want to stay buried in my sleeping bag forever. Alex was already up, boiling water for tea on the little stove, steam fogging his glasses as he squatted in the tent's covered entrance.

"Rise and shine, soldier," he called, and I groaned, but the smell of tea and the sight of his hair sticking out in seven directions made it impossible to stay mad.

I pulled on yesterday's socks, shivered into my jumper, and crawled out to the world. The air was pure and sharp, the kind that made your lungs sting and your eyes water. Around us, the forest dripped, needles glistening with the overnight soak. Above, a sliver of blue sky promised the rain wouldn't last.

We ate granola bars and debated the best route up Snowdon. Alex spread the map on a boulder, pinning it with a rock, and traced a line with the tip of his pen, "this one's steeper, but it'll get us to the ridge before lunch," he said, tapping a dashed path that looked more like a suggestion than a promise.

"Lead the way," I said, and meant it.

We packed quickly, leaving the tent staked, and set out. The first hour was a slog, boots sinking in mud, the track little more than a memory stitched into the moss. The climb forced the silence; there was no room for talk when your heart was pounding and your thighs burned. Now and then, Alex glanced back to make sure I was keeping up, his grin wide and wild when I caught his eye.

After the initial ascent, the trail opened onto a shelf of granite and lichen, the heather bruised flat by years of sheep and wind. In the distance, the peaks of Snowdonia knifed into the sky, still veined with dirty snow in the folds. To the left, a mountain lake glimmered, black glass, ringed with boulders and shreds of mist.

We detoured to the shore, the ground squelching underfoot, and sat on a rock to catch our breath. The surface of the lake was so still it felt wrong to speak.

Alex plucked a stone and skipped it, three perfect hops before it vanished. "I could live out here," he said, "if there was a Sainsbury's and a betting shop within a mile."

"I'd give it two weeks before you went feral," I replied.

He laughed, then looked at me, the mirth lingering but softening at the edges, "what about you? Think you'd survive outside the city?"

I picked a stone, flicked it; mine sank instantly, "I like the quiet," I said, "makes me feel less... on display."

He nodded, eyes on the water, "it's easier to be real here, isn't it?"

I thought about the dining room, the weight of a dozen invisible judgments, "yeah," I said, "it is."

We sat for a while, not talking, watching the clouds shred and reform over the summit.

Eventually, Alex broke the silence, "Dad wants me to do the internship in London this summer. Some barrister friend of his, all robes and Latin."

"Will you?" I asked.

He shrugged, "it's already decided. I just haven't agreed yet." He turned to me, the joke gone from his voice, "you ever get tired of being told who to be?"

"Constantly," I said, "but I think I do it to myself, too. Like, if I stopped trying to impress everyone, I'd just disappear."

He nudged my knee with his boot, "you'd be the only one who noticed."

I grinned, "that's the most backhanded compliment I've ever received."

"Get used to it. Law's nothing but backhanded compliments."

The path to the ridge was a scramble, loose rock and scree threatening to undo every gain. Alex reached down and hauled me up at one point, his hand firm around my wrist. We found the rhythm, he'd lead, I'd follow, then swap when the terrain flipped.

At the top, we stood alone by the stone cairn, and the world went huge. The sky was clear now, the wind whipping the sweat from our faces, the view stretching out all the way to the coast.

We flopped onto the ground, chests heaving. Alex rolled onto his back, arms spread wide, eyes closed to the sun.

"I never want to go back," he said.

"Then don't," I replied, the words out before I could think.

He opened one eye, looked at me, "you really think it's that easy?"

I didn't answer.

He sat up, brushing grass from his hair, "what would you do, if nobody cared what you chose?"

It was the first time anyone had asked me that, for real. I stared at the sky, searching for an answer.

"Teach, I think, do a *PGCE*, or maybe stay on, do a master's. I like the idea of being the one who's supposed to know things."

He smiled, a real one, "you'd be good at it."

We shared the last of the water, then started the descent. We took the direct route back down skipping across the scree slope - which was both exhilarating but also terrifying when gravity seemed to be master of the descent. On the way down, the conversation was lighter, jokes about the sheep, plans for dinner, speculation about the odds of surviving the next stretch without a twisted ankle. But something had shifted: a space opened up between us, honest and unafraid.

As the valley closed around us, Alex slipped on a wet rock and nearly took me down with him. He caught my arm, steadying himself, and his hand lingered just a beat too long before letting go.

"Thanks," he said, quietly.

We made it back to the village in time for the last light and to take a couple of drinks in the *Tanronnen Inn* across from the bridge. After we finished our third pint each, we headed out into darkness and back to the campsite. The only illumination was an almost full moon that broke through the tree canopy. It was the first time I had ever noticed moonlight shadows.

Had it not been for the distant orange glows coming from the three or four other tents we might never have found ours. It stood alone on the rise, the river a silver thread below. Alex reached inside the tent and lit the gas lantern, and I watched him shake out his damp hair. The air echoed the sounds of distant owls and nesting rooks, the evening alive with the knowledge that, for once, we didn't have to answer to anyone.

I sat on the log, boots unlaced, and felt the ache in my legs, the fresh one in my chest. I watched the ghostly form of Alex moving against the backdrop of trees, and for the first time, it didn't feel like a secret I had to keep from myself.

I wanted to reach out. I almost did. Instead, I let the night come, and the silence, and the long, slow comfort of being exactly where I wanted to be.

"I'm going to check out the shower block," Alex announced, peeling off his T-shirt and jumper. With theatrical flair, he tossed a towel over his shoulder and winked, "fill the kettle, put it on the stove, then come join me?"

I picked up the kettle, my stomach fluttering, should I have asked why he expected me to fetch water? I followed him around the corner, trying to sound casual as I turned the tap on the outside wall. My mind buzzed: he's naked soon. I'd never seen Alex completely nude. My pulse pounded.

"Don't use all the hot water before I get back," I called through the door, even though the thought of saving water barely registered. I dashed back to the tent, heart thumping. My washbag and towel felt suddenly weighty in my arms.

Steam billowed as I cracked the shower block door. Warmth washed over me, but adrenaline kept my skin prickling, "that you, Liam?" Alex's voice floated from one of the two cubicles.

"Erm, yes," I squeaked. The cubicle door swung open, and there he stood under the spray, soapy streams tracing every ridge of his body. My jaw dropped before my eyes could. A flush burned through me. My clothes vanished faster than I could process why I was undressing. His grin widened, almost predatory, and I felt an ache, an urgency, I'd never known. Part of me screamed to step closer; another part recoiled in guilt and fear. I wanted him and dreaded wanting him.

Then, snap, the outer door creaked. Someone approaching. Embarrassed and caught, I bolted into the empty cubicle, heart pounding so loud I thought Alex would hear.

The rush of conflict left me flustered. I forced a quick shower, rinsing away not only the suds but the weight of my desire and shame. Alex had emerged first, and was drying his feet on the bench. He looked up with that easy smile, "that was close! But don't worry, whoever it was has gone, just using the loo, I guess."

My cheeks burned hotter than the steam. He left me to finish drying myself, and I stumbled back to the tent in a haze, watching the sky churn with brooding clouds. No moon, no stars, just a roiling promise of rain. Inside, Alex handed me a steaming enamel mug of tea. We sat cross-legged in just our shorts under the flysheet; bodies now damp from the humid air. Our shoulders brushed. My skin tingled at the contact, torn between craving closeness and terrified of what it meant. In the lamp's glow, I noticed his fine golden shin hair and the darker, thicker hair covering mine, and felt absurdly self-conscious.

An hour later, a thunderclap split the silence. I was filling the kettle again when fat raindrops splattered my arms, the earth turning to mud, "get in, idiot! You'll drown out there or get struck by lightning!" Alex's shout jolted me.

I sprinted back, slipping slightly down the bank, soaked through to the bone. We tumbled under the flysheet together. Alex zipped us in, trapping the heat of our bodies, and my racing thoughts. Lightning cracked overhead and thunder rumbled the valley. In that charged hush, our laughter trembled between us, full of yearning, fear, and the messy pull of something neither of us was ready to name.

Outside, the rain came down in sheets, hammering the tent with a fury that made conversation impossible. Inside, the world was reduced to a cocoon, two bodies, one damp tangle of nylon and polyester, the only light the yellow glow of Alex's old camping lantern.

"Fucking hell," he said, shaking out his hair, "we might need a lifeboat before morning."

Then Alex reached across the tiny gap, his palm flat and hot on my knee, "come here," he said, voice swallowed by the drum of rain.

For the first time it started slow, an inventory of touch, his hands mapping my ribs, my arms, the nape of my neck. I could feel my own heart, fast and huge in my chest, the heat of his breath on my cheek. We kissed, the taste of rain and salt and something electric, mouths opening not in hunger but in wonder, as if we'd only just discovered how lips could fit together.

He pulled me down, onto the unzipped sleeping bags, and rolled on top, the weight of him pressing me flat. His thigh slotted between mine, pinning me in place, but I didn't mind. I wanted to be held down, to be known, to be written into the memory of this night like a name carved in stone.

We undressed each other with the patience of archaeologists. Alex took his time, never looking away, his gaze fixed and unblinking as if afraid I might vanish if he so much as blinked.

Skin against skin, the sensation was wild, overwhelming. I shuddered when his fingers grazed my hip, when his lips found the hollow of my collarbone. He traced a path down my chest with the tip of his tongue, pausing as if inch of skin was a revelation.

I reached for him, ran my hands over his back, the curve of his spine, the sharp planes of his shoulder blades. He gasped when I bit gently at his earlobe, and I felt the tremor run through his whole body.

"Liam," he whispered, not a question or a plea, just my name, soft and stunned and real.

We moved together, not frantic but with a slowness that felt ceremonial, sacred. I let him guide me, let myself be taken apart and rebuilt. The lantern cast our shadows huge and golden on the curve of the tent wall, so that it seemed there were four of us: two real, two spectral, flickering in and out with every movement.

The rain was a soundtrack, steady, relentless, drowning out the world beyond our shelter. I lost myself in it, in the sound of our breathing, the wet slap of bodies, the quiet muttered curses and half-laughed apologies when a knee or elbow hit the wrong mark.

At the end, when we came, it was together, a shared hush that pressed us closer, foreheads touching, mouths open in silent wonder. The aftermath was heat and heaviness and the sudden, absurd urge to cry.

Alex curled around me, his arms a vice, his legs tangled with mine. "Jesus," he said, after a while, "I think I pulled something."

I laughed, breathless, and wiped sweat from his forehead with the heel of my hand, "you'll survive."

"Only if you keep doing that," he murmured, eyes already closed.

We lay like that, not talking, the world reduced to the sound of the storm and the slow ebb of our heartbeats. I stared at the lantern, at the way its light also gilded the fine hairs on Alex's arm, the downy shadow of his jaw. I wanted to stay in that moment forever, the air thick with ozone and sweat and the conviction that nothing could touch us.

Outside, the rain hammered on, implacable, but inside the tent we were a single, perfect unit, safe, inviolable, and for once not needing to hide. I drifted to sleep with his hand on my chest, the rhythm of the rain in my blood, and the knowledge that the world outside had been washed away, if only for a night.

The next day we took on the challenge of *Moel Hebog*, Snowdon's (slightly) smaller brother. The climb was more challenging as the paths were not as visible or as established as those we had followed the previous day. We reached the summit just as the clouds broke for good, and the valley below flooded with gold. The river wound through it, swollen and furious, but from up high it looked like a ribbon someone had tossed away.

We found a flat rock, still warm from the day, and sprawled side by side. Alex pulled out a flask, unscrewed the cap, and offered it. The whisky tasted of peat and smoke and the promise of mistakes. We hadn't seen another person since leaving the road.

We sat in silence, drinking in turns, watching the sun catch fire on the lake. I couldn't remember the last time I'd felt so utterly at ease with another person, the space between us easy as breathing. I wanted to bottle the moment, to carry it with me, to live in it for as long as possible.

"Sometimes I think about quitting everything, just… disappearing. Find a town where nobody knows us, teach during the day, drink in the evenings, hike on weekends," I said quietly.

The words came out before I could stop them, and the second they landed I wanted to take them back. Alex's face froze and he seemed to almost physically recoil from me. The silence that followed was a knife, and I was the one holding the blade.

I stared straight ahead, counting the sheep on the hillside, the birds circling overhead, anything but the look on Alex's face. I concluded during this silence that Alex, either didn't share the idea of a future with me or that the concept of two men together was just too much.

He didn't speak. The quiet stretched, growing heavy, the only sound the wind through the heather and the distant bark of a dog. I gripped the edge of the rock, knuckles white, heart rattling in my chest. I wished I'd said nothing, wished I could unmake the moment, wished I wasn't so desperate to be wanted.

The sun dropped, the light shifting from gold to the bruised purple of twilight. I could feel the heat of Alex's thigh against mine, the solid reality of his presence, and yet I'd never felt more alone.

Still, I didn't move. I waited, braced for the answer I was sure would break me.

The air changed halfway up the valley on our return to *Beddgelert*. It wasn't just thinner; it tasted like cold iron and moss, a sharpness that cut through the sweat and made your lungs ache in a good way. I wasn't built for this kind of terrain, scree underfoot, the path zig-zagging up the mountainside until it disappeared into the cloud. But Alex set a pace as if he'd done it every weekend since birth, boots eating up the gradient, one hand in the pocket of his parka, the other occasionally steadying himself on a tuft of gorse. The only things that felt real were the ache in my calves, the sweet burn in my chest, and the quickening thump every time Alex turned to see if I was still alive. His silence though cut deep.

When we stopped for water, I doubled over, hands braced on my knees, trying to get my lungs to work again. Alex tossed me half a *Mars bar*, the wrapper flapping in the wind, and the silence was broken.

When he spoke, his voice was softer than I'd ever heard it, "before, what you said, that's not how the world works, Liam. That's not a world I would ever be allowed to live in."

I forced a laugh, bitter at the edges, "since when do you care about how the world works?"

He turned, expression unreadable, "since I realised it doesn't care about me."

We sat, the gap between us suddenly enormous, both of us pretending the wind was the only thing making our eyes water. I wanted to reach for him, to say something that would bridge the distance, but the words died in my mouth.

He broke first, "look, I'm not …" He stopped, gritted his teeth, then started again, "I like you. I do. But this has got to be temporary. You get that, right?"

I nodded, the movement tight and mechanical, "because of your parents? Or because of Caroline?"

He shook his head, exasperated, "not everything is about my family. Or yours. It's just …" He exhaled, long and slow, "there's no future in it. Not for people like us. Not now."

I wanted to argue, but all I could think of was the look on his father's face when I'd admitted to being in the *Socialist Society*, the way Mrs. Hughes's questions circled around my future as if I were a specimen and not a guest. I remembered the thrill of the night before, the heat of Alex's body on mine, and how even in that perfect moment, I'd been afraid to speak, afraid of what would happen if we let it all spill into the open.

He put his arm around my shoulders, pulling me close, "don't take it personally," he murmured, voice barely above the wind, "you're the best thing that's happened to me all year."

I laughed, which was the wrong reaction, but he didn't let go.

We sat like that for a while, pressed together against the cold, watching the sun punch through the clouds and paint the valley with shifting patches of gold. The light moved fast, one second it was on us, the next it was gone, sliding down the slope to ignite the next hill over.

I wanted to memorise every detail: the scratch of his jumper against my cheek, the smell of salt and sweat, the way his fingers traced lazy patterns on my arm. I knew this wouldn't last. Even if I tried to hold it in my head, it would fade, replaced by lectures and exams and the endless grind of pretending. But for now, it was enough.

He pressed his lips to my ear, his breath warm and ticklish, "we have now," he said, voice low and certain, "isn't that enough?"

I closed my eyes, willing myself to believe it.

The light was failing as we returned to the tent, Alex unzipped the flap and ducked inside, kicking off his boots and peeling away his jumper. The air inside was stale with old sweat and the chemical tang of waterproofing spray, but it was warm, and the wind was gone.

He lay back on his sleeping bag, arms folded behind his head, eyes fixed on the nylon ceiling, "we'll have to leave early tomorrow if we want to get back for lunchtime," he said, voice flat.

I nodded, tugged off my own boots, and crawled in beside him. For a minute, we just lay there, not touching, listening to the hiss of the gas stove outside and the faint hum of a generator somewhere down the valley.

Then, without warning, he rolled onto his side, pinning me with his weight. His lips found mine, urgent and hungry, the taste of salt and blood and something sweeter. His hands were rough, calloused from the climb, and they left marks wherever they landed, my ribs, my back, the inside of my thigh.

We fucked like it was the last time, which I thought it might be. There was nothing gentle about it, he bit my shoulder, fingers digging into my hips, breath hot and wild against my neck. I clung to him, nails raking down his spine, desperate to leave a mark that would outlast the morning.

When it was over, we lay tangled, his head on my chest, both of us slick with sweat despite the coolness. He traced slow circles on my stomach, each one a silent apology.

I stared up, at the way the lamplight turned the nylon into a shifting ocean, and tried to memorise the feeling, the ache, the heat, the impossible closeness.

Outside, the world waited. But inside the tent, there was only us, suspended in the narrow space between now and never. He fell asleep first, arm draped across my stomach, breath warm against my skin. I lay awake, counting the seconds, wishing I could freeze them forever.

The seconds slipped past anyway, silent and inexorable, until finally, I let myself drift, knowing that when the morning came, it would all be different.

The cold woke me. Not the polite chill of an English morning, but a deep, marrow-scraping cold that made my teeth hurt and my fingers ache even inside the double layers of sleeping bag. I reached out, expecting to find Alex's arm slung across my waist or his knee pressed into the backs of my thighs. Instead, the other bag was empty, a crumple of nylon and nothing else.

For a minute I lay there, counting the drumbeat of my heart and the tap of condensation as it dripped down the tent wall. My first thought was that he'd gone for a piss, but the silence outside was absolute; no footsteps, no zipper teeth, just the low hum of wind in the trees. I waited, listening for any sign, then unzipped the bag and shivered as the night air bit at my bare chest.

I fumbled for a jumper, yanked it on, and clumsily laced my boots with hands that didn't want to work. The torch was by the flap, but I left it. There was enough moon to see by, a sickly yellow that turned the world outside the tent into a negative of itself: black grass, silver rocks, the faint glow of the stream where it traced the edge of the field.

I found him maybe twenty yards from the tent, perched on a fallen log at the edge of the trees. He was hunched forward, elbows on knees, a cigarette cupped in both hands. The smoke caught the moonlight and curled around his face, ghostly and insubstantial.

He didn't look up when I approached. I thought about sitting beside him, but the chill held me back. Instead, I hovered at the edge of the little clearing, watching him watch the sky. His breath steamed in quick, white bursts, each exhale a countdown.

He finished the cigarette, ground it out on the log, then lit another, hands shaking just enough to make the flame dance. His profile was cut sharp against the night: jaw tight, lips pressed into a flat line, eyes trained somewhere above the horizon.

I wanted to say something, but nothing felt right. There was a dignity to his silence, a finality that made me want to stand at attention or take off my hat. I imagined the smoke signals drifting up, a private language of loss and anticipation.

After a while, I backed away, careful not to crunch any gravel, and slipped back into the tent. I crawled into my bag, curling up tight around the space where he should have been, and waited for the dawn.

He returned sometime later, I heard the zipper, the brush of cold skin as he slid into his sleeping bag, the soft clack of his teeth as he tried to stop shivering. I wanted to reach for him, to share what little heat I had left, but I stayed still, holding my breath so I wouldn't break the spell.

In the dark, I thought about the way he'd looked on the log: so small against the world, so different from the boy who had once filled every room with his laughter and his certainty. I tried to reconcile the two, to fit them together in a way that made sense, but I couldn't.

Instead, again, I memorised the scene, the angle of his shoulders, the flick of the lighter, the way the moon painted hollows on his cheeks. I pressed it into my memory, a keepsake for later.

I knew, even then, that this was the last time of it just being us. That when we left the valley and returned to the world, we'd fold back into the stories we'd rehearsed for everyone else. I'd go back to my parents, to Mum's polite questions and Dad's silent pride; Alex would go back to the Hugheses and to Caroline, to the long tables and the cold light of breakfast.

Maybe, in another world, we could have stayed on that mountain forever. But in this one, the only thing we could keep was the memory.

I listened to the soft rumble of Alex's breath, the tent walls trembling in the wind, and waited for the morning to make everything ordinary again.

CHAPTER 11: THE WARRINGTON DEMONSTRATION

February 1983

When we returned to university for our second year, we rented a shared house in Fallowfield with some other friends of Alex. There were four girls, and including us, four lads in total. Alex and I shared a room with two small single beds pushed to opposite walls, close enough that I could hear him breathing at night, far enough that I couldn't reach him without making a deliberate choice. Some nights I'd lie awake, both wanting him to cross that gap and dreading what might happen if someone walked in. Other nights I'd resent the very sight of him turning away from me. His fear of discovery strangled whatever we had, reducing us to whispered conversations and furtive touches that left me both grateful and hollow.

I'd convinced myself our new living arrangement would bring us closer, but by November, I was spending more evenings alone in our room while he lounged downstairs with the others, laughing at jokes I couldn't hear. Was he protecting us both, or simply using me when convenient? One evening I overheard Alex with his two mates in the kitchen. One had asked him why he had chosen me to share with them. Alex had laughed loudly and then said, "wasn't it obvious?". Although out of sight on the stairs, I imagined his mates' confused looks before I heard him continue, "Liam is no competition with the girls, not like you two." The sound of their understanding laughter followed me up the stairs to my room.

In the New Year, I returned with a resolve that felt both like betrayal and salvation: to stop measuring my days by his attention. *The Socialist Workers' Student* Society met in the basement of the *Union* building. Overhead, three strip-lights flickered with the sullen yellow of an old lager, casting shadows so sharp that when Diana took the floor you could read her silhouette on the wall behind.

She started in *medias res*, voice already hoarse from shouting down Tories on the steps outside, "we're not here to rehearse theory," she said, stomping her boot on a milk crate that served as podium. "We're here because if we don't stand up, the government will have us back in the workhouse before the term is out. Eddie Shah is the thin end of Thatcher's wedge, he breaks the print unions, she breaks us. Solidarity means showing up, not just talking."

There were two dozen of us more or less, spread along battered folding chairs that stuck to your thighs if you sat wrong. Half the faces were new to me. There was the girl with the safety-pinned denim who'd called me a "closet Menshevik" in tutorial; the tall boy from Law, his hair like a thatch roof gone to seed, lips already stained with rollies; and a trio of freshers whose eager, nervous posture marked them as the next generation of cannon fodder. I felt old by comparison, though I was only a second year and barely old enough to buy my own pints.

Diana held court with the confidence of a woman used to having to win the same argument twice. Her hair was cropped so close you could see the veins in her scalp, and the sharp planes of her cheekbones looked carved for head-butting. She wore a t-shirt with a portrait of *'Che' Guevara* stencilled across it, tucked into combat trousers held up with a tie-dyed scarf. She moved like a boxer, pacing, pivoting, never letting your attention wander.

"Tomorrow's the dry run," she announced, waving a fistful of red flyers overhead, "Warrington. Shah's got the *Messenger* going in spite of pickets, so we're hitting him where it hurts, on the gates, with the *NGA* lads. There'll be police, but we've got numbers. We leave from here at half eight. If you're not on time, you're not coming."

The air thickened. The girl in the denim asked, "are we bringing banners, or just bodies?"

"Both," Diana said, "but no party slogans. This isn't about point-scoring, it's about presence. If you get nicked, keep your mouth shut and ask for a brief. Don't give your real address unless you have to."

She began to pass the flyers around, one for every hand. The paper was rough, the print job uneven, but the black-and-white image of Shah's face had a tabloid clarity that felt more real than the man himself. Underneath, in block capitals, the words: *"NO TO UNION BUSTING. NO TO THATCHER. JOIN US."*

I took one, folding it neatly and sliding it into the back of my notebook, where the poems and the phone numbers went. I tried to picture myself on the line, chanting, maybe, or just standing, refusing to move, and it felt like a role from someone else's story.

Diana locked eyes with me then, a look so direct it felt like a dare, "questions?" she asked, scanning the room.

The Law boy raised his hand, then dropped it again, "if it turns nasty, what's the plan?"

"We hold the line. Nobody leaves alone. And if you see someone in trouble, you pull them back. Simple as."

She grinned, teeth slightly crooked, and let the silence roll.

"Don't get sentimental," she said, "we're not here for glory. We're here to make it impossible for them to ignore us. If you're scared, good. That means you're paying attention. I'll see you in the morning."

She hopped down, handing out the last of the flyers as people began to rise. Conversations sparked instantly: what to wear, where to meet, who'd bring sandwiches. Some of them looked giddy, others just tired. The girl in denim clapped me on the shoulder as she passed.

"Better than the history society, this," she said, "at least you get to yell."

I smiled, but it felt borrowed. I gathered my bag, checked the flyer again, just to be sure, and started for the door, but Diana intercepted me with a movement that was all muscle and intent.

"Liam, right?" she said. Her eyes flicked over my shoulder, as if scanning for witnesses, "you coming, or is this another 'for research' job?"

I felt my face flush, instantly defensive, "I said I'd be there."

She laughed, a dry rattle, "you say a lot of things. But I never see you when it counts."

That stung, because it was true. I'd spent the last year oscillating between radical and observer, taking notes for essays on activism but never quite letting go of the guardrails. My own father would have called it "sitting on the fence and getting splinters up your arse."

"I'll be there," I repeated. It came out firmer this time.

She stepped closer, lowering her voice, "reading Marx in your bedroom won't change anything, Liam." She pronounced my name with a deliberate flatness, like she was reading it off a police list. "You've got the brain for this. Now show me you've got the guts."

I nodded, hoping the gesture looked more committed than terrified. She searched my face for a second, then seemed to find what she wanted.

"Eight-thirty," she said, and clapped me once on the arm, so hard my elbow rattled. She moved on, leaving me at the edge of the circle of chairs. I stood there a moment, feeling the ache where she'd hit me, the tingle of something like anticipation in my gut.

Outside, the corridor was already empty, the posters on the walls warping in the damp. I climbed the stairs to the ground floor and emerged blinking into the late afternoon, the sun a flat disc barely clearing the scaffolding across the quad. For a second, I thought about heading straight home, locking myself in with a textbook and a mug of instant soup, but my feet pulled me toward the library instead.

The reading room was a different world, quiet, padded, the only noise the soft flip of pages and the tick of the clock over the loan desk. I found an empty table under the window, laid out my books, and pretended to work, but my mind kept skittering back to the *Union* basement and Diana's voice, her words crawling under my skin like a rash.

I wrote "Warrington 8:30" in the margin of my planner, then circled it twice. The next page was blank except for an assignment from Dr. Henderson: "Write on the decline of class consciousness post-1945," due next Tuesday. I almost laughed at the irony.

I tried to focus, but after half an hour my attention had dissolved, and I found myself doodling lines of barbed wire around Shah's photocopied face.

A tap on the glass behind me made me jump. I turned, half-expecting to see Diana's glare, but it was Alex, his hair still damp from showering, glasses smudged. He pointed at my stack of books, then mimed a question mark. I grinned, waving him in. He wove between the tables, casual as if the whole library were his living room. He wore a jumper that looked hand-knitted, the sleeves too long, the colour somewhere between lichen and old tea.

He dropped into the chair opposite, flicking his fringe out of his eyes, "you're a glutton for punishment," he said, nodding at the pile.

I shrugged, "work doesn't do itself."

He smirked, "you know there's a party at Davey's flat tonight? Henderson's essay can wait."

I shook my head, "I'm behind. I said I'd get a draft in before Monday."

Alex raised an eyebrow, "seriously?"

I hesitated. The lie tasted sour already, but it was easier than explaining the truth, "I just... want to get ahead for once."

He let it go, but I could see him filing it away. He picked up one of my books, scanning the back cover, then set it down, "you're not coming, then?"

"Maybe after," I said, knowing I wouldn't.

He leaned back, stretching, "suit yourself. But if you finish early, I'll be at Davey's or maybe at the *Green Man*. Probably both."

He started to rise, but then paused, studying me, "you all right?" he asked, voice pitched low.

"Yeah. Just tired," I said.

He nodded, eyes lingering on me for a second too long, "you need to get out more. You look like you're serving a life sentence."

I forced a laugh, but my chest felt tight.

He left, hands in pockets, humming some melody I couldn't place. I watched him go, then stared at the door long after it swung shut behind him.

For the rest of the evening, I alternated between trying to read and watching the clock. At a quarter to nine, I packed my bag, made a slow circuit of the library, and stepped into the night. The air was colder now, the streetlamps flickering on like warning signs.

I walked home alone, the red flyer burning a hole in my notebook. I rehearsed what I'd say to my parents if I got arrested, how I'd frame it as a learning experience or a "practical assignment." I wondered if Diana would notice if I chickened out, if anyone would.

Inside the house, the kitchen was empty. I made tea, left the mug steeping, and went to bed with the taste of vinegar on my tongue.

I lay awake for a long time, staring at the ceiling, listening to the sounds of my housemates drifting through the thin walls. Laughter, music, the distant slam of the front door as someone came in late. I tried to imagine the demonstration, the noise, the crowd, the feeling of doing something that mattered. I tried to imagine telling Alex about it after the fact, and what he'd say.

Eventually, the need for sleep won out.

In the morning, I'd be on the 8:30 train to Warrington, alongside Diana and the rest, ready to prove that theory meant nothing without the will to act. But in that moment, I was just a boy in the dark, clutching a red flyer, afraid and excited in equal measure.

Saturday came up grey and spitting. The train carriage was packed with the usual suspects, students, union lads in worn jackets, pensioners who looked like they'd been on strike since the forties and weren't about to stop now. The heat was up high, but the windows still steamed, so all you could see of the outside was a blur of brick and freight yards and the occasional glint of canal water. My seat was near the aisle, hemmed in by rucksacks and the pervasive smell of wet wool and cheaper cigarettes than I was used to.

Diana led our contingent, striding the length of the carriage in her boots, calling roll and distributing last-minute supplies from a battered satchel. She pressed a folded handkerchief into my palm, cotton, doused with vinegar, the kind of thing I'd read about in books but never thought would apply to me.

"In case of tear gas," she said, low so as not to scare the new recruits. "Press it over your nose and mouth, don't rub your eyes, and for god's sake don't touch the police unless you want your teeth kicked in."

Her hair was slicked back today, accentuating the fierce geometry of her jaw. She wore a heavy jumper over a *Clash* t-shirt and fingerless gloves, the nails painted black and already chipped from the morning's preparations. I turned the handkerchief over, sniffed, and instantly felt my sinuses recoil.

Diana grinned, "better than nothing."

The journey was short but jittery. Every time the train rattled over a bridge or stopped at a signal, there was a ripple of nervous jokes, about the state of *British Rail*, about what Shah would do if we actually blocked the press, about the inevitability of police horses turning up and shitting everywhere. But underneath was a buzz that I recognised from the all-nighters before exams: a mix of hope, dread, and the sense that, for once, the outcome depended on us.

The guy sitting next to me, a Politics major with a nose broken twice, by his own account, leaned in and asked, "you ever been on one of these before?"

I shook my head, clutching the flyer in my jacket pocket.

"Stick close," he said, "if it goes south, find the oldest woman you can and hide behind her. Cops won't swing at grannies."

I tried to laugh, but it came out tight.

We pulled into *Warrington Central* already late. The platform was a tide of banners and bodies, people funnelling toward the exit in a crush that made my ribs ache. Outside, a handful of police in hi-vis jackets tried to direct the flow, but they looked more harried than menacing. Diana led us down the stairs and onto the street, where the real crowd waited, hundreds, maybe more, the air buzzing with chants and the tinny wail of a distant megaphone.

Someone handed out armbands, red for students, blue for union, yellow for "civilians", but nobody explained what that meant, and soon everyone was swapping them like football stickers. Diana tied hers around her upper arm and barked at us to keep together.

The march started slow, a shuffling mass hemmed in by the police escort, but it gathered speed as we turned onto the main road. By the time we hit the roundabout, the noise was deafening: a mix of "Whose streets? Our streets!" and "No to Shah, No to Thatcher!" Sometimes the chants merged into a single incoherent roar that pressed against your eardrums from the inside.

I'd never felt anything like it. The girl from the meeting, now in a patched parka and a wool cap, grabbed my hand when the crowd surged, her palm dry and hot even in the cold, "stay close," she said, and I did.

Ahead towards Winwick, the cranes and steel skeletons of the printworks loomed like the fossilised bones of a future already gone extinct. The building was ringed with temporary fencing and floodlights, though the sun was barely up. You could see figures moving behind the glass: men in orange bibs, faces pale and watchful, some holding mugs or just standing with arms folded.

As we drew closer, the police line thickened, rows of officers in blue, some with batons already in hand. Their faces were blank, even bored, but there was an energy coiled in them, waiting. Behind us, the march kept coming, the head of it almost at the gates while the tail still snaked back toward the station.

Diana raised her voice, shouting over the clamour, "remember what I said, don't break the line, don't rise to provocation, and if it kicks off, fall back and regroup at the road junction!"

She moved through our group, checking faces, clapping shoulders, reminding us this was what we'd come for. I could see sweat at her temples despite the cold.

Suddenly, a flare went up, red, brilliant, painting the smoke and the faces with an unearthly light. The crowd whooped, and for a second it felt like a festival, like we'd come to watch a football match and not a battle for the soul of the trade union movement. The energy was infectious: people started singing, someone popped open a can of lager and passed it around, and even the police looked less sure of themselves.

That changed in an instant.

Without warning, a clatter of shields echoed from our right side. A wedge of officers broke formation and swept toward the gate, moving fast. The crowd bunched, people shouting and shoving as the police forced a path. The chant faltered, then split, some doubling down, others already trying to peel away.

The riot went from theatre to war in the time it takes to swear under your breath. I was shoved hard against a concrete barrier, the chill of it biting through my jacket even as the crush of bodies kept me pinned. All sound collapsed to a single, grinding roar, boots on tarmac, the barked commands of police, the shrill, panicked animal noise of a hundred strangers trying to occupy the same square metre of space.

To my left, a policeman's visor cracked, splintered by a thrown can of *McEwan's*; he staggered, then swung blindly, his baton tracing a black arc above the melee. Someone caught it full on the collarbone and dropped, legs buckling, lost instantly to the churn. Blood spattered the tarmac in neat, surgical drops.

I tried to duck, but the crowd had other plans. A wave of bodies heaved, slamming me sideways, and for a split second my feet left the ground.

Then the old man appeared. Grey hair wild, blue anorak zipped to the chin, a faded *NGA* badge clinging to the breast like an old wound. He was caught in the no-man's land between protesters and police, yelling something I couldn't hear over the noise.

The baton came down, a dull, final sound. The man reeled, hands up, then went down hard, knees first, then shoulder, then skull. He lay still, blood already pooling at the temple.

The world slowed. Without thinking, I scrambled toward him, scraping my own knees on the rough concrete. He groaned, tried to push himself up, then slumped again. The cops ignored him, already focused on the next target, another kid with a scarf pulled tight against his face.

I grabbed the man under the armpits, surprised by the weight, by the heat of him. My hands slipped on his jacket, wet with rain and blood. I hauled, legs braced, and managed to lever him upright.

"Come on," I said, voice barely audible, "we have to move."

He blinked, blood in his eye, but nodded. I slung his arm over my shoulder, felt the sag and tremor of him, the way his ribs rattled on every breath. For a second I was a child again, holding up my dad after the pubs closed, a memory so sharp it almost made me gag.

We limped through the bodies, the crowd parting just enough to let us pass. Someone yelled, "medic!" and a woman in a Hi-Viz tabard appeared, face fierce and focused.

"This way," she barked, steering us toward a folding table at the edge of the field, already crowded with the walking wounded. The old man sagged onto the bench, head in his hands, blood spattering the wood.

The medic snapped on gloves, dabbed at the cut with a pad, "you got a name?" she asked.

He shook his head, then found it, "Mike. I'm Mike."

She pressed the pad harder, "you'll need stitches, Mike. Sit tight." She turned to me, "you hurt?"

I shook my head, but she reached for my face anyway, thumb pressing under my jaw.

"Split lip," she said, "lucky. Any dizziness?"

I shrugged, adrenaline making it hard to judge.

She nodded, then handed me a water bottle, "rinse your mouth. Sit with him. If he slumps, yell."

I sat. The bench wobbled under us, every vibration echoing in my teeth. Mike's breathing was shallow, wet; his blood was everywhere, painting his collar and the back of my hand.

We didn't talk. Around us, others arrived, one with a broken nose, another clutching a wrist bent the wrong way. The medics worked fast, efficient, bandaging, taping, moving people along like an assembly line for human damage.

The air was cold and thick with the smell of sweat, antiseptic, and the faint, metallic tang of blood. My lip throbbed, and I realised I was shaking, full-body, unstoppable. I tried to grip the edge of the bench to steady myself, but my hands were numb.

After a while, Mike spoke, "I was at Saltley. Thought those days were done." I didn't know what to say, so I nodded, biting the inside of my cheek.

He smiled, a grim, bloody rictus, "thanks, lad. Couldn't have done it without you."

I stared at my knees, embarrassed. The world was slowly coming back into focus: the rise and fall of sirens, the distant whine of a police helicopter, the murmur of protesters regrouping.

A medic handed Mike a wad of gauze and told him to press hard. She glanced at me, then at my wrist, "you'll have a hell of a bruise," she said, voice almost kind.

We waited until the worst had passed. Mike finished his water, then wiped his face with a paper towel, folding it into a small, precise square.

"You need to get out before they start kettling," he said, "go out the back way, through the car park. They're letting people go that side." I stood, legs stiff, and helped him to his feet.

He gripped my hand, hard, sudden, and then let go, "be proud, lad. Not many your age would step in like that."

I wanted to tell him I'd been scared shitless, that I'd acted without thinking, that even now I wanted nothing more than to go home and never speak of it again. Instead, I nodded.

I found Diana at the edge of the field, arguing with a pair of officers who looked bored but slightly afraid of her. Her hair was half undone, face streaked with dirt and sweat, but she was upright and loud, every inch the general.

She spotted me, and her face cracked into a smile, "Jesus, Liam. You look like you went three rounds with the *Flying Squad.*"

I touched my lip, wincing, "old guy took a worse hit."

She nodded, eyes approving, "you see him to safety?"

"Yeah."

She grinned, showing all her teeth, "fucking hero."

We stuck together for the next half hour, picking our way through the aftermath. The ground was littered with flyers, broken banners, the occasional lost shoe. Some people were singing again, quieter now, and the police watched from a safe distance, maybe too tired to risk another go.

On the train back, the air was thick with exhaustion. Nobody spoke much. Diana sat next to me, her knuckles swollen, one bandaged. She flexed her fingers, wincing.

"First time's always the worst," she said, voice softer, "you did good, Liam. You're one of us now."

I wanted to protest, to say I'd only done what anyone would, but the words stuck. I stared out the window as the countryside blurred past, watching the printworks recede, the city drawing closer by the minute.

My lips ached. My ribs felt like they'd been stomped by horses. My hands wouldn't stop trembling. But underneath it all, a strange, fierce pride burned, low and steady.

I'd shown up.

I'd acted and, even if I never did again, no one could take that from me.

Diana nudged my shoulder, then dozed off, head lolling against my arm. I let her rest, staring at the darkening world outside, already planning what I'd say if anyone asked about the day. Maybe I'd lie. Maybe I'd tell the truth but for now, I was content to watch the city lights gather on the horizon, knowing that, for once, I belonged.

By the time I made it back to the house, the street was black and empty, every window drawn tight against the cold. My body had stiffened on the walk from the station, each step a jag of pain up my ribs, the split in my lip throbbing with every shift of air. I'd left Diana and the others at the pub, claimed I was too tired to celebrate, but the truth was I couldn't face even a single hour of noise and scrutiny.

I fumbled my key at the door, trying to turn it quietly, but the lock always stuck. The hallway was lit only by the orange glow of the streetlights through the door and window above it. My shoes left a faint smear of mud on the mat. I bent to wipe it, thinking if I just moved slow enough, nobody would notice I was home.

Alex did. He was waiting, perched on the top stair, face in shadow, knees drawn up like a child hiding from monsters under the bed. His voice cut through the hush.

"You're late," he said, flat.

I froze, "lost track of time," I mumbled, not meeting his eyes.

He stood. The light from the landing hit him at an angle, picking out the sharpness of his cheekbones, the line of his mouth pressed tight. For a second, he just stared, taking me in, the torn jacket, the stiff gait, the stain on my collar.

"What happened?" he asked.

I shrugged, "nothing."

He moved closer, then saw the blood at my lip. His hand came up, half reaching, then dropped, "you've been in a fight."

"Not a fight," I said, "a demonstration."

He stared, processing, "Jesus, Liam. You look …" He broke off, running both hands through his hair, then spun away, pacing the landing in three angry steps.

I climbed the rest of the stairs, each movement scraping along the edges of my bones. When I reached the top, he was waiting at our door, blocking the way.

"Where was it?" he demanded.

"Warrington," I said.

His jaw tightened, "you said you'd be in the library all weekend. You lied."

I laughed, dry, "guess so."

He opened the door, then followed me in, shutting it behind us with a click.

"Why?" he hissed, "you could have been arrested. Christ, you could have been really hurt. Do you have any idea what that would do to your future?"

I sat on the edge of the bed, cradling my ribs, "it wasn't supposed to get violent."

"But it did," he said, voice rising, "and you, what, you just ran toward it?"

I looked up, feeling the heat in my face, "someone had to, someone was hurt."

He scoffed, then started to pace the small room, arms folded tight across his chest, "this is exactly what they want. They wind you up, throw you at the police, and then watch from the safety of the pub while you get the shit kicked out of you."

I shook my head, "you don't understand."

He whirled, "explain it to me, then."

I struggled to find the words, to make sense of the feeling in my chest, the mixture of terror and pride, the sense that I'd done something that actually mattered, even if only for a second.

"They were breaking the line. The old guy, he went down. I couldn't just watch."

Alex's face twisted, "and now what? You're a hero? Do you want a medal?"

I stood, too fast, the pain making me gasp, "it's not about that. It's about …" I faltered, searching. "… about not letting them win. Not just standing by." Words my father might once have said I realised in a flash.

He turned away, hands clenched, "you're not making any sense."

I crossed the room, closing the gap between us, "maybe not to you."

He laughed, bitter, "you think you're so much better. Standing up for the working class, for the cause …"

I cut him off, "at least I don't pretend it's all fine, that we just have to play along and hope it changes itself."

His voice dropped, cold, "you think I don't care?"

I hesitated, caught, "I think you're scared."

He spun, eyes bright, "of course I'm scared! We're one mistake away from losing everything, one arrest, one article in the paper, and it's over. For both of us." The silence that followed was jagged, each breath a challenge. He looked at me, the edge of his mouth twitching, "not everyone has the luxury to get arrested for fun."

I barked a laugh, "fun? You think this is fun? Not all of us have a daddy to fix it if we fuck up."

His face went slack, the words landing like a punch, "that's not fair."

I let it hang.

He backed toward the door, jaw set, "you're impossible."

I slumped onto the bed, exhausted.

He stood there, as if waiting for something, an apology, a reversal, but I had nothing left to give. He left, shutting the door with a final, soft click.

For the first time since Christmas, I slept alone in the room. I lay on my side, knees drawn up, arm pressed tight against the bruised heat of my chest. The house was silent, the only sound the faint, wet tick of the gutters in the wind.

In the morning, the ache was worse. I rolled out of bed, shuffled to the bathroom, and caught sight of my reflection in the mirror: lip swollen, skin yellowing at the edges, hair plastered to my forehead. I looked like someone else's problem.

Downstairs, the kitchen was empty. A mug sat on the counter, last night's tea congealed at the bottom, the spoon left in as a tiny act of defiance. I poured myself a glass of water.

Alex wasn't there. The settee in the living room was rumpled, the blanket he'd used last night folded and set aside. His shoes were by the door, neat as always.

I sat at the table, listening to the radiator struggle to warm the house. For a long time I waited, certain he would come in, that we'd resume our old routine, coffee, grumbling, the slow, careful dance of pretending nothing was wrong. But he didn't.

The silence pressed in, heavy and unfamiliar. I finished my water, then got up and went back to my room. I sat on the edge of the bed, hands clasped, the red flyer from yesterday poking out of my jacket pocket. I smoothed it flat, tracing the blocky letters with my thumb.

NO TO UNION BUSTING. NO TO THATCHER. JOIN US'.

I laughed, once, soft and bitter. Maybe this was what solidarity really felt like: the pride of belonging, but also the pain of losing something you loved in the process. I lay back on the bed, clutching the flyer to my chest, and let the silence have me. I fell back into a deep, and I hoped, healing sleep.

A few hours later, I found the note when I woke, slipped under the door in the way people used to pass secrets at school, unfolded, but folded once, like it wanted to keep its message half-hidden even as it confessed. The handwriting was Alex's, of course: neat, even, blue ink pressed harder than it needed to be.

'Let's cool things for a bit'.

Nothing else. No explanation, no *'Sorry'*. Just the soft landing of a future tense meant to draw a clean line under what had come before. I sat on the edge of the bed for a long time, reading it and rereading, trying to make the words mean something gentler. They didn't.

For the rest of the weekend, I moved through the house like a revenant. My face had swollen overnight, the split in my lip now a hard, angry ridge, but it was nothing compared to the ache in my chest, the way my breath felt shallow, artificial. I dressed slowly, every movement dragging. The sound of Alex in the bathroom, a splash, a cough, the faint rattle of the toothbrush against the mug, came through the wall, each noise too normal, almost obscene in its banality.

On Monday, I avoided the kitchen until I was sure he'd left. Then I made tea, barely tasting it, and packed my bag with the day's books. In the hallway, I nearly tripped over his shoes, still lined up, still facing the door as if nothing had changed. It was the shoes that did it; I had to sit on the bottom step, breathing in shallow gulps, just to keep from crying.

At lectures, I could barely focus. The words from the front of the room slid off me like rain on Perspex, never sticking. My hand kept straying to my lip, pressing the split until it stung, as if to prove I could still feel something. Between classes I wandered the campus, killing time in the library or by the canal, anywhere but the *Union*. I told myself I was being stoic, but the truth was, I couldn't face the looks from the others: pity, amusement, curiosity.

On Tuesday I decided I would try to catch Alex in the corridors, just to see if he'd look at me. He did, once, in the refectory, from the far side of the lunch queue. His gaze was quick, precise, then gone. He'd taken to eating with the Law boys, the ones who dressed in rugby shirts and talked in loud, carrying voices about internships and summer placements. I wondered if he missed me at all, or if it was a relief to be rid of my drama.

At night, I couldn't sleep, so I read, old history books or dog-eared *Penguin classics*, anything that promised a world with clear rules and outcomes. I made it through all of *"Maurice"* in one go, tracing the love story with a cold, forensic interest. In the end, I closed the book, lay back, and stared at the ceiling until the world blurred.

A week passed. The bruises faded, replaced by greenish shadows that made me look sickly but not spectacular. My coursework improved, a side effect of having nothing to do but bury myself in deadlines. Dr. Henderson praised my draft, said it had "new clarity, new force." I imagined telling him why: that heartbreak is the best muse, that deprivation sharpens focus like nothing else.

I went to another *SWSS* meeting, this time alone. The room was the same, strip lights, sticky carpet, the air still soured by sweat and smoke, but it all felt at a distance, like a play performed behind glass. Diana greeted me with a nod, nothing more. We talked about the fallout from the Warrington action, the media blackout, and the arrests that followed. No one asked about my face, but a few glanced at it, then looked away. The camaraderie of the first meeting was gone, replaced by something functional, less welcoming. I wondered if that was how it had always been, and if I'd just missed it when I'd had someone to return to.

Afterward, I walked the city for an hour, circling the blocks near campus, past the shuttered shops and the all-night offies. I bought a can of *Coke*, drank half, threw the rest away. For the first time in months, I considered calling Amanda, just to hear her voice, to prove to myself I still could. I didn't.

On the eighth night, I came home late. The house was silent except for the wind under the eaves. I climbed the stairs, half-dreading what I might find, but my room was just as I'd left it: unmade bed, books on the desk, the red flyer still pinned above my lamp.

I dropped my bag, slumped onto the floor, and was about to turn on the radio when I heard a soft thud from the hallway. I opened the door. Alex was there, sitting cross-legged on the landing, back against the wall. He held a paperback in his lap, my copy of *Maurice* the spine now creased. He didn't look up, just traced the edge of the pages with his finger.

I knelt beside him, close enough to see the tired hollows under his eyes, the way his hair curled messily at the nape.

"Hey," I said, voice raw.

He smiled, a tiny effort, "hey yourself."

We sat like that for a minute, both of us staring at the book, as if it contained the answers we'd been too stupid to write down.

"I've been a dick," he said, finally.

"So have I," I said, "it's a talent."

He laughed, soft, "I missed you."

The words landed somewhere between my ribs and my throat, the ache blooming all over again. We sat in the hush, the cold seeping up from the floorboards. I wanted to touch him, but I was afraid the spell would break.

"I re-read it," he said, lifting the book, "all of it this time. The ending's…"

"Hopeful?" I said.

He shook his head, "terrifying."

We laughed, and then, without thinking, I reached for his hand.

He let me, his grip gentle but sure. We went back into my room together, closing the door behind us with the same care as if it were made of glass. We didn't undress. We lay side by side on my bed, facing each other, our hands linked over the coverlet. I could feel the heat of his skin, the tension still living in his shoulders.

"You really scared me that night, I knew where you had gone, and then I saw something live on the news. I just went into a spiral of worry," he said gently, "if anything bad had happened to you I could never have forgiven myself for not being by your side."

"What, my posh scouser with all those socialists?" I tried to lighten the mood by turning to face him. The faintest of smiles touched his lips.

"Yes, if it had kept you safe," he whispered. I believed him, and I felt I should have replied that I didn't need his protection.

"Thank you Lex," I said instead.

We didn't say anything more, not for a long time. He fell asleep first, as he always did, a faint smile on his lips. I watched him breathe, counting each rise and fall as if it were a promise kept.

In the morning, everything would be different again. There would be old wounds, new silences, the slow work of rebuilding trust.

But for that moment, in the small patch of night we'd carved out for ourselves, I let myself believe in possibility. That people could change, or at least that they could keep trying. My deepest and sincerest wish was that, maybe, Alex might be able to see that we could have a future together. Something beyond what he had described as 'temporary' on the mountain top. The longer he stayed with me, the more likely this was to happen I concluded.

I drifted off to sleep, Alex's hand in mine, the book between us. And, when I dreamed, it was not of barricades or red flyers, but of a future just uncertain enough to make me want to live it.

CHAPTER 12: DIFFICULT CONVERSA- TIONS

June 1983

I always thought time ended in June, the way it did at the edge of school years: days turning thick and syrupy, routines dissolving into the paste of summer. The last Saturday of term found us not in the pub or the park, but cross-legged on the faded rug in our bedroom, surrounded by the detritus of a life measured in semesters. Alex and I packed in a kind of daze, our hands orchestrating the dumb choreography of tape and salvaged boxes while our eyes avoided each other with surgical precision.

The room was almost smaller than the one I'd grown up in, the ceiling forever on the verge of peeling away in strips. The rented house smelled of bleach and failed ambition. A single shaft of sunlight cut across the narrow bed, catching in the dust motes and painting everything in the kind of honest light that made you wish for darkness.

Alex folded his T-shirts with military precision, stacking them into the battered suitcase his parents had gifted him for his seventeenth. I pretended to read the back of a *Penguin* paperback, but my fingers were tracing the creased spine instead, worrying it the way a tongue worries a chipped tooth.

"You sure about next year?" he asked, not looking up, "the new halls are meant to be grim. I heard the walls are made of cardboard."

I zipped the book into a side pocket, "I don't sleep much anyway," I said, "at least I'll be closer to the library. Less time wasted on the bus."

He smirked, but it didn't reach his eyes, "Christ, you sound like my mother."

I shrugged, which was easier than saying anything true, "maybe she's got a point. It is our finals year."

He reached for the next shirt, navy, the one I'd always stolen when mine were in the wash, and hesitated, rolling the fabric between his hands. The silence was loaded, a round in the chamber.

"So. We're both moving in September?" he said, tone flat.

I nodded, counting out the facts like coins, "yeah. They assigned me a single. Top floor, allegedly with a view of the refectory bins."

He smiled, thin, "luxury."

We worked in silence for a few minutes, the only sound the crinkle of bin liners and the scrape of tape against cardboard. I glanced at him, noticed the way his hair fell into his eyes, the constellation of freckles exposed by the early sun. There were a thousand things I wanted to say, but each stuck in the bottleneck behind my teeth.

He broke first, "are you seeing Amanda this summer?"

I laughed, more bark than mirth, "doubt it. She's staying in Scotland and pretending Stirling is the Paris of the north. You?"

He looked away, fingers worrying the zipper on his suitcase, "Mum's got us off to France for the whole break. Dad says it'll be good for me. Networking. Meeting some of his contacts." He pronounced the last word like it was a diagnosis. "Six weeks on the fucking *Côte d'Azur*. I'll probably die of boredom." I couldn't tell if he meant it or not. Maybe that was the point.

"It'll give me time to catch up on the dissertation," I said, and regretted it instantly.

He watched me, eyes narrowed, "you always do that."

I braced, unsure what was coming, "do what?"

"Hide behind work. Like if you just read enough, none of the rest of it matters."

I busied myself with the next box, "doesn't it?"

He exhaled, a long, theatrical sigh, "not to me."

We finished packing with the unspoken agreement that the less said, the better. When we ran out of things to box, we sat on the edge of the bed, knees nearly touching, the whole room a graveyard of half-said things.

"You could come visit," I said, the words brittle.

He grinned, but it was more wound than smile, "you know what my father would say."

I nodded, "yeah. Mine too."

We sat like that for a long time, the sun tracing slow-motion arcs across the peeling paint, the walls closing in by degrees. Eventually, he stood, stretched, and offered me a hand.

"See you in September, then," he said, as if it was that simple, and extended his hand. I shook it, holding on a fraction longer than necessary.

"Yeah," I said, but it felt like a lie.

He left, the door closing with a sigh. I listened to his footsteps fade down the stairs, then slumped onto the bed, staring at the ceiling until the cracks blurred into constellations.

I zipped my case shut, the sound final and loud in the small room, and wondered if time really did end in June, or if it just started over with less of yourself than before.

The summer of 1983 in Rochdale tasted like scorched tarmac and washing-up powder, the air heavy with the promise of storms that never quite arrived. I came home to the familiar dampness of our terraced house, the house bracing for the annual siege of ants and the shriek of bin lorries at dawn. The weeks unfurled with a monotony that was both numbing and, in some twisted way, reassuring.

Sarah was the first to break the silence. She met me at the station with a packet of crisps and a bottle of cheap lemonade, her hair newly cropped and dyed the colour of tobacco ash. She'd grown two inches since Christmas and looked at me with an appraisal that was somehow both mocking and affectionate.

"Back from the barricades, then?" she said.

I rolled my eyes, but couldn't hide the small pride at being noticed, "you'd have loved it. Tear gas, horses, Diana nearly punched a cop."

She grinned, offering me the crisps, "revolutionary hero. Mum's terrified you'll turn up in the paper."

Mum was, predictably, less impressed by my exploits. She delivered her warnings in the kitchen, hands busy with the bread knife and the radio turned up just a notch too high.

"I'm glad you're passionate, love, but don't be daft," she said, slicing sandwiches with the same relentless efficiency she applied to every household chore, "you can't change the world with shouting. You'll end up arrested, or worse. What'll that do for your future?"

I nodded along, taking the crustless triangles and stacking them three-high. She watched me, the weight of her worry as palpable as the scent of *Dettol* on her hands.

Dad, on the other hand, offered his rarest of commodities: approval. He came in from work the second day I was home, still in his boiler suit, oil stains mapping the years of wage slips and overtime. He poured himself a glass of tap water, then nodded at me, jaw set.

"Heard what you did," he said, "proper job, that. Not many would stick their necks out anymore." He didn't say he was proud, but he didn't have to. The absence of disappointment was as good as a medal in our family.

I spent the first week drifting between the car wash, eight hours of hand-scrubbing *Austin Maxis* and *Cortinas* for a pound a time, and the cool, musty sanctuary of the local library. It was only open three days a week, so I rationed my visits, making them last with the slow, deliberate joy of a penitent. I'd read the same sentences three, four, ten times, letting them fill the hours between sunrise and the next meal.

Sarah adopted me as her project. She'd bring me mugs of tea at midnight, sneak the radio into my room so we could listen to *John Peel* at the lowest possible volume, or drag me to the park on days the sky was marginally less grey.

"You can't just read yourself to death," she'd say, tugging at my sleeve as if I were a particularly stubborn dog, "come on. I'll race you to the canal." Sometimes I'd even let her win, just to see the flash of triumph on her face.

By the third week, the rhythm had settled: car wash, library, awkward meals, park. I learned to treasure the moments of calm, Sarah's running commentary on the lives of every neighbour, the private jokes about the invisible lines that separated our estate from the next, the way we'd walk home in perfect silence, twin shadows stretched along the pavement.

On Thursdays, Mum would make chips and beans for tea, and Dad would watch the news with the volume up. I'd pretend not to listen as the anchors talked about the miners' strike, the latest protests, or the ever-present spectre of unemployment. Sometimes Dad would make a noise, a low grunt or a click of the tongue, but he never commented directly.

Sarah, though, would jab her fork in my direction and say, "that's your lot, isn't it? The angry ones in the background."

I'd reply, "better than being the ones asleep at the front," and she'd cackle, beans flying off her fork. We were a proper family, for once. Or close enough.

Late in August, Sarah announced she was throwing an early birthday celebration at *the Greengate*. She turned eighteen at midnight and was determined to do it "like a grownup," which in Rochdale meant drinking cider in the least shabby corner of the pub and not throwing up in the alley.

"You have to come," she insisted, pressing me into a chair. "Dad says you're responsible. And anyway, my friends all think you're a genius."

This was a lie, but it made me smile. I agreed, partly out of curiosity, partly to see who would show up. The night was warmer than most, the sky streaked with the lurid orange of sodium lamps and the promise of an *Indian summer*. *The Greengate* was half-full, the jukebox stuck on a cycle of *Madness* and *UB40*, and the air thick with the smell of spilled lager and desperation.

Sarah's friends clustered at a corner table: three girls with matching perms, one lad in a trench coat, and a tall, sheepish boy who looked like he'd been hired to provide comic relief. They greeted me with the usual barrage of questions, *'what was university really like', 'did I know anyone famous', 'was it true the girls there were all slags?'* I answered with the practiced blandness of someone who'd spent years perfecting the art of not being remembered.

At nine, the new *'alcoholpops'* began to have their impact on the young crowd and the evening blurred. I found myself outside seeking a quiet moment or two, flicking ash into the wind and watching the traffic crawl past. I didn't want to be inside, didn't want to be outside, but standing still seemed like the best compromise.

Sarah found me by the backdoor, two drinks in her hand and a set to her jaw that told me she was about to start an argument.

"You're not even trying to have fun," she accused, thrusting a pint at me.

I took it, nursed the foam, "it's your birthday, not mine."

She leaned against the wall, arms folded, "why'd you come home, then?"

I considered lying, but she would know. She always did.

"Nothing left to do in Manchester," I said, "term's over. Alex is in France for the summer."

She made a noise, soft and curious, "you miss him?"

I shrugged, eyes on the headlights, "not really."

She scoffed, voice rising, "you're such a shit liar."

I smiled, "you're not supposed to swear on your birthday."

She ignored this, pushing on, "when are you going to admit you care about him?"

I laughed, low, "you care about your girlfriends at college, don't mean you want them to move in."

She let the silence hang, then said, "is that why you're so sad all the time?"

I turned, the motion too sharp, the pint sloshing up the side, "I'm not sad. I'm fine."

She sighed, a long exhale that said more than words ever could, "you're allowed to be, you know."

I didn't answer.

She reached out, grabbed my hand, and squeezed it. Her palm was hot, fingers sticky with beer, "I don't care if you're weird. Or gay. Or a revolutionary. You're still my brother, okay?"

The word hung between us, a challenge and a lifeline.

"Okay," I said, voice barely there.

She grinned, eyes wet, "good. Now come back in before you embarrass me." I followed her, the noise of the pub washing over me, the warmth of her hand still lingering in mine.

For the first time all summer, I felt less like I was waiting for something and more like I was part of something already happening. Inside, her friends cheered as we re-entered, the jukebox belting out *Don't You Want Me* at full tilt. I caught a glimpse of my reflection in the darkened window, hair wild, collar askew, the hint of a smile twitching at the corner of my mouth.

Sarah raised her glass and toasted, "to the best big brother in Rochdale, even if he is a pain in the arse."

I laughed, and this time it felt real.

The night wore on, the drinks multiplied, and by closing time *the Greengate* was down to the hardcore and the hopeless. Sarah and her friends crammed into a taxi, singing at the top of their lungs, and I walked home alone, the air cool and clean.

I stood outside the house for a while, looking up at the window where Sarah's lamp was already burning. I thought about everything I'd left unsaid, everything still to come.

I stubbed my cigarette on the step, went inside, and climbed the stairs to bed, already feeling the soft ache of hangover and the new, unfamiliar shape of hope in my chest.

The sun barely cleared the rooftops when Sarah crept into my room, her silhouette framed by the pale blue of morning. She wore an ancient *Manchester United* shirt and a pair of Dad's old tracksuit bottoms rolled to her ankles, the cuffs threatening to trip her with every step. She carried two mugs of tea, the steam writhing above them like smoke signals.

"Truce?" she whispered, voice still raw from the night before.

I nodded, pushing aside the paperback I'd been using as a shield. My mouth tasted of ash and cheap lager, my head ached with the memory of her friends' relentless banter. She set one mug on the bedside table, then perched herself on the narrow slice of mattress next to my hip.

"Now," she said, and it was both a threat and a comfort.

I sat up, pulling the duvet to my chest for armour. The tea scalded my palms, but I welcomed the pain. She watched me with that unsettling patience she'd perfected after years of being ignored by the rest of the world.

"Seriously?" I managed, eyes fixed on the swirling surface of my drink.

She nodded, swinging her legs under the covers as if staking out territory, "I want to know. All of it. No bollocks."

I took a breath, let it out slow, "you'll hate me."

She snorted, "doubtful. Just spill."

I started at the beginning, or as close as I could get: the late-night tutorials, the books traded back and forth, the slow, perilous drift from study partners to something else. I skipped the sex, the sweat, the half-whispered promises in library alcoves, but I didn't spare her the rest, the longing, the terror, the way every day felt like walking a tightrope over a pit of knives.

She sipped her tea, not once interrupting. Her face didn't change when I described the fear, the constant scanning of rooms for threats or witnesses.

"So, you just… hide it?" she said, voice soft, after I'd run out of words.

I nodded, staring at my knees, "Alex said it was safer. His dad would've killed him if he found out. Probably still would."

She traced a pattern on the duvet with one finger, "that's shit."

I smiled, hollow, "yeah."

She leaned in, shoulder bumping mine, "what about Amanda?"

I shrugged, "a shield. For him, for me. I don't know."

She let that sit, the silence only punctuated by the clink of her mug.

"Is it over?" she asked, finally.

I tried to answer, but the words wouldn't come. Instead, I just nodded, the movement too small to be convincing.

Sarah set her tea aside, then reached up and poked my cheek with a cold, bony finger, "you're lost, Li. Proper lost."

I laughed, a wet, miserable sound, "tell me something I don't know."

She pulled the covers higher, tucking them around us like a cocoon, "maybe you need to talk to him. Not just about essays and politics. About you."

I wanted to argue, to explain that it wasn't that simple, that the world wasn't built for honesty like that. But the words dissolved in the heat of the tea, the warmth of her hand on my arm.

She rested her head on my shoulder, hair tickling my ear, "we're the only ones who matter, you know. Family. I'm always on your side."

I blinked, the sudden press of tears blurring the ceiling into watercolour, "even if I fuck it all up?"

She squeezed me, hard, "especially then."

We sat like that until the sun filled the room, the tea gone cold and the weight of the secret lighter, if only by a fraction.

Eventually, she stood, stretching the stiffness from her limbs. She looked at me with a smile that was half mischief, half mercy.

"Next time, just tell me," she said, "it's easier than me beating it out of you all the time."

I grinned, wiping my eyes on the sleeve of my T-shirt, "deal, but please no one else can know?"

She nodded and padded out, leaving the door ajar and the scent of tea and salt behind her. I lay back, arms behind my head, and let the day come for me, knowing at least I wouldn't be meeting it alone.

The last weeks of summer crawled by in increments: each morning a copy of the last, marked only by the angle of sun on my bedroom floor and the slow expansion of the mildew patch above my desk. With Sarah back at college and Mum picking up more shifts at the bakery, the house went silent except for the ticking of the kitchen clock and the muffled rumble of Dad's telly.

I should have used the time for my dissertation, but instead I rehearsed conversations with Alex, each draft more desperate than the last. I started simple. I'd lock myself in my room, drawing the curtains and sitting opposite the spare chair I'd rescued from the skip behind the Methodist church. I'd stare at the chipped blue vinyl, pretend it was Alex: posture perfect, eyebrow cocked in perpetual scepticism, legs splayed with the carelessness of the privately educated. I'd grip the edge of my desk, fingers aching with the urge to squeeze the life out of something.

"Alex, I need to talk to you," I'd begin, voice too thin, too shaky.

Sometimes I'd make it to the second sentence. More often I'd freeze, tongue thick with the taste of failure, and the chair would stare back at me, mute and unimpressed.

By the third or fourth try, I upgraded to props. I dug out an old scarf Alex had left behind, a garish red-and-yellow stripe, meant for some rugby team neither of us could stand. I draped it over the chair, using it as a talisman, a conduit for the memory of his smell, the faint ghost of cologne and stale *Marlboros*.

"Alex," I'd say, wrapping the scarf around my wrist, "what are we doing?"

On good days, the words came easier. On bad days, I'd crumple the scarf in my fist, throw it across the room, and collapse onto the bed with the hum of the old fridge downstairs as my only company.

Occasionally, I moved the operation to the library. I'd sit on the steps outside, notebook open, watching the flow of foot traffic, mums with prams, pensioners in raincoats, the odd knot of teenage boys practicing their loitering skills. I'd pick someone in the crowd, assign them Alex's walk, his posture, the way he always checked his watch when bored.

Then I'd whisper into the cold: "we need to talk. Please, just listen." It felt less insane in public, as if the act of rehearsing in front of strangers might one day make it easier in front of the real thing. Back home, I filled entire pages with possible openers.

"Alex, I know it's hard …"

"Alex, are you even happy?"

"Alex, I can't keep pretending …"

I'd write them, tear them out, ball them up, and toss them into the bin. By the end of August, the bin overflowed with false starts, each one a record of my own cowardice.

Sometimes, in the bathroom, I'd practice in the mirror. I'd stand there after a bath, steam curling around my head, and force myself to look into my own eyes.

"Alex, I've missed you," I'd say, testing out the variations. "Alex, I can't do this without you." "Alex, I'm not ashamed anymore."

I'd repeat them until my jaw ached, until the words sounded less like a confession and more like a simple statement of fact. At work, I found myself rehearsing too. I'd soap up the windshields, buff them until my arms burned, and mutter under my breath.

"Do you still care about us?"

Sometimes the question would float up unexpectedly, raw and full of teeth, and I'd have to duck behind the car or fake a coughing fit until the heat in my face faded.

Sarah caught me once, mid-mutter, as I was scrubbing the hubcaps of a *Ford Escort*. She crouched beside me, hands stuffed into the pockets of her coat, and grinned.

"You're practicing, aren't you?"

I flushed, but didn't deny it.

She nudged me with her elbow, "he's going to say yes, you know. If he doesn't, I'll kill him myself."

I laughed, the sound surprising both of us.

When the garage closed early for the Bank Holiday, I biked home along the canal, letting the wind batter the doubts out of my head. The repetition, the endless loop of questions and answers, didn't feel pointless anymore. With every attempt, the sharpness dulled; the fear shrank, the words lost some of their sting.

By the second week of September, the bin beside my desk was filled to bursting. I dumped it onto the carpet, spread the crumpled pages in a rough circle, and sorted them into piles: the lies, the truths, the lines that almost worked. I made bullet points in the margins, tiny ticks for the sentences that rang true.

On a whim, I called the number for Alex's parents' house in the Wirral. His mother answered, voice frosted with perfect politeness.

"Hello, Hughes residence," she intoned.

"Hi, Mrs. Hughes. Is Alex home?"

She hesitated, just enough to let me know she knew exactly who I was, "he's not here just now, dear. Shall I have him call you back?"

I said yes, knowing she wouldn't.

It didn't matter. I'd done the hardest thing, made myself visible, if only for a second. That night, I stayed up late, copying the best of the lines onto a single, clean sheet. The ink bled where my hand trembled, but I didn't erase or start over. I let the mistakes stand, proof of effort.

I left the scarf on the chair, a kind of placeholder. When I finally crawled under the covers, I stared at the ceiling and mouthed the words one last time.

"Alex, I'm ready." It wasn't true, not entirely. But it was truer than it had ever been. I slept, and dreamed nothing.

In the morning, I woke with a headache and the faint taste of hope in my mouth. The sun was already up, bright and hot through the window. Sarah had put a note under my door:

'GO GET HIM'.

I poured a cup of tea, sat at the kitchen table, and rehearsed once more, not for the chair, or the mirror, or the crowd, but for myself. I was ready to talk.

CHAPTER 13: A REPRIEVE

The third-year hall was a glass box baked into the side of the campus, each window framed with a lattice of fake-modern brown. Inside, the furniture was institutional but new, veneer laminate, too-bright task lamps, beds built for compliance rather than comfort. I unpacked the way a prisoner unpacks: methodical, no wasted motion, everything counted and accounted for. Books lined up on the shelf in height order, each battered *Penguin* or *Virago* placed with mathematical precision. Spiral notebooks stacked by colour. The single cup and bowl I'd brought from home, chipped, unmatched, but familiar, nestled side by side atop the desk. I arranged my folders alphabetically, then reversed the order, then gave up and fished for my cigarettes instead.

Outside, the corridors reverberated with the echo of new arrivals and the groan of baggage trolleys, each slam of a neighbour's door broadcast down the cinderblock and into the marrow. The air was thick with ozone and possibility, but I wasn't feeling either. Mostly I was waiting for the next thing to go wrong.

A soft knock, so gentle it was almost apologetic, startled me mid-drag. I froze, exhaled slowly, then stubbed the cigarette in my cup. My throat had gone so dry it clicked when I swallowed. When I opened the door, he was already halfway inside.

Alex looked different, sharper somehow, summer-tanned and a little leaner, his hair grown out at the sides in deliberate defiance of both fashion and parental mandate. He wore a faded grey T-shirt that must have started life as white, and jeans so tight I could trace the movement of each muscle as he leaned into the doorway, grinning.

He closed the door behind him, took three steps, and pulled me into a kiss that felt like a fist through my chest. No preamble, no handshake or "Hi, how was your summer?", just the taste of salt and tobacco and a hunger that had been fermenting for ten weeks. His hands were in my hair, then cupping my jaw, thumbs tracing the stubble. I opened to him, the room tilting, the air going instantly thick and then clear as glass.

"Fuck I've missed you, Liam," he said, not breaking the kiss by more than a breath. His voice was different, lower, and rough with sleep deprivation or anticipation, I couldn't tell which.

I stood there, every nerve blazing, not sure what to do with my own hands. When he finally let go, I was giddy, off-balance, and probably grinning like a child. He cocked his head and looked at me, eyes all blue and wicked, then laughed.

"You just going to stand there like one of *Lewis's*, or do you want to help carry up the rest of my shit?" He flicked a hand toward the door, already moving past me into the room.

Outside, parked on the curb with an air of reckless illegality, was Alex's car, its rear seats stacked with black bin liners and loose crates. The only other car in the lot belonged to a middle-aged man unloading what looked like a month's supply of pot noodles for his pimply offspring.

I glanced at Alex, then at the car, then back at him, "no parents?" I asked, only half-joking.

He shook his head, eyes luminous, "fuck no. Have had enough of both of them for a lifetime this summer." The relief in his voice was almost as palpable as the earlier longing. He turned and kicked the front tire of the *Escort* with the side of his foot, then shot me a quick, conspiratorial look, "come on, these won't carry themselves."

We did it in two runs, each load heavier than it looked. He'd packed everything loose, in the manner of someone whose mother had abandoned hope of civilising him years before: T-shirts wadded into balls, every sock a singleton, textbooks crammed in with LPs and cassettes. The second crate was the heaviest. I grunted as I took it from the boot, only to nearly drop it when I saw the box's contents: a stacking stereo, complete with two enormous, free-standing speakers.

"Jesus," I said, "you rob a *Curry's* on the way here?"

He grinned, shouldering a duffel bag, "it's a guilt present from my mum for making me stay for two months. I was only allowed to come back if I agreed to keep the volume down and not drop out." He arched an eyebrow, "only one of those is a possibility."

We got the stereo to his room, next to mine, the last in the corridor, and set the crate on the floor with a satisfying thud. For a moment, I just stood there, listening to the wild racket of the corridor, the squeal of excited voices and the slam of metal fire doors. Alex plugged in the stereo, twisted the dial, and let *Stevie Wonder* pour out into the chaos at medium volume. He closed the door, then turned to me.

"Now," he said, voice pitched lower, "where were we?"

He had me backed against the wall before I could answer. The kiss was different this time, slower, deeper, all the summer's absence compressed into a single, long inhalation. His hands mapped me, one at the small of my back, the other sliding under the hem of my shirt, skin to skin. I reciprocated, clumsy and eager, feeling the sharp lines of his ribs, the dip of his waist, the faint scar near his hipbone that I'd memorised but somehow missed all summer.

He broke the kiss, breath hot against my ear, "door," he said.

I reached behind me and turned the bolt. He grinned, then, in a single motion, swept me up and deposited me on the narrow bed. The mattress squeaked in protest, thin, foam, already compressing beneath us. Alex followed, one knee on the edge, his body blocking out the rest of the room. He tugged my shirt over my head, then lay beside me, mouth finding my neck, my shoulder, the hollow at the base of my throat.

It was fast, messy, and desperate. Jeans half-unbuttoned, hands everywhere, mouths devouring whatever flesh came to hand. There was no choreography, just a scramble to get closer, to erase the intervening months and the weight of everything that had gone unsaid. He pushed his hand down the front of my jeans, fingers finding me already hard and aching, and stroked in a way that was both expert and insistent.

I gasped, the sound embarrassingly loud in the tiny room. He pressed his palm over my mouth, eyes dancing with delight.

"Keep it down," he whispered, even as he moved faster.

I arched into his hand, the heat and friction overwhelming, and came with a violence that left me gasping and boneless. He pulled back just long enough to lick his palm clean, then tackled me again, rolling us both sideways so we nearly fell off the bed.

We lay like that, tangled and half-naked, sweat cooling, the air in the room now thick with sex and anticipation and *Stevie Wonder* crooning from the stereo. I stared at the ceiling, chest heaving, the beginnings of a laugh threatening to escape. Alex lay beside me, head propped on his elbow, looking smug.

"Wow," I said, when I could breathe, "you really did miss me."

He grinned, wicked, "what can I say? My parents have a terrible effect on my libido. I needed someone to cure me."

I laughed, then swatted him with a pillow, "you're an idiot."

He caught the pillow, then used it to pull me close again. We kissed, slower this time, and let the rest of the world slip away.

Eventually we got dressed, half-heartedly, with the occasional groping detour and finished unpacking the last of Alex's things. He insisted on setting up the stereo properly, arguing over the best placement for the speakers, then rearranged his books so the "good ones" were closest to the bed. It felt, for the first time in months, like everything might be possible.

When the light faded outside, we sat on the floor, backs against the bed, knees touching, and let the music play. I reached for his hand, and he let me take it, fingers entwined, warm and sure. Neither of us said anything for a while. We didn't need to.

The next morning, Alex woke me with a knuckle to the ribs and the hiss of "recon." I'd been dreaming of infinite stairwells and endless corridors, and for a moment I wasn't sure which world was real. He was already dressed, hair still wet from the shower, the tip of his nose shining with cold.

I groaned, but he yanked me out of bed and into the hallway, where the light was a flat, bureaucratic yellow. The floors were already echoing with the stomp and shuffle of early risers, but Alex paid them no attention. He led the way down the corridor, pausing at each door like a tour guide with a secret agenda.

"Here's the lay of the land," he said, voice pitched for my ears alone, "fire door opposite my room. Opens onto the fire escape, which only matters if you want to sneak out. Next door down from you is the Czech exchange student, they say he's a gymnast, but I've only ever seen him in pyjamas."

We reached my own door, he stopped, bent close, and murmured, "a deaf neighbour, I believe." He winked, "couldn't have planned it better."

I snorted, then caught his meaning, "so you're saying we're safe?"

He nodded, solemn as a judge, "safer than before. As long as my door is locked and there's music on, we can do whatever we want."

He demonstrated by pushing open the fire door opposite my room, revealing a stubby hallway with a battered sign, *KITCHEN'* to the left. "And here," he said, "is the communal kitchen. Only six other rooms on this stretch, both empty most nights. If we're careful, nobody ever has to know."

He closed the door, then pulled me into a quick, covert hug before stepping back into his own persona, the one that could banter with anyone, blend in, disappear. He walked me back to my door, then gave a theatrical bow. "I expect you for dinner at nineteen hundred hours," he said, "bring bread rolls. And a sense of adventure."

The sense of relief in me was so huge it felt like helium, my ribs floated, my head went light. The anxiety that had haunted every day since that night on the mountain began to erode, just a little. We were still careful, always careful, but the new layout, the subtle choreography of the halls, made it possible to imagine a future where being together wasn't only a matter of luck and subterfuge.

We fell into a routine so quickly it scared me: classes, then late afternoons in the library, dinners together, then music and homework and each other in the evenings. Sometimes we'd argue over politics or debate the fine points of some half-read novel, but mostly we just sat side by side, Alex sprawled on the bed, me hunched over the desk, *Stevie Wonder* or some other *Motown* filling the space between us.

His new stereo became the centre of our social life, the speakers always set to *just barely not disturbing'* level. We discovered that certain LPs played at a certain volume guaranteed privacy: no one ever knocked during *Songs in the Key of Life*, and the resident tutor seemed pathologically afraid of *Stevie Wonder's* high notes.

Most nights I slept in Alex's room. We devised a system for mornings, I'd slip out at 6:55, next-door to my own bed, and wait for the official start of the day as people moved back and to the kitchen before returning to him. It was theatre, but it worked.

Alex made a rule, "always out by seven, never later" and enforced it with a playful severity that made me laugh, even on mornings when the alarm felt like a knife to the brain. Sometimes I'd come back to find him already up, showered, and deep into the previous day's *Telegraph* crossword, pen poised like a scalpel.

We started eating breakfast together in the little kitchen, taking turns making toast and instant coffee. The first few times, I worried someone would notice, but after a week, the sight of us together drew no attention at all. Final year students had no interest in gossip it seemed.

We got good at pretending, at being friends in public, at keeping our conversations just on the safe side of intimate. But in private, the pretence dropped away. We'd talk for hours, sometimes about nothing, sometimes about the future, where we might live, what we might do, if any of it could last beyond the bubble of university. Sometimes I caught myself believing in it.

My coursework improved. I found it easier to concentrate, easier to breathe. The raw ache of the summer faded into memory, replaced by the steadiness of Alex's presence, the comfort of his hand in mine, the knowledge that he'd always be waiting on the other side of the wall.

We still had to be careful, always careful but it didn't feel so much like hiding anymore. It felt like home. We never had the conversation *what happens next?*, because as we spent more and more time together, the more convinced I was that Alex must want to continue after graduation I thought. I had hope.

December arrived overnight, one day the quad outside was just tarmac and bin bags, the next it was glossed with a film of sleet and the faintest rumour of snow. The hallways went weirdly quiet, everyone head-down in essays or packing up for break. Alex and I fell into a nocturnal routine: working late, then lying side by side in his darkened room, listening to the gentle buzz of the radiator and the low purr of the stereo on its lowest setting. It was the safest time, when the rest of the world had gone dormant and the only thing left awake was us.

We never really talked about Christmas until the term was nearly over. There was a kind of superstition to it, like saying the word aloud might collapse the spell of the last three months. But two days before the last class, with the corridor empty and the world outside glazed in half-frozen rain, I found myself sprawled on his floor, sorting exam notes while Alex read the *Telegraph* and faked outrage at the letters page.

He lobbed a rolled-up section at my head, "do you think my parents have figured out I'm not coming home yet?"

I grinned, "is that why you haven't called them all week?"

He made a show of considering it, then grinned back, teeth catching the lamplight, "God, you know me too well. They booked the fucking *Canaries*, by the way. Dad says the Wirral in December is 'spiritually unacceptable'." He sighed and then added, "and why not, I can afford it."

I snorted, "what's your excuse?"

He stretched, cracking his knuckles in a way I found both disgusting and reassuring, "told them I had to prep for finals. Might have implied I was on the verge of failing. Dad's already sent two angry letters. He's convinced I'm having a breakdown."

I leaned back on my elbows, heart pounding faster than made sense, "so what are you going to do? Spend Christmas alone in the canteen?"

He shrugged, affecting nonchalance, "I'll survive. Maybe I'll buy a turkey sandwich and throw it at the telly for tradition's sake."

I let the silence hang just a second too long, then heard myself say, "come to Rochdale?"

The words were out before I could unthink them. I stared at the spot between us, as if my own voice had come from somewhere else.

Alex raised his eyebrows, genuinely surprised, "serious?"

I nodded, not trusting myself to talk just yet.

He sat up, crossing his legs under him, and studied me like I was an especially complicated crossword clue, "you want me to meet your family?"

"Just for the holidays. It's not like…" I trailed off, realising I had no follow-up, "you can bring the stereo if you want, and the *Telegraph*, but hide the newspaper from my dad. Keep your defences up."

He laughed, but this time it was softer, almost gentle, "wouldn't they think it's weird?"

I shrugged, "not if we're careful. My mum'll be thrilled and I'll give her the full sob story of how your parents have abandoned you for a bit sun. I'll make it sound like something *Dickens* might have written."

He looked at me for a long moment, then smiled, the kind of smile I'd have followed off a cliff, "okay," he said, quiet, "I'd like that."

We didn't talk about it again that night. When I left his room, my hands were shaking so badly I dropped my pen twice in the hallway. In the privacy of my own room, I sat on the bed and tried to imagine it: Alex in my house, sharing chips with Dad, bickering with Sarah, sleeping on the camping bed that was older than both of us put together.

The next afternoon, I called home. Mum picked up after two rings, as if she'd been waiting by the phone all day.

"Hi, love!" Her voice was bright, almost too bright.

"Hi, Mum. Listen, I've got a question."

She didn't let me finish, "you're bringing someone, aren't you?"

I paused, "what makes you say that?"

A muffled noise, probably Sarah, cackling in the background, "a mother knows. Is it Amanda, finally?"

I hesitated, then tried to steer the ship, "it's a mate. From my hall. The one from the Wirral I went camping with. His parents have left him to his own devices for Christmas so they can go on holiday, so I said he could stay."

She went quiet, just long enough for me to think she was disappointed, then said, "oh, love, that's awful. We've always got space. Tell him we're not posh, though."

I laughed, tension breaking, "he'll fit right in."

She handed the phone to Sarah, who immediately laid into me with a barrage of questions: "is it Alex?"

"Yes, I whispered," though why I didn't know.

"So, you talked then?" now she was whispering so as not to be overheard, a gesture I appreciated.

"No, in the end we didn't need too. Everything has been so good so far," I explained, "but sis, promise me something?"

There was a pause, "OK, what do you need?" she asked.

"Promise me you won't say anything to him, I think it might spook him if he thought someone else knew," I realised that this is exactly what would happen, "Sarah?"

"Of course, I promise." With that we said our goodbyes.

Afterwards, the elation wore off and a slow panic set in. I spent the next three hours pacing the length of my room, making lists in my head of every possible disaster: Dad's bluntness, Mum's ability to sniff out secrets, Sarah's capacity for emotional blackmail. The house was tiny, the walls thin. There was nowhere to hide.

I tried to imagine how it would look to the neighbours: Alex, blond, well dressed and talking like a posh Scouser, sitting at our kitchen table, eating Mum's roast potatoes, laughing too loud at Sarah's jokes. I pictured the awkward silences, the moments where I'd forget myself and let something slip, the inevitable questions about girlfriends, futures, marriage.

I rehearsed a dozen different stories, each more elaborate than the last: Alex was just a mate, Alex needed somewhere to crash, Alex was depressed and I was doing him a favour. I told myself I could keep it together for two weeks, that if I just acted normal, nobody would suspect a thing.

But the part of me that had spoken up in Alex's room, the part that wanted him there, was too loud to ignore. The idea of sharing my family with him, of letting him into that world, even if just for Christmas, felt dangerous, but right. Like stepping off the edge of a roof and trusting the snow to break your fall.

The night before the term ended, Alex came to my room after midnight. He was buzzed on whisky and half-frozen from the wind. He didn't say anything, just climbed under the covers and curled around me, cold feet and all.

"You're sure about this?" he whispered.

"Yeah," I whispered back, though I couldn't tell which of us I was trying to convince.

We lay there in the dark, the hum of the radiator and the slow tick of the campus clock counting down the hours until we'd go home. I listened to his breathing, steady and warm, and tried to map out the future, Christmas dinner, New Year's Eve, the long stretch of January and everything after.

I thought of Mum's laugh, Sarah's bad jokes, even Dad's grudging approval. I thought of Alex's hand in mine, under the table or in the safety of my tiny room. For the first time, I wasn't afraid of being found out. I was afraid of losing it.

The next morning, I woke to find him still there, still sleeping, the shape of his arm draped over my chest. I stared at the ceiling, the sun painting new lines on the wall, and waited for the feeling to pass.

It didn't.

CHAPTER 14: A ROCHDALE CHRISTMAS

The campus emptied with violence I hadn't expected. By noon the hallways were hollowed out, the only evidence of life was the trails of muddy boot prints and the tang of burned toast from the communal kitchen. I packed with mechanical efficiency, hands numb from the night before, not trusting myself to linger over the books or the T-shirts that still smelled like Alex.

I helped Alex to load up his car, and he wore a scarf I'd never seen before, a thick navy-and-white one, probably stolen from his father and kept his hands jammed into his pockets. We didn't talk much, but when we had finished, "I'll call you," he said and squeezed my hand hard enough to leave a mark.

Then he was gone, off to the Wirral for a week, to his parents and their Edwardian mansion and the rituals of a family that expected good news. I stood for a minute, watching the car recede through the exhaust and sleet, and wondered if it would hurt less or more to be the one doing the leaving.

The journey to Rochdale was slow, each stop more deserted than the last. I watched the fog crawl over the Pennines, devouring the horizon, until all that remained was the hiss of the heater and the monotonous flicker of sodium lights passing by at each small town. I tried to read, but my eyes kept drifting to the window, the shapes of the clouds and the trees smearing into something weightless and unnameable.

Mum met me at the station, her coat buttoned up to the chin and her cheeks red from the cold. She hugged me as if I'd just returned from a war zone, then immediately asked if I was eating enough. I lied, because that was easier than explaining the rules of our shared kitchen, the intricacies of toast hierarchies and the politics of the under-stocked fridge.

The walk home was a replay of every return from uni: the terraces were the same, the air still thick with coal smoke and chip fat, the ginnels behind the houses littered with discarded furniture. Nothing had changed, except maybe me.

Inside, the house was overheated and close, the hallway lined with muddy shoes and the faintest undercurrent of *Dettol* and damp. Dad was in his usual spot at the table, the remains of the evening's tea congealed on his plate, the day's newspaper already yellowing at the edges. He looked up when I walked in, grunted a greeting, then asked, "you make the grades?"

I nodded, dropping my bag by the radiator, "all good," I said.

He grunted again, but I could see the ghost of a smile at the corner of his mouth. Sarah was in the front room, legs curled under her on the settee, headphones jammed on so tight I had to wave to get her attention. She pulled them off, then fake-punched me in the arm, "took you long enough," she said, but her grin was real.

The rest of the evening was a replay of every homecoming: tea, telly, the slow, careful recalibration of the self to fit back into the old rhythms. I waited until Sarah went up to bed before going to the bottom of the stairs to call Alex.

He picked up on the first ring, "Liam?" he said, and his voice sounded tired but lighter than I'd heard in weeks.

"Yeah," I said, "you okay?"

He made a show of sighing, "barely. Mother's already grilling me about Christmas and New Year's, and Dad wants a full debrief on my coursework before the weekend."

I imagined him pacing his bedroom, the walls hung with rugby memorabilia and family photos, his suitcase already half-unpacked, "bet you wish you were still at halls," I said.

He laughed, "I'd trade for a night in your box room and a mug of instant soup. How's Rochdale?"

I glanced around, as if the house could overhear, "the same. Dad's still working weekends, Sarah's still refusing to eat vegetables, and Mum's already asked when you are arriving for Christmas."

There was a pause. Then, softly, "what did you say?"

I closed my eyes, leaned my forehead against the cool of the window, "that you're coming. If you still want to."

He didn't hesitate, "of course I do. I've planned my escape already."

I smiled, felt the knot in my chest loosen a little, "when?"

"Next week," he said, "parents are flying out to *Gran Canaria* on Saturday. Thought I'd drive over after dropping them at the airport, if that's all right? Their flight is early afternoon, so I guess I should get to you about four or five pm"

My heart hammered, "it's perfect," I said, meaning it.

We talked a little longer, about nothing, really, just filling the air with the comfort of each other's voice. When I hung up, the house felt less alien, less like a costume I'd outgrown.

The days until his visit crawled with the slow, aching precision of a clock winding down. I spent the time cleaning my room with a manic fervour: stripping the bed, dusting every flat surface, even sorting my books by subject rather than height. I made a list of the best places to go within walking distance (which was not many apart from *The Greengate*), and circled the ones that wouldn't draw attention or raise questions. I also planned out the menu for the week, cross-referencing my choices with the list of foods Alex had once admitted to liking.

The hardest part was the map. Rochdale's streets were a patchwork of dead ends and half-remembered shortcuts, so I drew it by hand on a sheet of graph paper, marking the safest routes from the M62 to our house. I added notes about the one-way systems, the tricky junction by the canal. I even sketched a tiny, wonky house at the end, labelled "Parry's (with bad tea)."

I posted it to him straightaway, triple-checking the address and handwriting. Friday night, I lay in bed and listened to the wind rattle the old sash window, my thoughts oscillating between what could go right and all the ways it could go wrong. I imagined Alex getting lost on the way, or showing up to find Dad in one of his moods, or Sarah taking one look at the two of us and calling the whole thing out before we'd even put our bags down.

Worse, I pictured Mum seeing straight through us, reading the nervous glances and the careful choreography of our movements. I imagined the look on her face, pity, or disgust, or the sharp, silent disappointment she reserved for things she couldn't fix. I rolled over and stared at the ceiling, counting the cracks until I lost track.

The morning of Alex's arrival I woke before the sun, the house still tight with the hush of winter. The camp bed lived at the back of the airing cupboard, behind the jumble of towels and the box of Christmas lights that never worked. It took me ten minutes of contortion to get it out, and when I finally unfolded it, the canvas stank of rubber and mothballs. I opened the window wide, letting the air bite at my fingers, and draped the sleeping bag over the radiator to chase away the cold. It was the same bag we'd used on holidays to Rhyl; the one Sarah had once thrown up in after a night on stolen cider. I brushed off the memory, tucked the pillow under the head, and stepped back to survey the scene.

It was still a child's room, no matter how much I tried to sand the edges. The evidence was everywhere: the poster of the 1980 Olympic Games, the model aeroplane half-glued and shedding dust, the stack of *Beano* annuals Sarah insisted were "collectibles." I thought about hiding them, then decided it was too late for reinvention.

Downstairs, the kettle was already boiling. Mum was in the kitchen, wearing her "best" cardigan, white, with a little brown stain on the sleeve from last Easter's gravy. She was dicing onions with the kind of precision usually reserved for state secrets.

"Thought you'd still be asleep," she said, not looking up.

"Too much to do," I said, and helped myself to tea.

She watched me over the rim of her glasses, then asked, "you nervous?"

I shrugged, but my hands were shaking as I stirred the sugar, "a bit."

She set down the knife, wiped her hands on her apron. "What's he like, this Alex?"

I pictured him in my mind, the easy smile, the way he made even the ugliest sweaters look cool, the laugh that could peel paint from the walls.

"He's all right," I said, then added, "posh, though. His dad's some sort of lawyer."

Mum made a noise, half sympathy, half warning, "you think he'll mind the house?"

I snorted, but there was a bite in it, "it's not a museum. He's just not used to… normal, I suppose."

She went back to her onions, but I could see her chewing it over. After a while, she said, "I'll make the stew I do for the church do's. That's safe, isn't it?"

"Yeah," I said, "and maybe don't mention Dad's *Union Man of the Year* trophy."

She laughed, bright and sharp, "he only brings it out when we have company."

"Exactly," I said.

She chopped in silence for a bit, then, quietly, "your dad can be…"

"Loud? Opinionated?"

She nodded, "but he means well. And so do you, love."

She looked at me, really looked, and I felt my face go hot.

"I just want it to go okay," I said, barely above a whisper.

She reached out and squeezed my hand, her skin dry and warm. "It will," she said, with the certainty of someone who'd already decided.

I finished my tea, then helped peel carrots, anything to keep my hands busy. At the door, Sarah lurked, her hair a mess, still in her pyjamas. She leaned against the frame, grinning.

"House ready for the Queen?" she asked.

"Shut it," I said, but I smiled anyway.

She wandered in, stealing a bit of carrot from the chopping board, "he's staying in your room, then?"

"Yeah. I've set up the camp bed."

She wagged her eyebrows, "don't tell him what happened in Rhyl!"

I tried not to rise to it, but she knew me too well.

Mum shot her a look, "enough, you."

Mum watched her go, then shook her head, "she'll be the death of me."

I leaned on the counter, "Mum, can you just… not fuss too much? And maybe steer Dad away from politics?"

She looked at me, a wry smile playing at the corner of her mouth, "I'm not daft, Liam. But you know what your father's like."

I nodded, resigned.

"He's nervous, too, you know," she said, "wants to make a good impression."

That surprised me, and I let it sit for a minute before answering, "he'll do fine."

She laughed, softer now, "you say that like you're not sure."

I shrugged, because I wasn't.

Upstairs, I made one last pass at the room. The bed was perfect, the camp bed passable, the air less like mildew and more like cold.

I lined up the shoes by the door, then sat at the desk and tried not to stare at the clock.

At noon, Mum called up that lunch was ready, just soup and bread, "to tide us over." I ate in silence, watching Sarah butter her bread with surgical precision, her eyes darting to me every few bites.

"You're acting weird," she said finally.

I glared at her, but she just grinned.

"Just don't embarrass me, all right?" I hissed, as we cleared the dishes.

She shrugged, lips pressed together in a secret smile, "I make no promises."

When I passed her in the hall, I whispered, "remember your promise." She rolled her eyes, but nodded, and I felt the knot in my stomach loosen by a notch.

Back in my room, I sat on the edge of the bed, hands clasped between my knees, and tried to steady my breathing. I thought about Alex, about the last time we'd been alone together, about the way he'd said, "see you soon" and how it sounded like a dare.

I wondered if he'd like the room, or if he'd laugh at the *Beano* annuals and the Olympic poster and the threadbare camp bed. I wondered if he'd want to stay, or if he'd make an excuse after a day and drive home.

I wondered if I'd have the courage to touch him, even just a hand on the shoulder, with my whole family only inches away. But mostly, I wondered if he'd see through the layers of nervousness and fakery to the person I wanted to be.

I took a deep breath, then another, and told myself it would be fine. If nothing else, the bed was made, the room was clean, and the worst that could happen was a broken camp bed and a new story for Sarah to tell.

I could live with that.

The window in my room was a relic, two panes separated by a warped strip of wood, the top sash stuck forever half an inch ajar. I spent the afternoon at my desk, pretending to read, but really just watching the street through the narrow slot between the houses. From this vantage, I could see the bend in the road where the terraces began, and the makeshift fence that marked the border between "our lot" and the pensioners' bungalows.

Mum vacuumed the stairs in a slow, deliberate rhythm, as if the noise might drown out the restlessness vibrating through the house. Sarah was nowhere to be seen, which meant she was either eavesdropping from her room or smoking a cigarette in the yard.

I watched the world outside, letting my mind spiral through every disaster scenario. What if Alex got lost, or the car broke down, or he took one look at the house and decided to turn back? What if the neighbours saw two boys bringing bags into the same bedroom? What if he hated it, hated me, for not being able to offer anything better?

I played them all out, one after the other, until the only thing left was the faint hope that maybe it wouldn't be as bad as I'd imagined.

It started to rain at half past two, just enough to gloss the slate roofs and make the cars look like beetles under the streetlights. At three on the dot, a blue Escort rolled into view, crawling slow as if unsure of the way. I watched it inch past the gap in the terrace behind ours.

My heart went wild. I let myself breathe once, twice, then stood and checked the mirror. My hair was a mess; I smoothed it with wet fingers, then wiped my hands on my jeans. Downstairs, the vacuum had stopped.

I moved quietly, the stairs creaking under my feet. At the bottom, I paused by the door, listening to my own breathing. The hallway was narrow and dark, the only light a patch of blue from the frosted glass.

I reached for the handle, hesitated. I opened the door, stepped onto the pavement. The rain was colder than I'd expected, the air sharp with the smell of wet tarmac.

He saw me, grinned.

"Found it then?" I called, trying to keep my voice steady.

He raised an eyebrow, "seems so," he said, then glanced at the house behind me. "Very… authentic."

I laughed, the sound too loud in the quiet street.

He closed the boot, hefted one holdall onto his shoulder and tossed the other to me. We stood there, face to face, a yard of pavement between us. I wanted to hug him, or at least touch his arm, but the neighbours' curtains twitched at the edge of my vision.

"Come in," I said, stepping back.

He followed, wiping his boots on the mat. Inside, the house felt impossibly small. I could smell onions from the kitchen, the fug of damp coats from the rack behind the door.

We stood in the hallway for a second, me listening to the creak of the stairs and the hum of the kettle, Alex shuffling his boots against the mat like he was afraid of scuffing the vinyl. From the kitchen, Mum called, "is that him, then?" Her voice was bright, with a hint of nerves she'd probably deny.

"Yeah, Mum, Alex is here," I called back, willing myself to sound normal.

"Lovely. I'll pop the kettle on," she replied, and the sound of a teaspoon against porcelain followed.

I gestured for Alex to follow. The stairs were steep, the banister slick with a decade's worth of fingerprints. As we climbed, I pointed out the landmarks: the bathroom in the middle ("careful, the lock's dodgy"), Sarah's room ("enter at your peril"), and Mum and Dad's at the front, door closed and hung with a souvenir scarf from Blackpool.

At the top, my room was straight ahead. The paint on the door was chipped, and the old sticker that read *KEEP OUT'* had faded to a ghostly outline. I pushed it open.

The room was rectangular and barely wide enough for the single bed along the right wall and the camp bed wedged alongside the bookcase on the left. The desk was jammed under the long, thin window, which looked out onto the backyard and the ginnel. At the foot of the bed, behind the door, stood a wardrobe, its door prone to popping open on its own if you slammed the door too hard. The chest of drawers was crammed next to the bookcase, leaving a channel of about eighteen inches between furniture.

Alex took it in with the curiosity of a naturalist observing a rare species in the wild, "a bit small, I suppose," I said, suddenly embarrassed by the faded bedsheet and the detritus of childhood lining the shelves.

He grinned, setting his bag on the camp bed, "let's say *'intimate'*," he said, giving me one of his winks, equal parts flirt and reassurance.

I relaxed a fraction, closed the door with a click, and watched as he poked around the perimeter. He stopped at the window, stared out at the patchwork of terraced roofs and the faint plume of steam from a neighbour's tumble dryer.

"Nice view," he said, still grinning.

"Best in the house," I replied, "you can see the chippy from here, if you lean out far enough."

He leaned, just to test it, then flopped onto the camp bed, which creaked alarmingly but didn't collapse. He bounced once, twice, then settled in, hands behind his head.

"It'll do," he said, and the ease in his voice made me want to believe it.

For a minute, we just sat in the small, bright silence, the only sound the low gurgle of pipes and the distant clang of the kettle being filled. I found myself tracing the lines of his face, how the shadow of his jaw looked darker in this light, how the curve of his lip bent in amusement when he thought I wasn't watching.

He noticed, of course. He always did.

I caught myself and looked away, pretending to check the time on my watch, "we should probably head down," I said, "or Mum'll think we're hiding."

He sat up, smoothed his hair, and stood, "lead the way, Macduff."

We squeezed past each other in the gap, his arm brushing mine. For a second, the air felt charged, like static in the moments before a storm, but then it was gone, replaced by the shuffle of feet and the faint smell of toast from the kitchen.

Mum had set the kitchen table with more ceremony than usual, a faded oilcloth, the "guest" mugs with the flowers, and a jug of milk sweating on a coaster. She stood by the sink, hands folded over the dish towel like a referee preparing to call time on a fight.

"Come in, come in," she said, shooing us to our seats, "nice to finally meet one of Liam's friends."

Alex slid into the chair, smiled like he was auditioning for the part of *Perfect Guest*. "Thank you, Mrs. Parry, for letting me stay. Tea would be just the ticket after the drive."

Mum looked at me, then back at him, "doesn't he speak nice, our Liam?"

I shot her a glare, but she ignored it, busying herself with the teapot.

She poured three mugs, milk first, the way Dad insisted. The clink of spoon against ceramic was the only sound for a moment. I felt the weight of the silence settle, the kind that accumulates before a big match or a parent-teacher conference.

"So, Alex," Mum said, adding a sugar cube to her own cup, "what are you reading at university?"

He answered smoothly, "Geography, mainly, but I'm starting to think the student bar is my real subject."

She laughed, the sound genuine, "well, you'll fit right in here. Liam's father says the only thing he learned at school was how to pour a pint."

"He did," I muttered, but the ice was broken.

The conversation pinged back and forth, where was Alex from, what did his parents do, was he enjoying Manchester, did he miss home. He fielded each question like a pro, never rattled, never flustered.

I watched Mum watch him, her eyes flicking over his answers, weighing them like a butcher at the scales. She asked about his plans after uni, and whether he had a "special girl" back on the Wirral. He laughed, said he was "between relationships," and left it at that.

She tried to get more, but he deflected with a story about the union protest at Warrington, and the sorry state I was in after it. Obviously, I knew the story, but the way he told it, hands flailing, voice pitching up at the funny bits, made Mum laugh so hard she had to dab her eyes with a napkin.

I thought, *this must be killing her, not to dig deeper*.

When the tea was gone and the conversation had run dry, she stood, wiped her hands, and said, "go on, you two, go get settled. I'll call you when it's time for tea."

We stood, Alex nodding his thanks, and headed back upstairs. In my room, he set his bag on the floor and stretched, "that went well, I think."

"She likes you," I said, "she only gets the guest mugs out for special occasions."

He grinned, "you didn't tell me your family was so intimidating."

I snorted, "you'll know real fear when my dad gets home."

He looked around, "so, what's the plan for some privacy?"

I crossed the room, opened the wardrobe, and demonstrated, "if you wedge this door here, it jams the bedroom door handle. No one can get in without a battering ram."

He tried it, then nodded, impressed, "ingenious. You've done this before."

"Never been caught having a wank yet," I said, deadpan.

He laughed, then looked at me with a gleam in his eye, "or kissing a man?"

I hesitated, but before I could answer, he stepped forward, closed the gap, and kissed me.

It wasn't urgent, more like a test, a question. I let myself sink into it, the taste of tea still on our tongues, the awkward angle of our noses. It was quick, but it left me buzzing.

I pulled away first, glancing at the clock on the wall, "better not," I whispered, "it'll be teatime soon."

He grinned, leaned in close, "more tea?"

I elbowed him, hard enough to make him laugh for real. "That's dinner for you, posh boy."

His poker face cracked, and he snorted so loud I thought Sarah would hear. We both collapsed onto the bed, giggling like idiots, the tension of the day dissolving in the sudden rush of relief.

For a while, we just lay there, side by side, staring at the water-stained ceiling. He reached over, laced his fingers with mine, and squeezed.

"Thanks," he said, voice low.

"For what?"

"For making it easy," he replied.

I snorted, "it's only day one. Plenty of time to cock it up."

He squeezed my hand again, and I wondered how I'd ever survive two weeks of this. But as the smell of the stew drifted up the stairs and the low rumble of Dad's voice announced his arrival, I felt ready for anything.

The smell of the stew was a clarion call, by six, the kitchen was thick with the promise of comfort food, and Dad's voice rumbled under the noise like distant thunder. He'd changed out of his work overalls, but still had the imprint of a week's labour on his hands, grease stained into the lines of his knuckles. He nodded at Alex when we came in, sizing him up with the narrow-eyed look he reserved for salesmen and coppers.

"You must be the geography lad," he said, as if the subject was a personal affront.

Alex grinned, shook his hand, and said, "yes, Alex Hughes. Thanks for having me here Mr. Parry."

Dad snorted, but there was approval in it, "you'll want to watch out. My lot's famous for grilling the visitors."

Mum shooed us to the table, set out the plates with a flourish. Sarah arrived last, slipping into her seat without a word. She shot me a look, calm, assessing, then nodded once, as if to say, *you're doing all right so far*.

The meal was a performance, Dad told stories about the factory, the union, and the time he'd nearly lost a finger in the press machine. Alex listened, asked good questions, even laughed at the jokes that didn't make sense outside of the north. He talked a little about his own family, his dad's job, his mum's obsession with French television, and managed to steer the conversation back to safe waters every time Dad probed too close to politics or religion.

Mum watched the interplay like it was a tennis match, eyes darting between the men, ready to intervene if things got heated. But it never did. The worst that happened was Dad telling a story about his own schooldays, the "bloody posh kids" who thought they were better than everyone and then realising who he was talking to.

He went quiet for a second, then laughed, "no offense, son," he said to Alex.

Alex just grinned, "none taken. We're not all that bad."

Sarah ate in silence, but I caught her watching the two of us, a small smile curving at the corner of her mouth. By the time we'd finished, the table was littered with empty plates, the remains of a loaf of white bread, and a graveyard of chip ends. Mum cleared the plates, then set out a bowl of tinned fruit and custard for pudding.

As we ate, Dad loosened up, telling stories about Rochdale before the motorway, the characters from the old neighbourhood, the time he'd met George Best in a pub and spent the rest of the night pretending not to recognise him.

Alex matched him story for story, trading in the wit and warmth that had charmed every teacher he'd ever had. By the end of the meal, Dad was talking to Alex like he was part of the family. He even offered him a can of beer from the fridge, which was a first for any visitor.

When Mum called time on the evening ("Leave some room for breakfast, boys!"), we retreated to my bedroom, the door closed behind us. The house felt suddenly quiet, the walls thinner now that the trial by fire was over.

I flopped onto the bed, exhaled.

Alex sat on the camp bed, his knees drawn up, watching me with a look that was both amused and gentle.

"You did good," he said.

I shook my head, laughing, "you did. I've never seen my Dad talk that much to anyone."

He shrugged, "maybe he sees himself in me."

I rolled my eyes. "Sure. Next thing you know, he'll be running for Parliament."

Alex grinned, then went quiet. After a minute, he said, "thanks for inviting me."

I looked at him, unsure what to say. The truth was, I'd never expected him to come, let alone fit in so easily. It made something in my chest ache, in a way that was both good and scary.

"Glad you're here," I said, and meant it.

For a long time, we just sat there, listening to the house settle around us, the faint sound of Mum's radio drifting up the stairs.

Safe, for the first time in ages. I closed my eyes, and for once, slept without dreaming.

The next morning, the house woke slow and warm, the usual gallop of the weekday suspended for the holidays. Mum made toast and strong tea for everyone, and we ate at the kitchen table in our pyjamas, the cold leaking through the single-glazed window but not touching us. Alex looked rumpled and a little dazed, but happy in a way I hadn't seen before.

Over the next week, routine settled on us like a comfortable old jumper. Most mornings we slept in, then hung around the kitchen in various stages of undress, Mum giving up on decency and simply telling us not to spill jam on the good cloth. Alex and I ran errands for her, fetching bread from the bakery, picking up bin liners from the corner shop, once even braving the supermarket in town, which was full of pensioners and sugar-rushed kids on the verge of riot. He marvelled at the efficiency with which my mum corralled the queue at the tills, the way she could turn small talk into a weapon and get the best bit of ham by sheer force of will.

Sarah, when not hiding in her room, roped us into helping her wrap presents. She had a system, I held the paper taut, Alex did the tape, and she added the bows. She was weirdly good at it, and by the third day had run out of family to wrap for, so she started doing fake presents and stashing them under the tree to "bulk it out for the photos." The tree itself was a battered artificial thing from the seventies, its green faded to yellow in places, but once the lights and tinsel were up it looked almost real, especially with the lights off and only the TV flickering in the dark.

On Christmas Eve, Mum cooked like she was feeding a battalion, even though there were only five of us. She handed Alex a wooden spoon and put him to work stirring the pudding, which he did with the intensity of a contestant on *Mastermind*. At one point, she told him, "just call me *'Maggie'*, love, everyone does," and he blushed, nodded, then said, "yes, Mrs. Parry ... er, Maggie." She smiled, and for a second I thought she might actually want to adopt him.

Dad was off work for the first time in years and spent the days fixing things around the house, leaky taps, the back gate, a banister that had wobbled since I was six. He grumbled about the price of everything, watched football on the telly, and at night read the paper in the front room. He never once mentioned the protests or the strikes, and if he noticed anything unusual about our "guest," he never said so.

The only time he ever pulled me aside was on the Thursday before Christmas. He found me in the yard, lighting a cigarette, and stood next to me in the shadow of the ginnel.

"He's a good lad, your mate," he said, looking at the sky instead of me.

I shrugged, kicked at a pebble, "yeah. He's all right."

Dad nodded, then said, "could do a lot worse for a friend," and went back inside.

That night, Alex and I stayed up late, sitting on the camp bed and listening to music on my battered tape player. He told me stories about his own family's Christmas, how his dad once got a tree so big it wouldn't fit through the door, how his mum always forgot to buy batteries for his toys, how his brother had broken his arm sledging on a frozen golf course and blamed it on "government negligence." The more he talked, the less posh he sounded, the more he seemed like he belonged.

On Christmas Day, we woke to the sound of Sarah playing *Slade* at full volume, the *'Merry Christmas Everybody'* chorus echoing through the floorboards. I found a pair of paper crowns waiting on the dresser, one gold, one green. I took the gold and left the green for Alex, who wore it all through breakfast, even when Mum took photos and Dad made fun of us for looking like "the world's worst royalty."

Presents were exchanged in the living room. Most were cheap or practical, socks, chocolates, a new diary for me, but Sarah had made Alex a homemade card with a joke about "geography boys" and he laughed so hard he almost dropped his mug of tea. I'd saved up and bought him a scarf, navy and white like the one he wore that first night, but thicker and less scratchy. He put it on immediately, then pulled me into a hug, clumsy but genuine.

Lunch was the main event: roast turkey, stuffing, mountains of roasties, carrots, sprouts and peas and gravy thick enough to stand a spoon in. At the centre of the table was a plate of pigs in blankets, sausages wrapped in bacon, a staple of Parry tradition. Alex stared at them, then looked at me, "what are those?"

I laughed, explained, then watched as he loaded his plate with half a dozen.

Mum watched him eat with the quiet pride of a chef seeing their dish vanish. "Never seen anyone take to them like that," she said.

Alex grinned, wiped his mouth with the back of his hand, "best thing I've ever tasted, Mrs. ... Maggie."

Dad pointed at him with a fork, "told you. Lad knows his food."

We pulled crackers, told the jokes, wore the crowns. Sarah did impressions of the Queen and made everyone laugh until Mum had to get up for tissues. It was noisy, silly, and perfect.

After lunch, we all collapsed in the front room to watch a James Bond film, one of the old ones, with Sean Connery and improbable gadgets. Dad insisted, as always, that it was "a tradition," even though we'd only started doing it when Sarah was ten. Mum kept the snacks coming: *Quality Street*, mince pies, more tea, and later, sherry for the grown-ups. By nine, we were all half-asleep, except for Sarah, who kept a tally of how many times Bond said something "sexist or gross."

As the night wore on, Mum and Dad drifted off to bed, then Sarah, leaving Alex and me alone on the settee. We watched the flicker of the fairy lights, the tree reflected in the window, and listened to the muffled quiet of a world gone still.

He turned to me, voice soft, "I could get used to this."

I smiled, "it's not always like this."

He shook his head, "doesn't matter. It's better than anything I've known."

We sat in silence, neither wanting to break the spell.

Eventually, we dragged ourselves upstairs, changed into pyjamas, and crawled under the covers. The window rattled in the wind, but the room was warm, the air filled with the smell of pine and old books and the faintest trace of Mum's perfume.

I turned off the light, rolled onto my side, "Happy Christmas, Lex," I whispered.

He shifted, reached across the gap, and took my hand.

"Happy Christmas, Li."

Then, in the darkness, he pulled me close, pressed a kiss to my lips, and held me there for a long, quiet moment.

"Thank you," he whispered, "for all of it."

I felt his breath, steady and warm, and for the first time in my life, I didn't worry about being caught, or judged, or losing what I'd found

CHAPTER 15: A NEW YEAR REVELATION

If Christmas had been a fever dream of domesticity, New Year was a different species of madness. Sarah started laying the groundwork two days early, planting the suggestion at breakfast, "you have to come out, both of you, it's tradition," then escalating her campaign with increasingly desperate tactics as the big night approached.

On New Year's Eve, she dragged us into the front room, where she'd commandeered the stereo and was practicing her "playlist." Her argument was that it would be a public relations disaster if Alex spent the entire break "being held hostage by Liam and the *BBC Two* schedule." When I protested, she snorted, "come off it, I've seen you both on the couch. If I have to witness one more hour of *Question Time*, I'll gouge my eyes out with a *Quality Street*."

Alex raised both hands in surrender, "I'm powerless before such persuasive rhetoric," he said, though I could see the flicker of nerves behind his smile.

She clapped her hands, satisfied, "sorted. I'll see if I can get us a table at *the Greengate*. But dress nice, yeah? If you turn up in trackies, I'll disown you."

I shot a look at Alex, "she's not joking. Last time, she made Dad walk home and change."

He nodded, "duly noted."

It wasn't lost on me that, in the months since leaving for university, Sarah had done everything in her power to reinvent herself as the kind of person who "curated" evenings out, even if the venues never got fancier than a converted old-man's pub with sticky carpets and last year's banners still up. Her efforts were a kind of personal branding, but it suited her.

When the time came, we layered up in the hallway, me in a borrowed shirt and the only decent jeans I owned, Alex in a midnight-blue button-down that somehow made him look even more out of place. Sarah emerged in her "statement" skirt and a black jumper, her hair wrangled into loose waves that looked unstudied but probably took all afternoon.

She led the way through the streets, boots crunching on the salt they'd scattered for the forecast ice. The town was lit up with the last dregs of municipal tinsel, strings of fairy lights dangling in loose, exhausted bows. People were already spilling from the chip shop and the off-licenses, hooting in the cold, but Sarah powered through the melee with the poise of a parade marshal.

The Greengate inside was a vision in brown, brown panelling, brown carpet, brown tables, all varnished to a dull sheen by decades of spilt lager and the slow seep of second-hand smoke. The ceiling was low enough to threaten taller drinkers with concussion, and the only reliable lighting came from yellowed sconces at either end of the bar.

Sarah pushed us through the crowd with the confidence of a local, landing us at a corner table already half-occupied by her college friends. The girl squad from her birthday was there, plus a few new faces, one of whom was the trench-coat guy from before, his coat now festooned with a dozen novelty badges and a suspicious stain near the hem. He gave Alex a once-over, then nodded, as if confirming a rumour.

Introductions were perfunctory, drinks were ordered by committee, and soon we were wedged tight between the wall and a human barricade of Sarah's mates. Conversation tumbled out in overlapping knots, old gossip, new scandal, the latest in music and TV and which teachers had gotten sacked for what. Sarah floated between orbits, sometimes pressed against my shoulder, sometimes shouting across the table, always keeping one eye on her guests.

Alex played the part of "mate from Manchester" with aplomb. He laughed at the right moments, asked clever questions, even managed to blag a free pint from the trench-coat guy by pretending to care about *Joy Division*. I watched him work the table, observed the way he adjusted his accent by a hair's breadth to match the crowd, the way he seemed both at home and apart at the same time. It was a party trick I envied.

I sipped my lager and let the din wash over me. Every so often, I'd catch Sarah watching us, her gaze flicking from Alex to me, then back again, like she was scoring some invisible contest.

As the night deepened, the air in the pub thickened into a haze of smoke and laughter. People shouted over the music, the DJ a volunteer with a taste for *ABBA* and *Slade*. The floor grew sticky with dropped pints and melting ice. Sarah's friends became progressively louder, their banter shifting from playful to predatory as the clock rolled toward midnight.

At some point, I lost track of Sarah. One moment she was at the table, arguing with the bar staff over the merits of vodka lime, the next she'd vanished into the crowd. I craned my neck, scanning the throng for her head, but the whole pub was a soup of faces, none distinct.

Alex leaned in, "she's probably just in the loo. Or getting hit on."

"Or both," I muttered, more anxious than I wanted to admit.

He grinned, "she can handle herself, that much I have learnt this week about your little sister. I'm more worried about us." He gestured at the room, "we are, without question, the two least cool people here."

I laughed, which made me feel better, "speak for yourself."

He raised his glass, and I clinked mine against it.

Time collapsed as it only does when you're in a place with no clocks. The world outside grew colder, darker; inside, the temperature ratcheted up by the drink and the press of bodies. I drifted in and out of the table's conversations, half-listening as Sarah's mates debated which club to hit later, who fancied whom, whether or not the new biology teacher wore a wig. Every so often I checked my watch, counting down the minutes to midnight.

Then, at a quarter to twelve, I spotted Sarah across the room. She was at the bar; arm draped around the shoulders of one of the lads from college, a rangy guy with a mop of brown hair and a smirk I recognised from her stories. She laughed at something he said, then tilted her head back to finish her drink in a single, practiced gulp. When she caught my eye, she winked, then went back to her conversation.

I felt a tiny surge of jealousy, irrational, probably, but sharp.

Alex noticed, "you okay?"

"Yeah. She's just… busy."

He nodded, "you want to step outside? It's loud in here."

I considered it, then said, "give me a sec." I flagged down one of Sarah's friends, a pixie-faced girl named Janine, and told her we'd be outside for a bit.

She eyed us up and down, then said, "don't freeze to death."

We made our way through the tangle of people and out the back, where the pub had a "beer garden" that was really just a patch of tarmac with a picnic bench. The cold bit instantly, shocking after the fug inside. I hugged my arms to my chest and watched my breath condense.

For a while we just stood there, the silence oddly comfortable after the noise. From inside, the muffled roar of the crowd built and broke in waves; every so often, a door would open and a snatch of music or laughter would escape before being smothered by the cold.

Alex shifted his weight, then said, "I like it here."

"In the barrel yard?"

He grinned, "in Rochdale. It's… real. Not like home."

I snorted, "you must be desperate."

He shook his head, "no, I mean it. I like the way people talk, the way they don't pretend to be better than they are. Even the pubs feel honest, somehow."

I thought about this, then nodded, "yeah. It's not much, but it's ours."

He smiled, then leaned back against the brick wall. "I'm glad you brought me."

I looked at him, surprised by the softness in his voice.

He said, "I know you don't always believe it, but you're good, Liam. You make things better."

I stared at the ground, embarrassed, "you should see me on a bad day."

He laughed, then let the silence stretch. Through the window, we could see the crowd inside surge toward the bar. I checked my watch, five minutes to midnight.

Alex flicked his cigarette into the gutter and pushed his hands deep into his pockets, "we should get back, or she'll think we've legged it."

I hesitated, "let's just stay a bit longer."

He cocked his head, "what's up?"

I searched for the words, then said, "do you ever… I don't know. Want to just… stop pretending for a bit?"

He looked at me, not understanding at first, then nodded, serious, "yeah. All the time."

I felt my chest tighten, "even here, it's like… I don't know who I'm supposed to be."

He reached out, touched my shoulder. His hand was warm, steady, "you're just you. That's enough."

I shivered, and not from the cold.

Inside, the pub started the countdown early. Someone had a whistle, and the DJ's voice cut through: "ten, nine, eight…"

Alex checked the windows, the alley, then turned to face me fully, "nobody's watching," he said.

I swallowed, my mouth suddenly dry. He stepped closer, arms folding around me, slow enough that I could have stepped away if I wanted. He didn't force it, just held me there, waiting, "are you sure?" he whispered, breath fogging the air between us.

I hesitated, every part of me screaming yes and no at the same time. Then I nodded, once.

He put his hands on my face, thumb grazing my cheekbone, and kissed me. It was gentle, no fireworks, just a long, quiet pressure, like the sealing of an envelope.

For a second I froze, heart pounding, then let go and kissed back. I tasted the smoke and the bitter edge of beer and something sweet that might have been hope. The noise from the pub built and peaked, then broke into wild applause.

I'd like to say the moment lingered, that we stood together in the cold, kissing like heroes on the stroke of midnight, but in reality we'd barely separated when the universe reasserted itself in the form of Sarah, elbowing through the back door and freezing mid-step at the sight of us.

She blinked twice, then started to laugh; loud, clear, unguarded. "Oh my god," she said, and then again, softer: "Oh my god." She walked over, weaving just a little, and regarded us with the up-down of a scientist about to name a new species. We both stepped back, as if caught siphoning petrol or pissing in the street.

She didn't miss a beat, "don't mind me," she announced, voice pitched theatrical for the benefit of any imaginary bystanders, "honestly, I think you're cute together." Then, without waiting for a reply, she grabbed us both by the shoulders, reeled us in, and planted a big, wet kiss on each of our cheeks in turn. "Happy New Year, boys," she whispered, so close I could feel her breath, "and don't worry, your secret's safe with me."

Then she waltzed back into the pub, humming *Dancing Queen'* at top volume. For a second we just stared at the spot she'd vacated. Alex's face had gone so white it looked like a negative. My heart thudded in my ears, the shock and terror doing battle with a strange, bubbling relief.

He found his voice first, so low I barely heard it over the music, "do you think she'll—"

I shook my head, hard, "no. That's not Sarah's style."

He looked at me, searching, then said, "are you sure?"

"Positive," I said, and for the first time since she'd caught us, I actually believed it. "She doesn't do drama unless she gets to be the star."

He snorted, the tension snapping, and muttered, "well, mission accomplished."

We shuffled our way back inside, the room now a riot of celebration, people hugging, singing, smearing lipstick and lager foam across each other's faces. Sarah was at the centre of it, arm-wrestling the trench-coat guy for ownership of a battered party hat. She saw us re-enter and flashed a thumbs-up, then turned her attention back to the contest.

I felt the heat rising to my ears, but nobody else seemed to notice or care. We rejoined the table, where Janine had replaced her cider with something violently blue and was now holding forth on the merits of "boys who can dance." Alex let her pull him up for a turn on the tiny patch of cleared floor; he lasted exactly thirty seconds before the physics of the thing broke down and they both ended up on their arses, laughing.

Sarah drifted over, her face still flushed. She plopped herself down next to me, thigh pressed against mine.

"You all right?" she asked, voice suddenly gentle.

I nodded, not trusting myself to speak.

She nudged my shoulder, "you're not as subtle as you think, you know."

I looked at my hands, embarrassed, "you won't tell anyone?"

She rolled her eyes, "Liam. I'm your sister, not an arsehole." She sipped from her glass, then said, "besides, you both looked happy. About time, if you ask me."

I risked a glance at her, and she smiled, broad and genuine, "I mean it, Li. Don't worry." I let out a long, slow breath I didn't know I'd been holding.

The party trundled on, devolving from celebration to endurance test. By one, people were starting to drift out in clumps, bracing against the cold as they called cabs or trekked to the next destination. Sarah's friends disappeared by degrees, hugging her at the door and promising to meet up in the New Year. Janine gave Alex a peck on the cheek ("for luck") and high-fived me on the way out. The trench-coat guy, now visibly pissed, tried to negotiate a sleepover in our living room, but Sarah fobbed him off with promises of "next time, promise!" before shooing him into a taxi.

By half-one, the place was nearly empty. Sarah came over, linking her arms through mine and Alex's.

"Time for you to take me home, I think," she said, her voice wobbling between bravado and exhaustion. We guided her through the freezing air, each of us a prop under her shoulders. She sang snatches of *New Order* and *'Auld Lang Syne'* as we shuffled along, feet crunching on the salted pavements. Now and then she'd lean her head on my arm, or try to pinch Alex's cheek, only to forget what she was doing halfway through.

At the front door, she fumbled for her key, missed the lock twice, then handed it to me with a conspiratorial, "don't tell Mum." Inside, the house was dark and silent, save for the faint snore of Dad through the wall. Sarah kicked off her shoes in the hallway and turned to face us, hands on our shoulders for balance.

"Good night, gentlemen," she said, and pecked us both on the cheek again, lighter this time, "Happy New Year."

She tottered upstairs, giggling under her breath. We stood for a moment, listening to the sound of her door closing and the muffled thump as she probably collapsed onto her bed.

Alex grinned, "she's a legend."

I smiled back, "told you."

We crept upstairs, shoes in hand, and I felt the weight of the night settle around me, not heavy, but strange and new, like wearing someone else's coat. The fear was still there, but less than before. I thought about Sarah's words, about the promise stitched into her laugh.

In my room, Alex sat on the edge of the camp bed, rubbing his temples, "I can't believe we got away with it," he said.

I crawled under the covers, too tired to undress, "you'd be surprised what people don't see when they're not looking."

He looked at me, blue eyes soft in the dark, "I saw you."

I blinked, caught off guard, "I saw you, too."

He smiled, and for a while we just lay there, silent except for the creak of the pipes and the slow, even breathing of someone at peace.

Outside, the sky was still black, but I knew the sun would come soon. And when it did, I thought, maybe things would look different.

I woke late, the world pressing in with the kind of insistent brightness that made it clear I'd slept through the best part of the morning. Alex was already up, gone from the camp bed, his side neatly made with the efficiency of someone who'd been trained never to leave a trace. I lay there for a minute, piecing together the night before, Sarah's laughter, the alley behind the pub, the warmth of Alex's hands on my face and then forced myself up.

Downstairs, the kitchen was bright with weak January sun and the hum of the radio, tuned to some station playing back-to-back hits from the last decade. Mum was already making tea, her back to the door as she loaded bread into the toaster. She wore the green cardigan today, the one with the stitched patch where Sarah had once set it alight leaning over the cooker.

She turned as I entered, clocked my face, and said, "morning, love. Or should I say afternoon?"

I grunted, still half-asleep, and slumped at the table. My head throbbed with the aftershocks of cheap lager and adrenaline. Across from me, Alex appeared from the hallway, hair still damp from the shower, eyes blue and clear as glacier run-off.

He slid into the seat next to mine, "I don't think I've ever slept so well," he said, grinning, "or so long."

Mum poured tea into three mugs, added milk to ours without asking, and placed them on the table with the authority of a general marshalling her troops. She sat, folded her hands, and regarded us both.

"I want to thank you," she said, and for a second I thought she'd seen us last night, had read our minds and come to deliver judgement. But then she added, "for looking after our Sarah. She's told me all about her knights in shining armour, dragging her home when she was half-cut and trying to argue with a traffic cone."

Alex laughed, relieved, "she did most of the dragging herself."

"She can be a handful," Mum admitted, sipping her tea, "but she's got a good heart. She always speaks well of you, Alex. Says you're a proper gent."

Alex blushed, looking down at his mug.

"And you, Liam," she continued, turning her full attention to me, "I think you're happier than I've seen you in ages."

I stared at the table, not trusting myself to speak.

She reached out, patted my hand, "it's good to see."

The toaster popped, launching the bread halfway across the counter. Mum retrieved it with a flourish, slathered it with margarine, and handed slices around. We ate in silence, the kind that felt less like absence and more like the pause after a well-told story.

Sarah emerged mid-meal, hair a wreck, sunglasses perched on her head like she was bracing for paparazzi. She plopped into the seat next to me and stole my toast.

"Morning, losers," she said, voice raw. She eyed Alex, then me, then grinned, "you both look like hell."

"Thanks," I muttered, rolling my eyes.

Mum made another round of tea, "are you alive, Sarah?"

She took the cup, sipped, and nodded, "barely. But I'll survive."

Alex leaned back in his chair, surveying the room like he was trying to memorise it. He caught my gaze, smiled, then glanced away, back to his mug.

After breakfast, Mum went out to the corner shop to pick up last-minute bits for dinner, leaving us to clear the table and rinse the dishes. Sarah stacked plates with the efficiency of practice, then lingered at the sink, waiting until Mum's footsteps faded before turning to face me.

"You all right?" she said, voice low.

"Yeah. Why?"

She shrugged, "you seemed... different. In a good way."

I wanted to say something clever, something that would make her laugh, but the words tangled in my throat. Instead, I said, "thanks for last night. For not making it weird."

She grinned, then nudged my arm. "Please. It was the highlight of my year." She looked at Alex, then back to me. "Don't cock it up, yeah?"

I managed a smile. "I'll do my best."

She left us to finish up. As soon as the door closed, Alex leaned against the counter and exhaled, long and slow.

"Do you really think she'll keep it quiet?" he asked, voice barely above a whisper.

"Yeah," I said, certain, "she's got her flaws, but she keeps promises."

He nodded, visibly relieved.

We spent the rest of the afternoon packing Alex's bag, fitting the odds and ends back into their original containers, trying not to look at the clock. Every so often, I'd catch him staring at the ceiling, or watching the play of sunlight across the faded carpet, as if willing the moment to last.

When it was finally time, we carried his things to the door, where Mum and Sarah waited, each of them wrapped in oversized scarves.

"Don't forget your coat," Mum said, fussing over him, "you'll freeze on the motorway."

"I'll be fine, Maggie," he said, smiling, "thank you for everything."

She hugged him, quick but fierce, then stepped aside.

Sarah lingered, then wrapped her arms around him, surprising both of us. She whispered something I couldn't catch, then let go. Alex turned to me, and for a second, the world went quiet.

I walked him to the car, helped load the bags into the boot. He looked at me, his face serious.

"I wish I didn't have to go," he said.

I swallowed, the words caught in my throat, "it's only a week. We'll see each other in Halls."

He smiled, the sadness fading, "yeah. I'll see you soon, Li."

He started the engine, rolled down the window, "take care of yourself." I nodded, then watched as he pulled away, his car shrinking into the distance.

Back at the house, Sarah and Mum stood in the doorway, arms wrapped around each other for warmth. Sarah grinned. I stood there, watching the empty street, the strange steadiness in my chest making me feel heavier and lighter at the same time.

The world, I realised, hadn't ended. It had just started up again, turning on an axis I'd thought would never move.

After the flurry of departures and goodbyes, the house settled into its usual rhythms: Dad in his chair with the newspaper, Mum orchestrating Sunday lunch, Sarah upstairs with her music leaking through the walls. On paper, nothing had changed. The clouds still hung low over the terrace roofs, the bin lorry still rattled past at half eight sharp, the radiators still knocked and hissed as if the pipes themselves were alive.

But as I moved through the rooms, collecting stray mugs and setting the table, I felt different, a tiny, almost imperceptible shift in the way I fit inside my own skin. The dread that had followed me home every holiday was gone, replaced by a kind of steady glow. Not happiness, exactly, but something more durable.

At lunch, Dad asked about Alex, how he'd liked the stew, whether he'd made it back to the Wirral without running afoul of the weather. I answered in detail, embellishing stories about the pub and the walk home. Sarah chimed in, snorting with laughter at the bits she remembered.

Mum caught my eye, and in that brief, unspoken glance, I knew she saw it too: the weight lifted, the air changed.

Afterwards, I retreated to my room, the old desk piled with books and notebooks and the blue scarf Alex had left behind. I picked it up, ran my fingers along the edge, and tried to imagine what he was doing in that moment. Probably sprawled across his bed, planning the next week's reading.

I opened my journal and wrote for the first time in months.

I wrote about the pub, about Sarah, about the way Alex made the world feel wider. I wrote about fear, and how it shrinks when shared, and about secrets that grow lighter in the open. I wrote about coming home and finding that, for once, I actually wanted to stay.

When I finished, I closed the book and set it aside. Outside, the daylight was already fading, the town sinking into its usual grey dusk. But inside, the glow held, quiet, steady, something to build on. I breathed, and let myself believe that this, finally, was what hope felt like.

CHAPTER 16: GRADUATION DAY

Our return to Halls in January hurled us into a whirlwind of lectures and dissertation deadlines. Alex and I constructed a careful routine around our schedules, studying side by side at the library until closing. The nights I spent in his narrow bed felt different now, tender but muted, like music played through walls. I'd catch myself watching him sleep, wondering if this quieter intimacy was progress or surrender. Sarah called it 'love' over Easter break, her voice tinged with envy. When she asked about our future, I changed the subject three times before admitting I hadn't broached it with him. Her eyebrows shot up.

"Aren't you afraid he'll just... leave?" she asked.

I was. Terribly. But raising the question felt like inviting disaster, like naming a fear might summon it. Some mornings I'd wake beside him seized by panic, mentally calculating how many weeks remained until graduation would force our hands. Other days, I'd convince myself our easy rhythm was proof enough we'd continue. As May approached, we buried these questions beneath textbooks and revision notes, our conversations narrowing to citations and exam strategies. Perhaps we both knew what silence protected us from.

My hand ached like it was being slowly unscrewed from the rest of my body. I'd stopped registering the pain after the fourth hour, after the fifth mug of vending-machine tea gone metallic from the tang of blood where I'd bitten my lip. By the time the clock in the reading room tolled eight, the edge of my thumb was ground raw from the slow attrition of pen on paper, and the knuckle of my middle finger throbbed in time to the twitch of the fluorescent lights.

I shifted in my seat, tried to get comfortable, but the chair was engineered for penitence. The library was full of people like me, some hunched so low their hair brushed the pages, others sprawled as if to absorb knowledge through contact alone. Here and there, the air thickened with the residue of sleepless nights, a haze of sweat and anxiety layered over old dust and furniture polish.

Stacks of books ringed my workspace like a rampart. *The Age of Capital'*, *British Socialism since 1884'*, a biography of Ramsey MacDonald so spattered with marginalia the original text was almost lost. My own notes, a chaos of loose leaf and graph paper, fanned out in concentric arcs, the corners smudged by too many passes of a nervous hand. The essay prompt glared from the top of the desk: *To what extent did the failures of the Labour movement after 1945 contribute to the rise of Thatcherism?',* I wanted to stab it with my biro, but I was on my last one, and the thought of running to the *Union* shop now was unthinkable.

The halls had gone silent after dinner. Most of the first years had quit for the day, off to the bar or to their beds, but in the library the only sound was the stutter of my pen and the turn of thin, greasy pages. Every few minutes, a librarian stalked past in a haze of boredom and antiseptic, eyes flat as billiard balls. Once, I caught the eye of the Law boy from my floor, his hair slicked into a helmet, hands wrapped in fingerless gloves as if preparing for combat, but he looked through me like I was just another fixture of the library, another note stuck to the carrel.

The words came hard, harder than I wanted to admit. I had spent three years training my mind to be sharp, to parse out the argument, but now it felt like trying to dig a trench with a wooden spoon. Every sentence I wrote, I wanted to go back and sand the edges, but I was running out of time, and my wrist trembled on every downstroke. I measured my progress not in pages but in millimetres of ink lost.

Outside, the sky had slipped to a thin, dirty blue. The branches of the oak outside the window were bare and black against the lamplight, but here inside, the bulbs made everything jaundiced and overexposed. I scrawled the last paragraph with a kind of brute force, the logic battered into place, and signed my name with a flourish that nearly cost me a muscle.

I sat back, hands limp in my lap. The ache travelled from my fingers up the length of my arm, a dull, industrial pulse. I stared at the sheaf of pages, expecting some wave of relief or triumph, but all I felt was the sour aftertaste of effort, the knowledge that three years had boiled down to these seventeen sheets of A4, stapled at the top and still warm from my skin.

A minute passed. Then another. No one clapped. No one cared. Across the aisle, a girl in an Icelandic jumper scribbled with her left hand and chewed the cuff of her sleeve with a fury that made my own struggle feel anaemic.

It was over. I had finished.

I stacked my books with surgical precision, re-capped the pen, and slid my dissertation into its battered manila envelope. For a second, I considered reading it again, but the thought made me want to tear the whole thing to shreds and start over. I stood, my legs unsteady, and gathered my notes into a single, shambolic wad.

The walk to the submission box was short but ceremonial. My trainers squeaked on the vinyl, every step announcing my exhaustion to the world. I dropped the envelope into the battered plastic crate, watching it settle on a bed of identical offerings. That was it. No fireworks. No parade. I glanced at the other envelopes, some names I recognised, most I didn't, and wondered if any of us would be remembered at all, or if we'd just be sorted and marked and filed into the abyss.

On the way out, I stopped at the vending machine, fed in the last of my change, and punched the button for coffee. The machine hiccupped, then dispensed a cup of liquid that tasted of burnt beans and old hope. I took a sip, winced, then let the cup warm my hand as I stepped into the corridor.

The cold air hit me like a slap. I inhaled, and for the first time in weeks, the breath came easy.

At the doors, Alex waited, back to the glass, hands in the pockets of his anorak, hair still unruly despite his attempts to comb it. He looked up when he saw me, his face a flicker of relief and something else. Pride, maybe, or just the exhaustion of watching me destroy myself for a cause he couldn't name.

"How'd it go?" he said, voice pitched low.

I shrugged, "it's done."

He grinned, the old, lopsided smile, "that's all they can ask for."

We walked back to halls in silence, the campus empty except for the stragglers: a couple clutching each other for warmth, a group of lads singing tunelessly from the shadow of the refectory. The ground was littered with the detritus of spring, discarded wrappers, exam timetables, the occasional lost scarf.

Inside, the corridor smelled of stale toast and anxiety. Someone had left the telly on in the common room, the volume muted but the faces on screen twisted in perpetual argument. I dropped my books on the desk and flopped onto the bed, staring at the ceiling and letting the fatigue leach out of my bones.

Alex sat beside me, his hand a warm, steady weight on my shoulder. We didn't talk. We didn't need to. The world was still spinning, but for once I felt no obligation to keep pace.

Tomorrow there would be more, more exams, more essays, more hours lost to the grind, but for tonight, I let myself rest. I closed my eyes, the pain in my hand a small price to pay for the simple fact of being finished, at least for now.

Sleep came hard, but when it came, it was deep and dreamless. I woke hours later to the sound of rain on the window, the sky outside heavy and new. I flexed my fingers, testing the damage, and found that they still worked. I rolled over, pulled the blanket tight, and let myself drift.

There was nothing else to do but wait.

The days after the last exam lost all definition. For the first time in three years, there was no timetable, no lectures, nothing but a void of waiting. I slept at odd hours, ate when I remembered, and spent long afternoons sprawled in the sun-blasted quad with a paperback I never bothered to read. Alex drifted in and out of his room, sometimes alone, sometimes trailing a conga line of acquaintances from the rugby club or the JCR. We floated in the liminal space between student and graduate, not quite anything yet.

A week in, the itch to leave campus became unbearable. Alex suggested a road trip, said it would "clear the rot." We took his car, and we drove west with the windows open, eating up the hours with bad music and worse jokes. The world outside the city seemed thin and brittle, fields already going yellow under the June sun, sheep packed into the shade of pylons, the sky a slab of cloudless blue. We stopped at every service station, bought snacks and cans of *Coke*, and dared each other to chat up the bored girls at the tills. Mostly we just laughed, then left, the awkwardness hanging behind us like exhaust.

On the Wirral, Alex was a different animal. His posture changed, looser; he stopped policing his vowels and a slight Scouse twang back into his voice. We camped one night on a stretch of abandoned beach, drank cans of bitter until our teeth felt furry, and lay flat on the pebbles as the tide crept up to our toes. I told him about the old quarry behind my childhood home, how I'd once convinced Sarah it was haunted, and he told me about the time he'd set fire to a golf course and gotten away with it. Our laughter bounced off the water and into the dark, unobserved and unstoppable.

The next morning, he drove us to a bakery in Hoylake where his grandparents used to buy him sausage rolls. We ate them on a bench, the grease congealing on our fingers, and for a second it felt like we could stay there forever, suspended in the buffer zone before real life started up again.

The trip ended in Rochdale, a planned but unspoken compromise. I could sense Alex's nerves as we got closer to the estate, the way he tapped his thumb on the wheel, the way he checked the mirrors more than the road. My mum had insisted he stay the night, even made up the camp bed for him. He needed to be reassured that Sarah would say nothing about her New Year discovery.

The house was exactly as I'd left it, same sagging curtains. Mum met us at the door, already flushed from the heat and the effort of being perfect. She ushered us inside, made tea, and sat us at the kitchen table where I'd once failed every maths assignment of my childhood.

"Lovely to see you again, Alex," she said, pronouncing it *'Al-ecks'*, all consonants. "I am guessing that you have both been very busy in your last term."

Alex smiled, the polite, careful smile I'd seen him use with tutors and new parents, "thanks for having me, Mrs. Parry. And thanks for the spread."

She beamed, poured more tea, then left us alone with the plate of toasted teacakes, "and it's 'Maggie', remember." A playful tone rather than an admonishing one reassured Alex.

We talked about the road trip, the weather, and the state of the roads up north. I watched my mother move around the kitchen, clocked the way she hovered on the edge of the conversation, never quite stepping in. Dad was still at work, and Sarah was in her room, the radio thumping through the floorboards.

After tea, beans on toast, simple and good, we watched TV in the front room. Alex and I shared the old settee, careful not to touch. The six o'clock news ran a story on the miners' strike, and Alex made a crack about Scargill's hair. Mum laughed, then glanced at me, a quick, assessing look. When Dad arrived after a late shift about eight pm, he sized up Alex in a single sweep, grunted approval, and spent the rest of the night pretending to ignore us.

In my room, the camp bed was up against the bookcase as at Christmas, as if that small strip of space would be enough to keep us decent. I flicked off the light and crawled under my duvet, listening for footsteps, for the sound of the TV or my father's snoring through the door. In the dark, I could feel Alex's breathing, slow, careful rhythm, like he was practicing not being noticed.

I waited a full hour before I finally edged off the mattress and onto the cool carpeted floor. My mind spun with everything I wanted to say to Alex, where we'd go from here, how we'd face our families, but when I looked at him under that thin sheet, his skin warm and familiar, all my resolve dissolved. Instead, we kissed, mouths clammy with nerves, hands moving in slow motion as if we were both bracing for a blow. Every touch was tentative, every breath hesitant. When we finally stilled, tangled together in the half-dark, I found myself staring at the single rectangle of streetlight shining through the curtains, as uncertain as I felt.

"I used to hate it here," I whispered, voice unsteady.

He pressed a careless kiss to my temple, a touch meant to soothe, I think, but it only made me twist inside, "it's not so bad," he said, but I could hear the question behind his words: do I hate what I've become?

Sleep didn't come for either of us. His steady breathing beside me became a reminder of the silence between us, a silence I was too frightened to break. Maybe he was waiting for me to say something real; maybe I was just terrified of the truth we might uncover in honest words.

Morning felt sharper than usual. Mum was bustling in the kitchen, frying bacon and fussing over Alex's hair as if she sensed how raw we were. Sarah sat opposite us at the table, eyes narrow and predatory, like she was dissecting every syllable we didn't say. After breakfast, she cornered me in the hallway, arms crossed.

"You're both quiet," she said, "is everything okay?"

My pulse thudded, "yeah. Fine," I lied, plastering on a smile that barely reached my eyes.

"Spill," she pressed. Her determination felt intrusive, and I was torn between relief at someone caring and panic at being exposed.

I sighed, "I'm not even sure what I'm doing after graduation."

Sarah's brow lifted, "but your PGCE …"

"I'll do that, of course," I snapped, hating how defensive I sounded, "it's just… Alex doesn't know where he's headed." My words spilled out, more than I meant to say, and I hated the way Alex's shoulders tensed.

Mum's voice called from the kitchen then, "what's all this plotting about?" she asked, peering around the doorframe. "Those two were always up to something when they were kids," she said to Alex at the table. I knew immediately what Alex would think we were whispering about, and of course he was right in way.

"I was asking Liam if I could go to their graduation," Sarah blurted, even as I felt my cheeks burn.

Alex laughed, too loudly, "I have to graduate first, remember?" His head tipped back, eyes forced shut. I saw mum had reached over to rest a hand on his arm, gentle but desperate.

"You'll do great," she murmured, voice soft around the edges, "you've already achieved so much."

"Thanks, Maggie," Alex whispered, but his next words cut the room in two, "I just wish my own parents felt that way."

"I'm sure they do," Mum reassured with squeeze of Alex's arm.

"Maybe," Alex conceded, "but not enough to ever tell me though."

There was a pause, heavy with everything unspoken and the defeat in Alex's voice, and Mum's face softened, "why don't you three pop down to *the Greengate* for a drink before you head back to Uni?" Her tone made it clear: this wasn't a suggestion. My heart fluttered with gratitude and guilt in the same breath.

I moved to the newel post, grabbed our coats, then hesitated before pinging Alex's across to him, "come on," I said, my voice both gentle and firm, trying to steady the conflict in my chest. For a moment, he flickered a real smile, and I wondered if I'd done the right thing.

"Wait for me!" Sarah called from the stairs. I grabbed Alex's hand, guiding him to the hall, then dared to look back at Mum. I mouthed a trembling "thank you." As we slipped out the door, every step felt like another crossroads, every choice both a relief and a heartbreak.

Alex and Sarah took a table in the corner of the pub. I lingered at the bar, watching them through the smudged mirror behind the bottles. Sarah leaned in toward Alex, her face a mix of concern and curiosity I recognised from childhood, the look that preceded either comfort or an inquisition.

"Is everything alright, Alex?" Sarah asked. He glanced toward me, then back at her, his shoulders rising and falling with a sigh I couldn't hear.

"Yes, I'm sorry about before," he said, voice barely carrying to where I stood, "I let my parents get to me." His smile flickered like a bad connection. "I usually manage to keep it inside, because..." His voice trailed off, and I found myself both desperate to hear and afraid of what he might say.

Sarah reached across the table, "because you didn't want to worry Liam?"

Alex nodded, and something in my chest tightened. I wanted to go to him, but my feet remained rooted to the sticky pub carpet.

"He didn't need to know about the shit with my parents," Alex whispered, "and how they've taken my life away from me."

I watched Sarah's face change, "what does that mean?"

"It means," Alex hesitated, twisting a beer mat between his fingers, "that my parents are probably sending me away."

The landlady appeared with our drinks. I gathered them, torn between rushing over to interrupt and lingering to hear more. Alex leaned closer to Sarah, "Liam said you're good with secrets. Please don't tell him. I need to be the one." As Sarah nodded, I approached the table, heart hammering against my ribs.

"What are you two looking so serious about?" I asked, voice too bright.

Alex's smile was thin as paper, "just warning your sister about my parents if she meets them on Graduation Day."

"I'm sure she will behave herself," I said, grinning while my mind raced through what I might have missed, "won't you, Sarah?"

She nodded and changed the subject to her summer plans. I pretended to listen while watching Alex's face for clues, hating myself for spying and for not asking directly what was wrong.

We left after one drink. Alex seemed lighter, but I felt heavier, weighed down by unasked questions. Dad's parting handshake felt like judgment: "you're not so bad for a posh boy, Alex."

In the car, the silence pressed against my ears. Near campus, Alex pulled over and killed the engine.

"You think they know?" he finally asked.

"Doesn't matter," I said, though it did, "they still like you."

His smile, for once unguarded, made me want to confess I'd overheard something—or had I imagined it? The moment to speak passed.

We sat longer than necessary, the radio playing some synth-pop about heartbreak. I wanted to reach for him but worried it would seem like prying rather than comfort.

Eventually, we went inside, back to our uncertain future. We were suspended between truth and pretence, together yet somehow separate. I told myself this was enough for now.

Results day arrived with the precision of a firing squad.

By ten a.m., the *Student Union* was thick with the smell of instant coffee and deodorant, the air sodden with collective dread. Everyone had dressed for the occasion, not in black tie, but in some subtle marker of hope: the lucky t-shirt, the new jeans, the jacket borrowed from a mate who'd survived the ordeal last year. I wore the same shirt I'd worn for my interview three years earlier. It had fit better then.

We milled about in the main lounge, herded by invisible boundaries. History and Politics in one corner, Law and Economics in another, the Arts majors drifting between the two with the easy detachment of the already unemployable. Every so often a rumour would spark: the lists were up, or not up, or they'd been delayed because of a clerical cock-up. We waited, nobody wanting to make the first move, as if the very act of walking toward the admin corridor might tip the scales one way or the other.

Alex found me by the vending machines, his face a shade paler than normal, hair still damp from the shower, "heard anything?" he asked, voice pitched for secrecy.

"Nothing reliable," I said.

He laughed, sharp and quick, "typical."

We loitered with the rest until a girl from Modern Languages came sprinting in, waving her hands and shrieking, "they're up!" The room emptied in seconds, everyone funnelling through the double doors and into the corridor.

The walls were lined with lists, taped side by side, neat as tombstones. The crowd pressed close, each person jostling for a glimpse of their fate. I found my course and ran my finger down the leftmost column, surname, initial, then a string of numbers that might as well have been a medical diagnosis. I traced the line to the first results block: nothing. Not even a third. My stomach dropped. I checked the spelling, convinced they'd managed to lose me in the shuffle. But no, I was not there.

I moved to the next panel, and the next. Still nothing. The sweat prickled under my arms, cold and sudden. My vision narrowed to a strip of yellow paper, the rest of the world a fog of elbows and muttered curses.

Then I saw it.

'Parry, L. J.', Far right, at the very end. *'FIRST CLASS HONOURS, HISTORY'.*

The words didn't look real, as if someone had pasted them on as a prank. My hand shook as I pressed it to the paper, half-expecting it to peel off. Around me, people whooped and wailed, the corridor suddenly a battlefield of joy and carnage. The lad in front of me punched the air and shouted, "get in!", while a girl near the back of the crowd sank to the floor, clutching her cheeks.

I stood there, numb, until someone clapped me on the shoulder, "you did it, mate," said Price, the boy who'd made my first term hell and then spent the next two years borrowing my lecture notes. He looked genuinely pleased, which was almost as shocking as the result itself.

"Thanks," I managed.

I scanned the corridor for Alex. It took a minute, but I spotted him at the far end, standing alone, his back against the wall. I pushed through the throng, catching snippets of congratulation and commiseration as I went.

When I reached him, he was staring at his own name. *'LOWER SECOND, GEOGRAPHY'.*

He looked at me; the smile already fixed in place, "at least I passed," he said.

"I'm sorry," I said, not sure what else to say.

He shrugged, "could have been worse. Could have been a third."

We stood in the corridor for a while, letting the noise wash over us. I didn't want to celebrate, not when he was hurting, but he nudged me with his elbow and said, "you have to go tell your mum. She'll want to know first."

I nodded, but the idea of calling home seemed impossible, as if speaking the words aloud might make them vanish.

We drifted back to the *Union*, where the party had already started. Someone had dragged a crate of *Carlsberg* onto a table and was passing cans around like communion wafers. I accepted one, snapped it open, and let the foam spill over my fingers.

Alex raised his can in salute, "to the future," he said.

I tried to match his tone, but my voice came out thin, "to the future." I knew my future, but Alex's was still unknown, at least to me.

The next hour was a blur. People I barely remembered slapped me on the back, demanded to know how I'd "pulled it off." Even Diana, the perpetual agitator, hugged me and said, "knew you were a closet overachiever." I laughed, but it felt like someone else's joke.

Every so often I'd lose sight of Alex, then spot him across the room, leaning against a pillar or sharing a smoke with someone from his course. He wore the mask well, but I could tell the news had winded him. His parents had expected more, always more.

At some point, the crowd thickened and the music went up, and I found myself outside, gulping air, the can cold in my hand. Alex followed, closing the door behind him.

"You alright?" he said.

I nodded, but the tears were already in my eyes, hot and stupid. He put his arm around me, pulled me in, and for a minute we just stood there, two bodies shivering in the June heat.

"I'm proud of you," he said, quiet and sincere.

"Me too," I said, and meant it. For the hundredth time I avoided the one question I needed to ask him.

We finished our drinks, then went back inside, where the music was louder and the laughter was real. The night blurred into morning, the hours marked only by the slow collapse of bodies onto sofas, the drift of conversation from results to what came next.

As dawn crept through the *Union* windows, I realised the world hadn't changed, not really, but I had.

Graduation Day dawned hot and close, the air already thick by nine. The university's great hall was dressed up for the occasion, banners hung from every rafter, the floors buffed to a high shine that caught the sweat on the faces of a hundred nervous finalists. We arrived early, herded through the staff entrance and up a back staircase to the robing room. The queue for gowns snaked around the stairwell, a parade of unfamiliar shoes and too-short trousers.

I waited my turn, shifting from foot to foot. When I finally made it to the front, the lady behind the table measured my shoulders with a cold tape and handed over a weighty black robe, the hood lined in blue and silver. The smell of mothballs was so strong it nearly made me gag. I slipped it on over my shirt and tie, tried to make the hood sit flat, but it kept slipping off my shoulder. The mirror on the wall gave back an image I barely recognised: gaunt, sleep-deprived, but unmistakably proud.

There was a moment, just before we walked out, when everything went silent. No one spoke. The only sound was the gentle shush of polyester on polyester as hands fussed with sleeves and hoods. I wondered if everyone else was as scared as I was.

The usher led us down a side corridor and into the main hall, where the families had already gathered. The space was immense: stained glass windows, carved wood, the stage set high so the Chancellor could gaze down on his flock. The first rows were filled with dignitaries in coloured gowns, but beyond them, packed in shoulder-to-shoulder, were parents, siblings, and more than a few bored younger children.

I scanned the crowd, heart lurching when I saw them. Mum in her best dress, the green one with the little white flowers that she wore to every "proper" occasion, Dad in his work suit, the only one he owned, the tie knot too tight and the cuffs a bit too short. Sarah was there too, perched on the edge of her seat, hair curled for the first time in years, her feet stuffed into a pair of borrowed heels that looked like they might shatter if she tried to stand.

We filed in row by row, taking our assigned seats. The ceremony was a marathon: an hour of speeches, all of them variations on the theme of "this is only the beginning." The Chancellor, *the Duke of Devonshire*, gave a long, rambling address about "duty to the nation" and "the rewards of effort," his voice curling around every vowel as if afraid to let the meaning escape. I tried to listen, but my mind was stuck on the listless heat, the slow creep of time.

Finally, the names began. Each one read aloud, each graduate walking across the stage to shake hands and collect a scroll. As I rose from my seat, the blood rushed to my head, making the edges of the room shimmer. I kept my eyes straight ahead, focused on the blue carpet. The Chancellor's hand was soft and cold, his ring a heavy glint of gold. He gripped my palm and said, "well done, young man," in a voice that sounded faintly surprised.

I stepped down, scroll in hand, and dared to look up at my family. Mum was already dabbing her eyes, the tissue she'd brought for "emergencies" clutched in her left hand. Dad caught my gaze and gave a little nod, his lips pressed so tight they were just a pale line. Sarah grinned and did a tiny, secret thumbs-up.

After the last name was called, we recessed to the quad, where photographers barked orders and everyone pretended they didn't hate having their picture taken. The Parrys were first in line, Mum insisting we take "a proper family photo." She stood between me and Dad, her arms hooked through ours, and Sarah hovered by my shoulder, the heels already dangling from her fingers. The photographer snapped three quick shots and moved on.

In the queue for refreshments, I spotted the Hugheses gliding through the crowd. Mr. Hughes looked like an advert for double-breasted tailoring, his tie a perfect half-Windsor, his hand resting on the small of Mrs. Hughes's back. She wore a cream suit that would have looked ridiculous on anyone else, but on her it was effortless. They shook hands with the Dean, mingled with other parents, never once breaking stride.

Alex hung behind, his gown rumpled, his hair escaping the careful parting he'd done that morning. When he saw me, he raised his cup and smirked.

"Nice hood," he said, reaching out to flick the lining, "very you."

I tried to laugh, but my mouth was dry, "I keep tripping over the sleeves."

"You get used to it," he said, even though this was his first time too.

We stood a moment, not saying anything. The sun beat down, reflecting off every glass surface. My Dad edged closer, extending his hand to Alex.

"Congratulations, son," he said, and the word landed with a surprising warmth.

Alex smiled, shook hands, then nodded at Mum and Sarah. "Thank you, Mr. Parry."

The Hugheses joined us, and the shift in air was immediate. Mr. Hughes introduced himself to my parents with a smoothness that made Dad's grip on my shoulder tighten. They exchanged the usual pleasantries, comparing careers and children, each staking out their place in the world with careful questions. Mrs. Hughes complimented Mum's dress, then turned to Sarah and asked about her plans for after college. Sarah answered with a muttered, "not sure yet," her eyes darting between me and the ground.

We posed for a few group photos, the two families together, then each on their own. The Parrys lined up stiff and formal, as if waiting for inspection. The Hugheses clustered together with a practiced ease, their arms resting lightly on each other's shoulders. In the last photo, Alex sidled in next to me, his hand briefly brushing the small of my back.

As we were about to leave, I spotted Dr Henderson and led my parents over to meet him.

"Dr Henderson, this is my Mum and Dad and sister," I said. He smiled warmly in recognition.

"You must be very proud of Liam," he said with no hesitation, "as indeed am I." I felt the heat rise in my cheeks at the compliment.

"Thank you for helping my lad so much," my Dad said sincerely, Mum nodded in agreement enthusiastically.

"Yes, thank you Dr Henderson for everything," I reached out and took his hand, "I couldn't have done it without you." We shook hands warmly.

"Oh, you could have my dear boy, you really could," he said quietly. He placed his other hand on top of mine and patted it, "make sure you pop in and see me next term, ok?"

"I will, I promise," and with that we separated and said our goodbyes.

"Oh, what a nice man," my Mum said.

"He is Mum, the best," I concluded. In that moment I resolved to never forget the many lessons I had learned from him, about the truth and intellectual honesty. I hoped that one day I might be the kind of teacher he was.

We moved off to a pub on Oxford Road for a "celebratory lunch," whilst the Hugheses went to a booked table at the *Midland*. I caught Alex's eye as we parted, and he mouthed, "later?" I nodded, and the word hung between us like a lifeline.

At the pub, Mum ordered a bottle of champagne, the cheapest on the menu but still enough to make her giggle every time she sipped it. Dad loosened his tie, looking at me with a pride I'd never seen before. Sarah poked at her chips and asked me if it was true what people said about "the parties" at university. I laughed and told her it was probably worse than she imagined.

We lingered for hours, retelling the day's events as if we'd lived different versions of it. Dad talked about the speeches and Mum replayed every detail of my walk across the stage, insisting she'd known I'd get a first "all along." Sarah said she wished she could have seen the Chancellor's face when I shook his hand, but the seats at the back were too far away for anything except the top of my head.

At dusk, we dad drove us back through the city. The streets were full of graduates, gowns flapping behind them like superhero capes. Every pub and cafe was jammed with families, voices spilling out onto the pavement. I felt hollowed out, stripped of nerves and ceremony, just a body floating through the crowd.

We reached the house just as the sun dipped behind the terraced roofs. Mum unlocked the door, then paused on the threshold, turning to hug me so hard I thought my ribs would crack, "we're so proud, love," she said, the words muffled by my shoulder.

Dad shook my hand again, more awkward this time, then went inside. Sarah hung back, looking up at the sky.

"You looked scared," she said.

"I was," I admitted.

She grinned, "you still did it." I ruffled her hair, which earned me a slap on the arm.

Inside, the house was quiet, the only sound the fridge humming in the kitchen. I changed out of the gown and into my old tracksuit, the fabric soft and familiar. I poured myself a glass of water and sat by the window, staring out at the street.

The day felt unreal, as if it had happened to someone else.

Later, Alex called the house phone. Mum answered, then passed it to me with a knowing look.

"You coming out?" he asked.

"Give me half an hour, dad said he would drive me back."

The evening air clung to my skin as I crossed campus, past the *Union* steps, the blank windows of the administration block. Most of the students had already vanished, gone home for the summer or the rest of their lives. The halls of residence stood silent, every light off but two: the duty porter's den, and one square of yellow on the top floor. Alex's father had told him that as he had paid for the room until the day after Graduation, he might as well use it. Alex didn't need another excuse not to hurry home to the Wirral.

Alex answered the door on the first knock. He wore an old t-shirt, faded blue, and jeans that had started to fray at the bottom. His hair was longer than I'd ever seen it, pushed back behind his ears. For a moment he just looked at me, unspeaking, then stepped aside to let me in.

The room was half unmade, boxes stacked by the door, a suitcase open and already sagging with the weight of clothes and books. The desk had been cleared except for a bottle of wine and two glasses. His bedding was rolled at the end of the mattress, exposing a patch of pilled cotton that looked almost obscene in its nakedness.

"Sit," he said, and I did, folding myself onto the edge of the mattress. He poured the wine with a practiced hand, sloshed a bit into each glass, then sat cross-legged, facing me.

For a while, we didn't talk. He handed me a glass and I drank, the wine sharp and cheap, the taste lingering in the back of my mouth. The silence wasn't uncomfortable, not really, but it was full, charged with all the things we'd put off saying.

He spoke first, "I kept this for us," he said, tilting his glass at the bottle, "thought it'd be nicer than the pub."

I smiled, small, "it is."

We drank, passing the bottle back and forth, the conversation drifting from memories ("Do you remember that night in Beddgelert?") to speculation about the futures of some of their fellow graduates. Finally, though, I could wait no longer and I had to ask the long-delayed question.

"Alex," I paused and fixed my gaze on his bright blue eyes, "what are your plans now?"

"You ever think about just… staying?" he asked. "Never moving on?"

"All the time," I said.

He nodded, as if I'd confirmed a suspicion.

"But we can't, can we?" he noted.

"You could sign up for a PGCE like me?" I maintained my gaze, "we could have another year together."

"My dad's lined up a job in London starting next week," he muttered, eyes fixed on the worn carpet, "legal clerk. Shit pay, but it's a start."

I sat on the edge of the bed, heart thudding, "when did you decide?" My voice sounded shaky, uncertain even to me.

He shrugged, gaze still down, "I didn't. My father did. He assumed I'd fail." Silence stretched between us. The words I wanted stayed tangled in my throat.

"You could refuse it," I ventured, voice almost a whisper.

He laughed, a brittle, uneven sound, "disappoint Dad and end up like my brother, you mean?" He didn't look at me. His shoulders slumped, the hurt in them raw. I remembered how his *golden brother* had dropped out of Oxford, cast out by their parents, forced into an exile.

I swallowed, "what about your mum?"

He laughed again, louder, and I flinched, "my mum," he said, voice suddenly tight, "refused to help after I told her about… us."

My pulse spiked, "you told her?"

He winced, hand rising to his cheek, "big mistake. She slapped me and called us *'disgusting'*. Said I'd wind up like my brother, with nothing, a stain on the family."

My stomach churned. We'd risked everything for each other, and here it was slipping away.

"I'm sorry," I whispered, reaching for his thigh. He brushed my hand aside gently but firmly, "maybe we can find another way, without them?"

He shook his head slowly, "I have to be realistic, Liam. We can't keep doing this. It was incredible, but it's over. It just has to be."

A lump formed in my throat, "is it? I love you, you … stupid posh scouser!" The words tumbled out, frantic, unguarded.

He looked at me as if unsurprised by my confession. Then his voice came, soft, "I know you do. I have for a while. Since Christmas, I think. In fact about the same time I realised I loved you."

Shock and relief hit me at once. Tears sprang unbidden. He blinked, tears gathering in his eyes too.

"Terrible timing to tell you, huh?" he tried to laugh but it came out as a sob. We fell into each other's arms, foreheads together, hands on each other's faces, drowning in grief and love. Eventually, the sobs eased, leaving a fragile quiet, broken only by ragged breathing. I dug a crumpled tissue from my pocket and wiped my face.

I stood, voice hollow, "so this is it for us?"

He opened his mouth, then closed it, finally whispering, "I'm sorry, Li. It has to be."

I lifted my hand to keep him at a distance as I stood. My heart ached at my own gesture.

"Goodbye, Alex."

He exhaled, a soft, broken sound, and I watched him sink back against the bed. The room grew impossibly empty. He didn't look up.

I walked the corridors alone, the echo of my footsteps the only sound. Outside, the air was heavy, the lights along the quad throwing long shadows across the grass. I kept walking, past the library, the lecture halls, the refectory where we'd once thrown mashed potatoes at each other. Every corner was a memory, and every memory was a wound.

At the edge of campus, I stopped and looked back. The residence hall stood dark, its windows blind, its secrets sealed away. I let the grief come, hot, choking, relentless. I wiped my eyes with the heel of my hand, breathing hard, until the worst of it passed.

By the time I reached the gates, the sky was almost as dark as my thoughts. The city stretched out before me, endless and empty. I started walking, not sure where I was going, but certain I wouldn't turn back.

CHAPTER 17: THE ROOM ABOVE THE PUB

August pressed the city down like a thumb on a bruise. By the time I reached *The Crown,* my shirt was pasted to my back and my shoes had scuffed a pale crescent through the dust of Wilmslow Road. The pub stood as it always had, a squat redbrick at the corner of a student estate, its sign cracked and paint-scarred, the *'C'* in *'Crown'* missing a chip so that, from a distance, it read as *'frown'.* Appropriate, I thought, as I shouldered my duffel and pushed through the door.

Inside, the air was a tangle of malt, bleach, and last night's smoke. The lights were dim, little amber pools that made the beer pumps glow like relics and cast the regulars in deep-cut chiaroscuro. There were maybe half a dozen bodies at the bar, all men, all shapes of worn out: a man with a grey plait and tattooed hands cradling a half, two lads in overalls hunched over darts and silence, and at the far end, a figure with a copy of the *Mirror* spread like a privacy shield in front of her.

She was the manager, Carol, we'd spoken on the phone. She set the paper down as I approached, squinting over the top of her glasses in a way that suggested she'd already sized me up before I'd crossed the threshold.

"You must be Liam," she said, voice like gravel left to soak in gin.

I nodded, shifting the duffel to my other shoulder. "Reporting for duty," I said, trying to sound less like I'd rehearsed it.

She grunted, then slid off the stool with a cat's economy of effort. Up close, she was all bone and nerve, with the kind of face you'd see on an old fifty-pence piece: sharp planes, the set of her mouth both resigned and undefeated. She wore her hair in a cropped wedge, silver at the temples, and a shirt with rolled sleeves that showed off a ring of blue-black bruises just below the elbow.

She looked me over, head to foot and back again, "you ever pulled a pint?" she asked.

"Once or twice," I lied.

"We'll see," she said, then turned and beckoned me behind the bar.

The space was smaller than I'd imagined, everything mapped for muscle memory: glasses racked above, drip tray below, a line of battered pumps with the old brands, *Boddies*, *Hydes*, *Worthington*, done up in fake brass. She handed me a damp bar towel and pointed to a stack of empty glasses, "first job, wash and dry. If there's lipstick on them, clean again. No one wants last night's mouth on their pint."

I set my bag down by the icebox and got to work. The heat behind the bar was relentless, amplified by the fug of steam from the hot water tap. I fell into the rhythm, scrub, rinse, dry, stack, focusing on the small satisfactions, the gleam of glass when held up to the light, the clatter as I set them in rows that would make my mother proud.

Carol watched me for a while, arms folded, then nodded once, "not bad," she said, as if conceding a point in a long argument.

She moved to the far pump and pulled a pint with a practiced flick, letting the head settle before topping it off with a flourish. She set the glass on the bar and gestured for me to do the same.

I took the next pump, *Hydes*, my father's favourite, and tried to mimic her motion. I misjudged the pressure, spraying a foam-blot onto my knuckles, but caught the glass before it could overfill. I let it settle, then topped up and wiped the lip with a towel, hoping she wouldn't notice the way my hand shook.

"Needs work," she said, "but it'll do." She took a sip from my pint, smacked her lips, and pushed the glass back at me, "you're drinking that. You pour it, you own it. House rule."

I tasted the beer: flat, but not as flat as my nerves. I set the glass down and focused on the row of taps, memorising their sequence like a code.

The regulars started ordering in slow succession, mostly halves, the odd bottle of brown. I counted out the change with a precision born of childhood sweetshop anxiety, always double-checking before dropping coins into the till. No one spoke to me at first, just nodded or grunted, but I recognised the language: newcomers were to be endured, not engaged.

Carol handled the food orders herself, sliding past me to reach the dumb waiter, her hips navigating the narrow space with unhurried authority. She had a way of moving that made you believe she'd built the place herself, brick by brick.

"Your shift runs five to close," she said, stacking a plate of chips under the heat lamp. "After that, you get a pint, a meal, and a fag on the back steps if you smoke. Room's up the stairs, second on the left. Don't touch anything that's not yours."

She caught my gaze, her eyes pale and unblinking, "questions?"

I shook my head.

She nodded, "you'll do, then." She flicked a glance at the clock. "Now, keep an eye on him," she jerked her thumb at the dartboard, where one of the overalled lads was weaving on his feet, "he'll be sick by half eight if he keeps up."

I made a note, then set about restocking the crisps, arranging the packets by colour and brand. The motions were familiar, soothing in their pointlessness. I watched the room as I worked, mapping the regulars: the pair in the corner playing cribbage, the man with the plait who nursed a single pint for two hours, the group of students who drifted in after seven, loud and anxious, radiating the kind of energy that made the old-timers roll their eyes.

The hours bled together, marked only by the diminishing level in the barrels and the slow, inevitable deterioration of the regulars' conversation. By half nine, the bar was sticky with spilt lager and sweat. The dartboard lad had indeed been sick, but made it to the toilets in time. Carol gave me a nod of approval as I returned from cleaning up, and even the man with the plait grunted something that might have been "good lad" as I passed.

At closing, I helped stack chairs on tables, wiped down the sticky surfaces, and swept up the clots of peanut shells under the stools. Carol locked the front door and counted out the till, her fingers quick and sure on the notes.

She handed me a battered fiver and a pound's worth of coins, "first night bonus," she said, "don't get used to it." I pocketed the money and thanked her, then hoisted my duffel and headed for the stairs.

The corridor above the pub was barely wide enough to turn around in, the carpet a faded tartan that sucked at your feet with every step. My room was as promised: second on the left, a rectangle just big enough for a single bed, a wardrobe with one functioning door, a small desk and a window that looked out onto the soot-blackened bricks of the takeaway next door.

I dropped my bag on the bed and sat beside it, letting the silence close in around me. The only sound was the distant hum of traffic and, faintly, the clatter of Carol doing the last sweep below.

I unpacked my things: a stack of textbooks, a sheaf of forms for the teacher training course, a photo of Sarah and my Mum in Scarborough, both squinting against the sun. I stood the photo on the desk, then laid out the training materials in a grid, careful not to let the edges overlap. My hands trembled as I did it, but I told myself it was just fatigue.

There was no room for decoration, no room for nostalgia. The window was stuck half-open, and the air that drifted in was thick with the smell of hot oil and cigarettes from the takeaway. I watched the yellow light from the streetlamps flicker on the wall, then closed my eyes.

I should have been thinking about tomorrow, the routines, the bar orders, the impossible number of new faces to memorise, but all I could see was the look on Alex's face as I'd said goodbye, the way his jaw had set as if he could bear anything but hope.

I tried to shove it aside, but the memory sat in my chest, heavy as stone. I ran my thumb along the edge of the desk, feeling the splinters, then got up and opened the training folder. I read the first page three times before I understood the words.

After a while, I stripped to my boxers and crawled into the narrow bed. The springs groaned under my weight. I lay flat, arms at my sides, staring at the water-stain on the ceiling that looked, if you squinted, like a continent breaking apart.

I thought about Alex, about the boys at the bar, about the way Carol's voice had softened, just for a second, when she'd said, "you'll do."

I thought about the months ahead, the endless parade of strangers and the slow accumulation of trust. Eventually, I slept, the smell of beer and bleach clinging to my skin, the sounds of the world outside dulled to a kind of mercy.

Three weeks in, I could pour a pint without thinking, or even looking. I'd learned how to break up a fight before the first punch was thrown, how to clear a glass with a single swipe, how to tell the difference between a rugby team's roar and the beginnings of a proper riot. *The Crown* became its own universe, ruled by the unspoken laws of shift work and regulars' entitlement, the night divided by last orders and the silent choreography of closing time.

My mornings were simple, wake at ten, toast and instant coffee in the kitchen, then a slow trudge through the day's reading for teacher training. By five, I changed into my work shirt, sleeves rolled up, a biro in the breast pocket for quick notes or tallying up, then descended to the world below.

If Carol was the brains of the operation, Jenny was its beating heart. She was just turned nineteen, already on her second adult life, with bleach-blonde hair and eyeliner thick as fence tar. Her laugh could start a chain reaction from one end of the bar to the other. She flirted with everyone, especially the postgrads who thought "banter" was a dialect.

She called me "lad," as in, "oi, lad, use the drip tray." If I fumbled a pint, she'd sing out, "I said pour, not drown the bastard," and when she caught me reading at the bar, she'd roll her eyes and say, "what's the point? It's all bollocks anyway." I liked her, but I didn't trust her with my insides.

The students came in waves, first the pre-drinkers, then the serious drinkers, then the afters crowd, loud and shiny with ambition and terror. I grew adept at clocking their stories in the space between orders: the ones who'd never been away from home before, the ones already missing it, the ones who acted like they owned the place but paid in fifty-pence coins. They wore their tribal colours on their sleeves: United, City, or, for the brave, Leeds. Their energy was relentless, their emotions always set to maximum.

The regulars ignored the students, except when they could not. The regulars lived at the bar, their hands permanently wrapped around a pint glass, their jokes so old they had to be watered to sprout a laugh. I watched them with the same fascination I'd once reserved for rare birds, beautiful, doomed creatures, surviving on nothing but habit and the stubbornness of their own stories.

One Thursday, we got a booking for twenty, no food required, just a "few" tables and plenty of ale. Carol didn't blink, "it's the miners," she said, as if this explained everything, "solidarity night. Keep the Union Jacks off the bar and they'll be fine."

The miners arrived at six, in a convoy of battered *Cortinas* and borrowed vans, boots caked in mud even in September. They took over the back room, three to a table, faces red and shining, voices too big for the low ceiling. Their leader, an older bloke with a nose like a caulking mallet, came to the bar and ordered a round, the coins from his pocket spilling out like ballast.

I poured the first pints, watching the way his hands shook just slightly as he lined up the change on the bar, "on strike?" I asked, knowing the answer.

He nodded, eyes steady, "day one-four-seven," he said. "But who's counting."

I slid the pints down the bar, taking care not to spill. Jenny leaned over, popping gum, and asked, "you raising money for the kids' fund tonight?"

He smiled, showing a line of broken teeth, "always are, love. We pass the hat, maybe some of these students will cough up, eh?"

"Put a tin on the bar," Jenny said, "we'll help you shake it."

They brought in the collection tins, a pair of old *Nescafé* jars with *"NUM"* scrawled on masking tape across the front. By seven, the jars were already half-full, and by nine, the miners sang so loud they drowned out the piped-in music. The students joined in, first as a joke, then not. Even the regulars raised their glasses, united in their suspicion of the government, their nostalgia for when things had been harder and therefore, they insisted, better.

Carol watched from the edge, arms folded, face unreadable. She had warned me once about getting involved, "politics is like beer, good until it's gone sour, then it ruins the night for everyone." I took the warning as a challenge.

After last orders, when the singing had turned to mumbling and the jars were clinking with silver and copper, I found myself alone behind the bar, clearing the last of the glasses. The mallet-nosed miner waited, a fresh pint in hand, the collection jars at his feet.

He held out a pound note, too much for a tip, not enough for a bribe, "thanks, lad," he said. "You did us proud."

I took the note, not sure what to say. The sincerity in his voice made my skin prickle. I remembered my father at the kitchen table, union letters spread out, the arguments that followed. I wondered if he'd ever felt as lost as these men, or as proud.

I said, "good luck," but it sounded hollow.

He nodded, patted my arm, then drifted back to the others.

I counted the take after they left, four hundred in loose change, an impossible sum for a single night. I showed the total to Carol, expecting her to check the maths.

She just nodded, once, and said, "you're wasted here, Liam."

I flushed, unsure if it was insult or compliment.

Closing was always a ritual: chairs upturned, floors mopped, the dregs of lager poured down the drain. Tonight, with the noise gone, the pub felt twice as empty. Jenny stayed to help, her hair tied up in a messy knot, her hands quick with the spray bottle. We worked in silence, side by side at the bar, until she said, "you ever get tired of pretending?"

I looked up, "pretending what?"

She smirked, wiping down a pump handle, "that you're happy, that this is enough. That you don't want to be somewhere else."

I thought about it, then lied, "doesn't everyone?"

She laughed, a soft, tired sound, "not everyone's smart enough to know it." She set down the spray, folded her arms, and regarded me with a look I'd never seen from her before, open, a little bit dangerous.

"Let's get out of here," she said, in her typically flirty way. Over the weeks we had developed a good working relationship and could put on a show for the regulars. She'd try to put ice-cubes down the back of my trousers when I bent over, or I'd try to flick one into her cleavage. In my mind it was playful fun, and I honestly began to enjoy my shifts with her.

We moved to the back steps, where we smoked and watched the neon *'Closed'* sign flicker in the wet darkness. She sat on the top step, knees drawn to her chest, the glow of her cigarette painting her face with slow orange. I sat next to her, close enough to feel the warmth from her skin.

She turned, eyes hooded, and said, "you're a good lad, Liam. Too good for this lot." Then she leaned in and kissed me, quick at first, then deeper, her hand cold and rough on the back of my neck.

For a second, I kissed her back, the muscle memory automatic, the taste of beer and smoke and lipstick. Then I pulled away, gently, not wanting to hurt her, but needing to breathe.

She studied my face, unsmiling, "you're somewhere else entirely, aren't you?"

I nodded, ashamed at the realisation that my playfulness had been misinterpreted as flirting. It reminded me instantly of the way I had lead Amanda on, and the shame I still felt about that.

She flicked her cigarette into the dark and stood, dusting off her skirt, "don't be sorry," she said, "just be careful, yeah?" She left me on the step, the night thick and close around me. To her great credit this briefest of romantic encounters didn't change the way we worked together, and I thanked her later for not "making things weird", to which she, typically, replied, "get over yourself lad!".

Back in my room, the hum of the city rolled over the rooftops, cars, laughter, a siren somewhere far off. I sat and watched the *'Closed'* sign buzz and dim, buzz and dim, until I couldn't see it anymore.

That night, I didn't sleep. I sat at my desk, the single bulb swinging overhead, and listened to the drunks bellowing down Wilmslow Road, the taxis crawling past like clockwork mice. My body felt oddly detached, as if my hands and eyes and heart belonged to three separate people. I made tea and let it go cold. I opened my course binder and closed it again. At some point, I found myself staring at the blank page of my journal, pen in hand, as if waiting for instructions. The page stayed blank for a long time.

When the words finally came, they came in a rush. I addressed it, *Dear Alex'*, then scratched that out and wrote just his name. The pen stuttered on the paper, my hand shaking with fatigue or something worse.

I wrote: *'I'm supposed to say I'm fine. I'm not';*

I wrote: *Every night, I try to remember the sound you made when you laughed. I'm losing it*';

I wrote: *Jenny kissed me tonight. I didn't feel anything. I wanted to, but I couldn't*';

I wrote: '*I can't be angry at you. But I wish I could*';

I wrote: '*This is what I wanted, right? To be my own person? To not have to hide?*';

I wrote: '*You said once that the world was cruel because it couldn't be any other way. I think you liked that about it*';

I wrote: '*I miss you. I miss hating you. I miss wanting you*'.

When I ran out of words, I signed it, then crossed out the signature, then signed again with only my initial. I folded the page, then unfolded it, then tore it into quarters and let the pieces fall into the wastebasket. I watched them drift and settle, wondering what it would feel like to be so light.

I slept for an hour, maybe two, then woke before the alarm, my throat raw and eyes stinging. I dressed for the morning studies, but before I left, I fished one of the letter scraps from the bin and tucked it into my pocket. It felt like a relic, or maybe a warning.

After breakfast, I walked to the barbershop on Oxford Road, the tips from last night's shift jangling in my fist. The shop was empty but for the old Greek man who ran it and pop music droning from a radio in the corner. I sat in the cracked leather chair and asked for a short back and sides.

He nodded, fingers efficient, and set to work. The scissors whispered around my ears, and I watched the hair fall, brown and spent, collecting on the white bib like years shed in handfuls.

When he finished, he brushed my shoulders, held a mirror behind my head, and said, "handsome boy." His voice was dry, like paper left out in the sun.

I looked at myself in the mirror: the cut made me look older, my jaw sharper, my eyes bigger and browner than I remembered. I looked like someone who didn't have time to care about who he used to be. I thanked the barber, tipped him too much, and left, blinking in the new sunlight.

The second step was the clothes. I went to the *Oxfam* shop by the station, knowing I could stretch a fiver into something almost respectable. I chose two button-down shirts, one white, one pale blue, and a checked jacket with the lining coming loose at the sleeve. In the changing room, I tried them on, layering the jacket over the shirt, turning this way and that in the cracked mirror.

The clothes changed me. In the jacket, I looked like I could stand in front of a classroom and not fall apart. I practiced my teacher's face, neutral, attentive, faintly amused, and realised how easy it would be to hide behind it. I could be sensible, credible, safe. I could be invisible, if I wanted.

I bought the shirts and jacket, had them folded in brown paper, and carried them home like a parcel of possibility. In my room, I hung them on the wardrobe, then sat on the bed and pressed my palm to the shape of the letter scrap in my pocket.

The rest of the day I spent reading, making notes for my first placement at the local school, copying out lesson plans until my handwriting blurred into a line. I didn't think about Alex, or Jenny, or the miners. I tried not to think at all.

That evening, I dressed in the new clothes and stood in front of the window, practicing my posture, my handshake, my smile. I watched myself in the glass, the old and the new layered like a double exposure. The longer I looked, the less I recognised the boy with the nervous grin and the sharp hairline, the boy who'd walked away from something he couldn't name.

I drew the curtains, then went back to my desk, switched on the lamp, and began again. Tomorrow, I would show up. I would stand straight, speak clearly, count out the change without trembling. I would be the person they needed me to be, even if it was only for one day at a time.

And, if I missed the sound of his laughter, or the taste of his skin, or the feeling of being wanted by someone who understood how lonely a city could be, I would fold that memory down to a scrap of paper and keep it safe, close to my heart, where no one could see.

I practiced my teacher voice one more time, then flicked off the lamp, the world going suddenly, mercifully, dark.

CHAPTER 18: LESSONS IN TEACHING

My first teaching placement started for five weeks in November. It was in an 11-16 comprehensive school in Old Trafford. Built in the early 1970s, when the school leaving age was increased to sixteen, the building was beginning to fray a little around the edges. It consisted of two three storey wings – one for years seven to nine and the other for the 'upper school'. The central block contained the staffroom, assembly hall, library and kitchens. A large, and modern, sports hall was detached and set in the playing fields to the rear.

My teaching career began with year ten English literature, and by the end of first period, the board was already an unholy mess, chalk dust stippling my knuckles and knifing the air like cigarette smoke. I was halfway through the "introduction" to today's lesson, Ted Hughes, *'Hawk Roosting'*, but the class's collective attention was off somewhere with the last drizzle of autumn, oozing out beyond the double-glazed windows. The fluorescent tubes overhead flickered in arrhythmic pulses, lending every moment the feel of a bad interrogation.

Thirty sets of eyes watched me, most with blank suspicion, some with open hostility, the rest busy writing in the margins of their exercise books, things that had nothing to do with hawks or poetry. A murmur rolled in unpredictable eddies from the back rows, always a seat ahead of my sightline, like a rat that only appeared when you looked away.

I cleared my throat, "right, class. Today's poem is about a hawk. Not a cartoon hawk, not a nice zoo one, this is a killing machine. Who's got a thought?"

An immediate, mass silence, each kid snapping shut their willingness like a trap. A lone hand, half up, uncertain, waved in the second row.

I pointed, "Shazad. Go on."

He hesitated, eyes darting to his mates, "it's about… being in charge? Like, the hawk's in charge?"

A ripple of laughter at the word "charge," which had become code for a fart in Year Nine, but I rode over it. "Excellent, Shazad! Top of the food chain. So, why's the hawk so obsessed with power?"

From the back, a low voice, Kevin, shot: "because it's a knob-head." Laughter. He slumped further in his seat.

Mrs. Blackwell, Head of Department, sat near the radiator with a notepad in her lap, the kind of old-fashioned spiral-bound thing I associated with police statements and my mother's shopping lists. She didn't move, didn't even blink, just flicked her biro once along a margin and fixed her gaze on Kevin.

I ignored the disruption, "possibly, Kevin, but let's try to keep our language professional. How about, *'arrogant?' 'Vain?' 'Narcissistic?'*"

Kevin grunted, folded his arms, and crumpled the worksheet into a tight little ball. The muscle in his jaw ticked.

I kept going, breaking the poem into lines, underlining words: *'hooked head', 'perfect kills', 'I hold Creation in my foot'.* The wall clock ticked like a slow leak. Somewhere, someone was sneaking *Haribo* under the table; the wrappers rustled with all the subtlety of a hedgehog in a crisp packet.

I worked the room, doing what the books called *'positive reinforcement'.* Every time someone ventured a guess, I said "Nice!" or "I like that!" even when the answer was more about winding me up than engaging the poem. It had taken only a week to realise these kids could smell weakness, and that my only armour was to pretend, always, that I was the most patient man in the world.

But even with all that, the class would revert. In every lesson, one kid, the canary, cracked first. Here, it was always Kevin. He was a study in antagonism: a permanent sneer, a mop of hair that defied any comb, hands tattooed in biro with band logos and football scores. He wore his school tie so loose it hung like a noose for a much smaller boy.

He muttered, "this is bullshit," loud enough for me and Mrs. Blackwell to hear.

"Kevin, could you share with the class what's so…bullshit about the poem?" My voice came out too teacherly, too canned.

He glared at me, then at the page, "just… it's made up. Who gives a shit what a bird thinks?"

This, at least, made the front rows laugh, and I felt the control slip another notch. I tried a softer approach, "okay, fair. But Hughes uses the hawk to say something about power.

About violence. Maybe even about humans. Can anyone tell me what that might be?"

Another silence. The clock dripped seconds. I could see Mrs. Blackwell writing, her pen moved with ruthless precision, like she was scoring a boxing match and I was already losing on points.

I decided to walk it back, slow things down, "tell you what," I said, "let's try reading it together. Kevin, you can start, just the first two lines."

His face flushed, "can't be arsed," he said, but his voice had lost some bite.

I knelt beside his desk. Up close, I saw the edges of his worksheet were torn, the handwriting inside was a mess, uneven, jagged, as if he was trying to mask his own struggle with the words. His pencil lay untouched atop the page, bitten in half. His lips moved, tracking the poem, but his eyes darted along the text, stuttering at the lines.

It clicked: the signs, from my university seminars and the special needs handouts. The way he "couldn't be arsed" was a shell; underneath, he couldn't read it clean. The letters danced for him.

I knelt lower, quiet, "want a hand?"

He shrugged, aggressive in the way only a child is when terrified of being pitied, "don't matter."

I covered the rest of the poem with my hand, leaving only the first two lines, "read these. Out loud, if you like."

He stared at the page, then at the ceiling, "I... sit in the... top of the wood, my eyes closed." He fumbled the 's' on "woods," squinted, but pushed through, "inaction, no falsifying dream."

I finished it for him, "between my hooked head and hooked feet." I let the silence sit for a beat, "that's good. That's what poets do, write how it really is."

He looked at me then, his face changed, suspicion replaced by something rawer, "does it matter?"

I nodded, "if you ask Hughes, it's the only thing that does."

He looked down again, tracing the margin with his pencil. The tension drained, just a little, from his body.

I stood, "class, let's do it together. I'll read; you follow. If you can't keep up, just listen." I started from the top, reading slow, giving each line a little more weight than necessary, hoping the rhythm would pull the class along. It mostly worked: the side conversations died down, and a few faces, the kids who never spoke, actually watched me.

I saw Mrs. Blackwell pause, her biro stilled for the first time.

When the bell rang, the noise level exploded, a flock of bodies and backpacks battering the aisles. I braced myself as Kevin swept past, waiting for the dig, but he just mumbled "cheers" and stuffed the worksheet in his jacket pocket.

When the last student was out, I leaned on the desk and let the quiet suck at my bones. My shirt stuck to my back, my hands shook from the strain of pretending calm. Mrs. Blackwell approached, notebook in hand. Her lipstick was a perfect line, her shoes the same black as the morning outside.

"Well done," she said, voice both dry and, I thought, slightly impressed, "you have the patience of a saint, Mr. Parry."

I smiled, then immediately regretted how sheepish it felt. She paged through her notes, "Kevin can be difficult. You handled him well."

"Thank you," I said, still uncertain if this was a trap.

She closed the notebook with a snap, "but you'll need to toughen up. The class senses kindness, and while that's not a crime, it's not always a virtue. You have the instincts, but sometimes kindness needs a backbone."

I let the words hang there, unsure what response was wanted. "of course."

She smiled, the faintest twitch, "we'll discuss the lesson in more detail later. Good recovery, though. Most of the new ones crack by the end of week one of teaching practice."

She left, the echo of her shoes ticking down the corridor like a metronome set too fast. I looked at the poem on the board, the smudges where my hand had failed to wipe the words clean. For a second, I thought of Alex, the way he'd once told me that "kids respect an honest bastard more than a nervous genius." I wondered if he'd ever read Hughes, or if he would have laughed at the bird's arrogance too.

The room was empty, but for the thrum of the lights and the drift of dust settling on every surface. I picked up the worksheet Kevin had left behind, smoothed its edges, and read the single word he'd written in the margin:

True.'

I folded the sheet, slid it into my jacket pocket, and made for the staff room, the feeling in my chest equal parts pride and dread.

My next class was in ten minutes, but for now, I let the hush surround me, and I let myself believe, just for a moment, that I was not completely failing at this new life. At least this next lesson, A Level history, was more likely to be well-received by its recipients.

After the final bell, the staff room had a post-mortem quiet, broken only by the odd clack of a mug set down or the muted drone of *Radio 2* leaking from a battered radio near the tea urn. I'd always imagined teachers as stern lifers, but in here, at least, they shed their armour: neckties slack, blouses untucked, voices low and sodden with the day.

Mrs. Blackwell beckoned me with a single crook of her finger. She already had two mugs lined up on the *Formica*, both filled to the legal limit with milk and a dusting of instant coffee granules, "you take sugar?" she asked, already spooning it in.

"One, please," I said, conscious of every move, like I'd been called to the head's office and told to 'act natural.'

She sat, arranged her skirt, and took a loud, slurping sip. I set my bag under the chair and tried to match her posture, upright but not rigid, hands folded around the mug. My fingers felt sticky from nerves and the previous lesson's chalk.

She took another sip, watching me over the rim, "do you have experience with special needs? Dyslexia, perhaps?"

"Some," I said, "we covered it at uni, but I haven't had much hands-on until now."

"Not many do," she said, "most just write them off as trouble-makers. Good to see a fresh perspective."

I nodded.

We sat a minute, the silence stretching. The staff room was a time capsule: corkboard full of faded photos, a shelf of *Reader's Digest* novels, a box of *Celebrations* on the windowsill with only the *Bountys* left. I looked at the far wall, where last year's exam results were pinned up, each name highlighted in green or red.

Mrs. Blackwell set her mug down, fingers drumming the handle, "tell me, Mr. Parry, is there someone at home waiting for you?"

The question hung in the air, casual as a landmine.

I felt my knuckles whiten on the mug. "Sort of," I said, slow, "my girlfriend's up in Scotland, doing her postgrad at Stirling Uni. We're long-distance, for now."

She smiled, just a hint, "that's hard, I imagine."

I shrugged, the way I'd practiced, "it's not ideal, but we manage. Calls at the weekend, the odd letter."

"You seem very devoted," she said, studying my face.

I forced a laugh.

Mrs. Blackwell nodded, as if confirming something, "my daughter's about your age. She's at York, studying English. She was always the reader in the family, taught herself to write poems at eight. I always thought she'd end up a teacher."

I smiled, trying to look interested and not panicked.

"She's still single," Mrs. Blackwell said, then added, "not that I'm matchmaking." She laughed, brittle, and for a moment looked almost embarrassed.

"Maybe you could introduce us," I joked, and she smiled, though her eyes never softened.

We drifted into safer ground, lesson plans, the upcoming open day, the football team's dire prospects this season. I found myself slipping into the performance, offering up bits of "Amanda" as needed: her fondness for Scottish bands, her collection of battered *Penguin* paperbacks, her allergy to cats. It was almost easy, the way the details layered on themselves, the same way I used to tell my mother about imaginary friends to avoid awkward questions.

Mrs. Blackwell pressed a hand to her mug, then let it go, "you're very convincing," she said.

"Sorry?"

"About teaching," she clarified, "you have a way of holding the class together, even when you're not sure yourself."

"Oh," I said, relieved, "I suppose I'm learning as I go."

She stood, gathering the empty mugs, "that's all any of us do. Learn, then bluff, then learn again."

I stood too, reaching for my bag. She waved me off, "leave it. I'll wash up. You look dead on your feet."

"Thanks," I said, and meant it.

As I left, she called out, "don't stay up too late. Early start tomorrow, assembly in the hall."

I nodded, the wordless affirmation of a man who would absolutely stay up too late. The corridor outside was cold and silent. I let out a breath I hadn't realised I'd been holding. The mask, the story, the whole careful scaffolding, it sagged the instant I was out of sight. My heart thudded, stupidly, as if I'd been running.

On the walk home, I tried to picture Amanda, her face, her voice, the tiny, perfect flaws of memory, but all I saw was the back of Alex's head, the way he never looked back in the corridors at uni, the way he could conjure a lie and never flinch.

I wondered what he'd make of Mrs. Blackwell. I wondered if I'd fooled her, or just confirmed what she already suspected.

I got to *the Crown*, ducked through the side door, and went straight to my room. I flicked on the lamp and sat at the desk; the day's lesson plan splayed in front of me. The words on the page blurred, and I realised my hands were still trembling, ever so slightly.

I set them flat on the *Formica*, watched the veins go blue with the pressure, and waited for the shaking to stop.

Saturday night, and Manchester thrummed with the urgent need to forget. The city centre choked on exhaust and sodium light, every pub a crucible for the week's disappointments. I'd spent the afternoon at the *Rylands Library*, the red-brick sanctum cool and shadowed as a confessional, but even its hush couldn't scrub the noise from my skull. By the time I stepped out, evening had spread itself across the pavements in a slick of January rain.

The walk to *Piccadilly* took me past the same battered parade: a snarl of minicab offices, charity shops papered with *'Closing Down'* signs, kebab takeaways advertising "authentic" meat. Above it all, the clock tower at *Town Hall* blinked midnight even when it was barely six. My jacket was wrong for the weather, second-hand wool, almost waterproof, only if you never went outside. Within ten steps I felt the cold at my collar, creeping down like the hand of a dead uncle.

I told myself I was heading home, but the city nudged me off course. I found myself on the edge of Canal Street, the light there a different species, brighter, meaner, pulsing out from the neon letters of gay bars with names like *The Rembrandt* and *Via Fossa*. The pavement glistened, each puddle a wonky mirror. I walked slower here, out of curiosity at first, then guilt, then something like nostalgia for a life I'd never lived.

I'd read about this stretch in *the Guardian*, how it was safer now, how the raids were less frequent, how you could even bring your mum for a drink at Pride if you wanted. But the men who loitered in doorways looked nothing like my mother's idea of community. They didn't look like Alex, either, or the version of myself I sometimes caught in the mirror after a double shift, hair wild and face gone hollow with hunger.

The Rembrandt was the first bar I passed. A bouncer in a quilted bomber jacket nodded at me, lips pressed thin, as if daring me to pretend I belonged. I kept walking, the warmth and music leaking through the door a physical force against the chill. At the end of the street I stopped, looked in the window of a takeaway I'd never noticed before, then looped back.

I circled the building twice more, each time getting a little closer, letting the press of strangers and the drone of wet traffic convince me I could slip inside and disappear. My palms were sweating, my breath short. On the third pass, someone called out:

"Oi, darling. Lost your nerve?"

The voice was rough with booze, but friendly. I looked up and saw a woman, no, a drag queen, full sequins, cigarette in one hand and pint in the other, leaning out of a doorway. Her wig was a dome of blue curls, lacquered to withstand a nuclear winter.

I flushed, "just passing through," I said, lamely.

She laughed, a sound that carried halfway down the street, "first time, love? Come in, we don't bite, unless you ask nicely."

A couple of lads in football scarves hooted. I felt their eyes on me, appraising. I was about to cross the street, make my escape, when the drag queen added, softer: "no shame in being nervous. We all start somewhere."

That nearly did me in. The kindness of it, the sheer fucking decency. But instead of walking in, I turned away, hands jammed so tight in my pockets I thought the seams might split. I heard another burst of laughter behind me, good-natured, not cruel, and the humiliation burned all the way up my neck.

I ended up at the university, ducking into the back entrance of the Arts Building, hoping to lose myself in its maze of corridors. The place was supposed to be locked up after hours, but the security was for show: any student with the right ID, or a bit of charm, could get in. I found the *Film Society's* screening room, its door propped open and a flyer taped to the wall: "Tonight: *'Paris, Texas'* – 7PM. Free to All."

I slipped inside, the darkness a balm. The only light was the spill from the projector at the back, its bulb making a square of gold on the far wall. The seats were two-thirds empty, most of the audience pairs or groups. I took one in the middle, far enough from the aisle that I wouldn't have to talk to anyone.

The film was already halfway through. On the screen, *Harry Dean Stanton* wandered a desert, eyes rimmed with sand and loss. The soundtrack was a single, unbroken guitar line, sad and beautiful as a last chance. I tried to lose myself in the story, but my mind kept skipping back: to the queen at *the Rembrandt,* to the shiver of shame when I'd run.

Someone a few rows down unwrapped a sweet, the noise so loud it broke the spell. I stared at the back of his head, willing him to turn around, to notice me, to ask if I wanted a sweet too. Of course he didn't. Nobody ever does, in real life.

On screen, the main character wandered through Houston, searching for a woman in a red dress. I found myself tearing up, furious at the film, at myself, at the world that made even sitting in a dark theatre feel like an act of treason. I thought of Mrs. Blackwell, her way of asking questions she already knew the answers to. I thought of the partially fictional Amanda, the made-up girlfriend I'd conjured into being, waiting patiently in Scotland for a visit that would never come.

I thought about *the Rembrandt,* and the queen who'd called me "darling," and how for half a second, I'd believed her.

The credits rolled. People shuffled out, talking in whispers about the cinematography or the ending. I stayed seated, letting the music play out, watching the light fade to black.

When the room was empty, I got up and walked home. The city was even colder now, the pubs letting out, the streets alive with the kind of energy that only comes from knowing tomorrow is Sunday and nothing bad can happen.

At *the Crown,* I let myself in through the back. The pub was dark, save for the TV's blue flicker in the front bar and the soft, intermittent clink of bottles as Carol did the till. Halfway to my landing I almost tripped over an envelope, face-down on the tread, paper slightly buckled from the damp that always crept in at this hour.

The address was in my mother's hand, written in the tight, careful print she used for bills and Christmas cards. Underneath, in a different hand, angular, impatient, blue ballpoint pressed so hard it dented the paper, was the original. I didn't need to see the return address. I knew it was from Alex. I'd recognise his handwriting anywhere: the aggressive slope of the capital *L*, the way the numbers all leaned to the right, like they couldn't wait to get on with it.

I hesitated, thumb sliding under the corner, then stuffed the letter in my back pocket and finished the climb. My room was cold and bright, the window left open by the cleaner. I filled the kettle and propped the letter against the battered teapot, forcing myself not to look at it as I made coffee. The ritual helped, sugar first, then granules, water only when it was boiling so the mix would bloom. I lit a cigarette and sat on the bed, watching the envelope out of the corner of my eye.

It had been three months since I'd heard from him. Not counting the postcard he'd sent in October, a picture of the Thames at dusk, with only *'Hope you're alive, London's fine, A'* written on the back, no address for reply. That had felt pointed, and I'd carried it around in my wallet for weeks before finally shredding it in a fit of self-respect. But this was different: thicker, heavier, obviously more than a single sheet.

I finished my coffee, stubbed out the cigarette, and finally picked up the letter. My hands shook, just a little. I peeled the flap open. Inside was three pages, densely filled. The opening lines were pure Alex, irreverent, insincere, desperate to prove he was thriving. He'd settled in his job, but *'don't tell anyone, or my father will make me stay forever'.* He'd moved into a flat in Camden with two other lads from Manchester; *'the place is a dump, but the kettle works and there's a Sainsbury's next door so I'll survive'.* He wrote about going to a gig in Brixton, how the crowd reminded him of the *'good old days'* at uni, which he pretended never happened. There was a bit about the miners' strike, how nobody in London seemed to care. *'It's all yuppies and actors here. People in Rochdale would punch them on sight'.*

The tone was cheerful, even flippant, but I could hear the effort in it, the strain behind the jokes. Every paragraph ended with a hedge, *'maybe I'll get used to it', 'could be worse', 'still not as bad as the school dinners'*. He mentioned dating a girl from work, *'don't laugh, she's actually quite clever, and no, I haven't told her about you, because why would I?'*. The parenthetical stung more than it should.

It wasn't until the bottom of the second page that he wrote what I'd waited months to read:

'Don't worry about me anymore. I'm all right. I've settled here, more or less, and I've made some new mates so you don't need to feel guilty, if you ever did. You always were the better person at this kind of thing. Or maybe just better at lying'.

The last page was shorter. He apologised for not writing sooner. He said he'd started a letter a dozen times but always binned it because *'I didn't want to sound pathetic'*. He said he hoped I was enjoying the teaching, and that *'your kids are lucky to have you, even the little bastards'*. The final lines were blunt:

'Thank you for the three years we had as friends and sorry if I hurt you when I left. Have a good life.

Alex'.

I read it twice, then folded the pages back into the envelope. I set it under the teapot, as if that might anchor it to the world and not my chest.

For a while I just sat there, breathing in the burnt-coffee air, the ghost of cigarette smoke hanging over everything. The silence felt huge, like the pause between thunder and the all-clear. I thought I'd feel relief, knowing he was okay. But it was something sharper, a mix of anger, longing, and a deep, unnameable shame. It pissed me off that he could move on so easily, that I was still sitting in a rented room above a pub, pretending to be someone I wasn't even sure I liked.

I got up and refilled the kettle. I made another coffee, then another. I chain-smoked three cigarettes, watching the streetlights carve shadows onto the wall. Outside, the city moved on without me, the bars closing, the night buses crawling past on a schedule I never bothered to learn.

At two in the morning, I pulled on my jacket and left the room. I walked back down to the street, past the empty bar, past the lockup, and out into the damp cold. The city was almost silent, save for the hum of distant traffic and the rush of the river a few blocks away.

I made my way to Canal Street. Even at this hour, there were stragglers, two men in matching denim, arms looped over each other's shoulders; a group of girls shrieking in the rain, mascara melting into the night. *The Rembrandt* was shuttered, but the light from its sign spilled onto the wet pavement, pink and gold and brave.

I stopped across the road and stared at the doorway. Nobody looked at me; nobody called out. I could have crossed, walked in, bought a drink, and been part of something. Instead, I watched the empty glass flicker in the neon, and felt the last of the anger drain away, leaving only the ache.

I stood there a long time, the letter warm in my pocket, until the city began to pale at the edges, hinting at morning.

Then I walked home, let myself in, and climbed the stairs again to bed. The envelope stayed on the nightstand, a small, stubborn proof that sometimes you have to let go, even if you never really learn how.

I lay awake until sunrise, watching the light slide across the ceiling, promising myself that next time, I'd find the courage to cross the street. And if I didn't well, that would be my own bloody fault.

CHAPTER 19: A DECISION MADE

The rest of this placement passed quickly, and I realised that the real purpose of it was to sift out the grossly incompetent and the non-committed. There was no 'pass' or 'fail' at the end of it, just an interview with your university tutor and a decision to be made.

On the final morning, the staff room looked like a crime scene. Not a drop of blood anywhere, but the violence was all in the way the chairs were flung back from the table, the mugs abandoned at mid-sip, the carpet splotched with a constellation of black tea and dried *Pritt Stick*. The December daylight pooled behind the frosted windows, blue as a hospital bruise. I sat at the edge of the battered *Formica* table, gathering my lesson notes in slow, trembling handfuls.

I collected my things and stacked my lesson notes by date, then by topic, then by how much I hated the lesson. *"The Enclosure Movement: How Fences Ruined the World,"* followed by *"Victorian Childhood: A Cautionary Tale."* Each sheet was limp from handling, the edges already curling like old sandwich bread. I flattened them again, then again, until the stack stopped fighting me.

My hands shook in anticipation of my meeting with Dr Henderson later that afternoon. Not the full palsy, just a light static, like my nerves had been stripped and frayed. I told myself it was the cold. I told myself I hadn't just flunked an observation the day before, that Mrs. Blackwell hadn't cocked her eyebrow when half the class pretended to be lost in the bathroom. That the grunting silence that followed my best open-ended question wasn't a referendum on my ability to teach, or to exist. I adjusted my tie, even though I'd already loosened it, and glanced at the clock above the sink.

I looked one last time at my planner, and the only thing on its calendar was *'Reflect. Prepare. Try Not to Fuck Up Tomorrow'.* I shuffled the papers lodged in the back cover again, this time by the colour of the pen I'd used to mark corrections. Red first, my default for sarcasm and rage. Green for "constructive feedback." Blue for notes to myself: "Don't get drawn into Kevin's games," "Use the board more," "Breathe." I ran my thumb over the blue-ink notes until it stung.

I'd been at this school for six weeks of "taster" teaching, a phrase the University used like it was a tray of *amuse-bouches* and not a crash diet. Each morning had started with the taste of adrenaline in my mouth, and each night ended with the same: a film of worry I could neither spit out nor swallow.

The windows looked out onto the playing field. Frost dusted every blade of grass, the white line boundaries wavering in the dusk. For a moment I saw myself as a child, running the perimeter with Sarah, both of us convinced that the world ended at the farthest lamppost. I pressed my forehead to the glass, felt the sting of the cold, and wondered if she'd made it home from hockey practice yet. It was possible she was already on the bus, slouched in the back, earbuds in, planning a future that didn't involve kids named Kevin or chalk dust or me.

A mug clattered behind me. The head of department stood there, cardigan buttoned wrong, watching me with a mixture of pity and relief.

"You're still here," Mrs Blackwell said, "putting off your meeting back at Uni?"

"I was just about to leave," I lied, though part of me wanted her to ask me to stay, to tell me I belonged here, "just getting my stuff together."

"You don't have anything to worry about Liam, you did well," she said kindly, though her eyes darted to the door, "so I shall say goodbye and wish you well."

"Thank you," I muttered, "and thanks for all your help and support." The words tasted both genuine and hollow in my mouth.

A shiver rolled through me. My shirt clung damp to my back. I clutched my arms, tried to wring out the tension, then gave up and just watched the frost creep up the glass. I thought of Alex, wondered what he'd say about my "crisis of confidence." Probably something snarky, probably something true. Probably something I'd both hate and need to hear.

I packed my bag, wanting to linger but knowing I shouldn't. I adjusted the tie again, tightening it, then loosening it. The clock said one-twenty. Dr. Henderson was waiting, but so was the safety of this staffroom, this limbo between student and teacher.

The staffroom doors closed behind me with a soft click. I was alone with the weak winter sun, and the sound of my own breath, and the knowledge that tomorrow would come whether I was ready or not, whether I wanted it or not.

The university was a mausoleum in the off hours, every corridor echoing with a cold and calculated indifference. I stalked the linoleum under the jaundiced wash of strip lights, the only sounds the slap of my own shoes and the distant, rubbery cough of a vending machine dying in the humanities block. My breath fogged a little, even inside, and I had to keep moving or the chill would have found its way into my bones.

The door to Dr. Henderson's office was half-open, as if he'd already weighed the odds of my arrival and decided to let fate sort it. I knocked and nudged it wider and stepped in.

He sat behind a desk layered in sedimentary bands of student essays, each pile threatening collapse at the merest exhale. The room's walls were a riot of shelving, every inch groaning with history texts and the odd totem: a pewter mug, a battered campaign sign, a fading photo of some student cohort where everyone wore the same sheepish smile. There was a worn patch on the carpet where visitors had nervously paced over the years.

"Liam," he said, eyes flicking up over rimless spectacles, "you look... alive."

I shrugged, "barely."

He gestured to the single unoccupied chair, already loaded with a pyramid of unsorted mail. I displaced it and sat, perching on the edge with my bag between my feet. The desk was vast, but the clutter rendered its surface a myth. Henderson steepled his hands, the gesture a trademark, and regarded me with an intensity that could have stripped wallpaper.

"So," he said, "first term in the trenches. Enlighten me."

I hesitated, unsure whether he wanted truth or performance. "It was..." I began, then stopped.

He let the silence fill, one eyebrow quivering with impatience. I tried again.

"I had a good discussion on the *Industrial Revolution*," I said, "Week two. Got them talking about working conditions, child labour, the shift from field to factory. They argued for a whole hour, almost civilly. I think two of them might actually have read the chapter."

"Miracle," Henderson said, "and?"

"I tried to handle a rowdy Year Nine class," I admitted, "failed, spectacularly. They sensed blood the second I walked in. Spent the entire lesson trying to convince me one of them was an actual orphan."

"Was he?"

"Not even close," I said, and Henderson's smile was swift and thin.

"And the best?"

I shifted in my seat, uneasy, "he was in Year Ten and dyslexic, as far as I could tell. I worked with him on reading aloud. He hadn't passed a single test all term. We spent a lunch period mapping timelines, markers, sticky notes everywhere. Next test, he nailed every date. He just stared at it for five minutes, like he couldn't believe it himself," my voice wavered.

Henderson inclined his head slowly, "that's something. Did you enjoy it?"

I hesitated, panic flickering, "enjoy? I … I don't know. It was work, right? Not exactly thrilling."

His eyes searched mine, "but did you feel anything? Satisfaction? That you made a difference?"

I stared down at my fingers, nails ragged, "sometimes," I whispered, "but… was it me helping him, or him pulling himself up? I'm not even sure."

He watched me as though weighing a verdict. The silence stretched too long.

"Good," he said at last, voice clipped. He ran a hand through his hair, his nervous tic sharpening his youth rather than his professorial air, "if you don't object, I have your next placement." He rifled through a pile of envelopes, then slid a plain brown one across the desk.

I picked it up, feeling a squeeze of dread and realised that I had "passed".

"Openshaw High," he said, "Start in February. It's rougher. Mentor's one of ours, Teresa Batty. I've asked for you to get some A-level exposure."

My throat tightened, "Openshaw…"

He leaned forward, lowering his voice, "take it seriously. They've burnt through plenty of good intentions there. If you want real impact, this is where you'll find it."

I nodded, turmoil churning in my chest.

He glanced at the clock, then at the grimy window where a weak December sun fought the winter grey.

"Any questions?" he prompted.

I exhaled, uncertain, "not yet. I'll … save them for when I inevitably screw up."

He cracked a grin, surprisingly warm, "don't worry. That's teaching." He paused, as if noticing my tension, "rest over Christmas and New Year. Come back to me in January; we'll go through the feedback from this term. See what we can learn from it."

"Thank you, Dr. Henderson. I… I'd like that. Maybe next time I won't feel so clueless."

He smiled, but it felt like a test, "that attitude will carry you forward. Now go, try to enjoy yourself."

I rose, the chair scraping across threadbare carpet. Henderson sank back, arms folded, already absorbed in the next stack of chaos. I tucked the envelope under my arm, torn between excitement and fear of what lay ahead.

In January, back in my room above the pub I sat at the single desk, a relic probably salvaged from a skip, its surface pocked with the ghosts of a hundred pint rings and the scratches of ex-lodgers. The air was heavy with the funk of old beer and the greasy sweetness of takeaway chips from the shop next door. On the desk: a half-dozen textbooks, lesson plans in various states of completion, and my own battered notebook, open to a page where I'd written "Openshaw High— Don't Die" in permanent marker.

I tried to focus on a reading about differentiated instruction, but every third word blurred into an advertisement for self-doubt. I made a note to myself: "Ask Henderson about behaviour management. Or at least how not to get stabbed", and then crossed it out, because that was tomorrow-Liam's problem.

The door crashed open without warning. Carol filled the frame, hair slicked back and an unlit cigarette wedged between her lips like a punctuation mark.

"When does your next teaching practice start then?" she asked.

"A couple of weeks yet," I replied, my stomach knotting at the thought.

"And this is the big one I am guessing?" she smiled.

"Yes, fail this one and I'll be asking you if I can stay on here full time and permanent," I said, half-joking, half-terrified by the possibility.

"Well, better make sure you pass then!" she teased, then laughed heartily, "but seriously, when you start I am happy to let you change shift pattern to weekend lunchtimes and Friday and Saturday nights," she said, voice now flat as the corridor carpet.

I blinked, torn between gratitude and the dread of juggling both commitments, "thank you, I think that would help a lot," I hesitated, "if it's not too much messing around for you?"

"not at all Liam," she said, "so what's this you doing?" She gestured to my desk.

"Teacher training stuff," I said, "homework for grown-ups." The words felt hollow in my mouth, like I was playing at being someone I wasn't sure I could become.

She grunted, then fished a lighter from her apron and set the cigarette going in a series of short, angry puffs, "I've seen fewer books in a bloody library," she said. "Don't forget. You're on tomorrow at noon. Can't have you falling asleep at the bar, can I?"

"Wouldn't dream of it," I said, already calculating how little sleep I could survive on.

With that, she was gone, door slamming behind her hard enough to make the window rattle.

I stared at the lesson plan, at the list of names I'd barely begun to memorise, and at the schedule now tattooed on my consciousness. For a second I considered the option of just… not showing up, to either job. I pictured a life in which I lay on the threadbare mattress for days, reading old paperbacks and letting the city do whatever it wanted outside.

Instead, I pulled the schedule off the wall, rewrote the next week in pen, and added the new shifts in block capitals for February. Then I set about copying my own notes, cross-referencing with the textbook, and drinking the tea cold and gritty, because the alternative was worse.

Outside, the city was gearing up for a Friday night of bad decisions. I could hear the crowd's shouts through the double-glazed window, each rising note a warning from my future self.

I ignored it. I sat at the desk, underlining phrases until the ink bled through the page, and willed myself to believe that in a few weeks I'd be ready for whatever the kids, or the pub, threw at me.

Openshaw High was a slab of 1960s concrete flanked by chain-link and the kind of patchy grass that never quite recovered from football season. The foyer stank of damp and disinfectant, and the kids in the corridor eyed every adult like they were either a threat or a promise of escape. I signed in at the office, and followed the directions on the memo: *Turn left at the mural of the miners, then right at the mural of the suffragettes, straight down to Room 209*.

Teresa Batty's office was a bombsite. Books in toppling stacks, student portfolios wedged between coffee mugs and potted ferns, windowsill choked with pamphlets and faded *Polaroids* from a dozen protests. The only clear space was her own desk, and even there a perimeter of coloured pens and mismatched staplers marked her territory. She sat with her back to the door, hair pulled tight in a silver streak, typing at a speed that made the keyboard sound like a hailstorm.

She spun in her chair, caught my eye, and grinned.

"You must be the new blood," she said, voice sharp but not unkind.

"Liam Parry," I said.

"Teresa," she replied, then turned back to the screen and finished her thought before gesturing me to sit, "ignore the mess," she said, "it's proof of life."

I took the seat across, careful not to unbalance a stack of yearbooks threatening to avalanche. She poured two mugs of coffee from a battered *Thermos* and slid one across. The liquid was so black it could have been used for photocopying, and I doubted it contained anything as gentle as water.

"I read your file," she said, "History, bit of English Lit, union kid from the North. Welcome to the trenches."

"Thanks," I said, and meant it, "you've been here long?"

She laughed, a bright rasp, "since Thatcher was in short pants. Was at Manchester before that, politics, then teaching, then thirty years of trying to convince teenagers to care about dead people."

She took a long pull on the coffee, then set the mug down, "so. Tell me about you."

I gave her the basics, where I grew up, the degree, the part-time job, the teaching placement that had left me with more questions than answers. She listened, head cocked, as if calibrating my story against a private scale.

When I got to the student activism, she pounced.

"You were in the *NUS*?" she said.

"When I could," I said, "went to Warrington for the *Messenger* thing."

She nodded, the smile turning conspiratorial, "I was the same. Back in the seventies we occupied the Vice-Chancellor's office over some bullshit about women's pay. Stayed three days. We nicked his brandy and played poker on his carpet. Got a caution and a footnote in the alumni newsletter."

I laughed, genuinely, "they never mention that in the prospectus."

She leaned forward, elbows on desk, eyes suddenly serious, "you'll need that spirit here. The kids, half of them are running on anger and sugar. They'll eat you alive if you let them. But if you fight for them, really fight, they'll never forget it."

I sipped the coffee. It tasted like burnt hope, "I'm trying to get the hang of classroom management. Last school, I had a few small wins, but mostly I just survived."

She wagged a finger, "survival is step one. Step two is giving them a reason to care. Sometimes it's history, sometimes it's you."

She drummed the desk, "tomorrow, I'll introduce you to your classes, and then you'll see why all the textbooks are a load of wank. After, we'll talk lesson planning. I like your notes, practical, not flowery, but you'll need a plan for every personality in the room."

I nodded, a flood of relief rising in my chest. She wasn't trying to intimidate; she was arming me.

She pointed at the mural on her wall: a photo-collage of women with fists raised, half of them in school blazers, "see that? Last year's strike. School lunches got cut for budget. Our kids picketed for a week. We got coverage in the *MEN*, even a bit on *Granada Reports*. The council caved. Not much, but it mattered."

I scanned the mural, trying to imagine being that brave at sixteen.

Teresa saw my doubt and grinned again, "you don't have to be a hero. You just have to not be a coward."

She stood, stretched, and pointed to the battered teaching schedule pinned to the back of the door, "you're with me for period two, then observation for three and four. Lunch in here if you want, or the canteen if you're feeling social."

She paused, sizing me up, then softened, "first days are always shit. Second days are worse. But after a week, you'll know who to watch and who to worry about. After a month, you'll be addicted."

I thanked her, then tried to stand without knocking over the stack of books. It wobbled, but stayed upright. She noticed, and a flicker of pride crossed her face.

At the door, she said, "where you living?"

"Above a pub," I said, "Wilmslow Road."

She cackled, "best place for a teacher. Dulls the pain. Just don't fail for being late."

I promised to try.

In the corridor, the kids flowed past like weather, all noise and motion, but I felt anchored. Teresa had mapped the terrain: messy, dangerous, and alive.

I took a detour on the way out, past the murals, and stopped at the one of the miners. For a second I thought about my dad, the way he'd measured every decision by whether it put food on the table. Then I looked back at the suffragettes, their faces pixelated but defiant, and I wondered which fight I belonged to.

Outside, the sky had softened, the light blue and brittle. I walked to the bus stop, thinking about tomorrow, about the lessons that might stick, about what kind of difference a single teacher could actually make.

The rain had been falling all day, not the defiant hammering of a winter storm but the thin, insistent variety that seeps in at the windowsill and stains the world a single, sodden colour. By the time I reached the pub, my coat was heavy and my feet squelched in their shoes, the edges of my trousers banded with water like an old tide line. The stairs were slick with the residue of a hundred careless shoes, and the air on the landing tasted faintly of damp concrete and old takeaway.

I let myself into my room, but after a day at Openshaw it felt like the antechamber to a cathedral. The warmth struck my face, followed by the chemical sweetness of the plug-in air freshener. I stood by the radiator, pressing my hands to its fluted body until feeling returned to my fingers. Then I noticed some post Carol must have put on my desk.

I shrugged off my coat, hung it over the kitchen chair, and picked through the letters. Bank statement, circular from the local Labour MP, a takeout menu in lurid pink. At the bottom of the pile, almost hidden, was an envelope with my name in familiar blue ink. The address was right, but the 'Liam' was in the old style, the capital L a swooping, optimistic curve that took up half the line.

Amanda.

My breath caught. Not much, just enough to mark the shift from background noise to full alert. I tossed it onto the bed, and circled around it as if it might detonate. I unbuttoned my shirt, traded it for a clean t-shirt, ran my hands through my hair. Then I sat on the edge of the bed, picked up the envelope, and ran my thumb along the seal.

It wasn't thick. Just two pages, maybe three, folded with the same precision I remembered from revision notes and mix-tape inserts. For a minute I stared at the handwriting. It was unchanged, still careful, still slightly left-leaning, the lowercase *e's* a little too round. I thought of all the notes she'd left me over three years: reminders to buy birthday cards for Sarah, to pick up her library books, to call her on Sunday because she missed my voice. I thought of the last letter, the one I'd written to her after everything with Alex, and the way I'd forced myself to be honest, even when it felt like cutting a tendon.

I cracked the seal. The pages slipped out smooth, smelling faintly of her, of soap, of pencil shavings, of the unnamed vanilla in her old parent's furniture polish.

I read the letter in silence. Every paragraph was a tight-rope: the opening apology (*'Hope you don't mind me phoning your mum to get your address'*) then (*'Sorry it's taken so long—life has a way of swallowing me lately'*), the hesitant updates about her family (*'Dad's knee is better, finally, and Mum's teaching a new reading scheme that's the talk of the whole town'*), a single line about university

('French is less glamorous when you're teaching Year Seven how to conjugate 'être' in a windowless classroom'). Then, finally, the part I'd braced for.

She wrote, *'I know you said I didn't owe you a reply, but I wanted to. I wanted to tell you in my own words that it's okay, that I'm not angry anymore. You always did have the hardest time forgiving yourself. I guess I've always been better at letting go'*.

I felt my jaw clamp. I tried to keep reading, but my eyes wouldn't focus. She continued, *'There's someone here. He's kind, and clever in a way that doesn't make me feel small. I didn't want to mention it, but you deserve the truth, after all of it. We've only been together a few months, but I think he might last. I'm happy, Liam. Or as happy as anyone ever gets'*.

I exhaled, a thin, wounded laugh. Of course she was happy. That had always been her superpower, despite my best efforts to sabotage that.

At the end, a postscript: *'Thank you for telling me the truth'*. Or at least my version of the 'truth' I immediately thought to myself, *'I think it took more courage than you'll ever believe. Please be gentle with yourself. You are not as alone as you think'*.

I set the letter on my lap and flexed my hands, trying to wring the ache from my knuckles. The rain hammered at the window, louder now, as if the city was determined to fill every silence.

I reread the letter, slower this time, letting the words settle. I imagined her hunched over the kitchen table, mug of tea gone cold at her elbow, writing and crossing out and starting again. I pictured the new man, his gentleness, his cleverness, his unthreatening smile, his honesty, and felt a little undeserved jealousy simmer, then dissipate, replaced by something closer to relief, once I realised my deceit had not had such as impact, as I so arrogantly assumed it would.

For a long time I just sat there, the letter open in my hands, the world outside reduced to the steady hiss of rain and the tick of the radiator. There was no accusation in her words, no blame. Just the calm certainty that it was over, that we'd both moved on, and that the best thing left was to wish each other luck.

I folded the pages, careful to align the creases. I slid the letter back into its envelope, then opened the drawer in my bedside table and set it on top of the old photos, the student IDs, the half-written lesson plans. I closed the drawer with a gentle push.

The room was still. For the first time in weeks, I felt the weight in my chest shift, lighter, maybe, but still present, a reminder of the spaces that letters leave behind.

I leaned back on the bed, closed my eyes, and listened to the rain. In the morning, I'd have to teach the Year Elevens about Shakespearean tragedy, and I already knew which speech I'd use. But for now, I let the quiet fill me, and I let myself believe, for as long as it lasted, that I could be happy, too.

The last day of my teaching practice started before sunrise. I woke to the distant sound of bins being wheeled out along the pavement, the hush before the city committed itself to motion. My room was cold, the radiator only ticking with residual heat. I lay in bed, listening to the world assemble itself: the rush of the 142 bus on Wilmslow Road, the staggered footfalls of Carol's boyfriend coming off night shift, the thin chirp of a radio through someone's open window.

Today was the day of my final assessment. The one lesson that mattered, the difference between "trainee" and "qualified." The one where Teresa and Dr Henderson would sit at the back of the classroom and decide my professional fate. I showered, dressed in my best shirt, white, with a collar that never quite sat right, and ate breakfast with the careful detachment of a man counting out last words on a condemned cell's calendar. My hands shook, but only a little. Practice had inured me to most of the terror.

Outside, the rain had faded to a sticky mist that seemed to press every surface slick and uncertain. I walked to the tram, rehearsing the day's script in my head: attendance, settle, Civil War introduction, the groupwork, the five-minute plenary to tie it all together. The class was Year Nine, bottom set, which meant half of them would be hungover from sugar or from rage, and the other half would be dead to the world until lunch. My only hope was that they'd be so busy tormenting each other they wouldn't bother trying to make me cry.

At Openshaw, the building squatted in the fog like a punishment. The walls inside were a patchwork of damp and motivational posters, the carpet worn to a granular shine. I said hello to the site manager, who grunted, "good luck, mate," with the sincerity of a man who'd seen fifty student teachers burn out on the spot.

In the staff room, the silence was electric. Someone had left out a tray of supermarket pastries, but the only thing that moved was the slow drift of steam from the tea urn. I checked my bag for the fifth time: lesson plan, handouts, the extra box of marker pens. At precisely 8:43, Teresa entered, her clipboard clutched to her chest like a life vest.

She wore her usual uniform, grey skirt, blue blouse, scarf knotted at the throat. Her hair, always immaculate, was held back with a single tortoiseshell clip. She nodded at me, neither friendly nor cold, then busied herself with the sign-in sheet.

"Morning, Liam," Teresa said, her eyes flicking over me like a checklist.

My chest tightened, "morning, Teresa," I managed, though my voice felt nothing like mine.

She studied my cuffs, as if cuff cleanliness could predict my performance today, "you ready for this?"

I forced a swallow, "I … I think so."

She glanced around the empty staffroom, "Dr Henderson will join us soon. You go up first and begin without us, don't wait." She tapped her clipboard, and I pictured her scrawled note: thinks he's ready. Probably panicking. Then she offered that practiced smile, "remember: they're not as clever as you fear, but not as stupid as you hope."

A rush of relief mixed with dread washed over me. I nodded, clutching that crumb of encouragement even as doubt gnawed at it.

The bell rang. My stomach lurched, then settled into a slow churn of mechanical dread, my constant companion these last six months. The Year Nine corridor was chaos incarnate: backpacks strewn like landmines, the scrape of trainers on lino echoing off concrete walls, a stifling haze somewhere between teenage deodorant and outright terror. I unlocked the door, flicked on the lights, and paused, heart hammering .

They were already there, the front-row know-it-all with folded arms and a mocking smirk, two girls at the back whispering secrets I'd never decode, and Billy, big-bodied, impassive, planted square in the middle. My throat went dry as I took the register, stumbling once over a fresh new surname. My pulse hammered in my ears. Was this really me, teacher now? I shook off the thought and plunged into the lesson.

"Right. Today: the English Civil War. Anyone know what that means?"

Silence. I felt my face heat. Had I lost them already? I pressed on, sketching a stick-figure king on the board, crown lopsided, my hand trembling so slightly I feared it showed. A ripple of laughter ran through the room, not at me, but at the cartoon absurdity. A small victory. I added a mop-haired figure labelled "Oliver C.", earning a reluctant groan from the front. Better that than total apathy.

Five minutes in, the door creaked. Teresa slipped inside, Dr Henderson at her heels, and both slid into the chairs I'd left at the back. Instantly, every head snapped toward them. Teresa pressed a finger to her lips, and the murmurs died.

"I'm over here," I said, choking down the lump in my throat. My voice had that practiced calm teachers teach you to fake. It worked and all eyes returned to me.

At the back, Teresa and Henderson sat motionless, notepads poised. Each time I glanced over, they looked busy writing, or staring just above my head, as if tracking the precise moment I'd collapse. My chest clenched, but I forced my shoulders back. Conflict still churned inside, fear, pride, imposter syndrome, determination, but I'd started now. And whatever happened next, I had to keep going.

The lesson sped by faster than I'd anticipated, and part of me rejoiced at how lively the room felt. Another part seethed at my own loss of control. I herded the students into groups, handed out the worksheets, then drifted from cluster to cluster, listening. When Billy tried to recast the English Civil War as "a punch-up between posh lads," I corrected him on the details but let the metaphor stand, partly to keep him hooked, partly because I was tired of policing every nuance. Guilty and gratified in equal measure.

Halfway through, a mini-uprising erupted over highlighters. I rationed them by group, feeling like a supply-line sergeant caught between fairness and chaos. My heart thumped as the students squabbled, was this the kind of learning I wanted to encourage, or had I gone too far in letting them loose? I'd seen veteran teachers navigate this orchestrated pandemonium with effortless calm. I was fumbling.

The last ten minutes blurred into a flurry of raised hands and rapid-fire questions. I felt exhilarated, then panicked, then oddly at peace, as if I'd stumbled into mastery by accident. When I rounded off with, "so, what was the English Civil War really about?" two or three kids offered answers that, while not strictly accurate, nailed the theme. Relief washed over me, laced with the worry, did I teach them anything real?

The bell rang, and the class dissolved, leaving a mess of paper scraps and snapped pen lids behind. I collected my things slowly, my mind fluttering between pride and self-doubt. Then I looked up at Teresa standing in the doorway.

She smiled, that cautious, half-smile that could break a dam, "good lesson," she said, "clear, lively. I liked your handling of Billy."

"Yes, Liam," Dr. Henderson agreed, "the pacing and vocal variety were spot on." Their praise felt warm and undeserved all at once, like standing in sunlight after weeks of storm. My shoulders, coiled for an hour, finally loosened. "Thank you," I muttered, afraid to sound too eager or too relieved.

Teresa closed her notepad, "there's room for improvement, tighten your timing, don't let the smart ones steamroll. But you've got this." Her words both soothed and unsettled me, I'd done well, but what if I hadn't? "Thanks," I said again, pitching my voice somewhere between disbelief and gratitude.

She headed off, then turned, "give us thirty minutes to wrap up the paperwork, then pop into my office for your feedback. For now? Breathe." She left. I sat at the teacher's desk, head bowed, letting relief, and an undercurrent of dread, wash through me. Outside, the corridor clamoured with locker doors and teenage grumbles, a reminder that calm never lasts long.

In the staff room, the pastries were gone. I made tea, gazed through the window at the mist lifting off the playground, and wondered, would Alex buy that I hadn't messed this up? Would Amanda clap me on the back, or just smirk and say "I told you so"? My chest tightened with hope and terror.

Thirty minutes later, I knocked on Teresa's door and found her and Dr. Henderson bent over triplicate forms. He peeled off the back white copy and handed it to me, Teresa tucked the yellow into a folder. I squinted at the sheet labelled *End of Placement Summary*. Three boxes:

'pass', *'fail'*, *'referral'*. A faint tick in *'pass'*. My breath caught, joy and panic collided in my chest.

"Congratulations, Liam," Teresa said, her eyes bright.

"Very well-deserved." Dr. Henderson reached out, shook my hand, "never in doubt." My chest pounded with relief so intense it felt like fear. I smiled, uncertain whether to believe them—or to brace myself for the next lesson.

That night, *The Crown* was packed, the usual mix of students outnumbered by the Friday evening regulars. Carol poured me a pint without asking. Jenny produced a cupcake with a sparkler jammed in the top. Someone taped a sign to my back reading, *'be gentle, newly qualified'*.

The noise was enormous, the heat sticky and close. People clapped me on the back, wished me luck, offered advice ranging from "don't let the kids see you bleed" to "always keep a spare shirt in your car." I took it all in, feeling buoyant and shellshocked at the same time.

Around nine, the crowd thinned. Jenny joined me at the bar, topping off my pint.

"So, you did it," she said, eyes sharp as ever.

"Apparently," I said, "didn't think I would."

She snorted, "neither did I. You seemed so nervous, but you surprised us all. Even Carol."

At the end of the bar, Carol raised her glass in my direction. I saluted, trying not to slop beer down my front.

Jenny nodded at the newspaper spread across the table, "looking for work already?"

I shrugged, picking up the jobs page, "just seeing what's out there."

She arched an eyebrow, then left me to it.

I'd bought the *Times Educational Supplement* on the way home, and moved immediately to the vacancies. The job ads were a litany of need: schools in London, Kent, the Midlands; salaries and scales in bold type; all wanting someone with a pulse and a certificate. I scanned the listings, half-interested, half-scared by the prospect of leaving everything I'd built in Manchester.

I circled a job in Camden, then one in Southwark, thinking of Alex and the stories he'd told about his new life there. I imagined myself walking those same streets, teaching kids whose names I couldn't pronounce, building a life out of nothing. The idea was both thrilling and nauseating. Then I thought it might be an opportunity to reconnect with Alex, maybe put everything behind us and start again, but then my mind's eye reminded me of the look of determination on his face on Graduation Day. My search moved on. I found an opportunity for a school in Stockport, just a few miles away. I circled it, too.

I set down the pen and stared at the page, weighing my options like a man with too many coins for the slot and no idea which one was counterfeit. After a moment, I grabbed the pen again and drew a thick, confident ring around the Stockport job. Then I folded the paper, tucked it into my jacket, and muttered, "coward."

Jenny must have heard, because she looked over, lips pursed, "nah," she said, "just loyal."

She went back to wiping the bar, I sipped my beer, feeling the warmth spread through me. The laughter in the room rose and fell, a tide that could carry you if you let it. I looked at the job page again, then at the faces around me. The fear was still there, but it was edged with something lighter. Hope, maybe. Or just the knowledge that, for the first time in a long time, I had a place to be, and a reason to get up tomorrow.

The pub door opened again and a group of regulars entered in their work clothes, boots caked in mud, eyes bright with the reckless optimism of a weekend beginning. I recognised the mallet-nosed leader, who grinned when he saw me.

"Hey up, lad," he said, "did you pass then?" he asked kindly. I nodded and smiled, "didn't I tell you you'd make something of yourself?" He smiled, and then added, "pity really, just as you'd learnt to pull a decent pint."

I smiled, then laughed, and raised my glass to him, to the locals, to everyone in the world who'd ever doubted they could. The night rolled on. I let it carry me, just for now, wherever it wanted to go.

Outside, the mist had lifted. The city sparkled under the streetlights, every brick and puddle etched sharp and clean.

Tomorrow, I'd start again. But tonight, I was happy, and I let the feeling hold me for as long as it could.

CHAPTER 20: STOCKPORT GRAMMAR

September 1985

I had applied for a lot of jobs, and my third interview was at the mixed grammar school in Stockport at the beginning of August. I'd left the interview feeling confident that at least I had performed better than previously. The job offer came in the post a few days later, and set in motion a flood of all the practical actions needed. This occupied my mind more than the significance of it for the rest of my life.

Sarah and I visited a few flats near the school. She chose one near the hospital while I hesitated, wondering if I should live closer to Manchester. It was on the first floor of a converted Victorian town house with high ceilings that made me feel both important and exposed. The lounge had a bay window that flooded the room with light I wasn't sure I deserved.

Once I had secured the tenancy, I gave Carol my notice at the pub. With Jenny we shared a quiet drink together after hours on my last night. The locals had been generous in their good wishes to me during my last shift, "I think some of the miserable old buggers might actually miss you," Carol said.

"Especially now they think they had got me trained to their standards!" I added, and we all laughed at the partial truth in my comment.

We concluded with a toast to "the future", and Jenny added, with a wink, "and don't be a stranger Liam."

Sarah came with me the next day as I moved my few possessions into my new flat, watching me arrange and rearrange them like chess pieces.

"You can buy a bed settee for the living room so I can stay over," she announced.

"One thing at a time," I replied, avoiding her eyes, "need my own bed first and then a desk."

"Fair enough," she conceded, "but you'll be earning a fortune now, so shouldn't be too long."

"A fortune?" I countered, "since when has £550 a month before tax been a fortune?"

"Since it's not £1.80 an hour working in a pub," she explained.

I nodded, thinking of Alex's London salary, "fair point, just may be a while until I have everything I need."

"I know, I just don't want you feeling that you have to be on your own the whole time," Sarah said and gently punched me on the arm.

"Thanks, lil sis, I won't." The lie tasted metallic.

My bank agreed, given my new job, a new overdraft for me and I also got my first credit card. Both of these were used to furnish my new home, a double-bed that felt too large for just me, but a deserved luxury I thought, an armchair I positioned facing the window, then the wall, then the window again, and finally, a bed settee for my sister that I placed where it would be hardest to see from the bedroom door. The rest came from my parents - kitchen appliances, crockery, and pots from under the stairs. "And that's why I never throw anything away," my mum had said as I unpacked her aid package, wondering how much else I was keeping hidden away.

My first day at my new school was a Monday. It was a day for teachers devoted entirely to planning. I chose to walk to work and left home in plenty of time on a bright early September morning. To be honest, I had not slept at all the night before, such were the hundreds of scenarios, I played out in my mind about how the day would go.

The corridors were old enough to have survived two world wars and at least two fire regulations. There was no heating at seven-thirty, and the air had that monastery-cold wetness that crept in above your ankles and set up permanent residence. I could hear the scuff of my shoes echoing down the passage, a clatter that sounded both desperate and eager.

The tweed jacket, the one I'd bought from *Oxfam*, and spent the weekend de-linting with *Sellotape*, itched at my neck, and I found myself picking at invisible threads as I went. At each turn, I rehearsed the words: "Mr. Parry, History." I tried to deepen my voice on the "Parry" part, to give it the punch of a real grown-up, a man who might one day own a houseplant that didn't die.

When I arrived, a caretaker directed me to the staff room and its entrance was a set of double doors, each with a diamond-shaped glass window too smudged to see through. I paused, adjusted my tie, then opened one just wide enough to slip in. The room was exactly as I remembered it from the interview day: tables battered smooth by decades of exam marking, a sagging sofa in one corner, the pungent haze of instant coffee and cheap air freshener locked in standoff. At the window, a man in a brown suit stood with hands clasped behind his back, surveying the schoolyard like a general preparing to send troops over the top.

He turned at the sound of the door and fixed me with a look. Not unfriendly, but not inviting either, a professional interest, as if I were a suspicious parcel that needed to be logged.

"Mr. Parry," he said, not a question. I recognised him from my interview a few weeks before. "Welcome. Harry Windle, Head of Humanities. Call me Harry, unless there's a parent in earshot."

I managed a handshake that landed somewhere between "firm" and "clammy."

He studied my face, then the lapels of my jacket, then my shoes, "not a bad choice," he said, gesturing at the tweed, "better than jeans and jumpers, though I doubt the sixth-form will appreciate it." He moved on, expecting me to follow.

Harry was built like a rugby forward gone to seed, thick neck, arms that strained the buttons of his shirt. His hair was military short, and when he walked, his shoes made no noise at all. I trailed behind, noting how the other teachers gave him a wide berth.

We stopped by the kettle, "first rule, lad, never smile before Christmas," he said, deadpan, "otherwise, they'll eat you alive."

I smiled, not sure if it was a test.

He shrugged, "your funeral."

I nodded, trying to school my face into something less desperate, "understood."

Harry poured two mugs, both black, no sugar, "you'll meet some of the rest once they arrive. Barbara, geography, she'll fuss over you. Daniel, Politics, don't take it personal if he ignores you. That's his way."

He led the way to a battered round table near the window, "sit," he said, and I did. The mug was hot enough to burn, but I took it gladly.

Just before eight, more teachers trickled in. Barbara Wilson entered first, a soft, rounded woman with a bun so tight it looked like it hurt. She wore a cardigan with *appliqué* cats and moved with a sort of ballet grace, even as she carried an industrial-sized *Tupperware* of homemade biscuits.

She took one look at me and beamed, "you must be the new history boy!" Her accent was Stockport, the vowels kind and rolling.

I stood, then sat again when she waved me down, "Barbara Wilson, geography and senior tutor. Here, have a biscuit, first day and all that." She thrust the tub at me. I fished out a shortbread, trying not to scatter crumbs on my tie.

She sat opposite, pouring herself tea from a tartan-patterned flask, "so, Liam, what did you make of Harry's welcoming speech?"

Harry grunted, eyes on the window, "told him not to smile until Christmas. Did you listen, lad?"

I nodded, mouth full, "absolutely."

Barbara winked, "ignore him, love. He only smiles after the third pint on a Friday. You'll be fine."

As if on cue, Daniel Cooper arrived. He was lean, angular, hair slicked back in a style twenty years out of date. He wore a suit, but the shirt beneath was so rumpled it looked slept-in. He went directly to the coffee jar, scooped a mound into a mug, then plopped into the seat beside Harry. He never looked at me, just unfolded a copy of *The Times* and started reading at the centre spread.

Harry leaned in, stage-whisper, "Daniel is probably on day four of a four-day hangover, which means you're lucky. He only bites when he's sober."

I nodded, though I doubted anyone would notice if I didn't. Barbara handed Daniel a biscuit; he took it without thanks, already paging through the news.

"So, Liam, are you local?" Barbara asked, her tone the gentle prod of someone who's spent a career coaxing answers from the shy and the recalcitrant.

I cleared my throat, "originally Rochdale, but I did university in Manchester. I've just finished my PGCE there. This is my first appointment."

Daniel made a noise that might have been a snort or just indigestion.

Harry smiled, not kindly, but not unkindly either, "the lower sets are all yours, then. Welcome to the trenches."

Barbara smacked his hand lightly, "don't tease, Harry. You'll have some lovely classes as well."

I smiled, rehearsed now, "I can handle the trenches."

Harry laughed, then sobered, "let's hope so."

Barbara turned her attention to my mug, "is that coffee? Do you take milk? You can't start a term on black coffee and nerves."

I hesitated, but she was already up and bustling to the tiny fridge at the end of the room. She poured a generous splash into my mug, then brought over a sugar pot shaped like a goose.

"Thanks," I said, accepting both.

As she sat, Barbara fixed her gaze on my hand, "no ring?" she asked, cheerful as you please, "girlfriend? Boyfriend?"

My brain froze for a moment, then defaulted to the pre-set fictional, "fiancée, actually. Amanda. She's up in Stirling, finishing her degree. We're doing the long-distance thing for now." What shocked me was not the lie, but the ease with which it came from my lips.

Barbara lit up, "how romantic! When's the wedding?"

"Next summer maybe," I said, and the lie rolled off so easily it almost surprised me. I tried to imagine a photo of Amanda, what she'd look like if she existed, and pictured the old black-and-white of my mother, hair in a plait, lips set in a smile that could have belonged to anyone. I felt my fingers tighten on the mug.

Harry said, "careful, Barbara. You know the union's got rules about romance in the workplace."

Barbara tutted, "don't listen to him, love. The last romance in this building was when the caretaker eloped with the PE teacher. She left him for a pool lifeguard in Tenerife." She shook her head in mock tragedy.

Daniel finally spoke, voice flat as a lecture hall, "I give it a year, tops. This place eats idealists."

Barbara snapped, "Daniel, hush."

I grinned, hoping to pass for *'taking the joke'*, "we'll see."

A silence settled. I sipped the coffee, now pale and sweet, and let the room's hum fill my ears. There were posters on the walls, *'Reading Is Power'*, *'Zero Tolerance for Bullying'* and a third, faded to the point of illegibility, showing a grim line of Victorian schoolchildren. The radiator ticked in slow, irregular bursts, a metronome for the start of term.

Harry drained his mug, then stood, "briefing in the Hall at eight-thirty. Find a seat near the back and try not to look eager. They can smell it."

Daniel folded his paper and followed, leaving the mug and a crescent of biscuit crumbs behind. Barbara patted my arm, "if you need anything, just ask. Staff toilets are through the door, two lefts, and there's always a biscuit jar. Don't let Harry scare you off."

I thanked her, then watched her waddle off, her bun bobbing with each step. Alone, I scanned the room, trying to memorise every detail. I felt the flush of adrenaline from the introduction, and the small, sour weight of the lie about Amanda settling at the back of my tongue. I ran a thumb along the rim of my mug, watching as a fingerprint smudge caught the light.

I told myself this was what adults did. They put on a jacket, learned the rules, and performed until it stopped feeling like a performance. I tried out my new name again, this time just in my head:

"Mr. Parry, History."

It sounded a little more real with each repetition. Maybe by Christmas I'd even start to believe it myself.

The first full staff meeting concluded quickly, with the headmaster introducing his new staff. I was invited to stand up when he announced my name, and my face burned with embarrassment.

I followed Harry to my first faculty meeting in a windowless office, grandly labelled as the *Faculty Resource Centre'*, that stank of old wood and books. There was no round table, strictly speaking, but a collection of rectangular ones that had been pushed together so many times the carpet beneath was worn thin, the pattern threadbare from a thousand shuffles. Harry stood at the end, hands on hips, surveying the assembled troops.

Barbara arrived early and set out a row of biscuits, precisely alternating chocolate and plain. Daniel appeared two minutes late, still reading the sports page, and managed to sit without once meeting anyone's eye. Two other staffers arrived, one a part-time history teacher called Mike, and a silent woman from Sociology whose name I didn't catch.

Harry started with the register: "right, let's not waste time. Parry, you're here. Good. Wilson, Cooper, present. Mike, thanks for gracing us, mate. Right, down to business."

He outlined the term's plan with military efficiency, "new Head wants more creative writing in lower sets. Expect pushbacks. *Ofsted* are on about cross-curricular skills, so if anyone's got ideas for projects, speak now or forever hold your peace."

Barbara piped up, "I thought we might do a World War One letters project? Kids could write as soldiers, or nurses. Empathy and historical context in one go."

Harry nodded, "good. Liam, you'll co-lead. You look like you've written a poem or two."

A laugh, good-natured, I thought, but Daniel's mouth twitched as if suppressing a sneer.

Barbara turned to me, beaming, "do you write, Liam?"

I nodded, "a bit. Mostly journals and angry letters to my MP."

She laughed, but Daniel caught my eye, "you'll fit right in," he said, his voice a dry, dead leaf.

Harry moved to exams and mocks, scheduled for early December, warned us about invigilating with "pissheads from science." The meeting blurred into logistics and who got which form group, which corridor would be renovated next, who was on playground duty for the first week back.

Near the end, Harry flicked on the battered radio in the corner, "always listen to the news at break," he said, almost apologetic, "keeps you one step ahead of the kids. Or the parents."

Barbara tutted, "it's nothing but bad news these days."

But Harry clicked it up anyway, and the room filled with the familiar drone of the *BBC*. For a while it was all strikes and unemployment figures, then the newsreader's voice changed: "American actor Rock Hudson has announced he has been diagnosed with *AIDS*."

The room stopped breathing. The word was still new, at least here, a distant panic from the tabloid headlines but not yet part of daily life. There was a beat, two, maybe three, before Daniel set down his pen and said, "Arse Injected Death Sentence."

He said it like he was announcing a horse race result, but Mike barked a laugh, and the Sociology teacher made a noise in her throat.

Barbara's face fell, but she just said, "that's not funny, Daniel."

He looked at her, then at me. "don't see the joke?" he asked, his eyes flat.

I shrugged, managed a smile I hoped read as *'too polite to laugh'*, or *'bit harsh, maybe?'*.

Daniel rolled his eyes, but Harry cut in, "enough. Let's get back to the syllabus, shall we? *AIDS* or not, the year nines still can't spell *'Versailles'*."

Barbara turned the radio down, her lips pressed in a line. She patted my arm, almost as if apologising on behalf of the others.

The meeting ended soon after. We filed out in awkward silence. In the corridor, I slowed to rearrange my notes and overheard two teachers, young, both PE, talking in urgent whispers.

"It's all over the telly now. They reckon it's contagious, like the flu. I'd keep away from them, if I were you."

"Who?" the other asked, genuinely confused.

"You know. The gays. That lot."

I kept my face blank as I passed, my grip tightening on the briefcase until the vinyl squeaked. I walked the rest of the hall without blinking, eyes fixed on the line of trophy cabinets, where a decade of teams, boys, always boys, the odd girl in net-ball kit squeezed into the margin, smiled from behind polished glass. I imagined being part of one of those photos, a ghost version of myself tucked into the background, smiling the regulation smile, secret invisible behind a layer of celluloid.

We moved to the humanities corridor on the first floor, and a tight knot formed in my chest with every step. Harry mumbled directions about classrooms and whispered judgments about colleagues he'd "approved" of, helpful, yet oddly condescending. I nodded along, torn between relief at his guidance and unease at his tone.

At the end of the corridor, Harry and I entered a classroom. It was immaculate: perfect rows of desks facing the front, polished floors, walls bare except for a single blackboard. I admired the order, but felt oddly intimidated by its precision. Harry swept his arm across the room, "this is my room," he said, pride and proprietorship in his voice.

At the back stood a windowless door. My pulse quickened as we stepped through. I expected a dusty storeroom. Instead, there was a snug little office: three desks pressed against the walls, two armchairs around a low coffee table, a kettle perched beside mugs and supplies under a large window, "and this," Harry continued, "is where we can hide." My stomach twisted, was he joking, or was there something secretive about this space?

He gestured to an armchair. I sank into it, grateful yet wary. He flicked on the kettle, "milk, one sugar?" he asked. The normalcy of the question caught me off guard. I hesitated, surprised at his courtesy.

"Erm, yes, thank you," I managed, my voice sounding shaky even to me.

As he busied himself with mugs and tea bags, he pulled a small brass key from his jacket pocket and waved it before me, "your staff master key for the Humanities Block," he said, tossing it into my palm. It landed with a light thud. "lose it at your peril!" he winked. I turned the key over in my hand, pride mingling uneasily with the weight of that responsibility.

I opened my induction folder and began jotting notes while Harry outlined the essentials: where the staff toilets were on this floor, where to refill the kettle, his duty to bring milk each day, mine to provide biscuits, and our shared task of alternating tea and coffee restocks. My pen trembled despite my best efforts to stay composed.

Next came my timetable. Harry handed me a crisp photocopy: mostly lower-form history, a few English Lit lessons, an O Level history class, and a shared A Level group. Excitement and dread warred in me, eager to teach, yet acutely aware of the unknown.

He leaned in, pointing at the A Level section, "British or European history?" he asked. I swallowed.

"I covered the French Revolution at uni," I offered, uncertain if that sounded too confident.

"Perfect," he declared with a broad grin, "I've always hated the *Frogs*. I'll take British half." His joke landed awkwardly, funny or rude? I couldn't decide, so I stayed silent.

"I think we're going to get along just fine," he added, stacking his papers with deliberate care. I forced myself into a small nod.

"Pick an empty desk in here," he said, motioning to the two vacant desks, "and your main teaching room is through that door." He pointed behind him.

"Thank you, Harry," I said, voice steadier than I felt.

He tapped the folder on my knee, "ignore the schedule in there. Take the afternoon to explore and settle in here and in your classroom. All the syllabi you need are at the back; recommended textbooks are on these shelves." I nodded, torn between relief and confusion, was I free to forge my own routine or being tested?

"And tomorrow?" I asked.

"Meeting in the main staffroom first thing," he replied, "then let battle commence. Years ten and up only are in tomorrow; seven to nine join Wednesday." I noted each detail, mind flickering between anticipation and apprehension.

Harry stood and drifted toward his classroom. He paused, turned back with a mischievous glint, "if anyone asks after me, say I've gone to my 'club'."

I raised an eyebrow, "club?"

He laughed softly, "the pub around the corner. They'll understand." With a final wave, he slipped away down the corridor, leaving me alone in the hush. I closed my eyes, heart thundering with excitement, suspicion, and a cautious hope all tangled together.

The rest of my day was lost to paperwork and a little panic. I spent the lunch hour setting up my classroom, arranging the tables into a horseshoe as instructed in my *'Effective Modern Teaching'* manual. The sun hit the windows just right, and for a moment the room felt warm, almost homey. I set my briefcase on the desk in the office, then pulled out the small frame I'd brought from home. The photo inside was of "Amanda," but really it was the real Amanda from sixth form. I noted the location of the textbooks I would need for my first two classes the next day.

I counted to ten, then turned back, scanned the room, and made sure every trace of "Liam" was hidden behind the mask of "Mr. Parry."

After a few minutes, I walked to the door, closed it gently, and sat behind the desk. I practiced again, this time just a whisper:

"Amanda, Amanda, Amanda."

The more I said it, the easier it became. With any luck, by Christmas, I'd be able to say it without shaking, or smiling.

At the official end of the day, I felt tired, so I caught a bus back to the flat. The driver gave me a nod, the only human interaction, until I reached my door. Upstairs, the room was colder than I remembered, the bed stripped bare from the morning rush.

I sat at the table, not turning on the light, and listened to the hush of the city through the window. It was louder than I'd have guessed, bin lorries, shouting drunks, a dog somewhere in the distance. In the kitchen, I boiled water for tea, then forgot about it and watched the steam dissipate into nothing.

I picked up the phone and called home by muscle memory. Sarah picked up on the second ring.

"Liam!" she said, voice bright as a bonfire, "how's the great educator?"

I smiled, really smiled, for the first time all day, "I'm surviving. First day over."

She made a noise, half sympathy, half glee. "How's your boss?"

"He's okay, so far," I said, "a traditionalist I think."

She cackled, then softened, "you sound tired."

I didn't answer for a moment, "I am, a bit."

She paused, then, "hope you not too lonely, Li?"

I hesitated, "it's just… it's a lot, you know?"

"I know," she said, "but you're good at it, aren't you?"

"I hope so."

There was silence, gentle and easy. I imagined her sat on the bottom stair. I wanted to be there, not here, where the only evidence of my existence was a mark book and a mug of cold tea.

"You should come visit," I said, the words out before I could edit them.

She didn't miss a beat, "I'd love that. Name the weekend once I get settled at Salford."

I felt my throat go tight, "I'll check my diary."

"You do that," she said, "and Liam?"

"Yeah?"

"You're not alone, you know. Even if you think you are."

I let the words hang, then said, "thank you."

We talked a little longer, about Mum, about the new dog, *'your replacement'*, about her run-in with the local vicar over the Christmas bazaar. When I finally hung up, the city's noise seemed further away, like it had retreated out of respect.

I made another cup of tea, drank it in the silence, and went to bed. The window was still open, the night air bracing, but I left it that way. Just before sleep, I tried saying Amanda's name one last time. It came out easy, practiced, perfect.

But when I dreamed, it was always someone else's voice calling me home.

CHAPTER 21: THE CHRISTMAS PARTY

By the second Monday in September, I was already losing track of the days. The first term, "Autumn" on the calendar, though the world outside seemed to leap straight from stifling summer to guttered dusk, was a constant low-level crisis, broken into fifty-minute increments by the clang of the corridor bell and the bruised-looking faces of each year group as they shuffled into my room. The kids came in tides: some loud and spitting, some drained pale by the weight of sleep deprivation and expectation, all of them testing, always testing. I learned to keep my back to the blackboard, eyes on the most dangerous corners, and to never, ever show if I was thrown. Harry's dictum, "never smile before Christmas," became both shield and mantra; I would sometimes mouth it like an incantation on the walk up from the bus stop, the words a taste on my tongue.

Lesson plans multiplied like viruses. Each night, I'd get home to my flat, still smelling of new paint, every surface hard and echoing, and collapse into my desk chair with my briefcase, spreading the day's detritus over the table. I'd revise my notes, rewriting them in a panic, trying to anticipate which line the kids would seize on for mockery, which fact would become the next meme in the undercurrent of the lower forms. I began to dream in O Level history: Stalin's moustache hovering over the duvet, the Treaty of Versailles leaking onto the bathroom tiles.

Harry was always first in, and last out, except Friday afternoons when he retired to his *'club'* for the afternoon. I quickly learned the sound of his tread, heel-heavy, uncompromising, echoing up the stairwell to our little office. Each morning, he'd hand me a mug of tea before I'd even dropped my bag, "you'll need that, lad," he'd say, with a nod toward the stack of red folders that awaited me. If I didn't take it, he'd stand and wait, blue eyes fixed until I relented. Sometimes I'd catch a smile lurking behind his bristles, but never quite at the surface. "Survive today," he'd say, "and you can die tomorrow."

The office became our trench. There was a window which allowed in some sunlight, though the view was a car park and the brick rear of the canteen. We'd sit in the semi-dark, muttering over the day's schedule, trading stories of students gone off the rails or the latest policy missive from the headmaster. Barbara would pop in at intervals, ferrying biscuits or news from the staffroom ("Daniel's on the warpath again something about lost funding, or lost marbles"), but most of the time it was just me and Harry and the scent of strong tea or coffee.

"Don't get soft, Liam," he'd warn if I tried to cut slack for a kid who'd missed a deadline or turned up *sans* homework. "You let one slip and they'll smell the blood for months." I'd nod, feeling both grateful and slightly bruised, but the advice worked; by October, even Neil from Year Nine had stopped testing the perimeter and started turning in his essays, grudging but complete.

I watched Harry handle his own classes with the same precision he used on the kettle. He ran the room with a quiet, deliberate force, never shouting, never pleading. His voice would drop, not rise, in anger, "you've got ten seconds to get your act together, or I'll send you to the Head. And believe me, you'd rather face me." It worked. Kids respected him the way you respect a wolf in a field, you watched your step, and you knew he could end you if he wanted.

If I showed any sign of panic, he'd take me for a walk at lunch, two circuits of the playground, just long enough to run through a scenario or offer a story of his own disaster as a first-year probationary teacher, "once lost an entire class on a trip to the *Imperial War Museum,*" he'd confess, shaking his head, "spent an hour searching for them before realising they'd nicked my sandwiches and were hiding behind the gift shop." I'd laugh, and he'd glance at me with something close to approval.

As for the rest of the staff, I kept them at arm's length. I turned down invites to Friday pub sessions, the first time with the excuse of lesson prep, the second because of laundry, the third because, by then, the idea of small talk over lager made my stomach lurch. I could see that Barbara took it personally at first, but then she started inviting me out only as a matter of ritual, the way a hostess might ask if you want more cake while already clearing your plate. Daniel, on the other hand, seemed relieved not to have a rival for the last seat at the bar, and greeted my refusals with a snort and a raised eyebrow, "suit yourself, Parry," he'd say, "more for the rest of us."

The real reason was less dignified. Even in the smoky safety of the staffroom, even with "Amanda" as my conversational shield, I couldn't bear the thought of the first time someone would clock the tell, the way I'd linger on a mention of a male actor in a lesson, or the hesitance with which I'd answer questions about my "fiancée." It was easier to keep them at a distance than risk the erosion, the thousand small cuts that would bleed me out long before anyone said a word.

So, I became the workaholic. I lived for my timetable, the A Level group on Wednesdays and Fridays, the O Level one Thursdays, the coveted Friday morning with the bright kids from Form Three who actually wanted to be there. I learned to love the routines: the rattle of the book trolley as Barbara wheeled it past, the scratch of Harry's fountain pen in the quiet after lunch, the unvarnished honesty of the student essays ("Hitler was probably insane, but not as mad as my dad after he lost his job at *B&Q*"). The only variable was me, the way I slowly began to fit the space around me, the way my voice, at first hesitant, then ironed flat for authority, became just another feature of the corridor landscape.

By the last week of term, I could sense the shift. The kids no longer greeted me with suspicion; instead, they rolled their eyes at my jokes, called me "Sir" without irony, even tried to bargain for extra marks with a candour that bordered on affection. My Year Ten group made me a card (*'To the best history teacher we've ever had'*, it read in four different hands, two of them misspelled), and presented it to me after class with the solemnity of a court summons.

I kept the card in my desk drawer, under the folder where I filed all the detentions and missing homework slips. When I looked at it, I felt a twist of pride and something darker, a knowledge that I was, in this context at least, enough.

At home, I'd sometimes sit by the window, watching the traffic in the street below. My new bed still felt strange, the sheets too crisp, the air too dry, but I'd grown to like the view: a strip of road, the brick line of a primary school, and beyond that, a line of skeletal trees that bordered the estate. In those moments, I'd let the armour slip and take stock.

I thought about the fictional Amanda, the shape she'd taken in my life. I'd filled her out with details: a scarf she'd worn in a photo from sixth form, a coffee mug she'd once carried to a debate, the way she'd signed her name with a loop that looked like a treble clef. When colleagues asked about her, I'd deploy the stories like small change, her love of music, her intolerance for cheap whiskey, her frustration with the wind in Stirling. I'd constructed her so well that sometimes, in the edge of sleep, I'd almost believe she was real.

And yet, the price was always there. I could feel it in the stiffness of my own posture at staff meetings, in the way I'd pre-edit every line of casual conversation. I'd become an expert at omission, at steering the topic away from myself, at deploying humour or feigned ignorance as needed. It worked, but at the cost of a constant, grinding vigilance, a tax I paid in silence.

One lunchtime in that last week of term, after a particularly bruising year eight lesson, Harry found me in the office staring out of the window. The sky was gunmetal grey, the wind looked sharp enough to peel skin. He didn't speak at first.

"You're doing well, Liam," he said, voice low, "better than most who start here."

I nodded, not trusting myself to reply.

He squinted out of the window, "but don't let it eat you up. You can't fix everything. You can't be perfect all the time. Just do the job, and let the rest go."

I almost laughed, he made it sound so simple, so survivable. But I understood what he meant. I wanted to say something about the weight of keeping it all together, but the words stuck, like cold in my chest.

"And no more excuses," he said, perhaps more firmly than he had intended, "you will be coming to Friday's do at the pub," and there was something in his tone that suggested he wouldn't accept any of my usual excuses to decline, "or Barbara will have my guts for garters."

"Yes, I will Harry, thanks for the invite," I submitted.

"Good man!" he barked and then he clapped me on the shoulder, picked up pile of exercise books and disappeared into his classroom.

Later that night, I sat hunched over my desk, the lamp's yellow cone flattening my shadow to a jitter on the paint-chipped wall. There were seventy-five exercise books in front of me, each a minor crime scene: graffiti in the margins, half-hearted attempts at the causes of the English Civil War, the occasional sullen confession of not having read the chapter at all. I marked in red, then doubled back and marked again, second-guessing my own comments, afraid of being either too soft or too severe.

When my eyes began to blur, I reached for a blank notepad in the drawer that had replaced my shoebox, anything to clear the taste of the day. The drawer stuck, then jerked open. A sheaf of old letters came loose, and with them, a folded letter fluttered out and landed face-up on the floor.

I recognised the handwriting before I even touched it. The slanted capitals, the way the lines crashed into each other, Alex, always in a hurry, even on paper. I sat for a minute, thumb tracing the edge, then unfolded it.

It was the last letter he'd sent, months ago. The page was creased, the ink smudged at the fold. I read it again, pretending I didn't know the lines by heart. I tried again to read between the lines, to find a thread of the old Alex, the one who'd lie beside me in the dark and narrate his dreams, the one who'd hold my hand under the sheets and say, "fuck 'em, we're smarter than all of them anyway." But here, in the careful prose of a letter he must have half-dreaded to write, there was only distance.

The first time I'd read those lines, they'd made me so angry I nearly tore the page in half. I hated the implication, that he was the keeper of my truth, the one person in the world allowed to see me without armour. But now, months removed, I felt only a dull warmth. If Alex was moving on, I could too. I was even starting to believe it.

I set the letter aside, carefully, then bent back to my lesson plan. It struck me then how little I'd written to him, since. I had not replied to this letter, or the postcard before it. I wondered if that was cowardice, or just the slow logic of survival. I wanted to believe it was the latter, that I was better off in my new routine, even if it meant letting go of the only person who'd ever really known me.

Still, when I shut the drawer, I couldn't bring myself to put the letter away. I left it on the desk, half-buried under worksheets, as if it might someday answer a question I hadn't yet learned how to ask.

Later, when the street outside had gone fully silent, I made myself a cup of tea, then stood by the window and looked out. In the flats across the road, a string of coloured lights blinked uncertainly in the darkness. I wondered if anyone behind those windows felt as empty as I did, or if they'd already grown immune to the cold.

I cradled the mug, thought of Alex, and wished him well. I wished him everything he'd ever wanted, even if it never included me again. Then, I drained the cup, washed it, and went to bed. For the first time in weeks, I slept straight through until morning.

On Friday evening, *The Red Lion* was already at capacity when I shouldered through the door, the fug of cheap lager and wet wool so dense it stung the inside of my nose. Christmas lights were looped in drunken spirals across the beams, tinsel wound round every column and banister, as if the staff were engaged in a personal war against good taste. Behind the bar, a battery of cut-glass decanters reflected the fairy lights in shattered bands, while the sound system cycled through the same ten holiday hits on what must have been the world's shortest playlist. I'm sure I clocked *'Merry Xmas Everybody'* for the third time before I'd even made it to the end of the bar.

I'd dressed as neutral as possible: shirt but no tie, grey V-neck, the least offensive jeans I owned. My jacket was left unzipped to display the shirt, a concession to professionalism I doubted anyone would notice. I ordered a pint, tried not to flinch at the price, and hovered by the entrance, half hoping I'd misheard the invitation and could slip away unnoticed.

No such luck. Barbara Wilson was there, radiant in a Christmas jumper stitched with actual bells and a brooch that looked like Rudolph mid-collision. She waved both arms in a semaphore of welcome, nearly upending her own drink in the process.

"Liam! Over here, love!" she called, voice slicing clean through the crowd. Heads turned. I felt the old prick of embarrassment, but there was nothing for it. I weaved through the knots of colleagues and spouses, clutching my pint like a shield.

Barbara caught me at the elbow, already beaming, "you made it! Didn't think we'd see you, even though Harry had said you'd come." I smiled, tried to look casual. She sized up my drink, then me. She laughed, nudged me toward the table.

Harry was there, of course, nursing a scotch and chatting to a woman I vaguely recognised from reception. He raised a hand in greeting, "evening, Liam. Don't look so nervous!"

I rolled my eyes, "I'll be fine after a few of these," I raised my glass.

He grinned, "good lad. The trick is to keep just sober enough to remember the gossip, but not the regrets."

Barbara had already moved on, corralling a cluster of staff at the next table: Daniel, still looking like a man handcuffed to his own disappointment; the Head of Maths, all teeth and nervous energy; a PE teacher whose name I never remembered but who always called me "Professor." They all called out in chorus, "Liam! Over here!" and I nodded, took a chair, and did my best to blend.

I worked my way through the pint in slow sips, listening more than talking. The conversation pinged around the table: inspection rumours, the new canteen regime, someone's disastrous attempt at a "fun" lesson using fractions and Christmas cake. I chimed in when prompted, defaulting to my Amanda stories when asked about the holidays, "she's in Scotland, still," I said, the lie now so smooth it required no effort at all, "we'll meet up in the New Year hopefully." Nobody questioned it. I was just the quiet, reliable one, the sort you invited to round out numbers, but never expected to carry the room.

The evening drifted on, the volume rising with every round. Just as I was plotting a graceful exit, Barbara returned, towing a stranger in her wake, "Liam, there's someone you absolutely must meet," she said, her tone pitched halfway between co-conspirator and matchmaker, "this is Simon Vance, used to be one of our top sixth formers. Now he's a superstar at the Royal Northern."

Simon offered a hand, his grip light but insistent, "hi. It's weird to be back as a civilian."

He was a little shorter than me, slightly built the best I could tell through his thick woolly jumper. His hair was longish, the colour of good honey, falling in a swoop over one eye and curling around the upturned collar of his woollen trenchcoat. I glanced down at his hand, there were calluses on the fingertips, the pads slightly ridged and blanched. Musician's hands, for real.

I held the shake an instant longer than necessary, "nice to meet you," I said, "what do you play?"

He shrugged, "violin for study. Piano for fun. I'm not as good at the latter, but I try to fake it."

Barbara patted his arm, "he's being modest, as always. Simon's won about every competition they'll give to someone under twenty-one. He was the heartthrob of Upper Sixth, weren't you?" She winked. Simon flushed, made a show of adjusting his sleeve.

"Barbara exaggerates," Simon said, his vowels drawn out with that familiar self-deprecation, "I was a complete nerd. Still am."

Harry, ever the soldier for good cheer, clapped him on the back, "ignore her, lad. Anyone who survived this lot can handle a concert hall." His grin felt rehearsed, like he'd said it a thousand times. Did he believe it? I wasn't sure.

Simon nodded, but the smile didn't reach his eyes, there was something in them I recognised: the quiet wariness of someone always bracing for disappointment. He settled across from me, set his glass down with care, and folded his hands. "So," he asked, "what's it like being on the other side of the desk?"

I forced myself to lean in, feeling the pull of his attention, and the weight of my own insecurities, "mostly like playing a fraud who's only one lesson plan ahead of the students. But they don't know that, so it works… for now." My voice wavered. I half expected him to ask for my lesson plan next.

He laughed, bright, easy, yet threaded through with something almost regretful. Those laugh lines made him look younger, absurdly so, as if all his grown-up anxieties were trying to shelter behind boyish features. Around us, the table erupted into its usual squabble about bar policy and rumoured staff indiscretions. Simon seemed to drift away, attentive only to the friction between my confession and the steadiness of my voice. When he asked his next questions about the best part of teaching, missing student life, concerts in the city, I felt the truths spill out, too small to hoard, too bitter to swallow back down.

After a moment, he slipped off to the bar, insisting on buying me a drink. Harry leaned in, voice low, "good lad, that Vance. Lost his dad a few years back, but never let it break him.

Bright, but too damned sensitive. Reminds me of you, if I'm honest."

I wasn't sure how to take that. I offered a tight smile, "he seems… decent." The word tasted hollow. Did I mean it? Did I even trust myself to mean it?

When Simon returned, a middle-aged colleague, Marj, perpetually perched on high heels, had snatched his seat, despite Simon's coat draped over the back as if she owned his personal space. He muttered at her, "be so quick in my grave, Marj?"

She shot back with a grin, "only when I'm in four-inch heels and my feet are killing me."

He set our pints down and nudged my knee, light, familiar, "budge up, then. Plenty of room for a little one." I shuffled along the bench, suddenly conscious of how long it had been since I'd pressed this close to another person. My thigh warmed where his touched mine, and my heart slogged through a tangle of relief and alarm. He leaned in, breath warm beside my ear, "that's better, now we don't have to shout to be heard" he murmured. And I believed him, even as a knot of something, longing? fear? tightened in my chest.

Shortly after, the landlady appeared with plates of mince pies. As she leaned over, she caught sight of Simon, "hello, Simon love! How's your mum these days?"

He straightened a little, "she's much better now, thank you." Then, nudging me, "do you know Liam here? He's Harry's new teacher."

Brenda beamed at me, "hello, Liam. Welcome."

I forced my own smile, swallowed the swirl of gratitude and doubt, "nice to meet you, Brenda. Thanks for your hospitality."

She moved on to another table. Simon turned his head and whispered, a playful spark in his voice, "you charmer."

I pressed a hand to my chest as if wounded, "moi? Surely not." My tone was light, but inside, everything felt weighted, his every look, the closeness of his shoulder beside mine.

Simon laughed, but I wasn't sure I joined him. I couldn't decide if I was relieved or terrified that he was still here, still leaning in. Either way, I knew I wouldn't be leaving this table unchanged.

He grinned, shaking his head, "you'd think people would figure it out by now, no such thing as a good mince pie."

I took the bait, "maybe it's the nostalgia. Everyone likes the taste of childhood disappointment."

He laughed, eyes bright, "that's almost poetic."

I shrugged, "most truths are, once you sand off the edges."

He studied me, then said, "you ever read Byron? *'Sorrow is knowledge: they who know the most must mourn the deepest'*."

I finished the line before I could stop myself, " *'the tree of knowledge is not the tree of life.'*" His smile went wide, genuine.

"Impressive," he said, "I never meet anyone who remembers the last part."

I tried to hide the rush of pleasure, but he must have seen it, "I also teach a bit of English Lit," I said, "you start with the easy stuff, then you can't stop."

He nodded, "it's the same with music. You learn one scale, and suddenly you need to master them all. Compulsion, or maybe just curiosity."

"Or avoidance," I said, then wished I hadn't.

He tipped his head, "of what?"

I considered the question, then shook it off, "never mind. I'm not even sure."

He let the silence grow, not uncomfortable, just full. Then, quietly, "I've enjoyed this tonight. Not many people make me feel… seen." He flushed, as if the word embarrassed him, but he held my gaze.

I wanted to say the same, but I worried it would sound like a line. I chose instead to simply enjoy the physical closeness. Barbara bustled up, already mid-sentence.

"Liam, you're not boring Simon with shop talk, are you?" she teased, her tone warm but tinged with that same gentle condescension.

He offered a tight smile, "not at all. I'm getting an education," he said, though a fraction of him wondered if he sounded ridiculous.

Barbara patted his arm as if to reassure a nervous child, then turned her attention to me, "I suppose all these middle-aged teachers might be a bit much for two young colts like yourselves."

Simon and I exchanged a look, lips twitching. *'Colts?'* We mouthed the word at each other, then exploded into giggles. Even as I laughed, a knot of unease twined itself around my chest.

I recalled Barbara's praise of Simon's concerts, the bright future everyone expected for him. I forced myself to lean forward, "what are you working on at the moment?"

His grin was infectious, unsettling, "you wouldn't know it, obscure post-punk, some Russian composers who make my tutor want to scream."

My pulse quickened, "try me," I said, though doubt fluttered in my stomach.

He rattled off names, *Magazine*, *Joy Division*, *Gang of Four*, and spoke of *Schnittke* with reverence I barely understood. I nodded along, naming bands of my own, and felt a spark of triumph when surprise lit his face.

"I didn't think anyone in Stockport knew about the *Au Pairs*," he said, almost reverent.

My chest swelled with pride and shame, "small town. Big record stores," I replied softly. "I spent my uni years hiding in the back of *Piccadilly Records*. Still do, sometimes."

He laughed, genuine and bright, then grew serious, tapping his pint against the table, "it's weird, isn't it? All the things you think make you odd, until you meet someone just as odd, and suddenly it's not lonely anymore."

I stared into my beer, the words echoing in my chest as hope and fear tangled together. Did he mean me?

Our conversation drifted, books we'd never finish, politics, revolts against bad school lunches, and the thrill of sneaking into a *Smiths* gig on a fake ID. Simon countered with a story about being chased off a wedding stage when the bride's father declared his violin "unholy." I laughed until I snorted beer, but part of me remained on guard.

An hour passed and a lull settled. My shoulders relaxed, my jaw unclenched, yet the tension lingered, like a breath I couldn't quite exhale.

"You ever feel like you're performing, even when nobody's watching?" I blurted, surprised by the tremor in my voice.

Simon froze, confusion and recognition flashing across his face, "all the time," he whispered.

Around us the pub noise swelled, drowning out our fragile connection. We sat in companionable silence, each wrestling with the same conflicting ache: relief at being understood, fear of being seen too clearly.

When Simon excused himself, Harry slid closer to me, whisky-scented and serious.

"He's a good kid, Vance," Harry said quietly, "looks after his mum, keeps his nose clean. I don't say that about many of them."

I nodded, unsure what he was aiming at.

"He could use a mate," Harry continued, eyes steady on mine, "someone who gets it. You're a good teacher, Liam. But don't forget to live, yeah?"

I wanted to laugh, live, like that was simple, but I only nodded, feeling the weight of his words settle on my shoulders. Simon returned and slid back in beside me, as if he belonged there. He gave me a small, hopeful smile.

"One for the road?" I asked, voice hesitant.

"Sure," he replied, relief lighting his face, "but you'd better promise to get me home, my mum will worry."

I agreed and went to the bar. I ordered two brandies and we drank in silence. The pause stretched out, not awkward but charged, like the moments after a final chord before the applause begins, full of possibility and the fear it might never come.

He set his glass down, glanced at the clock above the bar, "I should get going. Big day tomorrow, Mum expects me to help wrap presents for the cousins." He rolled his eyes, "that's the downside of living at home. No escape from forced festivity."

I nodded, feeling the weight of the same obligation. Sarah would want me back in Rochdale before noon the next day.

He fished in his pocket, came up with a pen, "you mentioned you hate Christmas parties, right?" He smiled, "I might have lied about there being no such thing as a good one. New Year's, though, that's different."

He grabbed a beer mat, wrote his number on it, underlined it twice, and slid it toward me, "some friends are throwing a party in Fallowfield. It'll be mostly music students. No Christmas jumpers allowed. No *Wham*. Probably a lot of awkward dancing and bad jokes, but it's safe. You should come."

I stared at the beer mat, the ink bleeding into the cardboard.

Simon must have read my mind, "no pressure," he said, "but I'd like it if you did."

I took the mat, traced the numbers with my thumb, "maybe I will," I said, voice quiet. "I'll call you when I get back from Rochdale."

He smiled, stood, and buttoned up his coat, "see you soon then, I hope."

The number burned in my palm as I watched him leave. I slipped it into my wallet, behind my bank card, just in case. When I finally stepped outside, the world had gone white. Snow was falling, slow and thick, already blanketing the pavement. The streetlamps turned each flake into a brief, golden spark. I noticed Simon was just ahead, footprints fresh. I followed the silence of the city wrapping me in its cold, clean arms. I called to him, "wait up!"

He let me catch him up and we walked in tandem for a few streets, neither of us speaking, the only sound our boots crunching in the snow. At the next corner, he turned toward his street, paused, and looked back.

For a moment, everything was still. The snow, the city, even the ache I carried under my ribs. He smiled, lifted a hand in farewell, and disappeared into the hush. I walked the rest of the way home with the snow dusting my shoulders, the city empty and expectant, waiting for something to start.

In the flat, I hung up my coat, set the beer mat on the kitchen counter, and stared at it for a long time. Maybe I'd call. Maybe I wouldn't. But for the first time in ages, I thought of something else other than school.

I went to the window, watched the snow gather in the orange glow of the streetlights, and let myself believe, just for tonight, that something new was possible.

CHAPTER 22: MIDNIGHT IN MANCHESTER

I met Simon by the bus stop, and we took the short ride to Fallowfield, then walked the last stretch past a launderette and chip shop, the night so cold it sandpapered my cheeks. Simon wore a parka with the fur half-ripped off the hood, hands in his pockets, steps loose and out of time with the pavement. He kept glancing over at me, a half-smile threatening but never quite making landfall.

I'd spent days deciding to make the phone call to accept Simon's invitation, and then an hour and a half choosing my outfit, dark jeans, casual shirt, the nice jumper from Mum for Christmas and my trusty weatherproof coat. The beer was a last-minute decision, the sort of grown-up thing my father would have called "proper manners." As we rounded the corner, I nearly dropped the six-pack, my hands so numb I could barely feel the plastic rings.

The house was a typical Victorian terrace, redbrick and sagging, a patchwork of condensation on the upstairs windows. The porch light flickered, illuminating the scraps of tinsel still wound round the iron railing. Even from the pavement, the bass was a physical thing, rattling the glass, the pulse synced perfectly to my heart. For a second, I wondered if we'd be able to talk at all, or if we'd have to shout across the gulf like actors in a very cheap play.

Simon pushed on the unlocked door and turned to me. "Ready?"

I shrugged, "not really."

He grinned, "good. That's the spirit."

The heat hit first: dense, almost greasy, carrying the smells of lager, deodorant, and old takeaway. The hallway was so narrow I had to walk single-file behind him, dodging around a coat rack overloaded with actual coats, not just the token two or three you'd see at a parent's dinner party. The banister was sticky, and the carpet squelched underfoot, saturated with some ancient spill that had never been cleaned.

At the far end, the kitchen glowed with the light of a hundred fairy bulbs, looped from the extractor fan to the fridge to the battered cupboards. The fridge door was plastered with cut-out photos: *Madonna, Kinnock*, random footballers I didn't recognise. There was a crowd gathered around the table, which was stacked with more bottles than I'd ever seen outside an off license. Every surface was a mess, half-finished pints, mugs of tea gone cold, a bowl of cheese puffs bleeding orange dust onto the laminate. No one looked up right away. The music came from the room next door, the sound warping whenever the crowd in there stomped in time.

Simon hung back, then pointed at a girl pouring shots with surgical precision, "that's Jade. She's hosting. Be nice, but don't challenge her to a game of cards unless you're ready to lose money."

Jade had shaved sides, the rest of her hair a black wave falling over one eye. She wore a denim vest, a strip of tartan tied round her throat, and what looked like three watches on her left wrist. She clocked me in a single, efficient sweep, then smiled, just enough teeth to be a warning.

"Simon! And you brought him. Nice." She looked me up and down.

I set the beer on the counter, not sure what to do with my hands, "hi," I said, "I'm Liam."

Jade raised an eyebrow, "I know. He's told us. We don't just invite anyone," she pointed a finger-gun at Simon, who mock-dodged, "you want a drink?"

"Sure," I said, instantly regretting my eagerness.

She poured me a half-measure of something clear, then topped it with *Coke*, handing it over in a sticky glass. I sipped, expecting the taste of paint thinner, but it was just sweet and flat.

Simon introduced me as "Liam," nothing more, no further explanation seemed necessary. I wasn't sure if that was a kindness or just the party's general lack of memory for context. It felt like I'd been let in on a secret or maybe smuggled across a border.

The living room was the epicentre: a human crush of bodies, all students, mostly art or music from the look of them. There were painted faces, spiked hair, safety pins in places that made my teeth ache. The ceiling was strung with more lights, this set coloured and blinking, lending everyone a weird, underwater glow. Smoke, both legal and otherwise, hung in the air, swirling under the lampshades and making the scene seem distant, half-dreamed.

We threaded through the crowd. Simon greeted everyone with a touch, a handshake, a slap on the shoulder, sometimes a low-voiced joke I couldn't hear. No one questioned me. The anonymity was disorienting, like I'd gone invisible, my whole history erased by the press of strangers.

In the corner, two girls argued over the turntable, each trying to out-obscure the other with their vinyl picks. When one finally won, the opening bars of *'Love Will Tear Us Apart'* blasted, and the room shifted in response: heads started bobbing, feet tapped out of sync, conversations dropped an octave to compensate.

Simon leaned in, his mouth close to my ear, "let's get out of the crossfire. I'll show you upstairs."

I followed him up the narrow staircase, dodging a couple making out so intensely they didn't notice us at all. The carpet was threadbare; the walls scuffed with the ghosts of a hundred moving days. Upstairs, the landing opened into a small room with a battered sofa bed, a lamp made from an old traffic cone, and a window that overlooked the ice-bright street. It was someone's bedroom, converted into a 'quiet room' Simon explained. There were only two people inside: a bearded guy with a notebook, and a girl cross-legged on the sofa, rolling a cigarette with expert flicks.

Simon flopped onto the windowsill, pulling his knees to his chest. I hovered by the doorway, unsure if I should sit or just stand like a coat rack.

He patted the space next to him, "you can relax, you know. No one here cares if you quote books instead of bands."

I sat, careful to keep my knees from knocking his.

He smiled, softer now, "they're all show-offs anyway. The real talent is being able to sit still for more than five minutes."

I tried to laugh, but it came out as a cough, "I don't think I've ever sat still at a party in my life," I thought for a moment and then added, "actually, I've not been to that many parties to know if that is true." It was a true confession about my student life, a tactic used to avoid any drunken moments of betrayal with Alex.

He looked at me, his gaze holding mine just a little too long, "you're doing fine then."

There was a pause. From below, the music shook the floorboards, each beat thudding up through the wood like an aftershock. I took a sip of my drink, found it already half gone.

The girl on the sofa rolled her eyes at the guy with the notebook, then flicked her lighter and let the cigarette hang from her lips as she exhaled.

"Never seen you before," she said, not looking at me, "you one of Simon's music freaks?"

I shook my head, "just a friend."

She shot Simon a look, "at the conservatoire?"

He grinned, "no, different scene. But he's got a good ear."

I wanted to say something witty, something that would signal I belonged, but my brain glitched. I settled for, "I'm more into books."

She nodded, as if that was the right answer, then held out the cigarette, "want a hit?"

I hesitated, then took it. The smoke was harsh, but I kept my face straight, passed it back. She smiled, the first hint of approval.

From the notebook, the guy muttered, "you're in the wrong room if you want normal. They're all lunatics in here." Then he looked up, his eyes bloodshot but kind, "I'm Jack. I write, mostly poetry. No one reads it."

I introduced myself, then asked what he was working on. He shrugged, showing the page. It was a list of words, some underlined, some circled in heavy blue ink: *'wound', 'ghost', 'fracture', 'midnight'*. He noticed me looking. "I just collect them," he said, "sometimes they make poems. Sometimes they just sit there."

I nodded, "I used to do that. Back in sixth form."

Jack smiled, "you never really stop. Even if you want to."

Simon reached over and stole a sip of my drink, then wiped his mouth with the back of his hand, "see? I told you, it's easy."

I wanted to say thank you, but that felt too formal. Instead, I let the moment stretch, the four of us passing the cigarette and the silence back and forth.

After a while, Simon stood, "you want to finish the tour?" he asked.

I nodded, and we left the poets to their darkness.

In the next room, the 'hard rock group', the noise was even louder. A group had set up a makeshift dance floor, the carpet sticky and treacherous. People danced with wild, loose abandon, not caring if they looked stupid or beautiful. I watched, transfixed, as a boy in a mesh shirt spun a girl who shrieked with delight, her arms flailing, her *Doc Martens* stomping out a rhythm all their own.

Simon grinned at me, then grabbed my wrist, tugging me into the edge of the chaos. We didn't dance, not really, but we found a patch of floor near the stereo and just watched. I felt the nerves buzz out of my body, replaced by a fizzy, uncertain giddiness. At one point, Simon leaned close and said, "you could show them up if you wanted to."

I shook my head, "I'd break something. Or someone."

He laughed, and I heard the affection in it, undeniable, unforced. For the first time, I allowed myself to be just another body in the crowd, no lesson plan, no mask, just the oddness of my own skin and the awareness of Simon at my side.

We stayed there a while, and then moved back downstairs, the hours dissolving into each other. I lost track of how many times I refilled my drink, or how many conversations I started and never finished. At some point, Jade reappeared, crowned with a string of party hats stapled into a makeshift tiara. She handed me a bottle of cheap fizz, then pulled Simon away for a group photo. I caught a glimpse of them through the crowd, her arm slung round his neck, both of them grinning like idiots, and for a moment, I felt a pang. Not jealousy, exactly. More like the ache of wanting something I'd never thought possible.

Later, when the clock in the hallway chimed eleven, Simon found me sitting on the bottom step of the stairs, my legs stretched out, head tipped back against the banister. He sat beside me, shoulder to shoulder.

"Having fun?" he asked.

I nodded, too tired to lie even if I had wanted to, which I didn't this time. He nudged me with his elbow, "you're a good person, you know."

I snorted, "that's debatable."

He looked at me, serious now, "I mean it."

The hush between us was a relief, a chance to let the world keep spinning without my permission. From the living room, a chant started up: "midnight, midnight, midnight!" It was still an hour away, but the crowd had given in to the inevitability.

Simon stood, then offered me a hand, "let's go watch."

I took his hand, let him pull me up. We drifted back into the party, the edge of the crowd. I felt his hand brush mine, once, then again, fingers just grazing knuckles.

For the first time in years, I didn't flinch. Instead, I leaned into the heat and the noise, and let myself believe that, for at least one night, I belonged.

The party slipped its gears after midnight started appearing closer to the horizon, the tempo inside ratcheting up as people realised they'd soon have to declare themselves, who they'd kiss, who they'd forget, who'd make it onto the night bus with them and who'd be left scraping up their dignity from the hallway floor. I floated from group to group, my pint glass always half-full and my brain running two conversations at once, one for the person in front of me, the other dedicated to Simon's whereabouts at any given second.

He'd vanished for a bit after another group photo, swept off by Jade and her circle of music students. I watched him from across the room, laughing at a joke he probably knew was at his own expense. He was good at that, absorbing the hit and turning it into something warmer, some new energy he'd toss back into the room. I admired it, and I envied it in equal measure.

I found myself wedged into a corner with a film student named Ben, his accent was as clipped as any I had heard from the Law students at uni, and insisted on calling me, "Manchester" because he'd forgotten my name after the first introduction.

"So, Manchester," he shouted over the thump of the bass, "top three films, go."

I hesitated, then named a couple of safe choices, *Taxi Driver*, *Blade Runner*, something French that sounded cleverer than it was.

Ben snorted, "you're such a teacher. All boys your age say *Taxi Driver.*" I shot him a look, then realised he didn't mean it as an insult.

Ben grinned, the kind of grin that dared you to be offended, "it's fine. You have a face for it. Dead serious. But you gotta have fun with it, too."

I said, "I'm working on it."

He raised his glass, "cheers to that, old boy." Then, abruptly, "you know Simon, right? He's all right. Bit weird, but all right."

I nodded, "he's the reason I'm here."

Ben eyed me, lips pursed, "he's got a type, doesn't he?"

I pretended not to hear, focusing instead on the room's pulse. The dance floor was thick with bodies, limbs tangled, all of them lost in the music or the people they were with. The air was full of sweat and vaporised gin, the kind of heat that made the world outside seem imaginary.

Every time I looked up, Simon was there. Not always close, but always in my line of sight. Sometimes he caught my eye and grinned, sometimes he looked away quickly, embarrassed to be caught watching back. We circled each other like dogs at a park, never touching but always ready.

I tried to enjoy the small freedoms the party offered: a smoke on the porch, a joke that didn't have to be explained, the chance to just exist without calculating every angle. I noticed myself getting braver, asking questions, making jokes, even dancing (a bit) when a song I recognised came on. Jade pulled me into a conga line at one point, and though I felt like a complete idiot, I also felt, briefly, like I'd been invited to the world's weirdest church.

At some point, my nerves burned out. The worry about being found out, about what people would think if they really looked, just… evaporated. No one here cared where I came from or what I did for a living. I could have told them I was a dog walker for the Queen and they'd have just nodded and asked if the corgis were as mean as everyone said. The freedom made me lightheaded.

I ended up back in the kitchen, alone for a minute. Someone had left the fridge open, and the cold air mixed with the heat of the party, making the room feel less like a room and more like the inside of a working lung. I took a seat on the counter, swinging my legs like I used to do as a kid when the rest of the family wasn't paying attention.

It was then that Simon found me. He slid in, closed the fridge door, and leaned against it with a bottle of cheap wine in one hand and two plastic cups in the other.

"Found you," he said, like it was a game.

"Didn't know I was hiding," I replied, but there was no bite in it.

He opened the bottle and poured two uneven measures, handing me the fuller one. When our fingers met, neither of us moved them right away. The touch was casual, the kind you'd share with a mate, but it was also charged, full of static and the promise of something more.

We stood there for a while, not talking. The kitchen window was open a crack, and the yard outside was empty and dark. Simon sipped his wine, then said, "I like you, Liam." It was so direct that I nearly laughed, but he said it with the seriousness of someone who'd never learned to lie about things that mattered.

I managed, "I like you too." My voice sounded wrong, all echo, but he seemed to like it.

He set his cup down and hopped up onto the counter next to me, so we were shoulder to shoulder, both staring out at the blackness beyond the glass.

"Do you ever wish you could just skip to the part where you don't care what anyone thinks?" he asked.

I thought about it, "sometimes I think I'll get there, but then something pulls me back. Like there's always someone watching, even when there isn't."

Simon nodded, "yeah. I know what you mean. But it's better here, isn't it? At least a little."

"It is," I said, "you make it easier."

He blushed, turning away so I could see the line of his jaw, "you know, I was terrified to invite you," he said. "I thought you might think I was a freak."

I shrugged, "you're not a freak. Or if you are, I'm worse."

He smiled, soft and a little sad, "we can be freaks together, then."

The party was getting louder. Someone had started a countdown, even though it was still fifteen minutes to midnight. The chant drifted through the house, losing steam then swelling again.

Simon drained his cup, then stood, "c'mon. You can't miss the countdown. It's the whole reason for the party."

I slid off the counter, knees wobbly. He steadied me with a hand on my shoulder, and for a second we stood there, his palm warm and reassuring.

"Thanks," I said.

He shrugged, then led the way back to the living room. The bodies were packed even tighter, the air thick with anticipation and whatever else people had been passing around.

We pushed our way to the middle, and suddenly I was at the centre of things, Simon at my side, the noise and heat and promise of the new year crowding out every doubt I'd ever had. I didn't know what would happen when the countdown hit zero, but for the first time I wasn't afraid of it.

Simon turned to me, his mouth close to my ear, "almost midnight," he said, voice low and steady.

"Almost," I said, and smiled. He smiled back, and the world spun just a little.

It happened all at once: the music died mid-song, and the living room surged with bodies, half the crowd raising their drinks as if to summon the next year by sheer force. Someone, Jade, probably, started the countdown at thirty, and the rest joined in, a messy, drunken choir echoing through the house. I felt the pressure of Simon's arm next to mine, warm and grounding, as we pushed to hold our ground.

It was suddenly claustrophobic, the air wet with sweat and breath, faces pressed close in expectation, everyone loud and laughing and unashamed of wanting something. For a second, I thought of every New Year's Eve I'd spent at home, the awkward ritual of hugging my parents, the quiet disgust at watching couples snog on the telly, the cold shame of wanting that kind of abandon for myself.

"Ten! Nine! Eight!"

Simon's hand found mine, just for a second, a squeeze of reassurance.

"Seven! Six! Five!"

He grinned at me, and I realised I'd been holding my breath. I let it out, and the sound of it was swallowed by the chant.

"Four! Three! Two!"

I saw his mouth form the numbers, his lips wet, a tiny scar on his lower one I'd never noticed before.

"One!"

There was an explosion of noise, screams, whoops, the unmistakable pop of at least one bottle ricocheting off the ceiling. A cloud of confetti showered down, the bits sticking to skin and hair and even, impossibly, to the walls.

Before I could think, Simon turned to me. No hesitation, no calculation, just a quick, certain movement. His hand was at the back of my neck, pulling me in, and then his mouth was on mine. Not a showy, performative kiss, but a real one, soft and solid, his lips opening just enough for me to taste the last of the champagne on his tongue.

I froze. The world stopped, all the noise replaced by the sudden roar of blood in my ears. I heard myself gasp, felt my own heart trip over itself. Simon pulled back, face flushed, eyes wide and uncertain.

I jerked away, instinct making me check the room for witnesses. But no one was looking. Two girls next to us were locked together in an embrace, their arms tangled in each other's hair. A boy in a dress shirt kissed Jade full on the mouth, and she responded by kneeing him gently in the thigh and laughing. Someone else had already started the next song, and the crowd was moving again, a single mass of heat and noise and indifference.

"It's okay," Simon whispered, leaning in so only I could hear, "no one cares here."

He smiled, the kind of smile that could shatter glass.

I looked at him. I looked at the room. Then, without thinking, I grabbed his face and kissed him back, harder this time, my hands pressed into the soft place behind his jaw.

He made a tiny sound, a whimper or a laugh, I couldn't tell and I felt it in my own chest. We broke apart, both of us breathing hard, and for a moment the room seemed to tilt on its axis, everything reorienting around this one ridiculous, impossible moment.

Simon wiped his mouth, looked at me like I'd just told him the best secret in the world. He said, "Happy New Year,

Liam," his voice full of hope and something else, something sharper.

"Happy New Year," I said, and it was the first time I meant it.

For the rest of the night, we didn't let go. He kept a hand on my shoulder, or the back of my neck, or sometimes just on the hem of my shirt, as if to remind me it had really happened. We danced, we drank, we talked to everyone and no one, and I realised the fear was still there, but it was smaller now, something I could name and put in my pocket.

I kept thinking about Alex, about the way he'd always warned me never to be seen, never to make a scene, never to want too much. I wondered if he'd ever had a moment like this, or if he'd always chosen the safety of distance over the risk of being known.

At two a.m., the party was still going, but Simon pulled me out onto the porch, into the cold air. Our breath hung between us like smoke.

"I'm glad you came," he said, shivering and not trying to hide it.

"Me too," I said, then added, "I'm glad you kissed me."

He grinned, "took you long enough to say it."

He leaned in and kissed me again, slow and unhurried, our foreheads bumping together as we laughed.

The street was empty. The whole city was ours.

Inside, the countdown had started again, a new group trying to turn the last moments of the night into something worth remembering. Simon and I watched from the threshold, together and apart, hearts beating in time to the muffled music.

When the next midnight came, I hoped it would be ours.

CHAPTER 23: THE ARRANGEMENT

January 1986

First day back was always supposed to be easy. You got through the hangover, traded war stories with the rest of the staff, handed out new registers, and prayed the students hadn't managed to forget how to open a textbook over the fortnight's break. That morning, I woke to my alarm, stumbled through a shower so cold it nearly unzipped my soul, then stood for a good minute in front of the mirror, searching for evidence of the previous week. There was nothing, really, no love bite or lipstick, no hickey tucked beneath my shirt collar. The only thing out of place was the look in my own eyes: sharper than usual, or maybe just frightened. I smoothed my hair, knotted the tie twice, then headed into the January morning.

The walk to school felt longer than usual, the cold sticking to my lungs and throat. A memory from New Year's, the taste of cheap wine on Simon's tongue, the shock of his hand on my jaw, kept worming its way into the edges of my thoughts. The whole week since, we'd only phoned each other twice. Once by me to thank him for Saturday night, and the other from him telling me he would see me on Friday in the pub.

The corridor in the Humanities block was colder than the street, the radiators giving off the faint suggestion of heat but not actually bothering to do it. I opened the office door, to find Harry already in his seat as usual, reviewing a stack of mock exams with the intensity of a man grading his own will.

He grunted in my direction, "morning, Liam. You look like hell."

I tried a laugh, "nice to see you, too."

He raised a mug of tea, then went back to the papers, "had you down for a man who could handle his drink. Shows what I know." And with that we resumed our established routine.

Classes began with the usual avalanche of forgotten books and sullen apologies. The lower years tested the perimeter, but a cold glare from me and a threat of a detention reestablished the natural order by the second period. Even so, my mind drifted: I'd catch myself staring out the window, missing three lines of the textbook while I replayed the New Year's kiss, the feel of Simon's palm on the back of my neck, the shock of being seen and wanted in a room full of strangers.

At break, I joined Harry in the staff room. He was reading *the Telegraph*, one hand wrapped around his mug like a life preserver. He watched me stir my tea for a solid minute.

"You all right, lad?" he said, softer than usual.

I nodded, but overdid the smile, "just tired."

He grunted, "better than being hungover, I suppose. You need to watch yourself, though. First signs of going soft and the kids'll be on you."

"Duly noted."

Harry went back to his paper. I sat, watching the condensation on the windows, and tried not to think about Simon or how many hours it was until Friday.

The rest of the day slipped past in stuttering jumps. In one class, I lost my place while reading a passage, had to start the page again. In another, I caught myself smoothing my hair in the reflection of the classroom window, then immediately checking my tie for straightness. At lunch, I ate alone in the office, staring at my sandwich as if it might reveal the right thing to say if Simon actually showed at the pub on Friday.

When colleagues asked about my holiday, I gave the same rehearsed answer, "quiet one, mostly family, party New Year's Eve, nothing dramatic," and avoided their eyes as much as possible.

The last period ended with a whimper: a year-nine boy sneaking out early, the rest of the class too dazed to even pretend at rebellion. I let them go a minute early, then sat at my desk, staring at the clock, counting the seconds until I could escape.

After the bell, I lingered in the office, pretending to grade papers but really just waiting for the halls to empty. Only when the silence felt complete did I pack up, lock the door, and make for home.

The sky was already slate-dark, the streetlights flickering on with the reluctance of a teenager on bin duty. My shoes slipped a little on the frost that had already started to film the pavement. I tried to focus on the cold, on the bite in the air, on the taste of my own breath, but every time, the memory of Simon's mouth, his smile in the shadow of the party lights, cut through like a song I couldn't get rid of.

By the time I reached my flat, I was wound so tight I nearly snapped the key in the door. I went straight to the kitchen, made a cup of instant coffee, and stared at the phone hanging on the wall. I wanted to call Simon and tell him about my day and ask about his, but this feeling was simply too new for me to know what to actually do about it.

I sat at the kitchen table, the flat silent except for the tick of the old radiator. I tried to make myself read, journal articles, the lesson plans for tomorrow, anything to smother the static inside my head. But Friday was only four days away I decided in the end. I could wait.

Friday at the pub felt like Christmas: same sticky floors, same table in the corner claimed by the school staff before the locals could invade, same battered fruit machine trilling a soundtrack of near-misses and disappointments. But the air felt thinner, the hum of conversation pitched an octave higher. My hands shook more than usual, so I gripped the pint glass with both, hoping the condensation might cool the heat in my palms.

Barbara was in her element, holding court at the head of the table. She'd brought in her own "special" sausage rolls, spiked with fennel and something else that made Harry cough and reach for his whisky. The first rounds went fast, and so did the stories: Daniel's car that wouldn't start, Harry's theory on the "inevitable decline" of the A Level syllabus, Barbara's running tally of her cat's New Year's "resolutions." I laughed where I was supposed to, but the noise pressed on my skull.

I side-stepped the expected questions about Amanda by explaining she had been unable to get away as her mother had been unwell over the holiday period. But every minute that passed, I found my eyes drifting to the door.

When Simon appeared, I nearly choked on a sip of beer. He wore a dark blue crew neck over a white T-shirt, hair tied back in a way that left his face completely open, cheekbones catching the glow of the fairy lights strung across the bar. He paused at the entrance, scanning the crowd, then spotted Barbara and raised a hand.

She shrieked his name, loud enough to hush half the room, and waved him over. Harry glanced up, eyebrows climbing. Daniel followed with a look I couldn't read, something between *'Christ, we're let-ting kids in here now?'* and *'Could've been worse, I suppose'*.

Simon reached the table, standing just behind me, and set down a small box, biscuits, probably, for Barbara. His hand brushed my shoulder as he slid into the empty seat next to mine. It was so quick I could have imagined it, but the skin burned for a full minute after.

Barbara made introductions, effusive as ever and entirely unneeded. Simon smiled, soft but genuine, and said hello around the table. His voice was lower than I remembered from the party, more deliberate, as if he were performing a role. He leaned back, crossing his arms, giving off the impression of being at ease, but I noticed his right foot tapping an irregular code beneath the table.

"So, Simon," Harry started, "how was your holidays? All glamour and gala dinners?"

Simon grinned, playing along, "just the odd party between making sure Mum was ok."

Barbara beamed, "I told you he was wonderful."

Conversation rolled on. Simon held his own, taking polite sips from the half-pint I'd nudged toward him, letting the talk wash over. Once or twice, I felt his gaze land on me, brief, then gone, but each time it left a tremor in my ribcage. I tried to keep my focus on the group, but the urge to turn, to really look at him, was almost unbearable.

At some point, the conversation turned to music. Daniel, who'd been mostly silent, perked up, "heard you're into the experimental stuff as well," he said, aiming it at Simon but keeping his eyes on the foam of his *Guinness*, "what's the deal with all these composers who don't even use melodies anymore?"

Simon shrugged, "there's melody, but you have to listen for it. Sometimes it's more about what isn't played."

Daniel snorted, "sounds like cheating to me. In my day, you either learned the instrument, or you didn't."

Simon smiled, unfazed, "maybe. But sometimes the mistakes are the best part." I liked the way he didn't let Daniel's cynicism get to him.

I caught his eye then, and he held the look, just for a second, before returning to the group.

The evening moved with the inexorable logic of all staff drinks, a round for every story, louder laughter with each hour. The table shrank as people peeled away, first the Head of Maths, then the Science twins, off to catch their bus. By half-nine it was just Harry, Daniel, Barbara, Simon, and me.

Barbara scooted closer to make room, nudging Simon and me together. Our knees touched under the table. It could have been an accident, but we both knew it wasn't. The sensation was electric, a charge that ran straight up my spine and made every other noise in the pub fade to static.

Harry stood to get another round, and Daniel followed, grumbling about the "new" bar staff. Barbara leaned over the table, her eyes dancing with some secret amusement.

"You two look like you're having a deep and meaningful," she said, just loud enough for us to hear.

I fumbled for an answer, but Simon beat me to it, "we were just being music geeks."

Barbara cackled, "I believe it. Liam's a dark horse for sure." She winked at me, then turned away. For a minute, it was just us, the hum of the bar and the warm, amber shadow on Simon's jaw.

He leaned in, voice barely audible, "it's good to see you," he said. I nodded, unable to trust my own voice.

The others returned, and the spell broke, but the contact at our knees remained. Simon poured a splash of his beer into my glass, a meaningless gesture, but the intimacy of it made my face flush. I couldn't stop thinking about the Saturday night out we'd shared, the way he'd kissed me, the line of his fingers on my skin.

When Harry announced, "right, last one, and then I'm off," the night felt suddenly, violently brief.

Barbara gathered her things, her face soft in the golden light. "I'll see you on Monday, love," she said, then, to Simon, "you should pop into school one day. We miss your energy around here."

Simon promised he would, but I could see in his eyes he was watching for my next move.

As we stood, Simon brushed my arm, "heading this way?" he asked, with a casualness that bordered on reckless.

"Yeah," I said, "walk you out?"

We moved toward the door. Behind us, Barbara smiled, a slow, knowing thing that made me shiver. She didn't say anything, but her eyes followed us all the way out.

Outside, the cold was total, wrapping the world in a kind of honest silence. Simon zipped his coat, and we fell in step, side by side, the streetlamp shadows spilling ahead of us. We walked without speaking, the only sound the bite of our shoes on frozen pavement and the slow exhale of our breath, visible as a pair of plumes that collided and drifted apart again. The residential streets were mostly dark, each garden bristling with frost and the leftovers of December's lights, now more ghostly than festive. I could feel Simon matching my pace, but keeping just a half-step closer than needed.

After a while, he tilted his head, voice low, "do you always walk this fast, or is it just to stay ahead of the gossip?"

The question made me laugh, too loud in the hush, "maybe I need to," I said. "I spent the whole Christmas break eating carbs and chocolate."

He smirked, "you look fine to me." The compliment hung in the air, awkward and pure.

We kept on, past shuttered shops and the occasional car with its windows crusted white. I wanted to say something meaningful, something that would explain the static in my chest, but all I could manage was, "so, how's college?"

Simon shrugged, hands stuffed deep in his pockets, "it's music school. Intense, but worth it. You know how it is, everyone competing, but also desperate for someone to listen. Sometimes I think I'd be happier in a shed with a decent stereo and a kettle."

"Sounds about right," I said, "that's most teachers' retirement plan."

He glanced over, a sideways look, "do you like it? Teaching?"

I nodded, then hesitated, "most days. I like the work, and the kids are better than they let on. But sometimes…" I trailed off, unsure if I was allowed to finish.

He filled the silence, "sometimes you wish you could be a different version of yourself."

That caught me off guard. I stopped, almost slipped on the curb, then recovered, "yeah," I said, "exactly."

We walked a few more steps in silence, letting that settle.

At the next streetlamp, Simon turned to face me, hair haloed by the jaundiced light, "I've been thinking about you," he said, the words flat and fearless, "since Saturday."

"I don't want to screw this up," I said, surprising myself with the honesty.

He looked at me, patient, "what's there to screw up?"

I weighed the question, then admitted, "I'm scared. Not just of being found out. I'm scared I'll get used to wanting things and then have to give them up again. Like at uni, or before."

He nodded, serious, "you don't have to decide everything to-night."

"I know. But if someone sees us, if a parent or a student ..."

He held up a hand, cutting me off, "let's keep it simple. Fridays, after school, with the others. Safe. Saturdays, in town, where nobody knows us, so also safe. If we want more, we'll figure it out."

The logic was so clean, so gentle, that it almost made me cry. Instead, I shoved my hands into my own pockets and said, "that sounds perfect."

At the next corner, Simon stopped again, just far enough from the main road that nobody could see. He pulled his hands out, rubbed them together for warmth, then, after a hesitation, reached out and found my hand.

His skin was cold, but the pressure was steady. I looked up and saw him smiling, a little bashful, a little daring. We stood like that for a second, not moving, just letting the night watch.

He squeezed my hand, then let go, as quick as he'd taken it.

"I should head back," he said, "Mum gets jumpy if I'm late."

"Sure," I said. "I'll walk you as far as your street."

We moved on, slower still. At the corner of his road, Simon stopped, then turned to face me, eyes searching for something.

"I told my Mum I may be out for the night tomorrow if that's ok?" he asked, "I'll call you in the afternoon to sort it."

I nodded, barely trusting myself to speak.

He smiled, then, just for a second, put his palm on my cheek. The touch was soft, but the meaning behind it was solid enough to hold me upright for a week.

Then he was gone, hands in pockets, head down, disappearing into the sodium glare and the silence. I watched until he turned into his house, then stood for a long time, the cold eating through my coat but leaving something alive and bright underneath.

I walked home alone, but every step felt like less of a risk and more of a promise. By the time I reached my flat, the fear had faded. In its place was the memory of his hand in mine, and the certain knowledge that, tomorrow, I'd get to feel it again.

Saturday, the sky was nothing but an unbroken slab of white. I woke early, unable to shake the sense of something looming, like Christmas morning, if Christmas involved the risk of being caught and ruined at any moment. Simon called mid-afternoon, and we arranged to meet later. I went through three combinations of jumper and shirt and still looked like a supply teacher bracing for a parent complaint. I checked the clock: too early, then too late, then exactly on time.

Simon was already on the platform when I arrived. He wore a denim jacket with the collar up and a scarf knotted so expertly I wondered if he'd practiced it. When he saw me, his whole face lit, and for a second I forgot how to breathe.

"Hey," he said, shifting his weight from foot to foot, "you made it."

"Wouldn't miss it," I replied, and it was almost true.

We found seats near the back of the nearly empty carriage, the ride to *Piccadilly* took six minutes, but I felt every second. We watched out the windows, both pretending not to notice the way our knees kept knocking. At the station, the city poured in, noise, colour, the distant siren call of market stalls and the rush of people who had somewhere to be.

Simon led the way through the maze of concourse and out towards Canal Street. He had a destination in mind, and we diverted to Chorlton Street towards the bus station. Underneath the multi-storey car park itself was a new venue called the *Thomson Arms*.

"Heard good reports," he explained, "mostly students and younger crowd. The DJ is meant to be good too."

"A gay bar?" I whispered, with a hint of dread.

"Don't worry, it's a mixed crowd and just trendy," Simon tried to reassure me, aware of my fears and doubts as he was, "we'll have one, and move on if you want to. It's not a problem." I let him take my hand and lead me through the double doors.

Inside was a riot of disco lights, a dance floor, intimate booths and an L-shaped bar staffed by the youngest set of bar staff I had ever seen. Simon pointed out an empty booth, "grab that table and I'll get the drinks." I sat down at the empty booth and scanned the room and prepared myself for the panic that would come if I recognised some-one. I didn't of course, so I relaxed. Simon slipped along the padded bench with our drinks and sat next to me, our thighs touching.

I lifted my drink, "cheers!"

"So," he said, "tell me something real."

I laughed, not sure where to start, "like what?"

He leaned in, elbows on the table, unafraid, "anything. Family. Secrets. Your first record. You decide."

I looked at the beads of condensation forming on my glass. "I'm from Rochdale as you know," I said. "Dad was a foreman at the mill until it closed, then worked night shifts wherever he could. Mum kept house and made sure we didn't starve. I did well at school because it was the only way out."

Simon nodded, encouraging.

"I read a lot," I continued. I suspected I was taking this far too seriously than Simon had expected, but continued anyway, "mostly to avoid talking to anyone. I never really fit in, so I just... waited for something to change." I paused, unsure if this was the right time to mention the part about liking boys. I let the silence stand.

He took it in, "do your parents know you're gay?" His tone was matter-of-fact, but his jaw tensed.

I shook my head, "not exactly. My sister does. But I've never said it out loud."

He took a sip of his drink, then said, "it's different for me. Mum always knew. Dad was gone before I got old enough to care what he'd think. My friends... they're all musicians. Nobody cares."

"Lucky you," I said, but it came out sharper than I meant.

He smiled, forgiving, "it isn't always easy. There's still the gigs where someone yells 'poofter' from the back row, or the old guys at the pub who think it's funny to say 'that one's a bit delicate' when I ask for a shandy. But mostly, it's okay. I like who I am."

I envied the ease of it, "I'm not there yet."

He looked at me, softening, "you will be."

We filled the time with talk: books, music, the best and worst concerts we'd ever seen. He made me laugh with stories of the orchestra ("violinists are the worst, catty as drag queens, but less self-aware"), and I made him roll his eyes at my attempts to explain the plot of every novel I'd ever loved. It was easy, the rhythm of it, like the way I'd always imagined a proper date would go.

He watched me talk, his gaze direct, "I've thought about you a lot since New Year's."

I swallowed, the bite sticking in my throat, "I've thought about you too."

He grinned and stretched his hand across the sticky table, pausing just above mine. My heart thudded as he let it fall, palm up, as if daring me. I froze for a moment, wishing I could pull back, but longing to close the distance, before sliding my hand into his. Our fingers intertwined so naturally it felt impossible, and tears pricked behind my eyes at how achingly simple it all seemed, and how terrifying.

We sat like that for a while, hands clasped between sips of half-cold beer and quiet tales of ourselves. Around us the bar buzzed, but no one paid attention, or maybe they did, and didn't care enough to intervene.

At last Simon broke the silence, "was there someone else before me?"

The question hit me like a punch. My grip tightened. I swallowed, "yes," I whispered, my throat dry, "someone from university… Alex."

He was silent, head tilted, absorbing it. I wondered if I'd just shattered something, if my past love was a crack in whatever we had. After a long beat he asked, quietly, "how long?"

"Almost three years," I said, and lifted my pint in a trembling salute, "my round," I managed, then pushed to my feet before he could reply. My legs wobbled as I threaded through the tables to the bar, heart hammering with guilt and relief in equal measure.

When I returned with two swaying pints, each now missing an inch of beer from my passage through the crowd, Simon greeted me with a soft smile and patted the seat beside him. He draped his arm around my shoulders, pulling me in close. Warmth bloomed in me, tangled with shame.

"Sorry," he whispered, voice low, "if you didn't want to talk about it."

I pressed my forehead against his arm, "no… I'm glad, it's just… I've never told anyone. It was a secret." I glanced at his chest, "except my little sister. She guessed everything last year."

"Thank you for trusting me then," he said softly.

I lifted my head to look at him, "your turn, then. Spill." I tried to mimic my sister's teasing grin, but it came out shaky.

He exhaled, eyes drifting to the amber beer, "I knew I was… different, weird as a kid, but nothing ever happened until *Freshers' Week* last September. I ended up in a bedroom with a third-year, total drunken fumble." He paused, as if embarrassed to own it. "I didn't even fancy him," he admitted, voice low. Then he reached out, cupping my cheek, turned my face toward his, "which is certainly not the case with you," he murmured.

My pulse jumped. I tried to hide my flush in the dim light, but I'm certain he felt it anyway. My gaze skittered around the bar, any familiar face, any potential hostile witness but something inside me snapped. *'Sod it',* I thought, and I leaned in, pressing my lips to his.

We hadn't even broken apart when a gruff voice beside us said, "you can get rooms by the hour in *the Rembrandt* for that." An older man in a rumpled coat slumped onto the bench.

We jumped apart and mumbled apologies. He waved a hand, "no need, I was only kidding, boys. Enjoy yourselves while you can." Relief flooded me and we all laughed, my tension easing as the stranger went on to make conversation.

He told us stories from his youth, shady bars, police raids, a night in a cell for simply being himself. His eyes glinted with bitter pride. As he stood to leave, he leaned closer, "ignore the bitter old queens you'll meet around here. They're just jealous you're living the life they couldn't." He gave a slow nod, "maybe see you again sometime?"

We exchanged uncertain smiles, "sure," we said in unison, each of us riding a wave of excitement, and fear, over what came next.

We eventually left the warmth of the bar and stepped into the city, the air even colder than before. Simon guided us down towards the junction with Canal Street, past the shops, takeaways and the shouting of the late-night crowd, and then, after a turn, into the heart of the Village.

Even in January, Canal Street pulsed with life: bars spilling bodies onto the pavement, laughter ricocheting off the canal walls, the scent of cheap lager and the sharper tang of anticipation. A-boards littered the pavement, variously promising *'Drag Bingo Tonight'*, or *'Happy Hours'*.

Simon slowed, then reached for my hand again, this time with no hesitation. We walked, not hiding. We passed couples: men leaning into each other, a woman in a tuxedo kissing her girlfriend beneath a blue-lit awning. Nobody stared. Nobody flinched. For once, I wasn't looking over my shoulder.

At the foot of the canal bridge, Simon stopped and turned to face me, our hands still tangled.

"This is nice," he said, and the understatement broke the last of my defences.

I looked at him, really looked. The hair escaping its tie, the flush in his cheeks, the way his mouth pressed shut when he was nervous. I wanted to remember every detail.

"It is," I managed, "it's the best night ever."

He grinned, triumphant, "wait until you hear me play. I'll ruin every other violinist for you."

We stood there for a long minute, neither of us willing to let go. At the edge of the Village, under a flickering sign for a club I'd never heard of, I turned to Simon, eyes serious.

"Coming back to mine?" I asked, voice barely above a whisper, "but only if you want to." My hesitation was a symptom of fear, habit, the ghost of all my old shame. The answer came quickly though.

"Of course I do. It's your place or a park bench cos I told Mum I would be staying out."

He squeezed my hand, and the two of us disappeared into the night, the glow of the city lighting our way home.

We took a night bus from *Piccadilly Gardens*. I remember the hum of the city through the window, the way Simon's thigh pressed against mine and didn't move even when we hit a speed bump near the station. His hand rested on my knee, casual as anything, as if we'd done this a hundred times. I wanted to say something, anything, but all the words collapsed before I could shape them.

We climbed the stairs to my flat, and I fumbled the key twice before managing the lock. Inside, the place was as I'd left it that morning: two mugs by the kettle, a stack of ungraded essays on the table, I switched on the lamp in the living room, yellow light pooling on the battered carpet.

"Coffee?" I asked, voice weirdly thin.

He nodded, "please." He walked over, brushed past me, and went to the fridge for the milk, "my Mum thinks I'm staying at a mate's tonight, after a party," he said, not looking up.

I laughed.

I watched him, trying to match his ease. The silence wasn't awkward, just fully charged, like the static before a storm. When the coffee was made, we sat together on the settee, knees touching, the mugs steaming between us.

He gestured at the stereo, "play something?"

I picked a record at random, Carol King's *Tapestry*. I put it on, and the room filled with her unique vocals, a voice I'd learned to love before I ever met Simon. He smiled at the choice, set his mug down, and leaned back.

After a while, the conversation dried up, not out of discomfort, but because there was nothing left that needed to be said. He reached for my hand, running his fingers along the back of it, tracing the lines like a secret. When he kissed me, it was slow and deliberate, his lips gentle, tasting of coffee and something citrusy, maybe the memory of the wine. I kissed back, learning the shape of his mouth, the warmth of his breath.

Simon shifted closer, thigh pressed to thigh, chest almost against mine. His hand drifted to my shirt, fingers curling around the first button. He paused, eyes searching mine for permission. He drew back, just enough to look at me, "this okay?" he asked.

"Yeah," I said, surprised at how steady my voice was, "it's perfect."

He kissed me again, deeper this time, his tongue teasing, his hands finding my waist and holding me there, as if afraid I'd slip away. We stayed like that for a long time, the record turning over to silence, the city outside a world away. The fear, the shame, all of it shrank to a distant murmur.

I thought, briefly, of Alex, of the way we used to meet in secret, the hurried touches, the constant vigilance, never daring to be seen or to want too much. With Simon, everything was slower, easier, like we'd been given permission to want and to take.

CHAPTER 24: CANAL STREET

April 1986

Saturdays belonged to us. Not by right, or by any proud claim, but by the simple fact that all the other hours of the week belonged to someone else. My students, Simon's mother, the staff at school, the dull drone of the city. But on Saturdays, after the lunch rush and before the onset of the city's evening mania, Simon and I would ride the train together, him with his coat unbuttoned, me pretending to read a magazine, both of us feigning boredom.

This time of year, the sunlight still felt like a promise. The air carried the raw, chemical tang of early spring, the trees threatening green, the pavements oily from the last rain. Simon always wanted the window seat, claiming he liked to watch the world scroll past, but really I think it made him feel protected, one less angle to be surveyed from. It left me on the aisle, acutely aware of the eyes, old women peering over shopping bags, students with *Walkman's*, men in suits that smelled of last night's beer. Sometimes we'd talk, usually about nothing: gossip from school, Simon's next concert, the absurdity of pop music, Thatcher, the miners, whatever. Never about us, not here, not in the daylight with strangers listening. It was safer that way.

When we hit *Piccadilly*, the city always seemed to exhale, a hot, dense breath of piss, exhaust, and the lurching hum of the main concourse. We let the other passengers off first, then stepped into the mass of bodies, navigating past the taxi queue and the cluster of drunks begging cigarettes outside the station. We kept a careful distance, never close enough to draw a line between us, but never so far apart that we risked losing each other in the tide. At the canal, Simon would always glance back, just to check. Then we'd cut east and make for *the Rembrandt*.

By now, we'd perfected the routine: up the side street, past the shuttered café and the curry house that only opened after six, then through the heavy doors and into the noise. *The Rembrandt* was both everything and nothing like I'd imagined it would be; men in cheap shirts, some in leather jackets, the floor sticky with a decade's worth of spilled lager and, for all I knew, tears. Posters of *Tom of Finland* torsos, a mural above the bar that was meant to be cheeky but just looked exhausted. The music pulsed but never quite took hold of the room; conversation always won out, the clatter of voices and the peals of laughter burying the synths.

We always sat near the back, not in the darkness but in the muted half-light, where the old dart board marked the edge of the "games area." Simon would order the first round, two pints of lager, nothing flashy, and I'd watch him work the crowd with that weird, offhand charm. He fit in here, somehow. Maybe it was his face, which could go from sly to cherubic in half a sentence, or the way he didn't bother with posturing, or maybe just the relief of being somewhere he didn't have to explain himself. I envied that.

Today, he'd promised to introduce me to "some legends", fellow musicians from a music group that were planning to put on a concert for an *AIDS* charity. I'd laughed it off, assuming this meant another bunch of first-year students with wild stories about drag nights, punk and not much else. But when we arrived, there were two men already at our usual table. They looked up as we approached, then David, Simon had whispered his name on the way in, stood and offered a hand.

He was in his forties, maybe older, with a thick beard and a greying ponytail. His partner, Michael, was slighter and younger, but not by much. Both wore denim, both smiled without suspicion. David's handshake was dry and firm; Michael's was shy, a quick squeeze and then hands folded again on the table.

"Simon's told us a lot about you," David said, eyes creasing with warmth, "though he made you sound about seven feet tall and made entirely of angst."

I blushed, aware of my height, the way my body never quite fit these spaces, "a long way from seven feet, but probably not far off with other," I said, and Simon snorted, almost spitting his beer.

Michael laughed too, "you must be the teacher. All the best men are."

I shrugged, "I try not to inflict too much damage."

"Don't be modest," Simon cut in, "Liam's an actual genius. He once won a pub quiz single-handed."

I shot him a look. He shrugged, as if to say, "you're allowed to be proud, you know."

Conversation came easy. They asked about work, about the latest school scandal, about the miners and the latest government scandal and whether I'd seen the new Terry Pratchett in *Waterstones* ("Of course he has," Simon interjected, "he nearly knocked over a pensioner to get the last one"). Michael talked about the hospital where he worked, David about his art projects and the time he'd spent on the scene before Canal Street was even called that. Every now and then, David's hand would slide across the table to rest on Michael's wrist, a gentle, habitual touch. Michael would lean in, let it stay for a minute, then return to whatever story he was telling.

Watching them, I felt a longing so acute it made me physically uncomfortable. Not lust, though both men had a confident ease that was undeniably attractive, but a hunger for the simplicity of their togetherness. The casualness of the affection. The sense that they had nothing left to prove to anyone, least of all each other.

Simon caught me staring and grinned, "don't get any ideas," he whispered, "you're stuck with me." Under the table, his knee pressed against mine, warm through the denim. I wanted to stay in that moment forever.

But nothing lasts. Not for us, anyway.

Halfway through our second pint, I got up to use the toilet. As I weaved through the crowd, I caught a flash of red hair and a too-familiar profile at the bar. My gut dropped, and I nearly turned back, but the traffic behind me forced me forward.

I kept my head down, eyes fixed on the dirty checkerboard of the floor, but it didn't matter. A voice rang out, loud and clear above the music.

"Aren't you that new teacher at my old school? Is that you?"

I froze. Slowly, I turned.

It was Jamie Turner, another of the school alumni that frequented the school pub on a Friday night He stood with another boy, a stranger, but clearly of the same tribe and both were grinning, half in shock and half in mischief. Jamie's face was flushed, his eyes glassy, but there was nothing blurry about the way he clocked me. If anything, he looked delighted.

"Didn't expect to see you here," he said, which landed like a slap. The other boy snorted, tried to suppress a laugh.

I stammered something, I don't remember what, maybe just a noise, and pushed past, into the toilets. Inside, I bolted to the end cubicle, locked the door, and slumped against the graffiti-laced tiles.

I could hear them out there, joking with their mates, probably already plotting the story they'd pass on to school on Monday. I pressed my fists to my temples, trying to will myself invisible.

A few seconds later, a knock.

"Liam?"

It was Simon. I exhaled, let my head thunk against the wall.

He waited, not pushing.

"You okay?" he asked, after a beat.

I tried to speak, but my voice cracked, "no," I managed. "I can't … I just fucking can't."

He rattled the door gently, "let me in?"

I slid the lock, and he squeezed into the narrow space, then closed us off from the world again. He didn't touch me. Just stood there, hands in his pockets, his face set in a look I'd never seen before, worried, but also a little angry.

"Talk to me," he said.

I shook my head, "outside. Jamie Turner. He saw me."

Simon's jaw worked, "what did he do?"

"Nothing, yet. But he's going to. He'll tell everyone. That's what people do."

He let the words settle, then, "you want to go?"

"No," I said, but I didn't mean it, "yes. I don't know."

He leaned back against the wall, folding his arms, "you can't keep living like this, you know."

I stared at him, hurt, "like what?"

He shrugged, "always running. Always acting like you're going to get caught, like it's some kind of fucking game of hide and seek." I caught the steely tone in his voice.

I wanted to snap at him, but my mouth just dried out, "you don't get it. If anyone at school finds out …"

"They won't, as I can't imagine it going down well with Turner's rugby crowd," he said, but his voice was softer now.

"Or if they do, and I very much doubt it, you'll handle it. You always do."

I scoffed, a dry, ugly sound, "easy for you to say. You don't have parents who … who …"

He interrupted, "no, but I have a mother who counts on me for everything. I have friends who would drop me in a second if they thought it would save them. I have to hide on the streets, same as you. But at least here, in places like this, I try to give myself a break."

I squeezed my eyes shut, "it's not enough."

"It's all we've got, Liam."

For a moment, neither of us spoke. The only noise was the sound of the hand dryer, wailing like a siren through the thin walls.

Finally, Simon nudged my foot with his, "I like you," he said, "but I can't keep being the secret one hundred percent of the time. Not forever."

I opened my eyes. His expression was raw, honest, maybe the most beautiful I'd ever seen him.

"We can have secrets," he said, "but we also need places to be real. Even if it's just a few hours a week, in a bar that smells like a urinal and plays shit music."

I swallowed, then nodded, slow, "okay."

He smiled, but there was something sad in it, "let's go back, before David sends a rescue party."

We left the toilets, and as we passed the bar, Jamie caught my eye again. This time, his smile was different, softer, almost uncertain. Maybe he'd seen something in my face, or maybe he was just surprised to see a teacher so rattled. Simon and I both nodded to him, "fake it until you make it, I was told once," Simon whispered in my ear. Either way, I didn't look away.

At the table, Simon squeezed my hand under the table. Just once, but it was enough. After a while, the panic receded. The music got better, or maybe I just stopped caring.

The rest of the evening passed in a gentle blur: more stories, more laughter, Michael losing a round of darts and blaming the "shit lighting," David making a crack about "kids these days" while giving Simon a look that was pure pride. Simon and I walked home in the dark, side by side, the canal on our right, the city's lights flickering on one by one.

At the bridge, on the way back to the station, I stopped. Simon turned, eyebrows raised.

"What?" he asked.

I hesitated, then, "thank you."

He frowned, puzzled, "for what?"

I shook my head, "for making me try."

He smiled, this time without sadness, "it's what we do, right?" He took my hand then, not caring who saw, and together we crossed into the growing night.

The following Friday, I woke to a headache and the thud of knuckles on the door. I ignored it at first, curling tighter into the half-warm duvet, but the knocking persisted, slow, measured, not the desperate staccato of a neighbour with a plumbing emergency. I'd barely peeled myself off the mattress when the letterbox flapped, and through it I heard a single, perfectly pitched word:

"Surprise."

My heart lurched as I opened the door. Sarah stood there, suitcase in one hand, an industrial tin of biscuits in the other, wearing that infuriating "don't argue" smile, the one that once convinced Dad to let her quit A-level Chemistry after a week. Part of me wanted to shove her back onto the pavement; another part, the one I barely admitted existed, melted at the sight of her.

"You're supposed to ring before you come," I said, my voice oddly flat.

"Where's the fun in that?" she breezed past me, nose lifting in an immediate inspection of the flat, "wow. You tidied up."

I pressed my lips together, "I didn't." I had of course, as I always did before Simon visited.

She sniffed, as if that explained everything, "really? Your bathroom is cleaner than ours on Christmas Day."

I watched her prod at the sofa cushions, her sofa now, I supposed, and swing open the fridge without checking. She leaned against it, arms folded, surveying my life with those sharp eyes.

"I'm here for the weekend," she announced, "Mum says hi, and Dad's off to the footy, so don't expect calls until Monday."

"Great," I managed, caught between relief and irritation. Because part of me was thrilled to have her here, but the rest of me was terrified of what having her here meant. Previously her visits had always been mid-week deliberately.

"Oh, and I brought biscuits," she added, as if that tiptoed her right past any argument.

She handed me the tin and hugged me, quick, elbow-first, full of awkward energy. I stood rigid, then returned it hesitantly. Her confidence and presence had grown, and I felt small beside her, even though she was supposed to be the little sister.

She made herself at home instantly: kettle on, tea bags hunted down on the top shelf, the one place I thought safe, and she flopped into the armchair like royalty, "so, what's the plan for today and tonight?"

My chest tightened, "I'm at work all day. I'm not a student anymore, so you'll have to fend for yourself until after I finish. Then you can join me and some colleagues at *the Red Lion*. If you want."

"Obviously," she grinned, dipping a biscuit into her tea.

"We usually head there around 4:30. Oh, and it's on the main road, turn right out the door and you won't miss it."

She nodded, already plotting her outfit in that mischievous head of hers. I poured my own tea, hands trembling. Not nerves, well, maybe a bit, but mostly the shock of Sarah stepping unannounced into my polished, private world. I kept glancing at the bedroom door, half-expecting Simon to stumble out, shirtless and dishevelled, wondering who'd crashed our weekend truce.

"What are you staring at?" Sarah challenged, mug halfway to her lips.

"Nothing," I lied, "just… thinking about not being late for work."

She squinted, but let it drop, "okay, what's the dress code?"

I shrugged, "it's a pub. Wear what you want."

She rolled her eyes, "dangerous advice. Watch me test those boundaries." She flicked back her hair, eyes dancing. My stomach flipped. I wanted to stop her. I wanted her here. I hated that I couldn't decide which feeling deserved to win.

"Now I need to get on and to work," I waved a hand around the flat, "make yourself at home, not that I doubt you will anyway, and there's a spare key on the hook by the door if you go out." With that I slipped back into the bedroom to get dressed.

The Red Lion was a half-mile away from school, an unremarkable brick wedge with a bent sign and the best jukebox in town. I got out a little early from work and Sarah was already inside nursing a drink. I was handed my 'usual' by the landlady, my order now merely required a nod.

Sarah grilled me about my classes, my students, my colleagues, and for each question I offered the bare minimum. She saw straight through me, of course, "always this boring?" she teased.

I forced a laugh, "absolutely."

"Phew. That would've been worrying if you weren't." She launched into tales of her first-year drama course at Salford, late nights, new friends, a freedom I envied more than I let on.

The bar was soon humming; teachers lined up at the window table, old men clustered around darts, a knot of ex-students prodding the fruit machine and testing the barman's patience. I searched the crowd for Simon, my pulse quickened, but he hadn't shown up yet.

"Come on," I murmured, guiding Sarah toward the back where the school staff gathered. My chest felt taut, as if I'd left something, or someone, out front.

Harry spotted us first, beaming with that well-practiced father-figure pride he perfected over thirty years of staffroom politics. He clasped Sarah's hand, "so this is the famous sister"

She blushed and then shot him a mature smile, "hi, nice to meet Liam's boss."

Barbara swooped in next, pearls gleaming, perfume trail lingering like a question you can't shake off. She peppered Sarah with inquiries, university life, future plans, O-Levels versus GCSEs, even muttering, "not that kids get a say." Sarah parried with surgical politeness, a grace born from too many obligatory family gatherings.

Daniel hovered on the periphery, nodding once, twice, sunk deep into the sports pages of his *Guinness*-stained tabloid. His detachment made me both envious and uneasy, was I the only one who felt edged toward meltdown?

We claimed the last two seats. I dashed off for drinks, craving the excuse to catch my breath. When I returned, Sarah was animatedly recounting the time I'd set the kitchen curtains alight. She left out my novel-reading distraction and the pan I'd abandoned, but the gist was there. I managed a tight smile.

I tried to sink into the banter, but every laugh felt brittle. I was bracing for something, someone, to tip the balance. My shoulders stiffened with each unfamiliar face, each burst of laughter.

And then Simon walked in. I'd decided not to warn him, convincing myself it'd be easier this way. He wore a white tee under an unbuttoned denim shirt, hair tousled like he'd just snapped out of a backstage blackout. The minute his eyes met mine, a slow half-smile eased onto his lips, and something fluttered in my gut.

I stood too quickly, "Simon, this is my sister, Sarah."

Sarah gave him a speculative once-over, one eyebrow hitching, "a bit young for a teacher, aren't you?"

He tilted his head, grin widening, "I'm one of the school's alumni, group of us still wander back on Fridays." He glanced over at the younger crowd, "that's how we met." Then he leaned toward Sarah, voice low, "he needed someone under forty in his life, I think."

Sarah snorted, "social work, was it?" They shared a laugh, and for a moment I felt the tension loosen. But as Simon pulled up a chair and settled in, I realised the relief was as fragile as the peace I'd sold myself on.

"Liam's told me a bit about you," Simon said. His tone was casual, but under it I heard the question I'd been dodging all night, what comes next?

She smirked, "has he, now?"

I cut in, desperate to change the subject, "Simon's at the Royal Northern. Violin."

Sarah perked up, "no way. I play piano. Terribly, but still."

Simon looked impressed, "we should duet sometime. Schubert's *Trout Quintet?*"

Sarah's eyes lit, "best bit is the fourth movement. I always trip up on the *arpeggios.*"

Simon shrugged, "me too. But if you play it badly enough, it's modernist." They laughed. I sat back, watching them, equal parts proud and but still terrified.

The night blurred in the way that good nights do; rounds of drinks, bad jokes, Sarah and Barbara debating which biscuit was superior ("*hobnob*, obviously," Sarah insisted), Harry and Simon discussing the politics of music education, Daniel asking Sarah which football team she supported and being scandalised by the answer.

At one point, I caught Sarah watching Simon and me, just a flicker, the briefest glance, but enough to make my ears burn. She looked away quickly, but I knew then that she saw more than I wanted her to. She jumped up to go to the ladies and I followed her into the corridor.

"Is Simon the new 'Alex'?" she asked in a flash. The truth was written on my face even before I spoke.

"Yes," I said, "but you know it's…"

"A secret," she finished for me, "don't worry Liam. Watching you squirm is fun, but seeing you happy is better." And with that she skipped down the corridor into the ladies.

Near eleven, Barbara declared it was time for her "beauty sleep," and the table broke up. Simon walked us home, hands jammed in his pockets, the three of us moving in a loose triangle through the night. At the door, he hesitated.

"You coming in?" I asked, aware of Sarah's presence behind me.

He looked at her, then at me, "sure, if you're up for it."

Sarah smirked, "don't mind me. I'm shattered anyway."

Inside, I made coffee while Simon and Sarah talked softly in the living room. From the kitchen, I could just hear their voices: Sarah asking about college, about his favourite composers, whether he'd ever played abroad.

"I went to Vienna for a competition last year," Simon said, "hated the judges, but the *schnitzel* was worth it."

Sarah laughed, "typical. All the best stories are about food, not the thing you went there for."

Simon agreed, "that, or the people you meet. Some-times both."

I stood in the doorway, mugs in hand, watching them. They sat close, not quite touching, Sarah with her legs curled under her, Simon perched on the edge of the settee. There was something easy about it, as if they'd always known each other. For a moment, I felt like an intruder in my own home.

I cleared my throat, passed out the mugs. We drank in silence for a bit, the only sound the gurgle of the ancient radiator and the faint drone of a late-night talk show from the flat above.

After a while, Sarah yawned, then stretched, "I'm dead on my feet," she announced.

I pointed at the settee, "I'll get you a duvet."

She grinned, "don't go to any trouble. I've crashed in worse places than this."

I fetched the spare duvet and a pillow from the cupboard, shaking out the dust before tossing them at her. She caught them, then flopped down, already half-asleep.

Simon and I stood, awkward for a moment.

Sarah looked at us through half-lidded eyes, "don't worry about me," she said, "go to bed. I'll be fine."

I nodded, feeling suddenly self-conscious.

"Goodnight, Sarah," Simon said.

She smiled, "night, Simon. Night, big brother."

We retreated to the bedroom, closing the door behind us for the first time. The room was dark, except for the yellow sliver of streetlight leaking through the blind. I kicked off my shoes, then sat on the edge of the bed, not quite sure what to do with my hands.

Simon slid in beside me, fingers brushing my wrist, "you okay?"

I nodded, but the air felt thick, "yeah. Just… weird, having her here."

"She's great," Simon said, "you're lucky."

I smiled, "she thinks I'm a disaster."

He laughed, "aren't we all?" he leant over and pecked me on the cheek, "did she guess or did you tell her about us?"

"Bit of both, as usual," I replied and I let my head fall onto his shoulder, the tension draining away. He turned, kissed me, slow and careful, as if learning the taste of my mouth for the first time. I let him, sinking into the hush of the room, the certainty that, for tonight at least, there was no one left to impress, nothing left to fear.

Outside, the city hummed on. But here, behind the closed door, the only thing that mattered was the warmth of his hand in mine, and the promise of morning.

The sun was bright through the gap in the curtains. It woke me by degrees: first the warmth on my cheek, then the faint hiss of the boiler, then the shadow of Simon's back as he sat on the edge of the mattress, already half-dressed and tuning the violin, with his chin tucked down like a guilty schoolboy.

He played a phrase, stopped, then another. The music was thin, half-whispered, but the effect was immediate, my heart started up again, thumping out of step with his scales.

I rolled over and watched him, "practicing already?"

He turned, lips pursed, "can't play the concert cold. Besides, it's Schubert."

I tried to act unimpressed, but the sight of him like this, focused, alive, caught between sleep and discipline, made me want to grab his shirt and pull him back into the covers.

Instead, I yawned, stretched, and asked, "do you want breakfast?"

He shrugged, "I can eat later. But I need to be at the hall by noon for final rehearsal."

From the other room, I heard the rattle of cupboard doors and the unmistakable sound of Sarah humming to herself as she made tea. I reached for a T-shirt, then thought better and just pulled the sheet up to my chest.

Simon grinned, "I'm guessing she fine with the idea of me and you?."

"Is she?" I wasn't sure I did, not really.

"Last night, she told me she liked you. 'He's softer than he thinks,' she said."

I snorted, "I'm not sure that's a compliment."

He set the violin down, crawled back into bed, and nudged my arm with his, "it is when you're you."

We lay there for a minute, the hush between us unforced. Then Sarah banged the kettle down and called, "tea or coffee? I made toast!"

I got up, found some tracksuit bottoms, and joined her in the kitchen. She stood barefoot, hair a nest, buttering toast in quick, surgical strokes.

"Morning, stranger," she said, then glanced at Simon behind me, "you too, maestro."

He grinned, "morning."

She slid two plates onto the table, then sat, legs folded under her as if she'd always lived here, "so what's the plan today?"

I hesitated, "Simon's got a concert. Benefit for *AIDS* charities, in town."

Sarah's eyes widened, "no way. Can I come?"

I blinked, "you want to?"

She shrugged, "why not? Unless you're ashamed of being seen in public with me."

I laughed, the knot in my stomach loosening, "of course not."

She grinned at Simon, "what are you playing?"

He answered, "Schubert's *Winterreise*. I'm the accompanist for a *lieder* set. Piano, violin, and a singer."

Sarah whistled, "impressive. Never got past Rachmaninov myself. Too many sharps."

He sipped his tea, then said, "maybe after, you can show me?"

She smiled, a small, private smile, "maybe I will."

We walked to the hall together, Sarah skipping ahead, humming to herself and glancing back every few steps as if to make sure I hadn't vanished. Simon had left hours before for rehearsals

Inside, the building was as cold and formal as a bank vault, all marble and hushed carpeting, but Sarah treated it like a playground, poking her head into empty rooms and reading the flyers tacked to every wall.

At the ticket desk, the volunteer looked us over, and handed us two tickets. We picked up programs with and found seats in the third row. The audience was mostly older men, some couples, a few women in pairs. There was a sense of hush, of reverence, as if everyone in the room was holding their breath.

When Simon appeared on stage, he looked transformed, back straight, chin high, his hands steady on the instrument. The pianist, a severe-looking woman with cropped hair, nodded to him. The baritone was Michael from *the Rembrandt* who nodded to them both, then began to sing.

The first notes were tentative, but then the sound blossomed: Schubert, rendered with a kind of longing that made my skin prick. I watched Simon's face as he played: the way his brow furrowed at a hard passage, the small smile when the baritone landed a tricky run. I felt a surge of pride, sharp and embarrassing, a desire to tell everyone in the row in front of me that this was my partner, the best part of my life.

But I didn't. Instead, I sat very still, hands folded in my lap, heart battering itself to pieces.

At the break, Sarah leaned over and whispered, "he's amazing."

I nodded, unable to speak.

She squeezed my arm, "you picked a good one, big brother."

In the second half, the pianist and singer were replaced by two other string players, and carrying a double-bass onto stage was David. The music from the quartet was a little more uplifting and light, classic chamber music. After their set, they stood and Michael and the pianist joined them to accept the applause. As the noise settled, Michael's booming voice called out.

"And please donate what you can on the way out!"

After the applause and the slow shuffling of the audience toward the doors, we found Simon in the green room, standing with a group of friends and strangers. He was flushed with adrenaline, laughing, shaking hands, accepting congratulations with the shy grace I'd never seen from him before.

When he spotted us, he lit up, "did you like it?" he asked.

Sarah pounced, "you were incredible. You should teach me how to do that with my face."

He laughed, then turned to me, "well?"

I looked at him, really looked, and for the first time I said it out loud, "you were brilliant." He grinned, and for a second I forgot anyone else was there.

We followed the crowd to a bar in the Village, one I'd only ever seen from a safe distance. Inside, it was warm, loud, and full of bodies, men and women and everyone else, all mixed together and laughing. The lights were dim, the music set to just above conversation level, and no one cared who touched whom.

Sarah soon vanished into a group by the jukebox, making friends in seconds. I stood near the wall, drink in hand, watching as Simon circulated. Now and then he'd glance over at me, our eyes meeting for a heartbeat, then he'd smile and turn back to his friends. I felt an odd sense of belonging, and also the ghost of old fears, what if someone recognised me? What if Jamie Turner was here, with a camera, with a friend, with the intent to ruin me? But the more I watched, the less I cared.

Later, I found Sarah with a knot of Simon's music friends, all of them gathered around a table littered with glasses and chip baskets. She was holding court, telling a story about our dad and the time he tried to fix the washing machine with chewing gum and almost burned the house down.

I stood at the edge, uncertain. Then I heard her say, "this is my brother Liam and his far too good-looking boyfriend Simon, right? That's the deal?"

She looked at us, eyebrows raised, daring us to deny it.

For a second, I froze. Then, in a single movement, Simon stepped closer, slid his arm around my waist, and I rested my hand on his shoulder.

"Hi," I said.

The table erupted into applause, good-natured and genuine. Sarah winked at me, as if to say, "you're welcome."

For the rest of the night, we didn't let go.

When it was time to leave, Sarah hugged us both, then ran ahead to flag a cab. We walked behind her, slower, letting the city's lights stretch out the moment. At the curb, Simon leaned in and kissed me, soft, but not shy, not anymore. I kissed him back, and it was easy, as natural as breathing.

Sarah watched from the taxi, grinning like a lunatic.

As the car pulled away, it felt like a journey to a new world.

CHAPTER 25: SUMMER REVELATIONS

May 1986

We took the train to Rhyl, connecting at Chester from Manchester, and I internally resolved to finally buy a car. The route took use along the Dee estuary, through Flint and onwards then to the North Wales Coast. The scenery was green not unlike the Pennines above Rochdale, but seemed softer, less extreme. I tried to imagine what it would be like to live here, the constancy of grey sky, the taste of salt in your mouth even on a good day. I wondered if the locals ever tired of the sound of the sea, or if, like me, they felt safest in the hush just after a storm, when everything was wrung out and ordinary.

Simon craned his head in the taxi we took from Rhyl station towards Kinmel Bay, "there's the sign! *Bryn Awel Guesthouse*', Christ, it's like something out of Agatha Christie." He grinned at me, the joke there for both of us, and the taxi pulled up outside.

The place was smaller than the one photo in the ad we had seen in the *Gay Times*: a whitewashed box with a wrought-iron fence and pots of dead geraniums flanking the door. The front window had heavy lace curtains, the glass behind it warped and pebbled with age. There were no cars parked outside, "are you sure it's open?" I asked, already second-guessing the booking.

Simon shrugged, "they confirmed everything on the phone yesterday. Two nights, breakfast included. Come on, it'll be fun." I paid the driver and collected our one holdall from the open boot.

We knocked, and the door was answered almost immediately. The man who greeted us was in his fifties, neat but not fussy, with the careful tan and silvered hair of someone who wanted to age with dignity. He wore a maroon jumper over a dress shirt and had a thin gold ring on his left hand, "you must be Simon and Liam," he said, and even though his voice was gentle, my pulse leapt.

"Yes," said Simon, shaking his hand with the easy confidence of someone who'd never had to explain himself, "thanks for having us."

"Pleasure. I'm Gareth. And this is my partner, Neil," he said, stepping back as a second man appeared from the hallway, this one shorter and built like a rugby hooker gone to seed. Neil gave a brief, appraising nod and offered to take the bags, which Simon surrendered, but I held on to mine a moment longer than necessary.

They showed us through the hall, narrow, lined with faded watercolours of the same craggy coastline we'd just driven, and up a short staircase to the first floor. "Room three," Gareth said, "it's cosy. The best view of the estuary, if the fog lifts. There's tea and coffee in the lounge anytime, and if you want to try the pub, it's a five-minute walk along the main road."

He paused outside the door, key in hand, "breakfast is eight to ten, but we're flexible. I'll let you get settled."

The room was exactly as described: a double bed, a battered dresser, a small window with a wedge of sea visible between slats of a ruined blind over the tops of countless caravans. There were two towels folded on the bed, and a glass vase on the dresser holding three limp daffodils. "Quaint," said Simon, then fell back onto beside it.

I set the bag down, scanned the walls for anything that might indicate threat or warning. Instead, I noticed the details: a rainbow sticker on the back of the door, a stack of *Gay Times* on the shelf above the radiator. The bedding was clean, but the blanket was older than both of us combined. There was a faint, persistent smell of lavender, like the ghosts of every couple who'd ever stayed here.

Simon bounced up again almost immediately, "let's go see the lounge. I want to meet the other guests."

We found Gareth in the small front room, tidying a tray of mugs. He straightened and greeted us as if we were old friends, "welcome to North Wales," he said, then poured two cups of tea without waiting for our answer.

Simon took his with a dangerous amount of sugar, then flopped into one of the mismatched armchairs, "we're here on a sort of retreat," he said, "he's a teacher, I'm a musician. We need somewhere to decompress."

Gareth smiled, "you've picked a good weekend. It's quiet. No children at the moment. The only other guests are two women who spend their days out walking."

He settled on the arm of the settee, just far enough away to avoid crowding, but close enough that I could see the rainbow enamel pin on his lapel, a detail that made my heart stutter. Simon, as usual, clocked it instantly.

"Nice badge," he said, a smile in his voice, "I've got one at home, but I'm too cowardly to wear it in public."

Gareth's eyes twinkled, "it's easier when you own the place."

Simon laughed, "is it always this friendly? I was nervous, well we both are if I'm honest."

"You're safe here," Gareth said, and though I doubted he could make it so, I wanted to believe him.

Simon slurped his tea, then glanced at the stack of *Gay Times* on the coffee table, "you actually get these delivered?"

"Every month," Gareth replied, "we've been in the guide for five years now. It helps." He looked at me, as if expecting a question, or maybe an objection, but I just nodded, grateful for the conversation to wash over me.

I sat, hands folded, and listened as Simon and Gareth traded stories: music, politics, the time the power went out during a wedding party and they'd had to light the entire ground floor with scented candles. After a while, Neil joined us, carrying a plate of Welsh cakes and a bottle of local cider.

"You'll want a drink before you try the village pub," he said, pouring Simon a generous measure, "landlord's decent, but some of the regulars can be old-fashioned."

Simon grinned, already half a glass in, "we can handle old-fashioned," he said, and I tried to believe it, too.

We spent the next hour in the lounge, trying to keep the conversation on safe ground. Every now and then, Simon would say something that nudged too close to us, to the nature of our trip, or the real reason we'd chosen *Bryn Awel*, but each time I found myself wanting, almost desperately, for Gareth or Neil to push the subject. They never did. Instead, they let us exist as we were: two men sharing a room, sharing a life, and nobody needed to say the words.

Eventually, the clock on the mantel chimed seven, and Simon stretched, "shall we try the pub?"

I hesitated, glancing at Gareth for a read. He smiled, "it's perfectly safe, really. You won't be the only out-of-towners."

Simon pulled on his coat, then held mine out for me, "come on," he said, "you need a proper drink."

The walk to the pub was short, the road was empty except for a single cat winding between bins. The air was heavy with the smell of rain and woodsmoke, the clouds pressing close enough to taste. The *Ty Coch Inn* was lit up like a stage, its windows spilling yellow onto the wet stone outside.

Inside, the pub was busy but not crowded, two old men at the bar, a cluster of farmers in one corner, and a table of walkers with mud up to their shins. The barmaid had a smile that bordered on real, and the beer was cold and flat in the way that made it clear they didn't cater to tourists that often.

Simon led the way to a small table near the window and ordered for both of us. I scanned the room, searching for any flicker of attention, but nobody seemed to care. The old men talked quietly, the walkers passed a flask of something stronger beneath the table, and the farmers just stared into their pints as if the world began and ended at the rim.

Simon raised his glass, "to not being noticed," he said.

I clinked mine against his, then took a long pull. The taste was sharp and bracing, the kind of drink that forced you to pay attention.

For a while, we sat in companionable silence, watching the rain start to chase down the glass of the window. Simon fidgeted with his glass, then rested his hand on the table, just close enough to mine that our knuckles nearly touched.

I drew back, then realised what I'd done, and forced myself to close the gap again. He noticed, but didn't push.

"Do you want to talk about it?" he asked, voice so low it was nearly a whisper.

I shook my head, "not yet."

He nodded, then squeezed my fingers, quick and gentle, before pulling back, "we don't have to," he said. "I just wanted you to know you can."

We finished our drinks, then ordered two more. The barman didn't blink at the order, didn't linger over the coins or look twice at us as we sat, knees touching, at the corner table.

After a while, the pub emptied out. The old men shuffled off, the walkers called a taxi, and the farmers disappeared one by one until we were the only ones left. Simon smiled, softer now.

"You know," I said, "I've never done this before."

"Done what?"

I shrugged, a little sheepish, "stayed somewhere as a couple. Had a weekend away. It always felt too risky. Or too fake."

Simon looked at me, really looked, "this doesn't feel fake."

I shook my head, "no. Not at all."

We walked back to *Bryn Awel* in the dark, our steps matching. The house was silent, the hallway light left on for us. At the door to our room, Simon paused.

"Thank you," he said.

"For what?"

He grinned, the mischief back in his voice, "for not running a mile."

I wanted to tell him that I'd never felt further from running in my life, but instead I just reached out and took his hand, right there in the narrow hallway with the faded watercolours and the faint, warm smell of lavender. He squeezed my hand, then led me inside.

That night, lying in the bed with the window cracked open to the distant sounds of the sea. I felt the smallest shift in the world, a lightness in my chest, a sense that I was no longer a visitor in someone else's life, but a willing participant in my own.

I woke to the metallic tang of the sea, and the screeching of seagulls. The air was dense and chilly even with the window barely open. Simon was still asleep beside me, his arm thrown up across his face, the sheet tangled in a way that left most of his back exposed to the chill. I lay for a minute, watching the soft rise and fall of his breathing, and wondered what it would be like to wake up like this every day, no performance, no dread, just the ordinary magic of someone else's presence in the dim light of morning.

Eventually, the growl of my own stomach won out over the inertia of comfort. I pulled on yesterday's shirt and jeans and padded down the hall to the bathroom, feeling for once like I belonged in the fabric of this house, like a second skin that had, overnight, become familiar.

The breakfast room was already set, sunlight spilling over the polished wood table, making a show of the fresh croissants and coffee. Gareth stood at the far counter, humming along to the radio as he arranged a platter of fruit. When he saw me, he smiled, not the brittle, professional smile I'd expected, but the warm, undemanding kind that asked nothing in return.

"Sleep well?" he asked.

"Best in ages," I said, and it was true.

He poured a mug of coffee and pushed it toward me, "Neil's making eggs, if you want. Or we've got yoghurt and muesli, but I won't judge if you prefer the full works."

I shrugged, glancing at the croissants, "this is more than enough. Thank you."

Simon appeared a few minutes later, hair damp and flattened from a quick shower, his shirt only half tucked. He greeted Gareth with the same ease as last night, then made a show of inspecting the bread rolls, as if he'd never seen baked goods before.

"So, what's the plan?" he asked me between mouthfuls.

I wiped a crumb from my lip, "there's a beach. We could walk? And maybe take a bus into Rhyl or go the other way towards Colwyn Bay?"

He grinned, "let's find the beach first, and maybe go for lunch somewhere?"

"Seems like a plan," I called over to Gareth and asked about the buses and he fetched me a folded timetable.

Once we were dressed, we ventured out to find the beach. We crossed the road and looked for a way through to the seawall that was visible in the distance, with what looked like a footbridge over the railway. Eventually we found a route that didn't cut through one of the large caravan parks. It was at a crossroads which had a few shops and arcades lining it. We turned right and followed the road to an open level crossing over the railway, the footbridge was a little further along.

For a while we just walked, the sound of our shoes sinking in the pebbles on the foreshore, the gulls overhead screaming at each other in voices too raw for song. Every so often, Simon would point out a jellyfish stranded above the tide line, or a crab shell picked clean by birds, his curiosity genuine, childlike, without irony. I found myself cataloguing the moment, trying to commit it to memory the way I'd once hoarded scraps of good days for later.

We kept our hands in our pockets, the wind too fierce for comfort. But at a bend in the beach, where the land curved in and the wind dropped, Simon slowed and reached out. His hand hovered, palm up, waiting. I felt the usual flicker of dread, what if someone saw? what if this was the moment everything fell apart?, but then I looked at him, really looked, and saw only hope.

I took his hand, and the world did not end. The sand went on, the sky went on, and our hands fit together as if it had always been so. For a long stretch we didn't speak, just walked in tandem, our joined footprints trailing behind us in two imperfect lines. The silence was not awkward, but full, the kind of quiet that comes when both parties are too content, or too afraid, to break it.

Eventually, Simon stopped at the edge of the tide and let go. He picked up a flat stone, skipped it once across the water, then turned to me.

"Do you ever think about just… disappearing?" he asked, squinting into the wind.

"Sometimes," I said, "but only if I can take you with me."

He smiled, but it was a crooked thing, touched with something I couldn't name, "deal," he said, and flung the stone again.

We walked back along the high seawall itself, letting the stiff breeze buffet us along. I walked close to Simon, occasionally grabbing him in a dramatic way when the wind took him close to the edge.

"My hero," he giggled, which provoked me into a hearty laugh each time. Our hair was wild and messy, our hands almost frozen, cheeks and lips burnt from the wind, yet I felt pure joy.

We got a local bus into Colwyn Bay and after a short walk found a little cafe that overlooked the sandy beach. Simon slid into the booth first, his foot instantly seeking out mine under the table. I nudged him, feigning annoyance, but left it there. We ordered, and when the drinks came, two hot chocolates, we warmed our hands on the steaming mugs. Then the waitress came by with our order of Welsh rarebit, grilled mixed cheese sandwiches.

We ate in silence, then lingered over our drinks, watching the sky close in over the headland. When the first raindrops tapped at the window, Simon grinned.

"Better be heading back I guess?" he said, opening his eyes wide in an invitation I recognised.

Back at *Bryn Awel*, the lounge was empty, the fire in the grate reduced to a soft orange glow. Gareth and Neil were nowhere to be seen. We stood for a moment in the hall, uncertain.

"Let's go straight up?" Simon asked, voice gentle.

I nodded, suddenly shy.

The room felt smaller in daylight, the damp seeping in through the window and pooling in the carpet by the sill. We stripped off our damp coats and crawled onto the bed, shoes left in a heap by the radiator. I lay on my side, facing Simon, our noses almost but not quite touching.

The rain drummed steadily, a lullaby for insomniacs and misfits. I heard Simon shift, felt the mattress dip as he rolled toward me and wrapped his hands around me. There was a pause, and then his voice, soft but certain.

"I think I'm falling in love with you," he said.

The words landed between us, solid and irrefutable. I gripped the edge of the mattress, my breath caught somewhere between my lungs and my throat. I wanted to say it back, wanted to more than anything, but all I could do was stare at the rain-streaked glass and hope he understood.

Simon waited, his breathing slow and even. The silence grew, then settled, then became a comfort in itself. After a while, he reached over and rested his hand on the small of my back, just enough to let me know he was still there. I didn't say the words, but I let myself believe, for the first time, that they could be true.

Dinner was almost an afterthought: we ate reheated a shepherd's pie in the pub. The evening passed in a slow drift, the kind of hush that only happens in places built for listening. We finished one more drink after the food and tiredness took its toll, so we decided to head back to the guest house.

Simon played a few phrases on the battered piano, a bit of Satie, a half-remembered theme from the TV, and Gareth, pretending to dust, lingered near the door for each note. There was a moment where it felt like family.

As we entered the clock was just chiming ten.

"Evening boys," Gareth shouted from the lounge, "had a good day?" We were invited in to join them for a nightcap. We recounted our day and how impressed we were with what we had seen, and how we hoped that we would come back one day.

"Well, we'd better let you two get some shut eye, no doubt you have an early start in the morning," Neil said. I stood and pulled Simon up with me.

"Thank you, both of you," I said.

"We'll definitely be back," Simon added, and we bade them goodnight.

Back in our room, we kicked off our shoes and flopped onto the bed side by side. Before exhaustion could take us, Simon propped himself up on one elbow.

"Can we talk for a minute?" he asked gently.

"Always," I whispered.

"You never talk about your ex. Not really," he started.

I looked into his eyes, thinking of all the ways to avoid the question, then let the old habits fall away.

"His name was Alex," I said.

Simon said nothing.

"We met at university. He was in my hall. We'd both …" I stopped, unsure how to say it, "we were good at hiding. Or I was, anyway. He made it look easy, being nobody's business but his own. But then, I don't know… at some point, hiding just felt safer than any of the alternatives."

Simon traced his finger along my nose, waiting.

"He was brilliant. Terrible at books, but he could talk his way into or out of anything. He was funny, but not in the way people expect. He could destroy you with a single line and then make it all right again in the next breath. He was the only person who ever made me believe I could be more than… whatever this is." I gestured at myself, at the night, at everything.

"Did you love him?" Simon's voice was gentle, not curious but kind.

"Yeah," I said, surprised at the ease of it, "I did."

"Why did it end?"

I closed my eyes, "because we were idiots, because we thought we could keep it separate forever, my family, his, the world at large. We pretended it didn't matter, that we didn't want what other people had. And then he was sent to a job in London by his father, and I stayed." I paused and recalled his last conversation with me, "he did tell his mother about me, in the hope she might change his dad's mind. She slapped him and threatened to kick him out and disown him if he ever mentioned me again."

Simon nodded, as if he'd already guessed the end of the story, "do you still talk?"

I shook my head, "not for years. He wrote, once or twice. I never replied."

Simon said, "you're allowed to be angry."

"I'm not," I said, but the ache in my jaw said otherwise, "well not anymore."

He let it sit for a while, the silence now edged with something sharper. Then he reached out, found my hand, and squeezed it tight.

"I had someone, too," he said, so quietly I almost missed it.

I looked at him, surprised, "the one you told me about?"

He smiled, but it was brittle, "yes, but I want to explain how it happened. My dad died when I was sixteen, and after that, Mum just... folded in on herself. I spent years making her tea, listening to her cry at night, doing whatever it took to keep the walls up. I didn't even look at a boy until I was at uni. Then, during Freshers' Week, there was the one I told you about, and that's it."

Simon shrugged, "Mum figured it out before I did. One night, as she was getting better, she sat me down and just asked: 'do you like boys, Simon?' I said yes, and she made me cocoa and told me she loved me no matter what. The next day, she went out and bought a copy of *Gay Times*, left it on my bed like it was homework."

I stared at him, "she just... accepted it?"

"Yeah," Simon said, "she said the world had enough secrets already, and she'd spent too long pretending everything was fine." He gave a small, awkward laugh, "she still tells everyone I'm single, though. Says I should 'play the field' before I settle down."

I couldn't help but laugh, too, "that's not how it works in my house."

He grinned, "doesn't have to be. You get to choose."

After a while, Simon said, "you don't have to tell your family if you're not ready. But you don't have to hide, either. Not from me."

I looked at him, really looked, and saw the truth in it, "thank you," I said.

On the journey back to Manchester, the air between us felt newly breathable, lighter, less freighted. We didn't talk much, but when we did it was with an ease I hadn't noticed before, as if the salt and wind and stories left on the Welsh coast had scrubbed away something stubborn inside me.

The city came up in its usual rush: red brick, fast-food wrappers, and the blur of late buses along the ring road. As we walked from the station and onto Simon's street, he said, "do you want to come in? Mum's probably making tea. She's …" He hesitated, uncharacteristically sheepish, "she knows I'm seeing someone. She says I'm smiling too much these days."

I tried to laugh, but my nerves stuck to the roof of my mouth, "if it's not weird?"

Simon grinned, "it's only weird if you make it weird. Besides, she'll like you. She likes everyone."

I followed him up the path, the house was terraced, with a chipped blue door and a fan of cracked glass above the frame. A faint smell of baking drifted through the bricks, and for a second I felt the urge to turn and run, not from the place, but from the tidal pull of all the ordinary things I'd never allowed myself to want.

Simon opened the door and called, "I'm back!" He kicked off his shoes, then led me down the narrow hall, past the photos of him as a child, first communion, violin recital, school trip to some stately home. The kitchen was at the back, painted a glossy yellow and crowded with plants, magnets, and the cheerful debris of daily life.

His Mum was there, folding laundry on the table. She was small, with neat brown hair and the same blue-grey eyes as Simon. When she saw me, she smiled, warm, reserved, but not unkind.

"You must be Liam," she said, and for a moment her accent put me in mind of my own mother, all the vowels pressed flat from years of economy.

"Yes," I managed.

"Sit down the pair of you, I've just made scones." She turned back to the counter, hands busy with kettle and cups, while Simon raided the fridge for milk.

I perched on a wooden chair and tried to look like someone who belonged at other people's tables. The kitchen was alive with small details, an old glass cake dome, a radio playing quietly, the clatter of a radiator pipe under the window. I wondered how many people had sat at this table before me, and if any of them had ever managed to say anything of substance.

"So, you're at the school?" Simon's mum asked, setting a cup in front of me.

"Uh, yes. I teach history. O-levels and A-levels." I replied, feeling the blush rise in my face.

She nodded, as if this explained everything, "you must know Mr. Windle, then? He was always good to Simon. Very strict, but fair." She shot Simon a look, half fondness, half exasperation, "he got my boy through some rough patches."

Simon rolled his eyes, but there was affection in it.

"He's a legend," I agreed, "keeps the place running. I wouldn't have lasted the first term without him."

She smiled, pouring the tea, "well, it's good to have you here. I hope Simon's not a terrible influence."

"Never," I said, and surprised myself by meaning it.

She joined us at the table, scone already halved and buttered, "so," she said, "tell me about your family, Liam. Where are you from?"

I told her about Rochdale, about my sister at Salford, my parents and the mill, the usual shorthand of biography. She listened, head tilted, eyes sharp. There was a kindness in her questioning, but also a measured quality, as if she were weighing every word for clues about who I really was.

Simon tried to steer the conversation away, "Mum, don't interrogate, you'll scare him off," but she only laughed and told him to mind his manners.

For a while, it was just tea and the soft, buttery warmth of scone. The conversation drifted: politics (she was Labour to the core), music (she asked after Simon's next recital), a little about the news, which she dismissed as "mostly nonsense, these days."

At one point, she asked, "are your parents proud you teach?"

I hesitated, not sure how much truth to offer, "I think so. I hope so. They don't really say."

She nodded, "it's not always easy, for them or you, now you have flown the nest. But it matters. The work, and the rest." She gave me a look so direct I almost missed the subtext, "it matters that you're happy."

I blinked, not sure if I was supposed to respond, but she was already refilling cups, her hands never still.

Simon sat quietly, eyes on his mum, then on me, a current of tension running beneath the easy talk. When the tray was nearly empty, she stood and said, "you'll stay for tea, won't you? I've a stew on the go, it won't take long."

I looked at Simon, who shrugged, then nodded. "we'd love to."

While she cleaned up, Simon and I slipped into the living room. It was smaller than my flat, the furniture worn but inviting. The walls were lined with books, and the window overlooked a tangle of back gardens. Simon sprawled on the sofa, pulling me down beside him.

"See?" he whispered, "told you she'd like you."

I relaxed, letting my head fall back on the armrest, "she's intimidating."

He laughed, "only if she doesn't approve. I think you passed." He nudged me with his foot, then grew serious, "thanks for doing this."

I shrugged, though the relief was real, "it wasn't that hard. She's... a good Mum."

He nodded, but didn't elaborate.

After supper, beef stew, heavy with carrots and thyme, Simon's Mum made coffee and set a plate of digestives on the table. We lingered, conversation looping back to the trip to Wales, then forward to Simon's concert next month. She asked if I'd be coming.

"Of course," I said, and saw the pleasure in her eyes, even as she tried to mask it. When it was time to go, Simon's mum walked us to the door. The evening was cold. Simon held back, leaving me alone with her for a moment.

She looked at me, eyes steady, "he's a good boy, my Simon. Sensitive. He cares too much, sometimes."

I nodded, not sure if I should say anything.

She reached out, squeezed my arm, "just treat him well. That's all I ask." Then, with a smile: "and you're welcome here, any time."

I thanked her, and Simon stepped forward to give me a peck on the cheek.

"Thanks for the weekend," he said.

The next Saturday, after another night out in Canal Street and a late-night taxi that seemed to float above the city, we ended up back in my flat, hungry but too tired to bother with toast or tea.

Next morning Simon lay sprawled across me, his cheek pressed to my chest, one arm heavy across my stomach and his knee wedged between my thighs as if he was staking out territory. He'd kicked off the covers in his sleep, and now the chill in the room made every inch of skin that touched feel like a secret.

I ran my fingers through his hair, slow and careful. It was a little tangled, soft in a way that never failed to surprise me. For a long while I listened to the hush of his breathing, the tiny whistles when he exhaled, the rhythm of his heart as it synched to mine.

Simon stirred, then blinked up at me, blinking the night from his eyes, "you awake?" he mumbled, voice thick and small.

"Barely," I whispered.

He shifted higher, resting his chin on my shoulders, "what are you thinking?" He asked it like a joke, but his eyes said he wanted the real answer.

I tried to find the words, and, for once, I didn't have to reach very far. "I'm not falling in love with you," I said.

Simon's brows drew together, and for a second I thought I'd screwed it up again. But I smoothed the hair from his brow, kissed the top of his head, and added, "because I already have."

Simon's breath caught, just for a beat, and then he grinned, slow, dangerous, and dazzling. He buried his face against my chest, making a sound that was half laugh, half groan.

"Idiot," he said, but the word came out warm.

We lay there, the city outside just a faint echo. At some point, I said, "you know, when I met your mum, I thought I'd have a panic attack."

He snorted, "you hid it well. She likes you, by the way."

I ran a hand down his back, feeling the curve of his spine, "I started thinking… maybe it's time I introduce you to mine. Mum and Dad. But not," I hesitated, embarrassed now, "not as my boyfriend. Just… as a friend."

Simon was quiet, tracing circles on my stomach, "if that's what you need," he said, "that's fine. Honestly."

"I'll talk to Sarah. She can help smooth things over, be my buffer. Mum's birthday is soon. Maybe then."

Simon lifted his head, met my eyes, "are you scared?"

I nodded, not trusting myself to say more.

He kissed my shoulder, "me too. But we'll do it together, okay?"

I smiled, and the last of the fear loosened its grip.

We stayed in bed most of the day, drowsing in and out, talking about everything and nothing. In the afternoon, Simon made coffee and burnt toast, and we ate it sitting on the kitchen floor, knees bumping, bare feet tangled.

I watched him, really watched, the shape of him in the washed-out light, the lines of his face, the way he curled his hands around the mug. I thought of the version of myself I'd been at university, at the start of all this, scared, careful, always waiting for the world to notice and punish.

Now, with Simon, I saw another possibility. The fear was still there, but smaller now, shrinking every time I let myself believe in what could be. As evening fell and the city lights flickered on, I called Sarah and told her my plan. She didn't laugh or sigh, just listened, then said, "I'll make sure it goes all right, big brother. Promise."

I hung up, and Simon sat beside me on the settee, his hand folded around mine. We watched the sky fade from blue to black, and when I finally said, "I'm ready," Simon squeezed my fingers, the answer already waiting in his palm.

CHAPTER 26: THE MINERS' BENEFIT

July 1986

It's a fool's errand, trying to get a hundred people to queue for anything north of the Mersey, but that was my charge: wrangling a crowd of miners, their wives, their impossible children, and the smattering of local lefties who showed up for the free beer and stayed for the raffle. The venue was a repurposed cotton warehouse off the main ring road, thick with the scent of chalk, old grease, and the ghosts of cigarette smoke embedded in every brick. They'd done their best to sweep up, but the floor still dusted your shoes with pale powder, and the stage was little more than a plank on cinder blocks. I felt at home in the mess of it.

Simon had organised the concert with a group from his college. It was a benefit for the families of striking miners who were still feeling the impact of a year-long strike that had ended twelve months before. It was a way to pass the hat without the shame of direct charity. The local branch secretary had thrown her lot in, promising "entertainment for the masses," and it was my job to make sure nobody nicked the instruments or died in the toilets before the interval. I manned the door with a bucket for donations and a notional guest list, though after the first ten minutes I stopped bothering to check names and let the tide in. People brought folding chairs, camping stools, or else just stood in the gaps, arms crossed, waiting for something worth listening to.

The banners were the best part: pit names in faded reds and golds, *'Unity is Strength'* in letters the size of my fist, slogans from the bad old days when union meetings risked the batons of mounted police. They hung off the rafters, motionless except when a draft caught them, and the effect was like being watched by a hundred eyes. Each banner had a history, and each carried a charge that made the music, later, seem both important and small at the same time.

Simon was backstage, if you could call the curtained-off alcove a stage at all, setting up with his quartet. They were all students, nervy and underfed, but Simon led them with the unflappable precision of a head chef plating a roast. The cellist was an ex-brickie whose hands dwarfed his instrument; the pianist, a girl with blunt-cut hair and an accent that hovered somewhere between Manchester and "posh." Simon

was the only one who looked genuinely at ease, running scales
with the casual elegance I'd once found insufferable in men like
him.

I took up a post at the side, near the table-top bar, three
tables pushed together, a makeshift barricade manned by two
pensioners who'd seen too many union meetings go south. I
watched the crowd, scanning for trouble or familiar faces, but
mostly I watched Simon.

The lights were cheap floodlamps, hung from scaffolding and aimed just above head-height, but when they hit his violin it glowed. He tuned without looking at the audience,
mouth set in a line of concentration. His hair, newly trimmed
for the occasion, looked paler under the blue wash, his jaw
shadowed by a day's stubble I knew was there but others probably wouldn't notice. I thought that it made him seem older, or
at least less breakable. When he glanced up, caught my eye, he
winked. Just a flick, invisible to everyone else.

The hush that fell when they began was absolute. The
miners had little patience for the classics, but they listened with
a kind of hard-earned respect, the way you'd watch a man fix
your car or set a broken limb. The first piece was slow, full of
open intervals and strange harmonies that made the room vi-
brate in sympathy. The second was faster, something with a
name I'd forgotten, but which Simon had played for me once at
the flat, after too many glasses of cheap wine. I remembered
the way his fingers danced over the fingerboard, how the sound
built and built until you felt sure the instrument would shatter,
and how at the very end he would hold the note just a little too
long, making you ache for the release.

Tonight, he played the ending softer, the final note almost drowned out by the creak of the folding chairs and a stray
cough from the gallery. I saw the way his chest rose, slow and
deliberate, and the way he bowed his head for a second before
the applause broke.

He looked up, and again, just for me, he smiled.

After the first set, I made a circuit of the floor, collecting envelopes and loose change, stopping to let a mother wipe
the snot from her toddler's nose with the hem of her own
sleeve. I did a quick headcount, then ducked behind the curtain.

Simon was adjusting the chin rest on his violin, hair clinging to his temple with sweat.

"How's it looking out there?" he whispered, voice low and threaded with nerves.

"Full house," I said, "and nobody's tried to steal the piano. Yet."

He grinned, brushing his knuckle across my wrist, "you're good at this. Logistics."

"I learned from the best," I replied, meaning my mother, but in the moment it sounded like a line. He ignored it, or maybe he didn't want to tease me in public. He leaned in and, briefly, our heads touched, just long enough for me to catch the soap on his skin and the warm fug of the room.

The break was over fast. The second half was shorter, lighter, designed to wake up the crowd. A medley of pop songs arranged for quartet, something that would let the miners hum along if they cared to. Simon let the other two take the lead, hanging back, blending in. He looked at ease, but I knew him well enough by now to see the tension in his jaw, the way his left hand flexed between phrases.

The applause at the end was louder than the music, hands clapping and feet stomping and the odd cheer from the back. Simon and his ensemble bowed, then retreated behind the curtain. I watched as a group of kids rushed the front, each clamouring to touch the violin or peer into the depths of the cello's belly. The brickie cellist showed them how the endpin worked, and the pianist let a girl in a puffy parka press a middle C, her face split by delight at the sound. Simon hovered, content to be an onlooker for once.

That's when I saw her, Diana, cutting through the crowd with the practiced precision of someone used to getting what she wants. She wore a navy blazer over a turtleneck, hair pulled back so tight it could have snapped a bootlace. She looked thinner than I remembered, but her presence hadn't diminished one bit. She scanned the room once, found me instantly, and zeroed in.

"Well, if it isn't the pride of Rochdale," she said, voice like the first sip of a gin and tonic, cold but bracing.

I laughed, "you're working for the union now?"

"Full time," she replied, "and loving every minute. Beats the hell out of committee meetings with third-rate academics."

She looked me over, then the room, then back, "you look happy, I am guessing the blond one is your boyfriend," she said, and the words, so simple, hit me harder than any compliment I'd ever fished for, "he's good for you."

I felt myself flush that she knew without being told, and then in that moment I didn't care. "He is," I said, "though he's not much of a revolutionary."

She smiled, a real one this time, and squeezed my arm, "you'll do more with kindness than a hundred bloody pickets. I'm glad you found someone."

"How did you know it was the blond?" I asked, genuinely interested in her answer.

"Oh feminine intuition," she winked and then added, "and there was that lad you were inseparable from at uni."

"Fair enough," I smiled.

"And, you can't kid a kidder," she let her comment settle before she added, "my girlfriend's here somewhere, I'll introduce you another time."

We stood like that, silent for a minute, the sound of the crowd dissolving into the background.

"So, what now?" she asked, gesturing at the chaos, "you going to ride the success, or run away before someone asks you to sweep up?"

I shrugged, "someone's got to mind the donation buckets. And anyway, I like it here. There's a kind of honesty to the dust and noise."

She glanced toward the stage, where Simon was talking to the kids, "you ever think of doing this for real? The organising, I mean."

I shook my head, "it's better as a hobby. Less risk of heartbreak."

She nodded, as if this explained everything, "if you ever change your mind, let me know. We could use more like you."

She left then, weaving her way toward the bannered men at the bar, already plotting her next move. I returned to my post, counting the takings and helping the pensioners distribute the last of the sausage rolls. Simon reappeared, hair slicked with sweat and a look of sheepish triumph on his face.

"You survived," I said, handing him a plastic cup of flat lager.

"Barely. The cellist's hands started bleeding during the third piece."

"Adds authenticity," I replied, and we both laughed.

He stood close, our arms touching. For a moment, I forgot the rules, forgot to check for watching eyes, and let my head tilt against his shoulder. He didn't pull away, just let the silence fill.

Then he leaned in, his mouth at my ear, "can we go home?"

I nodded, and together we edged through the crowd, hands almost, but not quite, interlaced. At the door, I looked back. The banners still watched, unmoved. I wondered what they'd make of us, and decided I didn't care.

Outside, the night was cool and clear. We walked to the station in silence, the echo of the music lingering in the crisp air. Just before we reached it, Simon stopped.

"What is it?" I asked.

He shook his head, "nothing. Just… I like being seen with you."

I felt the old panic stir, but this time, I let it pass.

"Me too," I said, and squeezed his hand, hard, before letting go, "so much so that an old friend from uni came over to me and she knew you were my boyfriend."

"Must have recognised the lust in your eyes," he teased.

That night, in bed, I lay awake long after he'd drifted off, the words of the day circling like moths. "He's good for you." "You look happy." I'd never thought to need that kind of validation, but now that I'd tasted it, I realised I wanted it more than anything. Not just the approval, but the ease, the right to exist without preamble or apology.

I watched Simon sleep, hair flopped over his eyes, mouth open in the unselfconscious way of children. I thought of the miners' banners, the certainty with which they declared their own worth. I resolved, then, to do the same.

Tomorrow we'd catch the train to Rochdale, flowers for my mother, a quick hello to my old man, and then maybe a weekend of pretending the world was less cruel than it really was. But for now, the flat was warm, and I let myself believe it could last.

The train rattled out of the city just after nine, a cold Saturday with frost dusted over every blade of grass as we headed north and the windows of the carriage breathing out miniature clouds. Simon insisted on carrying the overnight bag, which left me with the flowers: a cheap but artfully arranged bouquet I'd picked up from the station kiosk, the kind that announces, *'I remembered'* while also signalling *'I can't afford lilies'*. My hands gripped the paper so tight the cellophane crinkled with every jolt of the tracks.

Simon gazed out the window, chin in hand, the posture of someone who could drift through any landscape and emerge unchanged. He was humming something under his breath, probably a piece from the night before, or maybe just a nervous tic I hadn't noticed. I watched him from the side, cataloguing every detail, as if the journey itself might erase him by the time we reached Rochdale.

When the train slowed into the station, the old dread returned, the certainty that, no matter how long I'd been away, the air here would recognise me, would mark me out as a fraud for trying to live another life. Simon seemed immune; he set off at pace, marching the long platform with the air of a man going somewhere better than this.

Outside the station, a brisk wind cut through the concourse and up the road toward the estate. I recognised every bin, every empty bus shelter, and hated myself for the relief. We passed the old sandwich shop, shuttered, but still advertising bacon baps at 20p, and the undertaker's, black-curtained and unchanged since childhood.

Mum's house was only a few streets down. The front door opened before we reached the steps, and there she was, Margaret, in a housecoat over her dress, hair still in rollers but face set for company.

"About bloody time," she said, then pulled me into a hug so fierce my glasses nearly snapped. She let go just as quick, as if embarrassed by her own emotion, "and you brought a guest!" She offered her hand to Simon, who shook it like they were at a diplomatic summit.

I held out the bouquet, mumbling, "happy birthday, Mum."

She took the flowers, sniffed them theatrically, "lovely. But I'd have preferred a bottle of sherry. Go on, get yourselves in." She waved us inside, leaving the door open to let the cool air rush through the hall.

The interior was unchanged: smell of furniture polish, a runner on the stairs, three pairs of shoes lined up under the radiator. She ushered us into the kitchen, set the flowers in a vase, then whirled to face us, "your father's at the test match over in Leeds. He won't be back until he's suitably miserable or drunk, whichever comes first."

I felt the tension in my shoulders unwind by half.

She bustled to the cupboard, produced a *Tupperware* cake and set it, with a bang, on the table, "sit down, both of you." She poured tea with the speed and accuracy of a woman who'd done nothing else for forty years. Only after the cups were distributed did she actually look at Simon, her eyes doing a rapid up-and-down as if scanning for defects.

"So, Simon," she said, "what do you make of this one, then?" She jabbed a thumb at me.

Simon smiled, unphased, "he's the best. Runs rings round most people I know."

She laughed, a quick bark, and then, "you can't mean that. He's a lazy sod."

"Not really," Simon replied, "you'd be surprised." Simon then went through the help I had provided the night before.

Mum looked at me, as if seeing me through new glass, "well, I'm glad someone can motivate him. You staying the night I assume?"

Simon nodded, "if that's okay."

She waved it away, "I've made up the camp bed in Liam's old room. Sheets are fresh."

Simon shot me a look, barely suppressing a smile. I wanted to crawl under the kitchen linoleum.

Mum sipped her tea, watching us, and then turned back to me, "you hear from your old mate, Alex, lately?"

I felt the spike, sudden and sharp, "no. He's too busy in London with his new friends, I think. Hard to keep up."

She nodded, not pressing, "well, if you do hear from him, give him my love." She cut another slice of cake, slid it to Simon, "you need feeding up, lad. You're all bones."

The phone rang then, a loud, shrill intrusion from the hall.

"That'll be your sister," Mum said, "probably missed her bus or some other disaster."

She picked up the phone, spoke in a rapid-fire code only mothers and daughters understand. After a minute she returned, rolling her eyes, "yes, she missed her bus and is getting the Huddersfield one instead. She'll meet you at *the Greengate*."

I made a move to get up, but she put a hand on my arm, "stay a bit longer. I want to hear about your life, not just your friends."

So, we did, she asked about my job, about the flat, about the rent, about the bins ("do they collect weekly or not these days?"). She listened to Simon talk about music college, about his upcoming performances, about the time he saw a drunk audience member faint in the front row and played right through it. She laughed at all the right places, then fixed me with a look so pointed I nearly squirmed.

"I like him," she said, blunt as always.

I looked at Simon, and he grinned, cake crumbs on his chin, "thanks, Mum."

After going up to my room, we unpacked the few things we had brought for the night. Simon stood over the desk looking out of the window over the backs, "not so different to my house," he said almost to himself.

An hour or so later, we left the house, the echo of her approval ringing louder than any rebuke she'd ever given. As we walked toward the pub, Simon took my hand for just a second. I checked the street; no one was watching.

The Greengate sat on the main road from Rochdale to Huddersfield, with a convenient bus stop right outside. It's outside was white-washed, but clearly hadn't seen a new coat of paint since decimalisation and wore its nicotine stains like a badge of honour. We ducked in out of the impending rain, and found a table near the back, where the wallpaper peeled like dried skin and the radiators clanged with every rush of hot water. There were only a handful of regulars in this early, hunched over their pints, muttering in the slow, deliberate dialect of men who measured time in drinks.

I'd sat down by the time someone appeared behind the bar. Simon fetched us two pints of lager and slid into the booth, so we were wedged together, hip to hip. The moment felt too normal, so I kept my eyes on the deep groove in the table where generations of customers had carved their initials or, more often, just gouged out of boredom.

A shrill voice came from behind the bar, "hiya Liam love!" the middle-aged landlady called, "your Sarah coming in?"

"Hi Madge, sorry didn't see you on the way in," I excused my failure to say hello, "Sarah's on the bus as we speak."

"I like it here," Simon said, settling in, "it's honest. No one pretends to be anything else."

I snorted, "they wouldn't know how."

He tipped his glass, smirked, "you say that, but you're still the king of pretending."

I glanced at him, then away, "that's not fair."

He shrugged, "you're right. Sorry."

A silence. He sipped his beer, then leaned in, voice low, "I'm glad your mum likes me."

"She never says what she doesn't mean," I replied.

He laughed, the sound soft in the low ceiling. His thigh pressed against mine, and I let it stay there.

After a while, he said, "have you thought about us moving in together?"

The words startled me, less for their content than the ease with which he said them. I blinked, stalling, "not really. I mean, my flat's barely big enough for me. You'd have to practice on the landing."

Simon grinned, "we could find somewhere else. Castlefields, maybe. One of those flats by the canal. Plenty of space for a piano."

"A piano?"

He shrugged, "why not? You can afford a flat, I can afford a piano. It's the eighties, Liam. Dream big."

He held my gaze, and I saw he wasn't entirely joking.

"I'll think about it," I said, quieter than I meant.

He let the conversation drift, content with the promise of maybe. We sat with our pints and watched the locals play a silent, stubborn game of dominoes at the next table, the clack of tiles a background rhythm to our own private world.

It was a quarter past seven when Sarah barrelled in, cheeks flushed, hair wild, the air around her carrying the scent of rain and new cigarettes. She spotted us instantly, waved like a drowning swimmer, and charged over, unbuttoning her coat as she went.

"There you are," she said, breathless, slumping into the bench opposite, "missed my first bus. I thought I'd drown waiting for the Huddersfield one."

She pecked Simon on the cheek, then grabbed my hand and squeezed, hard, "you're a sight for sore eyes, both of you. Liam, you look like you've seen a ghost."

I shrugged, "just tired, is all."

She rolled her eyes, "he's always tired," she said to Simon, "that's his way of saying he's worried about something but won't tell anyone."

Simon smiled, "I've noticed."

Sarah ordered a vodka and coke, "so what's the occasion? You never come home on the weekend unless something's up, whereas I come home to get my washing done," she lifted and then dropped the holdall next to her.

I looked at Simon, unsure how much to share. He nodded, almost imperceptibly.

"Just a visit," I said, "Mum's birthday. And to see you, obviously."

She raised an eyebrow, but let it drop, "well, I'm glad you did. You missed Dad's epic meltdown last Sunday."

"Football or cricket?" I asked.

"Cricket, it's the summer supposedly!" she replied.

She launched into a tale of Patrick Parry's latest sporting outrage, voice shifting to a perfect imitation of his accent, every curse delivered with the precision of a stand-up comic. I laughed, despite myself, and Simon grinned, genuinely entertained.

When the story ran out, Sarah turned to Simon, "so what's it like living with this one?" She jerked a thumb at me, "he as moody as he used to be at home?"

Simon pretended to ponder, "sometimes. But it's not the worst. I think he likes having someone to argue with."

Sarah snorted, "that's because he was bored for most of childhood. I tried my best to keep him on his toes, but ..." she stopped, looking at me with a sudden seriousness, "I'm glad you have each other."

I felt a lump in my throat, but managed a smile. "Thanks."

We fell into the easy talk of siblings: old teachers, town gossip, who'd run off with whom, which classmate had been arrested for shoplifting. Simon mostly listened, adding the odd observation that showed he'd learned our family history better than I had his. It was late when the talk circled round to the subject I'd been dreading.

"Are you ever going to tell Mum?" Sarah asked, voice careful.

"Tell her what?"

She gave me a look, "about you and Simon. About… all of it."

I hesitated, then, "what's the point? She'd just worry. Or worse, she'd try to fix it."

Sarah nodded, but not in agreement, more in resignation, "she might surprise you, Liam."

"Maybe," I said, "but Dad …"

She grimaced, "he might be a lost cause. Still makes those comments every time *AIDS* is mentioned on the news. Like it's a punch-line."

Simon's face went flat, "it isn't, though."

Sarah reached across and touched his wrist, "I know. I wish it were different."

A silence grew, heavy and unresolvable.

Sarah broke it, brightening, "well, sod him. You've got us. And Mum, even if she pretends not to."

I looked at Simon, then at Sarah, then at the pitted table, "maybe next time," I said, which was as close to a promise as I could manage.

We finished our drinks and called a cab. Outside, the air had gone cooler, the rain bouncing off the cars parked along the kerb. The driver eyed us in the mirror but didn't say a word as we piled into the back seat, Sarah in the middle, head already lolling with sleep.

At the house, Mum was still up, watching TV with the sound off, a crossword in her lap. She looked at us over her glasses, then at Simon, and nodded once, as if confirming an internal calculation.

"There's bacon for the morning," she said, "don't eat it all before I get up."

We all said goodnight, then split to our rooms. Sarah's light went on for a minute, then off. I found Simon in my old room, already half-undressed, sitting on the camp bed and picking at the edge of the duvet.

He looked up when I came in, "you okay?"

"Yeah," I said, "it's just… never gets easier, does it?"

He pulled me down beside him, head on my shoulder, "maybe it's not supposed to."

We lay in silence, the moon painting the far wall in a cold rectangle of light. I closed my eyes and drifted, the memory of the day folding in on itself.

That night I dreamed of Alex. It was the first time in months. He stood at the edge of a train platform, face in shadow, hands in his pockets. He called my name, but when I reached him, he turned away and vanished into the crowd. I woke to the hush of the house, the faint creak of pipes, and Simon breathing softly beside me.

I watched him for a long time, the shape of his nose, the way his hair curled at the nape. I thought of all the years I'd spent hiding from myself, from everyone, and wondered what it would feel like to stop.

In the morning, we'd go back to my flat, our lives. Maybe I'd tell Mum, maybe not. Maybe I'd let the world see us, even if only for a second.

The next morning, I woke to the smell of bacon and the sound of my father berating the *News of the World*. The kitchen was already humid with steam, Mum banging pans and tutting at the state of the bin, while Patrick sat hunched over the table in his dressing gown, yesterday's football scarf still looped around his neck like a bandage.

He grunted at me when I walked in, "thought you were never getting out of that pit," he said, then eyed Simon, who trailed behind, hair still sleep-creased and face bare, "and your mate. Hope he doesn't mind a bit of burnt bacon."

Simon shook his head, murmured, "thank you," and sat at the table. He looked younger here, less the polished musician and more a teenage cousin dragged to an unfamiliar family Christmas.

Mum swept in, set plates down with military precision, "eat up, boys. We don't waste food in this house."

Patrick stabbed a rasher, then turned to me, "you treat this place like a bloody hotel, Liam. Rolling in after hours, and Sarah's no better, expecting your mother to do her washing. One day you'll have kids of your own and see what it's like."

The line hit me harder than it should have. I looked at the table, then at Simon, who kept his eyes on the food.

Sarah shuffled in, knotted hair and a hangover visible even in silhouette. She grunted a greeting, then reached for the tea, "morning all. Dad, you're not even dressed."

"Got overtime at the depot," he said, "but I'll finish the paper first." He flapped it open, hiding behind the tabloid masthead.

Simon tried to catch my eye, but I was busy counting the tiles on the kitchen floor, willing the moment to pass.

Mum, sensing the drop in temperature, turned to Simon, "you want some more toast, love? You'll need it if you're going on the train."

He smiled, gratefully, "thank you, Mrs. Parry."

From behind his paper, Patrick grunted again, "never thought I'd see my son with so many posh friends, a musician Maggie says. Next, you'll be voting Tory."

The joke was so on-the-nose it almost circled back to being funny. I forced a laugh, but it scraped my throat raw.

Sarah, ever the peacemaker, rolled her eyes, "Dad, Liam's a teacher, not a prince."

After we finished, Patrick stood, drained the dregs of his mug, then checked his watch, "better shift. You kids clear up." He folded the paper, on the page he'd just been reading and tossed it on the table. At the door he paused, looking back at us, his face gone soft for a second, then he disappeared upstairs and was out of the front door within five minutes.

The paper he left behind landed face up. There, in black letters that seemed to shout, was a full-page advert: *'AIDS—It Could Happen to You'*. Underneath, in red, *'Especially male partners'*. There was a photo of a man, mid-thirties, gaunt, shadowed. The kind of image meant to scare old men into fidelity and young men into silence.

Simon saw it too, and for a long moment neither of us moved. The kitchen, usually so full of life and noise, felt as sterile as a morgue. Mum swept the ad away with a practiced hand, replaced it with a plate of toast.

"Eat up," she said again, and it was both an order and an apology. She looked at Simon, "don't worry about Liam's dad, he went all the way to Leeds to watch the cricket and it rained most of the day. Always makes him grumpy."

We left a couple of hours later, after the obligatory group photo in the garden and a ten-minute debate over whether we'd have time to make the train. Mum hugged me at the door, squeezing tighter than usual, then did the same for Simon, who looked surprised but managed to return it.

"Next time, stay longer," she said, as if the future was already certain.

On the train, neither of us spoke for a while. The rhythm of the carriage, the blur of empty fields, did its job of numbing thought. Only when we were nearly back to Manchester did Simon break the silence.

"I like your mum," he said, voice low.

I looked at him, "she liked you too."

He smiled, but there was a sadness in it.

"Your dad's not ready though, is he?"

"No," I said, staring at the seat in front, "not even close."

He reached over, squeezed my hand, "does it bother you?"

"More than I want to admit," I replied.

He nodded, as if that was the answer he expected. Then he let go, and we watched the scenery pass, the closer we got to the city, the greyer everything seemed.

That night, in the flat, we sat side by side on the sofa, watching a game show and eating instant noodles. Neither of us brought up the weekend. We let the noise of the television fill the silence.

Then, during a break, the screen cut to a public information film. It showed a tombstone, huge and cold, growing out of the ground as a voiceover intoned: *'AIDS. Don't die of ignorance'.* The words hung in the room, heavy as stone.

Simon tensed beside me, "it's just meant to scare people," he said, voice too loud.

"Yeah," I said, "and guess who'll be the whipping boys?"

He looked at me, the old fear in his eyes, "we'll be careful," he whispered.

We watched the rest of the show in silence, the weight of the advert pressing down. When it finished, we went to bed, but neither of us slept for a long time.

Instead, I lay awake, listening to his breathing, wondering how long we'd be able to hide, and whether the world would ever let us stop.

In the morning, the first thing I saw was the grey light leaking through the blinds, and Simon beside me, still asleep, the lines of his face softened in the hush. I reached out, touched his hand, and decided that, no matter what, I wasn't letting go.

CHAPTER 27: SECTION 28

February 1988

It had rained all night, and I'd barely slept. The morning bus was packed with the usual mix: mothers dragging sullen kids, men in *Day-Glo* overalls and black-fingered gloves, a pair of sixth formers smacking each other with their rucksacks and pretending not to notice me. The cold hung on everyone like an extra layer. The only thing warm in my hands was the newspaper, and the headline *'THATCHER: SCHOOLS TO UPHOLD FAMILY VALUES'* stared at me in block capitals, ink bleeding slightly where a wet thumb had pressed the page.

When I stepped off outside school I then marched across the slick car park and into the side entrance, the one staff used to avoid running into students first thing.

The corridor smelled of bleach and wet wool, and a radiator was clanging a death march for its own slow demise. I paused by the noticeboard: a new cartoon, cut from some Sunday supplement, depicting a flustered headmaster in mortarboard, besieged by scruffy kids waving pink triangles. Someone had written *'SECTION 28 IS FOR REAL MEN'* in biro underneath. The joke, apparently, was on all of us.

The staff room was already humming at seven-thirty. Barbara had the window table, as always, red lipstick barely smudged by her first mug of the day, feet up on the battered copy of the *Oxford Dictionary*. Daniel was perched on the radiator, legs spread, tie already askew. Two of the newer teachers huddled by the kettle, pouring instant coffee and not making eye contact.

Harry was in his usual green tweed, was pouring over *the Times* crossword with the brow-furrowed gravity of a surgeon at a war hospital. He grunted hello at me without looking up. I nodded, hung my coat on a peg, and sat at the edge of the table nearest the door, out of splash range but within earshot.

Barbara was the first to say it, "it's in the news again," she announced, holding up a page like the world's most disappointing Christmas card, "government's on about *'protecting the young'* from the evils of perversion. Eight a.m. and I've already had enough." She flicked her cigarette into the old saucer she used as an ashtray, then topped up her coffee with a glug from the hip flask she pretended no one noticed.

Daniel leaned in, voice pitched to reach the farthest corners, "well, maybe they're right. Last thing we need is this place crawling with little poofs and lesbians. Wouldn't be able to get through a lesson without tripping over the rainbow." He cackled, expecting someone, anyone, to join him.

The two new teachers smiled weakly, then went back to their coffee. Harry didn't even look up.

Barbara set her mug down with a violence that made everyone flinch, "grow up, Daniel," she said, her vowels crisp enough to cut glass. "You're forty-three and still think bumming jokes are the height of wit. Maybe the government can pass a law against tragic adolescence."

Daniel made a face, but didn't reply. He had an instinct for when he'd lost the room.

Harry set down his pen, finally, and sighed, "if we're done with the playground banter, some of us are trying to work out the answers to seventeen across. And if you're desperate for a row, Daniel, go take it up with the sixth formers. They'll eat you alive."

Daniel sulked, then folded his arms and scowled at the window, where the rain was starting up again in earnest. I kept my face neutral, like I'd practiced in the mirror, but my gut was coiled tight. I could feel the blood in my neck, in my hands. I looked down at my own mug, the rim stained from yesterday's tea, and tried to breathe through my nose, slow and even.

Barbara glanced at me, her expression softened by a kind of tired sympathy, "you alright, Liam?" she asked, *sotto voce*, the words just for me.

I nodded, not trusting myself to speak.

She patted my arm, then stood to fetch more coffee. Her presence left a gap at the table, a negative space that drew the others in for a moment, before they drifted apart again.

The early-warning bell clanged in the corridor, announcing the imminent arrival of the first wave of students. Daniel took the cue to leave, stomping out with the forced bravado of a man who'd never once been questioned, let alone found wanting. The two new teachers followed, then Harry, who grumbled something about "the bloody pointless in-service," and shuffled off with his half-solved crossword.

I lingered, counting backward from fifty in my head, before getting up and walking, deliberately, carefully, to the little staff toilet at the end of the corridor. I locked the door, slid the bolt, and sat on the toilet lid, elbows on knees, head in hands.

For a minute, I did nothing but listen to the drip in the cistern and the distant scrape of chairs in classrooms, the world going on just as it always had. Then my breath started to come back, ragged and wet. I could see my hands shaking. I pressed them together until the knuckles went white, then let go.

When I felt steady enough, I stood and looked at myself in the small mirror above the sink. I practiced the teacher face, the one that said "business as usual," the one that could endure three periods of Daniel's jokes and a double with the third form without cracking. I smoothed my tie, ran wet fingers through my hair, and held my own gaze until the person in the mirror looked plausible again.

Then I washed my hands, twice, and went out to face the day.

That evening I walked the long way home, tracing side streets and lingering at newsagent windows, buying time before I had to face my flat. The air was raw, the sodium streetlights swimming in puddles, and by the time I reached our building my hands were numb enough to forgive the memory of Daniel's laughter.

Inside, the heat was barely holding. A radiator hissed in the hall, more for show than effect, and the stairs up to the third floor were lined with the debris of other people's weeks, junk mail, takeaway cartons, a single child's shoe abandoned on the landing. I turned the key quietly, out of habit, but Simon was now always waiting.

There were music scores scattered across the coffee table, pencils rolling in the gutter between sofa cushions, a broken metronome perched like a sculpture on the windowsill. The faint smell of burned toast always hung in the air.

Simon was cross-legged on the floor, sheets of paper spread around him like lily pads. He looked up as I entered, his eyes already set to "I have an idea and you're going to hate it." He wore my old jumper, the one with the hole at the elbow, and his hair was sticking up in uneven tufts as if he'd spent the afternoon yanking at it. "You're late," he said, voice clipped but not quite angry, "staff meeting run over?"

I shrugged, dropped my bag by the door, "just needed some air."

He stared at me for a second, then turned a page in *the Guardian*. "You see it?" he asked, not waiting for an answer. "Section 28. It's in every paper."

I slid onto the sofa, exhaling slow, "hard to miss."

He reached behind him and grabbed a handful of pamphlets. "There's a march in Manchester on Saturday. Starts at *Piccadilly*, ends at *Albert Square*. They want as many as can make it. Even my tutors are going."

I leaned back, closed my eyes, and listened to the pipes judder in the wall, "Simon, you know I can't. Not with the risk."

He stood, picking his way through the litter of music and newsprint, and sat down hard on the edge of the coffee table. His knees pressed up against mine, insistent, "this isn't the time for hiding," he said, and his voice was quieter than before, but more dangerous for it. "They're trying to erase people like us, Li. Not just in London, not in some abstract way, but here. Now. You want to teach kids to think for themselves? You think that means anything if you're not willing to stand up when it actually counts?"

His words were a blow, and I flinched, "it's not the same for you. You're not …"

"Not what?" he snapped, "not a teacher? Not responsible for keeping up appearances? Not scared?" He barked a laugh, "you think I don't care about risk? You think I want to be in some photographer's lens and get my Mum's house firebombed?"

I clenched my jaw, tried to breathe slow, "it's not about courage, Simon. It's about survival. If someone from school saw me on the telly, if it got out …"

He cut me off, his face set hard, "so we let them win by default?" He thought for a moment, then added, "you stood up for the workers in Warrington, you've helped the miners and the *AIDS* charity. So it is about courage, even if you don't see it like that."

A silence filled the room, thick enough to drown in. Outside, a car alarm yelped once, then died. Simon broke first, dropping his gaze to the floor. His hands found a music score, and he crumpled the corner of the page without seeming to notice. When he looked up, his eyes were damp.

"If we don't stand up now, when will we?" he said, barely above a whisper.

I looked at him, really looked, beyond the mess and the anger, to the shake in his hands, the way he'd never quite learned to hide. I saw myself reflected there: the kid in the school library, the university student skulking out back doors, the teacher too careful to say a word that might betray him.

I tried to speak, but my mouth was sand. When I finally managed it, my voice was so soft I almost didn't recognise it.

"Alright," I said, "we'll go."

Simon blinked, caught off guard, "you mean it?"

I nodded, though the dread in my chest was a stone.

"But," I added, and now it was my turn to hold the line, "we go at the back, and I wear a scarf and hat, and if anyone points a camera in our direction we duck. I can't … I won't lose my job for one day of grandstanding, Simon."

He reached out, caught my hand. His fingers were cold but his grip was solid.

"That's fair," he said, "we'll be careful."

I tried to laugh, but it caught in my throat, "I don't think that's possible anymore."

Simon squeezed my hand, and in the hush that followed, I found myself staring at the coffee table littered with scores and leaflets and half-drunk mugs of tea. I let myself imagine, for the smallest moment, that the march would change something, anything. That maybe, if enough of us showed up, we'd be harder to erase, just as I had felt in Warrington years before.

I felt my shoulders slump, as if the day's weight had finally settled in all at once.

"Alright," I repeated, the word flat but final, "Saturday. We'll go."

Simon let out a long, shuddering breath and leaned into me, his head on my shoulder, our arms tangled in the debris of hope and fear. We sat like that for a long time, neither of us talking, the silence a ceasefire and a promise both.

The morning of the march, Simon was up before the alarm, brewing tea and pacing the flat like a man waiting for the verdict on a life sentence. I watched him from the bed, the sheets still clinging to my legs, and let the scent of cheap *Assam* and sour milk remind me of every childhood morning before going to school.

By eight, the city was already stirring. From our window I could see the usual Saturday shamble, shop girls in lime green uniforms, pensioners walking dogs with the unhurried defeat of people who know rain is inevitable, not optional. But today, something was different. The air thrummed. Below, you could see the clusters gathering, even this far out: rainbow flags half-hidden under jackets, placards carried flat to avoid early detection, the nervous glance of someone sure the world will stare.

Simon emerged in full kit: denim jacket over a T-shirt with a faded Bowie print, and a scarf so garishly red that it seemed to pulse in the gloom. I pulled on a parka and an old beanie, one size too large, and checked my reflection twice before daring the street. The plan was simple: head for *Piccadilly Gardens*, blend into the back, and if things got ugly, duck out before anyone could point a finger.

Simon's hand found mine the second we cleared the stairs. He squeezed once, as if to say, "we're really doing this." I nodded, kept my face down, and tried to match his stride.

Outside the station, the flow was obvious: people, hundreds, moving as a single current toward the city centre. Some walked in silence, others in tight knots, voices low and urgent. There were banners rolled up under arms, a clutch of pink balloons, a pair of teenage girls in matching *Doc Martens* and denim skirts, their hair shorn close on the sides. For every face painted with purpose, there were ten more hiding in plain sight, just trying to make it to the square without being noticed.

By the time we reached the gardens, the crowd had swollen to thousands. The grass was slicked with mud, the pathways lost under the churn of boots and trainers and the occasional stiletto. There were drag queens in fur coats, lipstick perfect even in the mist; men in leather, arms linked with women in blazers and silk ties; student unions waving hand-lettered signs, *'NO TO SECTION 28'* and *'LOVE IS A HUMAN RIGHT'*. There was laughter, but it was nervous and brittle; every joke sounded like a dare.

Simon pulled me through the first ring of marchers, toward the statue at the centre, where a group had started up a chant, something crude but clever, the words lost in the roar of bodies. I could feel the panic rising, the certainty that at any moment I'd see a student, or worse, a parent, or a teacher from the school with a camera. I ducked deeper into the collar of my coat and let the din wash over me.

Next to the statue, a man in a rainbow sash was handing out leaflets. His nails were painted yellow, and he wore a gold earring with the confidence of someone who'd been punched in the mouth for it a hundred times and decided to stop caring. Simon took a leaflet, grinned, then tucked it into my coat pocket.

"Smile, Li," he said, his voice pitched for me alone, "it's history."

I tried to smile, but my teeth were chattering, "easy for you to say."

He laughed, then turned and pointed, "look," he said.

Near the edge of the square, a line of police was forming. Not riot gear, not yet, just standard issue, neon jackets and black hats, but their presence was enough to send a ripple through the crowd. The chanting got louder, the banners lifted higher. Someone threw confetti, and it stuck to the wet pavement in little explosions of colour.

For the first hour, it was just noise and movement: people chanting, hugging, singing, taking turns at a battered megaphone that barely reached the first few rows. A woman in her seventies took the mic at one point, her voice shaking but relentless, "I have waited my whole life to love in public," she said, and the crowd went mad for her.

As the march began to move, slowly, at first, like a beast waking from anaesthesia, Simon held my hand tighter. We fell in with a group of students, and I tried to look anywhere but behind me, afraid of seeing someone I knew. Every so often Simon would let go to clap or wave, but then he'd grab my wrist again, his grip urgent.

We made it fifty yards before the first confrontation. A group of lads in football scarves stood on the steps outside a betting shop, shouting "benders" and "poofs" and other names that still made my stomach flip, even after all these years. I saw a face I recognised, one of the dads from school, maybe, or a neighbour from my own estate. He glared at the march, then at me, and I froze. But Simon didn't. He kept walking, head high, and when I stumbled he caught my elbow and steadied me.

"You're alright," he said, "they can't do shit. For once there are more of us"

We kept going, and with each street the fear eased, or maybe I just stopped noticing it. There was a rhythm to the protest, a sense that the crowd itself was a shield, if you moved with it, let its energy carry you, nothing could touch you. Simon started chanting along with the others, voice rough but determined.

"No more silence, no more lies, we are equal in their eyes!"

At first, I mouthed the words, barely audible. But as we crossed the next junction, I heard myself shout, the sound torn from my throat raw and feral. I felt Simon's eyes on me, proud and a little startled. We joined the chorus, moving as one mass through the city, past shops and banks and the rows of terrace houses where I'd grown up.

The route twisted towards the town hall, and as we approached *Albert Square*: the police lines here were thicker, and a row of cameras flashed from the opposite curb. Simon squeezed my hand again, but this time I didn't look away. I let the cameras see me. I let everyone see.

At *Albert Square*, the crowd stopped. There were speeches, but I couldn't hear them; my ears rang with the echo of voices, my body buzzed from the adrenaline. Simon pulled me in, arms tight around my ribs, and for a moment it was just the two of us, surrounded by a thousand strangers with the same fire in their hearts.

Then the photographers came closer, weaving through the gaps. One raised his camera and pointed directly at us. I tensed, ready to duck, but Simon held me fast.

"It's okay," he whispered, "let them."

The lens found us, and I felt my own fear crystallise and break, like a pane of glass hit by a hammer. I turned, looked straight into the camera, and lifted my chin. The shutter clicked, again and again.

When the photographer moved on, Simon kissed me, not a big, cinematic kiss, just a quick press of lips to cheek, but it was enough. Around us, people cheered and clapped, some crying, some just grinning through tears.

"That's it," Simon said, voice hoarse but steady, "you did it, Li."

I didn't know if I'd done anything, really. My heart was still pounding, my hands still shook, but for the first time I felt something like relief, or maybe a strange, fragile pride. I was here. I'd shown up.

As the rally faded and people drifted away, I looked at Simon, really looked, and saw him as if for the first time: not just a partner, not just someone to hide behind, but a person who'd dragged me, half-willing, into the light.

We walked home that afternoon from the station, my arm on Simon's shoulder, then off it, then on again. I kept picturing my face in tomorrow's paper, imagining Daniel's smirk or Barbara's concerned phone call.

"Chippy tea?" I asked as we passed the fish shop, my voice surprisingly bright.

"Sure, why not?" Simon replied. Ten minutes later, we were back at my flat, sitting cross-legged on the settee. The vinegar smell filled the room, making me dizzy. I couldn't taste the food as my mind was racing.

"Best chips in Stockport," Simon said, "but don't tell my mum we ate them out of the paper." He flashed that smile, the one that usually melted me but now made my stomach twist with something like resentment at his easy contentment.

"How big's that piano you want?" I asked suddenly, surprising myself.

Simon stopped mid-chew, "what?"

"If we get a place in Castlefields," I said, the words tumbling out before I could reconsider, "we'd need room for one, wouldn't we?"

"A place? Together?" His eyes widened.

"Well I don't need a bloody piano, do I?" I snapped, then immediately regretted it, "sorry, I just ..."

"You're serious?" Simon set down his food, studying my face, "after today, you still want ..."

"I don't know what I want," I admitted, my throat tight, "but I know I'm tired of being afraid all of the time." I reached for his hand, then pulled back, then reached again, "the time's right, I think. Maybe. Probably."

We started looking at flats during Easter break. By July, we'd signed a lease and I had crafted a careful lie for work: economic necessity, a flatmate to split costs so I could afford a car, nothing more. Only Mum and Barbara knew it was Simon. "Such a nice boy," they both said, while I nodded and wondered if I was making the biggest mistake of my life or finally getting something right.

Now, for better or worse, it was done.

CHAPTER 28: THE LETTER FROM LON- DON

August 1988

We spilled into the flat just past midnight, still riding the voltage from the festival, Simon jittery from too much *Red Bull* and communal elation, me wrung out and giddy in the aftermath. I hung his jacket on the bedroom door, then flicked the light switch in the hall three times before it would finally comply, illuminating our not-quite-luxurious Castlefields living room with the sickly hue of a dying moth. Our lives were scattered everywhere: Simon's music sheets colonising every surface in loose drift, my lesson plans rigidly stacked on the desk like an accusation, the air pungent with the leftovers of last week's Chinese. We had still not completely unpacked despite it being two months since the move.

Simon collapsed on the sofa, arms stretched like a basking cat, and whistled a bar from the last set at *Love Rights*, "we absolutely killed it," he announced to the ceiling, then reached for the TV remote and, without looking, tossed it onto the armchair where it landed with a small, perfect thud, "come sit. Or did you have another parade to organise before bed?"

I ignored the jab and began the postmortem, collect the crushed water bottles, line up the record sleeves against the shelf, turn the mail pile so the envelopes faced the same direction. Simon watched, a lopsided grin forming as he propped his bare feet on the edge of the coffee table.

"Relax," he said, eyes following my methodical sweep, "you look like you're prepping for *Ofsted*."

"Old habits," I muttered, scooping up the mail and flipping through it, bank statements, a threatening letter from the TV licensing people, a catalogue Simon would never order from, and then, in the middle, a pale blue envelope, thicker than the rest, postmarked London but redirected via Rochdale in my mother's careful hand.

I paused, the sharp edge of the envelope biting the pad of my thumb. The handwriting wasn't hers; it was unfamiliar, too elegant, the slant hurried but deliberate. A shiver ran up my neck as I turned it over. Simon must have sensed the current because his voice softened.

"What's up?"

I shrugged, not trusting myself to speak, and slit the envelope with a thumbnail. The letter inside was a single sheet in the same unfamiliar hand as the envelope, and the first thing I noticed was the scent, faint, chemical, and almost but not quite like hospital disinfectant.

The words jumbled at first. Then they fell into place.

Dear Liam,

We've never met, I'm Pat (you can call me Patricia Delicia if you prefer), and I share a flat with Alex in London. This letter is awkward and likely unwelcome, but I felt you should know that Alex is not well—seriously not well, the kind of not-well you may not bounce back from no matter how much you want to. He didn't want me to contact you, but I found your address on an old letter he'd kept. If you want to come, I think you should. If you don't, that's your right too, but you at least deserve the choice.

He's at the flat, mostly, but sometimes the hospital. If you need the address, ring the number on the back. I'll keep an eye out for you, if you do show. I hope you do.

Yours truly (and I mean that, darling),

Pat

My hand shook a little as I refolded the letter. The air in the room thickened, heavy as a gym sock. I became aware of every small detail, the faint static on the telly, the sticky ring on the coffee table, the way my chest seemed to be working twice as hard to do half as much. I sat, hard, on the edge of the sofa. Simon instantly abandoned his feet-on-table act and slid to my side, "Liam. What is it?"

I passed him the envelope. He read in silence, the tip of his tongue wetting his top lip every three or four lines, a tell he'd never managed to break. He finished, and set the page down on his thigh.

"Fuck," he said, and the word came out so soft it was almost kind.

For a moment we just breathed, two men in a flat that suddenly felt too small for either of us. I kept my eyes on the floor, tracing the worn spot in the carpet between my feet.

"Are you going to see him?" Simon finally asked.

I ran both hands through my hair, then let them drop, limp, "I don't know." It was a lie, and he could tell.

He nodded, slow, "when?"

I checked the letter for some secret instruction, some escape hatch, but there was only Pat's phone number and the address, "soon. Maybe tomorrow."

Simon rested his palm on the back of my hand, just for a second, "do you want me to come with?"

That nearly broke me, but I managed to shake my head, "no. He probably wouldn't want that. I mean …" I stopped, voice crumbling, "I need to do this myself. If that's okay. Just to find out what's going on with him."

He withdrew his hand, but it hovered above my knuckles, not quite letting go, "whatever you need."

We sat, silent, the TV droning through highlights of a rugby match neither of us cared about. I could feel Simon watching, but I couldn't return the gaze. Instead, I picked up the letter again, reread it, and felt the blood drain from my head all over again.

"Do you want to call?" Simon asked.

"I will in the morning, from *Piccadilly* before I get on the train," I said, surprising myself with the decisiveness, "I should… I should see him before I lose my nerve." The words felt like someone else's, and maybe they were.

Simon nodded, "want me to make you some tea?"

I almost laughed, but the urge died in my throat, "sure," I said, though I knew I wouldn't drink it.

He left for the kitchen, and I listened to the click of the kettle, the measured clink of mugs on the worktop. I looked around the flat, at the mess, at the artifacts of our life together, and thought about all the times I'd packed a bag and run, only to end up here, with Simon, in the only place that ever felt like it belonged to me.

When he returned, he handed me the mug, then settled beside me, close enough that our shoulders touched. He didn't try to talk. He just sat, radiating patience.

I forced myself to drink. The tea was too hot, bitter and sweet all at once. We went to bed late. I lay awake, the letter on the bedside table, the address and phone number copied in my neatest hand into my wallet. Simon lay beside me, arm draped over me, his chin resting on my chest, the way he always did when he wanted me to know he was there. I wanted to say something, anything, but all I managed was, "I'm sorry."

He looked up at me, eyes bleary, "for what?"

"For making you live in my past. For not letting you move on."

He snorted, then reached over and traced a line down the side of my face, "I'm exactly where I want to be, you idiot."

I let him hold me, let the warmth fill the cracks left by the letter. But in the morning, when the alarm rattled us awake, the first thing I did was check the train times to London.

Simon noticed, but didn't say a word. He only pulled on his jeans, then kissed the top of my head before leaving for rehearsal.

When the door closed, the silence roared. I picked up the blue envelope, folded it tight, and slipped it into my jacket pocket.

Then I made myself ready.

I called Pat from a payphone and told him I should be there about noon. He told me the directions on the underground and how to find the flat. The 8:14 from *Manchester Piccadilly* hummed with the kind of tension reserved for exam days and early funerals. I found a window seat in the "quiet carriage," but nothing in the world was quiet, not the lurch of the brakes, not the polyester scrape of a businessman's suit, not the dull throb behind my eyes that refused to sleep. I pressed my forehead against the glass and watched the city turn into fields, then the fields into the indistinct, silvered blur of the Midlands, all of it sliding past like a film I couldn't pause or rewind.

For two hours, I rehearsed conversations with Alex. I tried to remember what his voice sounded like, what jokes he'd make, how he'd scold me for being dramatic or for carrying too much emotional luggage. I pictured him healthy, then frail, then gone, and every permutation made the air inside my chest colder. I cycled through memories, his laughter at two in the morning, the way he could make even the dullest lecture sound thrilling, the day he told me he'd never settle for ordinary. All of it seemed so far away, and yet it crowded me so hard I nearly missed my stop.

Saturday in London was a shock of bodies, everyone in motion, nobody looking anyone in the eye. I fumbled my way to the Underground and wedged myself between a man in paint-splattered overalls and a student with headphones so loud I could make out the rhythm. The train shot through tunnels, the darkness broken by neon platforms and the flicker of fluorescent ghosts. At *Leicester Square* I surfaced into a city that smelled of burnt sugar and diesel, both sweet and lethal.

Soho was awake even at eleven-thirty in the morning. Bars just finishing their cleanup, cigarette butts swept into pyramids by men who looked like they'd never wanted this job and never would. I walked past strip clubs with cracked pink awnings, past a bakery whose window cakes sweated under the lamps, past the old men hawking racing sheets to no one in particular. I stopped in front of the address from Pat's letter: three floors of peeling stucco, the windows streaked with last night's rain, an intercom that buzzed when I pressed the button.

The front door clattered open and out stepped Pat, or, as she'd signed her letter, Patricia Delicia. If I'd expected subtlety, I was a fool, she wore a sequined sheath dress in a shade of purple so loud it nearly silenced the street, her hair a cloud of impossible platinum, her makeup half-applied and glimmering even in the dull early afternoon. Her heels were weapons, and as she leaned into the doorway, she gave me a once-over that left me pinned in place.

"Liam, darling!" she shrieked, voice a decibel north of healthy, "get your arse in here before the paparazzi get wind." She air-kissed my cheeks, leaving a whiff of hairspray and gin in her wake, "let me look at you, no, don't speak yet, I want to preserve the mystique."

I blinked, "hi, Pat … um, Patricia?"

She winked, "Pat to my friends, Patricia to my enemies. Come on, we've got an hour before the next drama kicks off." She led the way up a flight of stairs so narrow I thought my knees would graze the rail. The walls were plastered with old gig flyers; some so faded the bands were a rumour more than a memory. At the first landing, Pat turned and, lowering her voice, said, "he's gonna be really pissed off with me for contacting you, you know. But even a dying man doesn't get everything he wants, does he?"

The words hit me like a physical thing, I flinched, and my vision tunnelled out for a second, the oxygen in the corridor thinning. Pat steadied me with a hand on my shoulder. Her grip was shockingly strong.

"Now is not the time for half-truths or misunderstandings," she said, more quietly, "you okay, love?"

I nodded, unable to answer.

We moved up one more flight and Pat pushed open a battered green door with her hip. The hallway inside was dim, choked with the faint staleness of old cigarettes and something medicinal underneath. She gestured for me to wait in a tiny lounge that doubled as kitchen and sitting room: a battered sofa draped with a Union Jack, a kettle on perpetual boil, and a goldfish in a bowl that looked as resigned to its fate as I did.

Pat vanished down the hall. I heard a rapid-fire exchange, her voice, then another, lower, angry but too muffled to make out. When Pat returned, her face was freshly powdered, but the lines around her eyes were deeper.

"He'll see you," she said, "he's still in bed. Doesn't get up these days. You want coffee?"

I shook my head, "I'll go in."

She patted my arm, "brave boy," she murmured, and ushered me toward a door at the end of the hall.

I stood outside, hand hovering, then knocked. Once, twice, then I just went in, because to do anything else felt like betrayal.

Inside, the light was thin, barely making it through the closed curtains. The room was smaller than I expected. There was a bed, rumpled, and a lamp on the nightstand, casting a pool of yellow across the duvet. Alex lay propped up by pillows, his face sharp with angles I didn't recognise, his hair gone nearly white at the roots. He looked up, and for a moment the room was silent except for the faint tick of the clock and the hiss of the city below.

He smiled. Or maybe he tried to, but it didn't quite reach the eyes, "I told her not to tell you," he said, voice raw but steady, "Pat never listens."

I stepped in, shut the door behind me, "hello, Lex."

He laughed, a sound dry as a cough, "nobody's called me that in years. Sit down. You look like you're about to faint."

I found a chair and perched on the edge, hands knotted in my lap. I couldn't think of a single thing to say. I wanted to apologise for not coming sooner, for never writing back, for every silent hour between now and the last time I saw him, but the words were powder in my mouth.

He let me stew for a minute, then said, "you look good. Teaching suits you."

"How did you ..." I stopped, "never mind."

He closed his eyes, then opened them, "Pat has her ways. She's kept tabs on you since I moved down, more out of insecurity than any thing else. She'd make a decent spy, if the drag circuit ever dries up."

I laughed, but it sounded false.

Alex coughed, harsh, racking, and when it ended he pressed a tissue to his mouth. I looked away, focused on the dust motes in the windowlight. He noticed.

"It's not contagious, you know," he said, with a bitterness that was almost funny, "I checked."

I blushed, furious with myself.

"Sorry," I managed. "I'm just ..."

He waved a hand, "it's all right. I wouldn't want to touch me either, if I had a choice."

I tried to meet his eyes, but he was already looking elsewhere, at the photos taped to the wall, at the half-empty bottle of *Lucozade* on the nightstand, at the future he didn't have.

We sat in silence for a while. Finally, I asked, "are you... okay?" The stupidity of the question stung.

He smiled, this time for real, "define 'okay'." He stretched his hands, long and elegant, the knuckles more prominent now, "it's *AIDS* Liam, but it's not so bad, most days. Pat makes sure I'm fed, and the hospital has a bed with my name on it whenever I fancy a holiday. They give me drugs, some of which actually work. Sometimes I even get visitors."

I nodded, not sure how to proceed, "I missed you," I said, because it was true.

He tilted his head, "did you?"

I bit my lip, "yes. All the time."

He studied me, as if he was searching for a lie, then seemed to accept it, "not enough to write, obviously."

"I didn't know what to say, I was angry when I read about your new life here."

"You could have said anything, even that," he replied, and then smiled again, gentler this time, "it's fine. Nobody teaches you how to do this. Nobody knows what to say when they know how it ends."

I looked at the walls, at the photos. There were a few of us from university, Alex in the centre, me off to the side, always half-in and half-out of the frame.

"I should have come sooner," I said, and now the words fell out easy, like blood from a cut, "it took over a week for Pat's letter to get to me."

He reached over, hand shaking slightly, and touched my wrist, "I hope you understand why I ran off to London. Easier to be anonymous. Easier to fuck things up where nobody knows your name. Easier it seems to catch *AIDS*." There was no bitterness, just resignation and his diagnosis confirmed my worst and unspoken fears.

He told me, then, about the years in London. The good bits first, working at a job his father arranged, getting his own place, living free for the first time. The bad bits followed, too many good times, too much booze, too many drugs, losing his job, losing his father's money, the parties that got wilder and lonelier as he moved from club to club, the friends who disappeared or turned out to be ghosts in borrowed clothes. The last year, he said, was a blur of doctors and missed calls, of hospital rooms and forms and the dawning realisation that this, whatever "this" was, was going to be the rest of his life.

He stopped talking, and the silence that followed was thick and absolute. I tried to find words to fill it, but I knew there were none.

After a while, he smiled again, "you should go. Trains back to Manchester get unreliable later in the day."

I shook my head, "I'll stay. I can get a late one."

He seemed startled, then pleased, "I'd like that."

We sat, watching the dust move in the light, talking of nothing and everything.

When I finally left, the corridor seemed colder. Pat was waiting at the door, still in sequins, but her hair now pulled back in a severe ponytail, her eyes careful.

"Did you say what you needed to?" she asked.

"No," I said, "but maybe I will, next time."

She nodded, "I'll let you out. London's a maze for newcomers." She offered her arm, and together we went down the stairs, the click of her heels echoing like a metronome in a song I never wanted to end.

"I'll come back soon," I promised, "please let me know if there is any change."

She nodded, "he talks about you. The only time he gets sentimental, really." She looked at me, suddenly serious, "if you know how to contact his mum, maybe you could? But be sure. No taking it back."

"I'll think about it."

I blinked, then looked at the floor, "thank you. For looking after him."

She squeezed my shoulder, "can't help who you fall in love with, eh darling?" She winked, then closed the door.

I put my hands in my pockets, feeling the letter I'd folded there, and started the walk to the station. I'd come back, as long as he needed me.

CHAPTER 29: A FINAL RECKONING

The train home took the colour out of me. By the time I hit Manchester, I'd faded to a kind of wet-newsprint grey: a ghost in the commuter mob, my hands still faintly reeking of disinfectant from Alex's room and cheap drag queen hairspray. I walked the last half-mile to Castlefields, and every footstep was a little mercy, one moment more before I'd have to say the words out loud. One more minute of nobody knowing what I now knew.

Our flat looked exactly as I'd left it. Simon's violin case lay open on the settee, the dark wood gleaming against the corduroy cushions. The heating was on, but the place felt cold, colder than I remembered, colder than even outside, the kind of cold that gets in behind your eyes and makes them sting. Simon was home, in the kitchen, standing with his back to the door and both hands braced on the countertop like he was keeping the world from collapsing.

He turned when I came in. For a split second, he smiled, that pure, unguarded Simon smile, then he saw my face and the whole room dropped a few degrees. He closed the distance in two steps, caught me by the elbows, and searched my eyes.

"How was he?" Simon asked, voice already bracing for the answer.

I tried to find the right word, "broken," I said, and it wasn't even close.

Simon nodded, and pulled me gently down onto the sofa. I sat, feeling the shape of his hand on my arm even after he let go. I didn't want to say anything, not yet. But the silence turned into a kind of pressure, so I opened my mouth and let it out.

"He's dying," I said. "*AIDS*. There's no way around it." I waited for Simon to flinch, but he only blinked and leaned forward, as if to catch the rest before it hit the floor, "he's got a flatmate, Pat. Patricia Delicia, if you please. She's the one who wrote me. She's looking after him now. There's nothing else they can do."

Simon pressed the heel of his palm against his temple, hard enough to blanch the skin, "how long?"

I shrugged, "a few months. Less, maybe. He barely eats. He's on so many drugs they don't know what works and what doesn't, and those that don't make him worse."

He nodded, like he'd already considered what might be wrong and just needed confirmation, "was he scared?"

I thought of Alex, of the way his face had changed at the end, the moment he stopped joking and just lay there, counting the spaces between the words, "no," I lied, "he was just tired."

Simon stood, walked to the kitchen, and I heard the kettle click on. I stared at the pile of music on the table, Kreisler, Beethoven, some bastardised Vivaldi arrangement that Simon always bitched about, but still played for the money. When he came back, he set two mugs on the coffee table, both of them steaming, and sat cross-legged at my feet.

"We should go down together," he said, not a question but a map of the future, "next time."

I wanted to say no. I wanted to keep Simon away from all of it, from the illness, the smell, the fact that *AIDS* was now not just an urban legend, but a thing that could reach through the television and into our lives. But I saw how he looked at me, and I couldn't say no.

"Okay," I said, "but not for a week. Let's just... stay here for a bit."

He nodded, picked up his mug and blew across the top. His hands shook. It was a small, almost imperceptible tremor, but once I saw it, I couldn't unsee it. The tea sat between us, cooling. Neither of us drank.

After a while, Simon spoke, his voice quieter now, "are you scared?" he asked.

I wanted to make a joke, or to say that I was fine, but instead I said, "yes. More than ever."

He moved closer, set his head on my shoulder and let out a slow breath, "me too," he whispered, "it's not supposed to happen to people we know."

I almost laughed, "who's it supposed to happen to, then?"

He shrugged, and the movement was so slight, I barely felt it, "somebody else."

We sat in that silence, the tea long gone cold, and I traced the line of his wrist with my finger, counting the tiny blue rivers beneath the skin.

After a while, Simon asked, "what did you say to him?"

I tried to remember, "I told him I missed him. That I wished it could have gone different."

"Did you mean it?" Simon's eyes were closed, but I felt him tense as he said it.

"Yeah," I said, "I did, but just because he doesn't deserve what's happening to him."

He relaxed again, and the tension ebbed away from his body. I leaned into him, and he leaned right back, the two of us balanced on the fulcrum of the sofa, neither willing to let gravity win.

We went to bed early, not because I felt like sleep, but because the day had wrung every colour out of us. I lay on my back, staring at the ceiling, counting the cracks in the plaster while Simon traced patterns on my forearm. We didn't talk about *AIDS*, or Alex, or what would happen next. We just held onto each other, as if something in the clutch of our bodies could hold back the future.

But, when I woke in the middle of the night, Simon was awake too, his eyes shining in the dark, and the air in the room was heavy with the unspoken. I rolled over, buried my face in his neck, and breathed in the warmth of him.

"It's not going to happen to us," I said, barely more than a whisper, though I wasn't sure if I believed it. I thought for a moment before I added, "I need to go and tell his mother tomorrow I think." I paused, wondering if I was making a terrible mistake. "She has a right to know, doesn't she? Even though she'll probably slam the door in my face."

"I'll go with you then," Simon said, his voice gentle but uncertain. He kissed my forehead, his lips lingering a beat too long, "try to sleep." But as he held me, I felt the slight tremble in his arms, and I wondered if either of us would close our eyes again that night.

Simon insisted on driving at first, but I made him hand over the keys before we hit the motorway. He had only passed his test a few weeks before. The need for control was physical, a tremor in the palms, a chattering in the jaw. I tried to explain, but he just smiled and said, "you're the boss," then sank into the passenger seat and fiddled with

the tape deck until the car filled with the decadent blare of
Spandau Ballet and their shallow, sunless voices.

The *Golf* had bad brakes and a rattle in the left door
that I could never fix, but today it felt solid, grounded by the
weight of what we carried. Outside, Manchester's brutal blocks
gave way to sprawl, then the green-spined rise of the *Cheshire
Ridge*. The rain came in, a thin, needling sort, just enough to
smear the windscreen into impressionist shapes. Simon
watched the landscape, silent except for the occasional click of
the indicator when he grew nervous.

At the turnoff for the Wirral on the M56, the fields
were blanched with sheep and mist. Every so often a clump of
houses would appear and vanish again, pubs named after kings,
petrol stations that looked like time capsules from the sixties. I
gripped the wheel until my knuckles shone, the ridges gone
bloodless.

"Are you sure you want to do this today?" Simon asked,
his eyes on the hedgerow racing past.

I nodded, not trusting my voice.

He reached over, found my hand, and held it there, his
thumb tracing the back of my wrist, "I'll wait in the car," he
said.

I smiled, "I'll be fine."

"You're allowed to be not fine, you know," he replied,
and it was so perfectly Simon that I almost laughed.

Heswall was posher than anywhere I'd ever lived or felt
comfortable visiting. The houses stood back from the road, behind walls and gates and long, ornamental gardens. The
Hughes' home was at the top of a slight rise: a Victorian beast
with bay windows and a turret on the corner, the brickwork
dark from years of salt air. The front garden was as neat as I remembered, the rhododendrons bruised and sagging against the
railings. The door was blue and shiny as I remembered it from
before.

I parked halfway up the drive, engine ticking with heat.
Simon squeezed my hand one more time, then let go, "go on,"
he whispered, "she'll listen to you."

I doubted it. But I got out and walked the path, every
step a rehearsal for what came next.

At the door I paused, took a long breath, and rang the bell. I heard footsteps inside on the tiled floor of the entrance, a careful, measured tread, and then Mrs. Hughes was there, framed by the heavy glass and the shadows behind her.

She looked smaller than I remembered. Her hair was still neat, still fixed in that impossible helmet, but her face was paler, the skin around her mouth stretched tight as if she'd spent the last year clenching her jaw. She took one look at me and her eyes hardened.

"Alex doesn't live here anymore," she said, voice flat as a closing door.

"I know," I replied, "but I just need a minute. Please."

She hesitated, fingers hovering over the latch like she wanted to slam it and be done, "if that boy is in trouble," she said, "then I don't want to know about it. His father's not home."

I let the words hang, then said, "you need to know what I have to say. I won't stay long."

She stared at me, and I could see the war playing out in her head, the urge to tell me to fuck off, and the need to know what was so important I'd come all the way from Manchester to her front door. She relented, just barely, and opened the door another inch.

"Fine," she said, "we'll do it in the drawing room."

She stepped back, and I followed her through the dark foyer. The air inside was thick with polish and the memory of last night's lamb roast. The drawing room was as I remembered it, grand and impersonal, all brown leather and heavy curtains, a gas fire unlit in the grate. There were family photos on every flat surface, none of which featured Alex after age fifteen.

Mrs. Hughes stood by the mantle, arms folded, watching me like I might run off with the silverware.

"Well?" she said. A clock ticked somewhere out of sight, but otherwise the only sound was the hush of rain against the bay window. The carpet was a pale blue, so clean that my boots left prints on it.

I stood, hands jammed in my pockets, and tried to remember what Pat had told me, something about there being times for half-truths and times for the real thing. This was not a house that tolerated ambiguity. Every surface was either glass, marble, or lacquered to a blinding shine.

Mrs. Hughes nodded at me, once, as if daring me to get on with it.

I said, "Alex has *AIDS*." The words didn't echo, "and he's dying. I thought you should know."

There was a pause so long it became a second kind of noise. Her face didn't change at first, but her left hand flexed open and closed on her arm, knuckles whitening, and then releasing, like she was trying to pump life back into them. I kept my eyes on the wall behind her, the framed print of St. Paul's and the Thames, the gleam of the silver plate on the shelf above.

She said, "I see." The words dropped like a coin in a well, "I wondered why you came all this way. Now I know."

I took a slip of paper from my pocket, the one with Pat's name, the address, and the hospital number, and set it on the table next to a heavy glass ashtray, "this is where he's being looked after. By a friend."

She didn't touch it. Her eyes moved to the fireplace, where a photograph of her wedding day, her in white, Alex's father young and dark-haired, stood slightly askew.

"You're the reason," she said, softly at first, but louder the second time: "you're the reason he turned out this way."

I let it pass. There was no point to arguing. Instead, I said, "he might not have much time. If you do want to talk to him, that should be soon."

She shook her head, once, sharp as a slap, "no," she said, and now there was a tremor in it, "if he cared for this family, he'd have told us himself." I had to work hard to suppress a laugh and the words that were forming in my mind, *what, so that you could slap him again for his honesty*.

I turned to go. At the door, her voice followed, thin and brittle, "I blame you, Liam, for leading him astray at University!"

I didn't answer. I just walked, boots leaving ghostly prints on the blue carpet, and didn't stop until the air outside hit me in the face. My hand shook as I opened the car door. Simon was there, hands tight on the steering wheel, waiting to drive us home.

A couple of days later, my heart thudding, I reached for the ringing phone and heard Pat's voice crackle through, charged with an agitation I'd never encountered, "that bloody woman, who does she think she is?" he spat, anger and hurt tangled so tightly they sounded like a single scream.

A rush of guilt warmed my cheeks. Had I done this? "You spoke to Alex's mum, then?" I ventured, striving for neutral calm.

Pat inhaled sharply, "now I understand why Alex begged me not to tell her a thing." He launched into their conversation: accusations that I'd fabricated Alex's illness, that I harboured some vile vendetta against him, that people like me deserved the flames of hell. Each insult sank in like a stone in my stomach.

I swallowed, "was she… upset?" I asked, as if a trace of maternal concern might have pierced her fury.

His laughter rattled me, "upset? No, just seething with hatred. From what Alex told me, she's all fur coat and no knickers anyway."

A hollow laugh escaped my lips. Relief clashed with shame, I was glad Pat saw her clearly, but I hated that I'd thrust him into this, "and what does she intend to do then?"

He paused, quoting her next words as if they were sharpened blades, "she said she'd refuse to visit him while he's living with a 'disgusting transvestite pervert' like me."

I closed my eyes, conflicted between outrage and fear. "I … I'm sorry I told her. You didn't deserve that for caring for him."

"No, darling," Pat's voice softened though it still trembled, "you did the right thing. I can look after myself." He hesitated, then added, "she's planning to call the hospital, have him transferred up north."

My pulse pounded, "can she actually do that?"

"Not while I have breath," he replied firmly, "Alex named me next of kin. So there's nothing she can do unless me and Alex agree, and I know he won't."

A wave of relief followed by fresh guilt washed over me, "good. He needs you more than that witch."

I hesitated, conflict knotting my throat, "um, Simon, my other half, wants to visit with me next weekend. Would that be okay with Alex you think?"

Pat's tone shifted, there was seriousness, sincerity, even warmth, "absolutely. He needs to see you're happy."

Even after all this? My chest tightened, "even after all these years?"

"Especially after all these years," Pat said, "Alex's deepest regret is how he thinks he let you down."

I felt tears sting my eyes, "we let each other down."

"I know, darling. I just want him to know that too."

With that, our conversation wound down and we arranged the next visit, each of us caught between worry, guilt, and the fierce bond holding us together.

Simon did come with me once that next weekend. After we arrived at Pat's, I introduced him to Alex as 'my boyfriend'. Neither said much to begin with, but, without thinking it seemed, Simon sat on the edge of the bed and just held Alex's hand and stared out the window. I couldn't decide if I wanted him there or not, grateful for his support but uneasy watching my past and present collide in this sterile room.

Eventually, Alex found some energy and asked, "does he still sometimes argue just for the sake of it?"

"All the time," Simon replied. Alex smiled, and I felt a stab of something like jealousy, they were bonding over me.

"And still a revolutionary?"

"A little bit, perhaps," Simon replied, launching into stories about the demonstrations and charity work we'd shared. I shifted in my chair, wondering which version of me Alex was picturing, and if it matched who I'd become.

"Good, he needs a cause to fight for," Alex's words were barely audible, his energy fading.

After a few minutes more, I decided it was time to leave. Barely able to lift his arm, Alex beckoned me closer, pulling my head down to his.

"Don't let this one go," he whispered, glancing at Simon by the door, "he makes you happy I think."

"He does, very happy," I said. I kissed his forehead, hating how my lips registered the fever beneath his skin. "I'll see you again very soon." He nodded slightly and let me go, eyes closing.

On the train home, Simon cried silently. I pretended not to notice, torn between comforting him and maintaining the wall I'd built between my grief and his. Sometimes I forgot he was four years younger and less practiced at compartmentalising, more honest with his emotions. I both envied and feared that rawness in him.

Over the next month or two, the trains journeys blurred together. By late November, I knew every tilt of the West Coast line, every platform kiosk, every chemical trick that made coffee taste more like soil than water. The flat in Soho grew smaller with each visit, Pat in her gown or his robe, Alex stretched across the bed like a cast-off shadow. The first time, Alex made jokes about his prognosis, calling it "the elegant way out," and winked when Pat told him to shut up. The second time, he barely managed a smile.

December brought new drugs and new rules. The hospital wouldn't let us all in at once. Pat started smoking outdoors. Alex's hands shook too much to hold a pen, so I read his post for him, even the bills, even the junk. There was never a letter from his family. Not even at Christmas. Pat had not heard anything further from Alex's Mum.

The last time I went, it was January and the city was locked in a mean, clinging cold. Pat answered the buzzer and let me up. "He's not here," Pat said, voice brittle as icicles, "they took him last night. Sorry, I should have called you, save you the journey down. His mum's in charge now. She doesn't want visitors."

"Don't worry about me," I reached forward and patted his arm. How could she do that?" I asked.

"Legally, apparently, as a non-blood relative, and obviously not his wife or husband, I have no rights unless I have a power of attorney or something." I let the words settle.

"That's not fair," I muttered.

"Since when has life been fair darling," a statement not a question. I could hear the hurt and desperation in his voice, but I had no words that would help him. "One of the nurses on the ward has promised to let me know how he is doing though." This was not much consolation, but it was all I could take away with me.

I stood on the steps for a while as I left, hands in pockets, watching someone pedal past on a bike. I wanted to go to the hospital and demand to see him, but I knew it would be pointless as Pat had already tried.

The last time I saw Alex, I remembered he'd said, "don't come again, okay?" He smiled, teeth as white as the rest of him. "I want to remember you as the clever one, the one who always gets out in time."

I told him I'd come back anyway, and he tried to laugh.

Three days later the call came from Pat. He was at the hospital, the *Charles Bell Ward* at the *Middlesex*. "I'm sorry Liam," Pat said, voice pitched to survive a hurricane, "he's gone."

He told me that he'd passed in the night, peaceful, no pain, and that the family was "handling arrangements." I hung up before I could ask what 'arrangements' meant.

Pat called again that night, "his parents are going to say it was cancer," he said, the fury leaking out with every syllable, "they're taking him to bury him at home. None of his friends here are invited and not you specifically. Can you believe that?"

I could. I could believe anything.

I waited until the flat was empty of sound, even the traffic outside flattened to a distant murmur, before I dialled the Rochdale number. Simon watched from the next room, pretending to organise the bills, but really just waiting to see if I'd go through with it.

Mum picked up after two rings, her voice a balm and a blade at once. "Maggie here. Hello?"

I said, "hi Mum, it's me," and immediately heard the shift in her breathing, she could always tell when something was wrong.

"Liam, love, is everything alright?" she asked, and the tremor in it nearly finished me off.

I tried to keep my voice level, "no, not really. I … I need to tell you something. About Alex."

Silence, then a careful, "go on, then."

I closed my eyes and pressed my thumb against the table so hard it left a dent, "he died last night. In hospital. It was… sudden, but not a surprise."

Mum inhaled, sharp and quick, "oh, love. I'm so sorry. Was he alone?"

"Only his mum was there," I managed, "she didn't want… visitors." My throat burned, "his family's saying it was cancer, but it was *AIDS*."

I waited, half-hoping she'd leave it at that, let the shock settle over everything like a dust sheet. But Margaret Parry wasn't built for comfortable fictions.

She said, "he was more than just a friend, wasn't he, Liam?"

The air left the room. My chest seized up, the words trapped somewhere behind the bone. I nodded, uselessly, then remembered she couldn't see me.

"Yes, Mum," I said, "a lot, lot more than just a friend."

There was no judgment in her reply, only the sound of tears she tried to swallow down, "you don't have to say anything else, love. I think I've always known, or thought it a possibility."

Something inside me cracked open. I sobbed, silent at first, then loud enough that Simon could hear. He stepped into the kitchen, wrapped both arms around my shoulders, and held on. I pressed the phone to my ear and tried to breathe.

Mum waited for me, didn't rush, just let the noise run itself out. When I finally spoke, the words came in stuttering fragments, "I'm sorry, I should've told you …"

"No, darling. You did what you thought was best. That's all any of us can do."

Simon squeezed me tighter. I felt him reach for the phone, and I let him take it.

He said, "hello, Mrs. Parry, it's Simon. I'm here with Liam. Don't worry, I'll make sure he's alright."

Mum laughed, the sound ragged but real, "thank you, Simon, love, for being there with him. You're a good one, I can tell."

Simon nodded, "I promise," he said, "we'll look after each other."

Mum's voice softened, "just tell him everything will be alright, and that I love him… as I know you love him and he loves you. That's all a mum wants, in the end."

Simon smiled, "he heard you," he said, then passed the phone back to me.

I didn't have much left to say, "I'll visit soon," I told her, "but not just yet."

She sighed, "take your time, Liam. And let me tell your father, will you? It'll be easier that way."

"Okay," I said, and the relief was so huge it made me dizzy.

We hung up. For a while, neither of us moved. Then Simon pressed his cheek against mine and just breathed with me, matching pace for pace, until my heart slowed down.

After a while, he said, "you did the hard bit. The rest is easy."

I almost believed him.

Two weeks slipped by with the grace of an amateur magician: all misdirection, everything vanishing just as you reached for it. I spent the days teaching, the evenings either at home with Simon or shuttling between our flat and the music college, and the weekends marking until my eyes blurred. Each morning, I woke with the certainty that I should call Pat, and each morning I didn't, not yet. My finger would hover over the last digit, then retreat. Instead I waited, and in waiting, found an odd kind of peace, a liminal state between two lives.

When I finally called Pat, my hands shook so badly I misdialled twice. We talked about Alex and our shared experiences of him, though half the stories made me want to hang up and pretend I'd never known either of them. I invited him to come up to Manchester so that we could drive over to the cemetery to pay our respects to Alex. "Any excuse for a girl to buy flowers is good for me," he replied, his voice both comforting and terrifying in its boldness.

During that conversation, and the ones that regularly followed, I began to understand why Alex had been drawn to such a big character, even as I worried what my neighbours might think of Pat's voice carrying through our thin walls.

It was during one of those phone calls that Pat asked me if I had come out at work yet. When I said that I hadn't, he simply said, "why not?" The question lodged in my chest like a stone. Afterwards I asked Simon what he thought, and he gave me one of those looks that said "about bloody time," though I couldn't tell if I was more afraid of his disappointment or his hope. This look was previously reserved for when he was trying to teach me something musical and I finally got it after the fourth or fifth attempt.

"If you're asking the question of whether or not, then I think you already know the answer," he said in a gently teasing tone that didn't match the gravity I felt.

"Really?" I asked sarcastically, though my heart was hammering, "and lose my job? Have the kids call me names? Have their parents complain?"

"Yes, really," Simon placed a hand on my cheek, "it's what you always do with the difficult stuff." His thumb stroked my cheekbone, and then he added, "it's one of the many reasons I love you. No secrets, no surprises."

I swallowed hard, torn between the safety of silence and the promise of something else. "Monday, then," I said.

CHAPTER 30: TO NOT BEING LOST

So, on the Monday after May half-term, I arrived at school before seven. I climbed the stairwell, the smell of disinfectant stronger than coffee in the air, and unlocked my classroom, which was exactly as I'd left it, blank blackboard, desks in the horseshoe shape I preferred, my battered briefcase sagging on the teacher's chair. I stood in the hush, letting the shape of the room settle around me, then crossed to the cupboard.

The drawer stuck, as always, and I wrenched it open with a violence that sent the contents skittering, lesson planners, a bottle of aspirin, and, on top, a cheap photo frame in faux-gold plastic. The picture inside was Amanda, or rather the girl who unknowingly played Amanda from my sixth form days. In the image, her face was turned to me, lips parted mid-laugh, my own hand resting on her shoulder with the uncertainty of a novice actor. I'd kept it there as armour: a shield for nosy colleagues, a prop to fill the dead air of staffroom gossip. I'd told myself it was just until I found something better.

I sat at my desk and looked at the picture, the memories it pretended to hold, and then I pried the backing loose. The photo slipped out easily, like it was relieved to be finished with the charade. Underneath, in the same sleeve, was a new photograph: me and Simon, caught on Canal Street at the end of last year's Pride, arms slung over each other's shoulders, half drunk and fully alive. We'd found a random stranger to take it, and the man's finger had smudged the lens, leaving a fog over the upper corner. I remembered, too, the panic afterward, the hurried pat down for witnesses, the instant regret at so much exposure. But now, in the quiet of my room, the only thing I felt was how right it looked.

I slid the photo into the frame, clicked the backing in place, and set it in the middle of my desk. The edges caught the morning light, and the two of us, me, hair a mess and smiling without irony, Simon squinting into the sun, stared back at me with the stubbornness of the truly reckless.

By eight-thirty, the school had filled with bodies: students in various states of uniform decay, teachers herding them along the corridor currents, the deputy head barking over the tannoy about lost property and late registers. I pretended to review my lesson notes, but in

truth I watched the door, counting the seconds before someone would come in, see the frame, and upend everything.

The first to arrive was Harry Windle, his tie already
stained with what looked like marmalade, his moustache slicked
down to an aerodynamic point.

"Morning, lad," he grunted, shuffling through the door
and setting a stack of battered exercise books on my desk. He
didn't look at the frame, didn't look at me, just thumped the
top book and said, "forty-seven unmarked essays, compliments
of 4A. Some of them even write in English." He sniffed, wiped
his nose on the back of his hand, and finally caught sight of the
photograph. There was a second, a beat so tiny you might have
missed it, when his eyes lingered, then flicked up to mine. "Are
you sure that's what you want to do?" he asked. There was
something in his eyes or his tone that suggested the picture was
merely a confirmation of something he already knew.

"Yes, Harry," I replied firmly. He smiled.

"It that case, just be careful around the kids," his voice
was gentle, almost encouraging.

"I will, and I won't broadcast it to them of course, but
if they ask, I won't lie any more, life is too short." I had told
him what had happened to 'a friend in London' one day after
he had noticed my sadness.

"I understand, Liam," he replied. He reached down and
squeezed my shoulder, "I'm proud of you, I really am." I
couldn't look up at him though, otherwise all my doubts and
fears would have flooded out.

"Thank you Harry, that means a lot," was all I could
manage.

"Nay bother lad," he added before removing his hand.
"Shall we get on with the day then?"

"Yes, sir!" I barked giving him a military salute.

The rest of the day played out in variations on the same
theme. Some colleagues didn't notice, some noticed but pretended not to, and a precious few, like Daniel, who had once
bet me a week's lunch money I wouldn't last a year, paused for
an extra second, gave a half-smile, muttered, "you've got balls
lad, I'll give you that," and then moved on. Nobody said anything mean, or crude, or even pointed; instead, there was a kind

of stealth acceptance, as if the school had always known and was only now admitting it to itself.

I called Simon at lunchtime and left a message on the answer machine we had recently invested in, "mission accomplished: pic on desk. No riots. See you tonight."

That Friday, as was tradition, the usual group of staff went to *the Crown*, which was as much a staffroom as the actual one in the school. I'd told Simon to meet me outside at 4.30, after he'd finished rehearsals, but he arrived early, hair still wet from the shower, shirt untucked in a way that made him look both younger and more dangerous.

We stepped inside together, abandoning our usual separate, non-suspicious liaisons. The warmth and the reek of spilled lager hit us at once. The bar was crowded, mostly with teachers and a scattering of the local hard cases at the fruit machine. I'd barely closed the door before the buzz at the tables dropped, just a half step, not hostile, more a collective intake of breath.

I hesitated, feeling the old panic surge, but Simon just nudged me forward, he leant into me and whispered, "time to make us official". We approached Harry's table where he was holding court. He glanced up from his pint and smiled at both of us.

"About bloody time," he said, "it's good to see two happy young men together," which provoked a chorus of approval from the table. Even Daniel looked up from his newspaper and *Guiness* to nod his approval. Barbara, was just Barbara, and she leapt out of her chair and to hold us both in a tight hug planting a kiss on both of us.

"I could cry," she finally said, and wiped her eyes to prove it. "Harry's right, it is about bloody time, that you two confirmed what we've all been thinking for at least two years since that New Year party."

"How'd you know about that?" I asked.

"You think Simon is the only musician I know?" she genuinely sounded insulted by my question.

"But you never said anything?"

"Wasn't my secret to tell, love." My face flashed red, and in my mind I couldn't help but think "does everyone know?". Then I decided, very quickly, that I just didn't care anymore if they did.

Simon squeezed my hand stood next to me. I squeezed back, suddenly aware of how easy it was.

"You did right, lad," Harry said once Barbara released us. "The world's a bastard. Might as well tell it to fuck off and be happy while you can." He pressed a crumpled twenty into my palm, as if I were still a schoolboy and he the benevolent tyrant, "go get the drinks in, the pair of you, before all this joy shatters my reputation for being a miserable bugger."

The table burst into laughter, and even Barbara, eyes rimmed with red, managed a snort, "oh Harry," she said, "trust you to spoil the moment."

I stood, Simon beside me, and as we crossed to the bar, I caught our reflection in the smoky mirror behind the optics: two men, side by side, visible and seen. This, I thought, is what comes after.

Towards the end of term, Simon travelled to London for an audition with an orchestra. We didn't talk about it much beforehand; the prospect was too big, too unlikely, and we both harboured the suspicion that even hoping for it might jinx the chance. I pretended it was just another gig, a way to impress his tutors, a weekend away from the grind. But when Simon packed his battered violin case and the single suit that fit him properly, he spent the evening before cleaning the instrument, wiping every curve with a rag and then, when he thought I wasn't looking, buffing the buttons of his shirt with spit and thumb. I knew then that this was real, that if he didn't get it, nothing else we did in Manchester would be enough.

The audition was for the *Academy of St Martin in the Fields*, one of the only places in Britain, or anywhere, that could make a permanent seat sound like a life sentence and a lottery win all at once. They wanted young talent, but not too much nerve; brilliance, but never arrogance. Simon's teacher had said he was a long shot, but a "contender," and I'd clung to that word as if it might transform into certainty through sheer repetition.

He took the train at six in the morning, the carriage empty but for a pair of grizzled businessmen and a girl with purple streaks in her hair, hunched over a manga comic. I watched the train depart, waited until the lights were swallowed by the next station, then drove home in a daze, the city looking unfamiliar, even a little hostile. Without Simon there, I noticed the silence in our flat, the way the morning sun filtered through the blinds and caught the floating dust. I made tea but didn't drink it, and instead paced the floor, mapping the scuffs and snags on the laminate as if they'd somehow changed overnight.

I didn't hear from him all day. By six in the evening, I was vibrating, torn between ringing the college, the London number he'd left for emergencies, and Pat's Soho flat, even though I knew perfectly well she'd still be asleep. Instead, I walked the city for an hour, up and down *Deansgate*, watching the student crowds and the packs of football kids already half-drunk on end of week excess. The city seemed to have a pulse, and each time I thought it would stop, it only beat harder.

When I finally got home, the answerphone was blinking. My hands shook as I pressed play. Simon's voice, hoarse but triumphant: "I got it. They said yes. They want me back for rehearsals next month. I don't … Liam, I don't even know if this is real. Am getting the 7pm train, shall be home 10 o'clock or so. Love you."

The next call was to my mother. She whooped so loud I had to hold the phone away from my ear, then spent five minutes plotting train routes from Rochdale to London, as if the gig would only matter if she could attend every single one. My father, in the background, grunted his approval, then added, "long as it pays, lad," which made Simon laugh when I relayed it.

We celebrated that night, not in the pubs or the clubs, but at home, with greasy takeaway and a bottle of cold *Chardonnay* I'd been saving for nothing in particular. Simon played a little, his fingers too excited to stay in the right key, and we spent most of the night tangled on the settee, each daring the other to say, "what now?" before the words had any shape.

What now, of course, was London. Or nothing at all. I stared at the ceiling, my stomach knotting. Manchester was the only place I'd ever felt safe. I'd built something here, a life, respect, routine.

"I could find supply teaching work down there," I said finally, my voice catching, "that's if you want me to come with you?"

"I can't do it on my own," he said, voice smaller than I'd ever heard it.

"Then it's settled," my external confidence was for Simon's sake. Inside I considered everything I had built the last few years, and what I would leave behind. The decision was of course simple, once I realised that none of it would mean anything without Simon by my side.

I called Pat the next day, asking if we could stay with him while we found our own place. His enthusiastic "oh darlings, I insist!", made my hands shake as I hung up. If I concentrated on the practicalities, I reckoned, everything else would slip into place in their own time.

The next month blurred. Simon finished his studies with barely a nod to finals, already halfway to London in his mind. I gave notice at school after the official resignation date, my letter of resignation sitting for a day on my desk before I finally submitted it. Harry said not to worry and cleared it with the headmaster, but I saw the disappointment behind his eyes.

Packing up the flat was a lesson in what we could live without: most of the furniture, the kitchenware, the years' worth of unread junk mail, all the mismatched towels and mugs we'd accumulated by accident. We kept the vinyl collection, Simon's music, my battered *Penguin* paperbacks, and a few photos from the last two years. It didn't seem like much, but it filled the car to bursting.

On our last night in Manchester, we did what we'd promised each other, years ago: we went to the pub with all the Canal Street crowd. Not just the usual suspects, but Harry and Barbara, and a few of the other teachers. The music college lot, of course and pretty much everyone we'd known, even some we'd barely tolerated; David and Michael from *the Rembrandt*; Karen from the record shop, hair dyed green this week, chain-smoking with her arm draped over a shy, sweet-faced girl she introduced as "my latest fuck-up, Hayley." The place was mobbed, a din of voices and laughter that only grew as the beer went down.

The pub hadn't changed, still sticky-floored, still lit like a crime scene, still staffed by the same two barmen who could pull a pint in under six seconds and eviscerate you with a single line if you so much as hesitated with your payment. We squeezed into the back room, the old dart board now more patch than cork, and Simon immediately took over the jukebox, stacking it with a weird mix of *Soul* and *Bronski Beat*. He was holding court, arms around the necks of anyone in range, his laughter floating above the hubbub. I watched him and thought: *'this is the end, and it's perfect'.*

The night blurred, the way only the good ones do. There were rounds of tequila, rounds of bad karaoke, an impromptu game of truth-or-dare that ended with Simon doing a lap of the bar in nothing but socks and shorts, cheered on by three middle-aged men in matching Hawaiian shirts. Harry made a speech that was half insult, half tribute; Michael tried to teach me to waltz and nearly had my toes broken; even Barbara, lush with white wine, pulled me aside and said, "you saved that boy, you know. And yourself, too. Don't ever forget it."

Somewhere past midnight, as the crowd thinned and the staff started stacking the chairs, Simon found me in the back room, sat on my lap, and put his head on my shoulder.

"We did it," he whispered, not a question but a benediction.

"We did," I said, and closed my eyes, letting the sound of the pub and the heat of his skin sink in.

At closing, Harry led the remaining crew in a final round, the pints raised high enough to slosh onto the table.

"To new starts," he said, "and to the lads who showed us how it's done."

"To the journey and who you share it with," I added, and the words came out so clear, so unforced, that even I was surprised by them. Simon grinned, then kissed me, right there, in front of everyone.

Nobody blinked.

We left at two, arm in arm, and walked the empty streets home. The city was slick with rain, neon reflected in the puddles, the air dense with spring and the last sweet traces of night. The buildings rose and fell in shadow, but I felt them less as walls and more like something that cradled us, proof that we had been here, that we mattered.

Back at the flat, we lay on the floor amid the last of the boxes, the windows open to the city's hush. Simon played a few quiet notes, then set the violin aside, and for the first time in a long while, we didn't talk. We just listened, to the wind, to the heartbeat of the building, to the way our breath tangled and separated in the dark.

In the morning, the world was waiting. London, the future, all of it. But for now, I let myself be still, and realised that I was not lost, not anymore. I had given up everything I thought was necessary, ap-proval, safety, the old dream of being normal, Alex, and found that what was left was better than I'd dared imagine. It wasn't perfection, or even peace, but it was real, and it was ours; as were the inevitable struggles to come. One thing I knew for absolute certainty was that I had chosen the right man to fight life with.

When we left Manchester, I didn't look back.

Some people lose themselves and never come home. Me, I lost everything and found exactly where I was supposed to be. And with whom.

Sat in our heavily laden car, Simon squeezed my hand, and we watched the city dwindle behind us, the road unwinding a new story ahead. He leaned in, soft as a secret, and said, "ready?"

"Yeah," I said, and meant it.

"Let's go."

THE END

ALSO BY THE AUTHOR

The Forbidden Love Series:
Book One
Two young friends are drawn together when their mothers die, embark on a personal journey of discovery about the nature of their friendship. One the son of an earl, the other of a German prince.
They reunite in the early summer of 1914 in London, but are soon sent to the family's country estate in Norfolk where they enjoy an idyllic summer together - largely oblivious to the gathering storm clouds of war in Europe.
With the imminent declaration of war they are summoned back to London by their fathers - and one has to return home to Germany.
Now on opposite sides, each serves their country with distinction.
Will fate allow them to be reunited in peace?

Book Two: Thomas' Tale
In the shadow of Langley Hall, young Thomas Cooper navigates the complexities of friendship, duty and love in Edwardian England. As the son of a tenant farmer, Thomas forms an unlikely bond with Lord John Langley and Prince Christian, two boys from vastly different worlds. Their shared adventures and deepening connections are tested by the rigid boundaries of class and the looming threat of war in the summer of 1914. When tragedy strikes, Thomas is thrust into a role that demands unwavering loyalty and discretion. As he rises through the ranks of service, he must confront his own desires and the painful secrets that haunt him. "Thomas' Tale", is a poignant exploration of love, loss and the enduring power of friendship in the face of society's constraints. Spanning seven decades of British history, Thomas' story chronicles his life from the fields of Norfolk, to a post-war life that includes a liberating road trip across the United States, and also reflects the many changes in social attitudes towards the LBGTQ+ communities.

Book Three: The Author's Story
Book Three intricately explores the life of John Williams, focusing on his journey through trauma, identity struggles, and the pursuit of belonging and reconciliation. Set against varied and evocative settings, from the historic Langley Hall estate and its surrounding village to the urban landscapes of Manchester and London, and the vibrant Greek islands. The narrative weaves themes of personal growth, love, and acceptance into a deeply reflective and emotional story.

ABOUT THE AUTHOR:

John Williams is a retired teacher of history from the north-west of England in the United Kingdom. He is a published local historian, and author of the "A Forbidden Love" series of historical fiction books.

Check out his other work at:
https://linktr.ee/john.williams3599